AnneMari ‖‖ ‖ ‖‖‖ ‖‖‖ ‖‖‖‖‖‖ ‖‖‖‖‖ ‖‖‖‖ ‖‖

KT-210-043

1

The Slum Angel

Published novels:

Historical

Kitty McKenzie
Kitty McKenzie's Land
Southern Sons
Where Rainbow's End
Isabelle's Choice
Nicola's Virtue
Aurora's Pride
Grace's Courage
Eden's Conflict
Catrina's Return
Broken Hero
To Gain What's Lost
The Promise of Tomorrow

Contemporary

Long Distance Love
Hooked on You
Where Dragonflies Hover

Short Stories

A New Dawn
Art of Desire
What He Taught Her

AnneMarie Brear

Dedication

To my lovely readers.
Thank you.

The Slum Angel

Chapter One .

York 1871

In her bedroom, Victoria leaned against the window seat cushions and stared out at the passing traffic on Blossom Street heading into York. Not that there was much to watch, just the odd hansom bringing home a lady from her shopping, or a private carriage coming in to the city from the country. A pedestrian walked by, but her uncle's house was set too far back from the street for Victoria to see if it was someone she knew.

She gazed up at the white clouds scudding across the sky. Delicate pink blossoms sprouted on the trees bordering the garden though the weather was still cool for April. She felt listless, wishing she had more to do with her time, but since falling ill with a bad chest cold weeks ago, she'd used up all her resources of timewasting.

Kilmore, her uncle's old gardener, walked across the lawn, back bent, hoe in hand. A weed dared not sprout in his garden. She watched him work for a time, her chin resting on her hand. She hoped summer would improve her mood, banish her boredom.

The book she'd been reading, *Emma* by Jane Austen, slipped from her lap and onto the floor. She sighed and bent to pick it up as the bedroom door opened and her cousin, Stella, marched in.

'Why are you in your room in the middle of the day?' Stella demanded.

Victoria smiled secretly. No matter how many times she told Stella that she enjoyed her own company, her cousin refused to believe it. 'I am reading.'

'Why?'

'What a silly question.' She shook her head. 'Mr Hubbard was instructing Jennie and Dora on how *not* to clean the drawing room's windows. I wanted somewhere quiet and came to my room.'

Stella went to the dressing table and patted her short brown curls in the mirror. Her looks were the most important thing to Stella. 'Well, I've had the dreariest time visiting this morning. I really am tired of listening to Mama's friends talk about nothing of importance. I need you to come with me. You always make it bearable. You ask them interesting questions and remember their family members' names. It's been months since you came out with me. Oh, I know you've been unwell, but you are better now, aren't you?'

'Yes, I'm better and I'll start making calls next week.'

Watching her, Victoria wondered how they could possibly be related. Stella was her opposite. She was loud, opinionated, vivacious, stubborn, difficult and had a beauty that was hard, but defined. Her brown eyes would flash with irritation or smoulder with a hidden secret. She was spoilt and petted by the family and used that power to her advantage at every opportunity. Yet, Victoria saw through her antics and would simply smile and let her get on with it. Stella was easier to deal with if one simply allowed her to have her way.

Bored with looking at herself, Stella spun to face Victoria. 'Papa has such tedious people coming to dinner tonight. I might plead a headache and not bother making the effort to dress.'

'We both know you will not.' Victoria rose from the window seat and placed the book on her bedside table. 'Your father's dinner parties are usually very entertaining.'

'Says you. You find *everyone* interesting. Will you join us tonight?' Stella walked to the walnut wardrobe and opened both doors.

'Yes, my cough has gone, I'm certain of it. I can sit through a meal now and not embarrass myself by coughing continuously.'

'What will you wear then?' Stella pulled out a gown of soft yellow with white lace detail that flowed down over the bustle. 'This one?'

Victoria sat on the bed, gazing at the beautiful dresses she owned. 'Perhaps the blue silk.'

'I was going to wear blue.' Stella pouted. 'We can't wear the same shade, you know that.'

'Then I'll wear the pink.' She sighed. 'I don't really mind.' Sometimes it was better to let Stella tell her what colour to wear.

7

Stella frowned in thought. 'But pink does go better with my colouring. Perhaps I should wear my pink striped sateen?'

'Everything you wear looks lovely,' Victoria soothed, wishing she had Stella's ample curves instead of her own boyish figure.

Her favourite gown was an off the shoulder duck egg blue silk shot with silver thread. However, she'd never mention it for Stella would instantly decide on wearing her silver.

Over the years she had learned how to play Stella at her own game.

Closing the wardrobe, Stella headed for the door. 'Come down for some tea. We can talk about it. Mama should be home soon.'

Knowing she'd get no peace if she didn't follow, Victoria left the bed, but paused in front of the mirror. She stared at her reflection. Nothing she did would give her bigger breasts or more rounded hips, but thankfully the latest fashions helped define what little shape she did possess. Disappointed in her body as always, she stifled a sigh and went downstairs.

In the drawing room, Stella was instructing the maid, Jennie, to bring in a tea tray. Victoria sat on the dark red velvet sofa, mentally preparing herself to spend an hour listening to Stella's nonstop chatter. Thankfully, spring was replacing winter, and she'd be able to leave the house and take long walks – walks that Stella refused to join her on. The chest cold she'd suffered through the winter months had kept her housebound more than she liked, but now she was well again, she was determined to take the long walks she enjoyed so much.

'I don't like that dress you're wearing.' Stella sniffed with dislike.

Victoria glanced down at the peach coloured day dress she wore. It was a few years old, granted, but pleasant enough. 'It's perfectly acceptable for being at home. I knew there would be no callers today. I'm not going to spend Uncle's money unnecessarily.'

Stella flicked through *The Queen*, one of her mother's magazines. 'Papa gives you a good allowance.'

Inwardly squirming at the mention of her Uncle Harold's generosity, Victoria pasted a smile on her face. 'Uncle is very kind, and I will not abuse his good nature.'

'Papa has plenty of money. He has never seen you go without in the past, has he? He treats you the same as me, and I'm his daughter.'

Victoria frowned, noticing of late how Stella would refer to their positions in the family. Stella was the *daughter* of the house, no one needed reminding, least of all Victoria. She knew all too well that she'd been taken in as an orphan. Stella had never been jealous before, when they were children, so why would she start acting it now?

Stella tossed the magazine aside as Jennie brought in the tea tray. 'Did you bring some of Mrs Norman's sponge cake?'

'Yes, Miss Stella, and also shortbread. Mrs Norman said it needs eating up as she wants to make a new batch tomorrow.' Jennie placed the tray on the small table beside the sofa. 'Shall I pour, Miss Victoria?'

'No, I'll do it, thank you, Jennie.' Victoria poured the tea while Stella filled her plate with the delicious delights of Mrs Norman's cooking.

The door opened again and Todd, Stella's older brother, walked in.

'Todd! What are you doing home?' Stella accused him as though entering the house was a foreign situation.

'What a welcome, sister.' He laughed.

'You're not expected.'

'I thought I'd spend the night here before heading back to Oxford tomorrow.' He flopped his long frame down beside Victoria and gave her a cheeky grin. 'Jennie is bringing in another cup. Don't eat all the cake, Stella.'

Stella stared at him and swallowed a mouthful of sponge. 'Be quiet. Mrs Norman didn't put enough on the plate. Have the shortbread.'

'How was Scotland?' Victoria asked Todd. Her handsome cousin was the apple of his mother's eye and could do no wrong, despite his poor attendance at university and dreadful exam results. Victoria wondered what he would do with his life. At the moment he seemed determined to waste each day in selfish pursuits.

'Scotland was cold. Edinburgh dismal.' Todd shuddered dramatically and a long dark curl dropped over his forehead, which he pushed back with one hand while reaching for shortbread with the other. He smiled at Jennie as she brought in another cup and saucer. 'I think I barely left the taverns at all. They are the warmest places to be.'

'It's not only the warmth that kept you there, I'm sure,' Stella scoffed, eyeing him haughtily. 'You went there to study. Papa won't forgive you if you have another bad term.'

'Don't start harping at me. I have enough of that from Papa. This is my last term and then I'm free of Oxford and books for good.'

'What will you do then?' Victoria asked, pouring tea for him. 'Go into the bank with Uncle Harold and Laurence?'

'Heavens no.' Todd stuffed more shortbread into his mouth.

'Papa won't want him, anyway.' Stella laughed.

'I'll go into the navy I think.' He sipped his tea nonchalantly as though the announcement was as simple as choosing what socks to wear.

Victoria stared at him, shocked. 'You've never mentioned the navy before.'

'Why didn't you tell us?' Stella snapped.

'Well, I have now. Mama's feels it'd be a fine thing to occupy my time. Papa has contacts so I'm put on a good ship. But first I'm going to Italy for a month in July with some chums.'

'I want to go to Italy!' Stella huffed. 'Why do you and Laurence get to go to exciting places? Laurence has been in London for months. Victoria and I have to remain stuck here at home all the time.'

'That's because you are mere girls.' Todd finished off the shortbread. 'Our older brother is a man of the world. Papa has Laurence at his beck and call doing bank business. I, dear sister, will not become a bank lackey.'

Victoria frowned. 'It provides a very good living, Todd. Don't dismiss it out of hand. Your father is a wealthy and influential man because of the bank he started.' Though she was sorry that Laurence hadn't inherited uncle's charm. She was most content to have her older cousin lodged permanently in London.

'And yet, it is not for me!' Todd stood abruptly.

'But the navy is?'

He shrugged. 'Who knows? I'm going to freshen up and sort out my luggage. I feel like I'm coated in a layer of soot from the train. Are we entertaining tonight?' he asked from the doorway.

'Yes. Papa's invited some dreary people.' Stella poured more tea, unconcerned. 'There's always someone at our dining table.'

Victoria nibbled at her piece of cake. Once Todd had closed the door, she looked at Stella. 'How can Todd know that the navy is right for him? Has he even been on a naval ship to see what it is like?'

Adding sugar to her cup, Stella stirred it. 'Oh, you know Todd. By the time he's returned from Italy, he'll have decided to do something else. He'll do as he pleases until Papa threatens to cut off his allowance.'

'Men have it so easy.' Victoria placed her teacup back on the tray. 'They have so much freedom. I envy them.'

'We'll have more freedom once we marry. I'm determined to choose a husband who will leave me to my own devices, and I'll make certain I have a honeymoon somewhere exotic!' Stella ate the last of the cake. 'And I'll have a cook as good as Mrs Norman.'

The longcase clock in the entrance near the front door chimed three o'clock.

Victoria glanced out of the window as she heard carriage wheels on the short driveway from the road. 'Aunt Esther is home.'

'I do hope Mama has brought me the silk samples from Miss Thatcher's Salon. I want to order some new summer gowns. You need to as well, no arguments. You aren't embarrassing me by wearing last season's styles. The invitations for summer are arriving daily and I refuse to be in your company while you're wearing last year's dresses.'

A few moments later, Esther Dobson entered the drawing room, frowning as she pulled off her gloves. 'Jennie tells me Todd has come home? I thought he was going straight to Oxford?'

'He changed his plans, Mama,' Stella said impatiently. 'Where are the samples?'

'Jennie gave them to Dora to put in your room.'

'But I wanted to look at them now.'

Aunt Esther raised her chin, her eyes narrowing. She looked an older version of her daughter. 'Then go upstairs and do it. I don't want them cluttering up this room when we have company coming in a few hours.'

'Oh, Mama!' Stella flounced from the room, muttering her displeasure as she went.

Aunt Esther smiled worriedly at Victoria as she unpinned her small black hat. 'Is your cough better, dear?'

'Yes, thank you, Aunt.'

'Your uncle has invited a doctor to dine with us tonight. Although it is highly irregular to impose on a guest, but perhaps we should ask him to examine you to make sure you are fully recovered?'

'There is no need, really. I am truly well now, I'm sure of it. I've not coughed at all today.' Victoria stood, feeling guilty at the attention. 'May I ask Dora to pour me a bath? I'd like to wash my hair and dry it in plenty of time.'

'Yes, dear, but have her light a fire in your room first to take the chill off the air. We mustn't take any chances with your chest.'

'I will. Shall I ask Jennie to bring you in some fresh tea?'

Aunt Esther rubbed her eyes tiredly as she sat on the sofa. 'I've already asked her as I came in.'

Victoria paused by the door. 'Was your day very exhausting?'

'You know how it is. Too many committees. Everyone wants you to help with their fundraising, and as much as I would like to assist them, I simply cannot do it all. It's very demanding. I return calls to ladies whose conversation repeats itself and I sit there worrying about all that I have left to do in the day.'

'Stella mentioned something similar about making calls.' Victoria smiled.

'Your cousin has no patience. Yes, it can be wearing, but still, I must do my duty as a reputable banker's wife and listen to those who need our help.'

'Yours and Uncle's influence is greatly respected by the people of York,' Victoria said proudly. 'You both do so much for others. Now I am well again I can re-join you in your efforts.'

'I do welcome that, my dear, as you are far better at it than Stella, but only if you are certain you are up to it.' Aunt Esther wiggled her booted feet. 'I must get new boots. These make my feet hurt.'

Victoria opened the door wider to allow Jennie to come in carrying another tea tray. 'I'll leave you to rest, Aunt.'

'Victoria?'

'Yes?'

'While you are bathing, have a moment to think about what you want to do for your birthday next month. Perhaps a party? You'll be twenty-one.'

'Yes, I'll think about it.'

Her aunt's words whirled about her brain as she bathed. Dora had brought the tin bath into the bedroom and after numerous trips down to the kitchen had filled it with hot water, scented with drops of rose oil. A small cheery fire crackled in the grate. Uncle was keen to install one of those new bath rooms that were the fashion, but Victoria liked having a bath in the privacy of her own bedroom.

Slowly washing her body with a soapy cloth, Victoria relaxed, enjoying the water lapping over her. But her mind kept returning to the thought of her birthday.

Since coming to live in the Dobson house when she was twelve years old, she'd always been treated as though she was another Dobson child. Yet, despite this, she felt as though she stood on the edge of the family, a part of it, but not a part of it, too.

When her mother and younger brother died from pneumonia within two days of each other, her father had brought her here, away from the house of death. She'd stayed ever since. Uncle Harold was her mother's brother, and he'd loved his sister dearly. He'd transferred that love to Victoria, while Aunt Esther had gathered her to her bosom like a hen gathers her chicks. Victoria had wanted for nothing. Still, there were times, like her birthday, when she missed her mother very much.

She glanced at the mantelpiece and the small portrait of her mother that stood on top of it. She had no image of her father and little brother, they were gone from memory.

Try as she might she couldn't see their faces, but her mother's beauty shone from the artist's touch and she looked at it every day.

Her father had gone to his grave within six months of burying his wife and son. His heart broken, she'd been told, he'd lost the will to live. Victoria hadn't been enough for him to want to take care of himself and after one visit he stopped coming to see her. If he'd continued to see her perhaps she'd have been able to give him the will to keep going. It didn't make sense to her why he gave up so quickly. In time she'd have been his companion and run his home, they could have survived, together.

She moved her legs in the water, feeling it lose its heat. She should get out, but the apathy that was on her today lingered.

Next month she'd be twenty-one. An adult in the eyes of the law. An adult living in her uncle's house with very little purpose or direction. How many more birthdays would she spend here, feeling adrift?

Annoyed with herself, she stood up in the bath and reached for the towel. She hated self-pity. It frustrated her that she couldn't shake it today.

Drying the top half of herself quickly, she stepped from the water and dried her legs and feet.

What was wrong with her? She had a lovely home and a nice family. She should be grateful. She *was* grateful!

Angry now, she donned her shift and began drying her hair in front of the fire. She had to stop these long days of inactivity. With her health better, she needed to throw herself into keeping busy. Aunt Esther did so much, she would follow her example.

A sharp knock on the door sounded before it opened and Stella walked into the room. 'I'm wearing the pink sateen with white flowers on it. I'm not wasting one of my better dresses for stuffy old bank people.'

Victoria, her head bent so her hair could fall freely in front of the fire to dry, glanced at her. 'You'll look very nice in it. Are the samples from Mrs Thatcher's any good?'

'Passable.' Stella flopped onto the bed. 'There's a rose silk I quite like, and I thought you might like the white and lavender stripe. We could get new hats, what do you think?'

'Sounds interesting.'

Stella reached over and, taking the towel, began rubbing Victoria's hair. 'I wish my hair was this colour. Look how the reddish gold catches in the fire light. It's as though it's alive, like the flames.'

Astonished that Stella had said something so nice, so poetic, Victoria was stumped for a moment on how to reply. 'You have beautiful hair, Stella. All those curls. Mine's straight and far too thick to be fashionable.'

'My curls are rather splendid, true. I just don't like the brown colour of them. I'd much rather have your deep copper colour, though I suppose it is a bit common. Half of York is overflowing with Irish poor who have a similar shade to you.'

A bubble of laughter escaped Victoria before she could stop it. Only Stella could give a compliment with one hand and instantly take it away with the other.

Chapter Two

Gentle laughter drifted out of the drawing room as Victoria went downstairs to join the party. She'd left Stella getting ready in her room, driving poor Dora mad with demands of making her curls sit just right. The guests had arrived half an hour earlier and Victoria was conscious of being rudely late to join her aunt and uncle. Stella could get away with it, but she didn't want to be seen as discourteous.

At the door, she paused and ran her hands over the soft grey satin gown she wore — selected by Stella. She'd lost weight over the winter and the dress fitted well over the corset which Dora had pulled tight to emphasise her narrow waist.

The off-the-shoulder style was edged with white lace four inches long and more white lace flowed over the small bustle at the back like a cascade.

Dora had fashioned her hair up in thick long loops entwined with silver ribbons. Stella said she looked pretty, so she was happy with that. She'd long ago come to terms with the fact she'd never be allowed to outshine Stella, not that she could anyway.

Taking a deep breath, she raised her head high and entered the room with a smile on her face.

Soft lighting from the frosted gas wall lamps and the golden glow from a roaring fire gave the room a welcoming atmosphere. Glasses clinked, polite chatter ebbed and flowed. Aunt Esther was talking to her friend, Mrs Hewitt, a very overweight woman, who had donated some of her late husband's land to the city for the building of an almshouse for the poor. Next to the fireplace, Uncle Harold was talking to two men, one she knew as Mr Belton, an alderman like her uncle. The other had his back to her.

Laughing with her cousin, Todd, was a pretty young woman called Alice Thorpe and her small, pasty-looking husband, Percy. Victoria and the family had attended the Thorpes' wedding last summer. The Thorpes' relationship wasn't a love match. Everyone knew that Alice had only married Percy for his money and the life he could give her. Victoria hoped she'd never have to make that compromise, but who was she to judge others?

'Lord, I didn't know *they* were coming,' Stella whispered from behind Victoria in the doorway. 'I'd best not be sitting next to Percy. The Thorpes bore me.'

'I'd rather him than Mrs Hewitt,' Victoria whispered back. 'She is nice, but she takes most of the food.'

Sharing a secret smile, they linked arms and swept around the room smiling widely to everyone.

After greeting the Thorpes and Mrs Hewitt, Victoria stood next to her uncle and nodded politely to Mr Belton before turning to be introduced to the newcomer.

'Victoria, dear, this is Doctor Joseph Ashton,' Uncle Harold said jovially. 'and this is my niece, Victoria Carlton.' He smiled proudly.

'How do you do?' She held out her hand, staring at the man before her. Along with Todd, he stood the tallest in the room at about six feet, but it was his eyes that held her attention for they were clear blue and rimmed with thick black eyelashes, the same colour as his hair.

'Miss Carlton. A pleasure to meet you.' Doctor Ashton held her hand firmly and his warm smile reached his impressive eyes.

'And you, Doctor.' She returned his smile, admiring his handsome face.

Movement at the doorway made them look as Mr Hubbard nodded to Aunt Esther, who announced dinner was served.

They all made their way across the hall to the dining room opposite and took their places. Victoria sat on her uncle's left side, Stella on his right, while Aunt Esther occupied the other end of the table with everyone else sitting between.

Smiling generally, but strangely disappointed that Percy Thorpe sat next to her, Victoria felt a little stab of jealousy when Doctor Ashton sat next to Stella. It was, however, pleasing to have him on the other side of the table to look at. She found her gaze drawn to him. He had a quiet magnetism that compelled her.

Before the first course had begun, Stella was talking animatedly to Doctor Ashton and Percy felt the need to discuss with Victoria the opening of the Royal Albert Hall in London.

'Will you travel down to see it, Miss Carlton?' Percy asked.

'The Royal Albert Hall?'

'Yes, I believe it is rather splendid. It would have to be, wouldn't it, being named after the late Prince? The Queen wouldn't have it any other way.'

'Indeed. I imagine it would be something of great interest to the Queen.' She started to eat her soup of leek and potato. 'I doubt I'll visit anytime soon though. Will you go?'

'Absolutely, yes. Alice and I might go in the summer and attend a concert.'

While Percy continued to talk about things to do in London, including buying a new hat, she only paid half attention to him as Doctor Ashton was now talking to Uncle Harold about fundraising for the Union Workhouse. Only last week, her uncle had become one of the guardians of that particular workhouse.

'Do you work at the Union, Doctor Ashton?' Victoria asked, keenly aware Percy had abruptly stopped talking as she spoke. She blushed, being rude wasn't something she enjoyed being, but she'd had enough of Percy for the moment.

Ashton lowered his spoon. 'When asked, I offer my time and knowledge, Miss Carlton,' he answered. 'It is only one of the places where I'd like to do some good.'

Uncle paused in sipping his soup. 'It was at the Union that I first met Doctor Ashton. He has only recently come to live in York, my dear,' Uncle told her. 'He's been here less than a month and already in much demand. The Board would like him to become the Medical Officer there, but Ashton has rejected our offer.' Uncle smiled to show there were no hard feelings about it.

Ashton quirked his lips. 'You know my reasons, Harold. I feel I can be of better use spreading myself around, and not just concentrating on one place.'

Victoria wiped her mouth with a napkin. 'No doubt there are a great many places in York which would benefit from your services.'

'I hope so. Sometimes I feel there isn't enough hours in the day to do all I wish to. I am most interested in assisting women and children who have fallen on hard times.' His eyes held hers until Stella coughed.

Doctor Ashton concentrated on his soup while Stella gave Victoria a stern glare.

'Where are you from originally, Doctor Ashton?' Victoria asked him, ignoring Stella's sharp look.

'Lincolnshire. Lincoln to be precise.' Ashton sipped his soup. 'My family have long been wine merchants on my father's side and held landholdings on my mother's side.'

Stella tilted her head. 'I've never been to Lincoln. I should like to though.'

'It has a magnificent cathedral on the hill, and there's a castle too.'

'Papa we must visit Doctor Ashton's home one day. In the summer I think.'

Uncle laughed deeply. 'I'll try and find a moment spare, dearest, to take you.'

'You must call on my family if you do venture there. My parents would be delighted to welcome you.'

'How charming!' Stella beamed. 'We will definitely go now, won't we, Papa?'

'What made you decide to become a doctor?' Victoria asked, her soup going cold. The doctor was the most interesting man.

He gave her his attention with a small smile. 'The need to want to help others, to make a difference in some small way.'

'That's admirable.'

'My brother has taken over the family company, which didn't really interest me to join him even though I am a shareholder. I wanted to travel and see the world. However, I went to university instead, at my mother's urging, for she was worried I'd waste my life if I wasn't dedicated to something.' He grinned sheepishly, amusement in his eyes when he looked at Victoria.

Stella lifted her wine glass. 'Oh, I am empty, Doctor Ashton. May I have a refill?' She gave him a dazzling smile, effectively drawing his attention away from Victoria.

'Certainly, Miss Dobson.' Ashton lifted the decanter.

Uncle Harold waved towards Todd, who was engrossed in conversation with Alice Thorpe. 'That is a current problem we are facing in this house, Doctor. Your mother is correct in leading you to worthwhile endeavours. Young men need to be directed by wiser heads or they lose motivation to lead a worthwhile life.'

Aunt Esther laughed suddenly at something Mr Belton said at the other end of the table. Victoria glanced down at her bowl not really hungry as her stomach seemed tied in knots. Percy once more started a conversation with her about the state of York's roads.

Throughout the meal, Victoria did her best to listen to the conversations around the table, but repeatedly her focus came back to Doctor Ashton whenever he spoke. She guessed him to be around thirty years of age, he looked no older than that.

She watched Stella grow bored whenever Uncle and the doctor spoke of the parishes' needs and helping the poor. She had nothing to add to the conversation, as her aunt had not allowed the girls to visit the poor areas, but Victoria was fascinated by Ashton's enthusiasm for the improvements needed.

'It is a waste of money,' Percy unexpectedly said, interrupting Uncle Harold as he spoke of donations required for a new almshouse close to the River Foss.

'A waste of money?' Ashton asked with a puzzled frown. 'How so, Mr Thorpe?'

Percy leaned back in his chair. 'It's been proven over the years how little these people respect the help that is given to them.'

Ashton stared at the man. 'I beg to differ, Mr Thorpe. Many lives have been saved due to almshouses and workhouses being available to them. Those institutions largely operate by donations. The poor are indeed grateful and know that without those charitable donations they would starve to death.'

'They die anyway, usually from drinking too much or childbirth.' Percy sniffed with distaste. 'They have no morals or self-respect.'

'You are generalising, Mr Thorpe. A dangerous thing to do.' Ashton's mouth thinned to a tight line. 'Unless you walk in their shoes how could you possibly make such a statement?'

'The evidence is quite clear, Doctor. One visit to those slums shows how they prefer to live their lives. They have too many children and are idle. What money is earned gets frittered away on drink and gambling and loose living.'

'And when was the last time you visited the slums, Mr Thorpe?' Mrs Hewitt boomed from the end of the table, her eyes beady in a flushed round face.

'I have no need to be amongst that populace to know of the dens of immorality and drunkenness,' Percy defended, his manner righteous.

'It is not something they choose. It is how life has treated them.' Ashton spoke with an undercurrent of frustration in his voice. 'Do you honestly think they would prefer to live as they do? If there was enough work, there would be enough money to provide for their families. Would any mother want to see her baby cry from hunger or die from disease?'

'Can you, Doctor Ashton, honestly say that every one of those people would give up their slovenly ways to work hard and provide for their family if the chance to do so was there? You are a fool to think so!'

'*I* am a fool?' A dangerous tone entered Ashton's voice.

Uncle Harold held his hand up. 'Now, Percy—'

Leaning forward, Percy refused to be quiet. 'Doctor, you who works amongst them, must see the true character of those people. There will always be those that *choose* to be lazy and unaccountable for their actions. They have no self-respect or self-control. Why else would they have so many children knowing full well they cannot support them? Where is the abstinence? They do everything to excess when they don't have the finances to back it up. They flood into cities from the counties expecting to be given work and houses and when it doesn't happen they turn to vice. It is life. No one can change that.'

'I'm going to try.' Ashton ground out. 'I believe those of us who have been dealt a better life have a duty to help the people less fortunate.'

Percy banged the table. 'Why should we? Is it *our* fault we have had forefathers who worked hard to ensure their future generations don't suffer? Constantly giving the poor our money doesn't seem to alter the situation at all. We'd be far better off investing in opportunities to advance the classes who appreciate it.'

'Such as?' Victoria asked, mortified by Percy's opinions.

'I'm more than happy to donate money to universities and schools for the families who work hard so they can educate their children properly, or to donate to the town to build parks for us to enjoy and museums to visit. All good causes.'

Victoria folded her napkin. 'Yes, they are, but what about the underprivileged who cannot afford to send their children to those schools?'

Percy smiled patronisingly at her. 'My dear, what you don't understand is that the poor are too stupid to go to school, anyway. Manual labour is all they are good for.'

There was a collective gasp around the table and Ashton jerked in either shock or anger, Victoria wasn't sure.

Before anyone could respond, Aunt Esther rose from her chair. 'Ladies, we shall withdraw and leave the men to their port.'

With reluctance, Victoria left the room with the women and entered the drawing room. Dora served tea in the subdued atmosphere.

Aunt Esther, her eyes like ice, pretended the rudeness of Mr Thorpe had not happened and enquired of Mrs Hewitt where she obtained the gemstone brooch she wore which was fashioned in the shape of a butterfly.

Alice Thorpe leaned forward eager to hear Mrs Hewitt's answer, her cheeks flushed and her gaze darting about the room as though she longed to escape.

'I've never seen Percy Thorpe so voluble,' Stella said, surprise making her whisper louder than it should be.

'Or so senseless!' Victoria muttered harshly. 'He embarrassed everyone at the table with his unfounded opinions. Poor Doctor Ashton, to be so insulted. He must have thought us as very provincial and miserly.'

'Indeed. Doctor Ashton must think York society very small minded if Percy Thorpe is an example.' Stella sipped her tea. 'Papa will inform him otherwise.'

'I hope Uncle makes Percy apologise.'

'That will not happen. The Thorpes think themselves above doctors. Percy would rather eat his own necktie than apologise to Doctor Ashton.'

'Well I shall refuse to speak to the man again until he does.' Victoria stirred her tea vigorously.

'You cannot do that!' Stella stared at her. 'Mama would be angry with you.'

'I think Aunt Esther feels the same as I do.'

Stella giggled. 'Mama is extremely upset. Look how stiff her shoulders are.'

Victoria refrained from commenting as the men joined them quicker than was usual. She looked at the doctor, his expression natural, but her uncle's sharp movements showed he was annoyed, while Percy appeared fit to burst. Only Todd seemed jovial as he spoke to Ashton about something.

Aunt Esther instantly went into motion as the perfect hostess and smiled brightly at the doctor, took his arm and steered him well away from the Thorpe couple. 'Doctor Ashton, will you be living here in York permanently now?'

'Yes, I believe so, Mrs Dobson. I feel I can do much good here. I've done a lot of study on the situation of the poor in London and Manchester and when I was offered the opportunity to work in York, I took it.' He smiled his thanks as Victoria passed him a cup of tea.

'And where are you staying? Do you have family or friends in the city?'

'I know only a few people here and wouldn't impose on them. I'm currently staying at the Station Hotel.' Ashton gave Aunt Esther his full attention. 'I will, of course, have to seek something more substantial for the long term.'

'I insist on helping you with that dilemma, Doctor, for I know everyone.' Aunt laughed gaily, if a little forcibly. 'You must allow me this indulgence.'

Ashton bowed. 'If you are certain?' He looked helplessly at Uncle Harold.

Uncle chuckled, resting his hands on his large stomach. 'Let her have her way, Ashton, I beg you, or I'll never hear the end of it.'

The doctor smiled warmly. 'I'll be honoured to accept your assistance, madam.'

'Excellent.' Aunt Esther beamed.

Within the hour, their guests had left, and the house quietened down. As Victoria and Stella made their way up to bed, Todd yawned on the staircase behind them.

'What a bore Thorpe is.' He yanked at his cravat. 'I thought the good doctor was going to throttle him at one point.'

'Mama will not invite them back in a hurry.' Stella yawned as well.

'Shame, as his wife is charming.'

Stella groaned theatrically. 'Nonsense, Todd. Alice is as dull as he is.'

'But pretty.'

Stella turned sharply to him at the top of the stairs. 'She's a muddle-headed doll who should have quietened her husband with a meaningful look to save everyone's embarrassment. They deserve each other.'

Todd laughed. 'I pity your poor husband when you find one! Good night.' He blew them a kiss and went to his room.

'Any husband of mine wouldn't dare to be so rude to a guest at the table. We'll probably never see Doctor Ashton again!' Stella kissed Victoria's cheek. 'I'll send Dora to you once I'm finished with her.'

'Very well. Goodnight.' Victoria entered her bedroom and began to take the pins out of her hair. She knew from experience that Stella would have Dora for a good half hour.

Sitting at her dressing table, she stared at her reflection and thought of the good-looking doctor. She certainly hoped they'd see him again.

Chapter Three

A week later, Victoria was sitting in the drawing room sewing a new piece of lace ribbon onto one of her summer hats. It wasn't a favourite hat, but she remembered the day a gust of wind nearly ripped it from her head, and she'd stuffed it away. The damage had been to the lace and she'd been in two minds to replace it or do away with it altogether, but then promptly forgot all about it, until this morning when she was searching through her hat boxes and came across it.

The front door bell rang, and she wondered who'd be calling. She heard Mr Hubbard answer it. To her astonishment, Doctor Ashton was announced into the room.

She stood and held out her hand. 'Doctor Ashton, this is a pleasant surprise.' Inwardly she hoped she looked presentable. Her day dress of narrow lemon and white stripes was last season, not that the doctor would know that.

'I am not disturbing you, Miss Carlton?' He raised his eyebrows in question.

'Not at all.' She waved towards the hat and ribbons. 'This can always keep.' She glanced at Mr Hubbard. 'Tea, please.'

He bowed and left them.

Suddenly nervous, Victoria sat down and indicated for the doctor to do the same.

'I'm sorry for calling unannounced. I was visiting St Thomas's Hospital and thought that since I was close by I'd call and collect the list of houses your Aunt has kindly put together for me to view.'

'Oh, I'm not certain where she has left the list. Perhaps it's in her secretary.' She went to stand, but he held up his hand to stop her.

'There is no rush. I can call again.' He smiled warmly, the lines crinkling around his lovely blue eyes. Her stomach dipped in response.

Jennie brought in the tea tray and left Victoria to pour.

'Milk? Sugar?' Her hands shook, mortifying her. Why was she acting like this?

'Just a little milk, please.'

'St Thomas's has only aged women staying there, is that correct?' She passed him the cup and saucer. 'I think my aunt has visited on occasion.'

'Yes. I wanted to see how it is managed and to observe the state of the patients. My old tutor at university is interested in my findings. He wants me to write a paper.'

'A paper? Is that a report of some kind?' She passed him a plate of coconut squares and date pinwheels.

'Yes. Such reports are published in medical journals.' He took a coconut square. He bit into it and rolled his eyes. 'Lord, this is delicious!'

'We have the best cook in York, I'm sure. Uncle would double Mrs Norman's wages if she ever decided to leave.' Victoria chuckled. 'I'm surprised she hasn't tried to do that yet and see what she can get from him.'

He laughed with her. 'I do enjoy eating coconut. It was in France that I first ate it. I've tasted such delicious food in Paris, they have such imaginations.'

'When were you in France?' She also took a coconut square. 'I have yet to visit the country.'

'I've been often. My father has many French business contacts in the wine industry. I think I have been at least once a year since I was a child. My brother is married to a French woman, Mariette. She is delightful.'

'Do you miss home, your family?'

'I am committed to my work, but I do miss my family, especially in the evenings when I am alone in my room. Our house was always a happy one. My parents are still very much in love even after all these years and it creates a comforting home that is a joy to be in. That is what I miss.' He smiled self-consciously. 'But my work is important. I cannot complain.'

'Can you not have both, your work and a family of your own?'

'I would like to think I could, yes.' His gaze held hers.

Heat rose in her cheeks. She acknowledged that this fine-looking man would be someone she'd like to marry. She faltered on what to say next.

'What are your dreams, Miss Carlton?'

'Oh dear, I don't think I have any of great importance. However, to travel widely is something I'd like to achieve.'

'Travelling is a fine ambition.' He sipped his tea. 'What exotic destinations do you long to explore?' he murmured softly.

She shivered at the intimacy of his voice even though the words were innocent. 'I-I am not certain…'

'Perhaps we could go for a walk when the weather warms, Miss Carlton. You can show me parts of York I haven't seen?'

A fission of happiness flowed through her. She felt her cheeks grow warm at the idea of just the two of them walking together. 'I would like that very much, Doctor Ashton. There are some lovely walks out into the countryside where I could take you.'

He smiled and drank his tea. 'I look forward to it.'

Noise in the hallway interrupted them as seconds later Stella entered the room. Victoria groaned inwardly, annoyed her time alone with Doctor Ashton was at an end.

Stella stared at Victoria and the doctor with narrowed eyes. 'This looks very cosy indeed. But we are here now, so Victoria you mustn't monopolise the Doctor for another minute. How dull it must be for him to only have you to talk to.'

Swallowing back a sharp retort at her rudeness, Victoria merely smiled and sipped her tea.

'Miss Carlton has offered to show me some country walks, when the weather warms.' Ashton placed his cup and saucer on the tray.

'Walks?' Stella laughed. 'Dear Victoria is a great one for walks. No, Doctor Ashton, I shall save you from such dreariness.'

Victoria gave her a sharp look.

'We shall ride the train to Scarborough and savour the delights of the seaside! Mama and Papa would introduce you to some of their friends. Papa has a great friend called Doctor Fisher.'

As Aunt Esther walked into the room, Stella turned to her. 'Mama shall we not take Doctor Ashton to visit Doctor Fisher in Scarborough? I think they would enjoy each other's company very much.'

'Oh indeed! Charles Fisher is a man of vision.' Aunt Esther nodded enthusiastically.

Ashton smiled. 'I have heard of Doctor Fisher and read a book he wrote on natural medicines. I would like to meet him.'

'Wonderful. I'll make the arrangements.' Stella beamed.

Nothing more was said about walking in the country.

~ ~ ~ ~

After weeks of being cooped up in the house, it was a pleasant change for Victoria to be out shopping in the weak sunshine. April showers had washed away the dirt and coal soot from thousands of fires and now flowers were beginning to bloom while blue skies replaced the grey ones.

In Coney Street, Victoria waited patiently outside a confectionary shop as Stella purchased a box of Terry's candied peel. They'd spent an exhausting morning buying ribbons and new gloves for a ball being held at the Assembly Rooms next week.

'Miss Carlton?'

Victoria turned and smiled at Doctor Ashton. 'How nice to see you.'

'You are well?' he asked, stopping beside her.

'Yes, thank you. And you?'

'Very much so. Especially since your aunt secured me a little cottage on Bootham that suits my needs perfectly.'

'Oh, she didn't mention you had settled on a house. That is good news.' Victoria wished Aunt Esther had spoken of it. The doctor hadn't been far from her thoughts. He was all she thought about.

'It happened only a few days ago.' He smiled kindly. 'Her help has been invaluable. I've been too busy to see to anything myself and your aunt sorted everything out. I took lease of it yesterday.'

'It's probably her way of apologising for our rude guests!' Victoria blurted it out before she realised. She slapped a gloved hand over her mouth. 'I didn't mean that! I am so sorry! I didn't mean she did it only for that reason. She'd want to help you, really she would.'

His laughing stopped her flow of words. 'I understand your meaning, Miss Carlton. Your aunt isn't to blame if one of her guests is a trifle ignorant.'

'You are too kind, Doctor. Percy though is *greatly* ignorant.' She grinned.

He leaned closer. 'I suspect he's not on the next list of guests?'

She laughed. 'Not for some time I would imagine!'

The shop door opened, and Stella sailed out full of smiles for the doctor. 'Why, Doctor Ashton, is my cousin being a joke? I could hear you laughing from inside the shop.'

'Your cousin is most charming, Miss Dobson, and no joke.' Ashton gazed intently at Victoria and she felt a fission of awareness tingling along her body.

'Really?' Stella stared in surprise at Victoria, a nerve ticked along her jaw. 'What on earth have you been saying?'

'We were merely discussing Doctor Ashton's new accommodation that Aunt Esther acquired for him.'

'I see.' Stella watched them.

'I am most grateful for her help, for I am too busy with my work to think of such things.'

'Mama is most attentive to those she feels are in less fortunate situations, isn't that so, Victoria?'

For some reason, Victoria felt that statement was directed more towards her than the doctor. 'Aunt is the best of women.'

'Yes, Mama enjoys taking chicks under her wings, just like she did when Victoria became an orphan.'

Now she knew the comment was aimed at her. Sometimes Stella liked to remind her that she came into the family in dire circumstances. Frowning at Stella's comment, she forced a smile in the doctor's direction. 'How are your studies coming along?'

His gaze went from Stella to Victoria. 'I'm kept extremely busy, which I prefer. There are not enough hours in the day.'

She allowed herself to stare at his handsome face for a moment, to memorise his features to think of later. 'I would like to help in some way too, if I may?' she suddenly blurted out.

Stella stiffened beside her. 'We do help already, Victoria. We spend many hours fundraising for Mama's charities.'

Victoria glanced at her, sensing her irritation. 'It's not enough though. I'd like to do more.'

'You could always volunteer at one of the hospitals or almshouses, Miss Carlton. Tomorrow, I'm at Wilson's Hospital, an almshouse for women. I could offer a tour of one of the hospitals for you to see for yourself where you could be useful?'

'No, she could not!' Stella snapped. 'Mama wouldn't allow it. You could catch anything and bring it home.' Stella linked her arm through Victoria's, her manner sharp. 'Good day to you, Doctor. We must be going, much to do.'

He hesitated. 'It was just a thought, Miss Carlton.'

'Thank you, Doctor Ashton.' Furious at Stella's disrespect, Victoria wanted to say more, but Stella dragged her away.

'Oh, Doctor Ashton,' Stella turned back fleetingly. 'We are to go to Scarborough next Saturday. Mark it in your diary. I've gone to much trouble to organise it so you cannot let me down.'

'I wouldn't dare, Miss Dobson. See you then, ladies.' Ashton bowed his head in farewell and crossed the street.

Irritated with Stella, Victoria withdrew her arm. 'I do not need you to speak on my behalf, Stella! I am most interested in helping wherever I'm needed, just as Aunt Esther does.' She marched away, angry as she'd ever been.

'But you are not Mama! You are unmarried.' Stella hurried to catch up with her. 'You simply cannot traipse around hospitals on your own. It's not done!'

Victoria jerked to a stop and faced her. 'I will not let that prevent me. I will help for I cannot sit being idle all day every day.'

'Mama and Papa will not allow it.'

'You forget, Stella, next month I am of age. I'll do as I please!'

'You live by my family's generosity! You'll *not* do as you please.'

'Why do you constantly bring up that fact into conversation?'

'Because you forget yourself!' Stella snapped.

'How do I?' Staggered by the contempt in Stella's tone, Victoria stepped backwards, wounded. 'I am just as good as you.'

'You think so? You think you can gain the attention of Doctor Ashton? You are fooling yourself. He'd never look at you, an orphan with no dowry, living by the goodwill of her uncle. What can you possibly offer him?'

Stunned by the venom in her words, Victoria crossed to the opposite side of Coney Street where she knew the horse tram stopped to pick up passengers.

'Where are you going?' Stella demanded. 'Come back here.'

'Home.'

'But we have more shopping to do.'

'I don't want to go shopping with you!' she barked. 'I'm tired of shopping, of wasting my days, of being at your beck and call.'

'Be quiet, you're making an exhibition of yourself.' Stella glanced around. 'Thank goodness no one we know is close by.'

Victoria heaved a long sigh, not caring who saw or heard her. Stella hadn't even realised how much her words had hurt her. 'I'm going home.'

Stella stamped her foot. 'I really don't understand you at times!'

~ ~ ~ ~

Joseph put his pencil down and stretched his back. The light was fading and he needed to light the gas lamps on the walls, but he was too stiff to move.

With slow movements, he folded the letter he'd just finished writing to his mother and slipped it into an envelope. He'd written about his work, his new home and the people he'd met.

His thoughts strayed to Miss Carlton, although he tried hard not to. She'd been on his mind far too much since meeting her at the Dobson's dinner party.

He'd enjoyed the family's hospitality, though the daughter, Stella, was a little highly strung for his tastes, but the elder Dobsons were good people and Miss Carlton was...

What was she exactly? Attractive, certainly, but there was something more within her that he'd only just glimpsed. A fire burned behind her eyes. He sensed her frustrations at having questions but not knowing the answers for he was a lot like that.

Perhaps that's why medicine consumed him in the way it did? He was always searching for answers to questions. Why did people catch diseases? How could he cure them? What made the human body function the way it did? His mind buzzed with thoughts and ideas and in Miss Carlton he hoped he saw a kindred spirit. Perhaps not about medicine as such, but certainly about general topics and the need to have answers.

On the few occasions he'd spent time in her company, she gave him no reason to think she was an empty-headed miss only looking for a husband, which most young women of his acquaintance did.

He smiled as he stood. Yes, coming to York had been the right move.

He could do good work here, and if he was invited to dinner parties where the likes of Miss Carlton attended, then his transition to the city was only going to become brighter.

A cat jumped up on the windowsill outside, startling him out of his daydreaming. He glanced at his thick medical tomes. He had some studying to do and more letters to write, but first, he would eat the simple meal the housekeeper had left out for him before she finished for the day.

As the carriage clock on the mantelpiece chimed five times, he headed into the small dining room and poured himself a glass of wine. The silence of the room was tomblike.

He sighed as he sat down and took a sip of wine. Despite his happiness regarding his work and the people he'd met, there were times like this when he longed for company. Perhaps it was time he married.

~ ~ ~ ~

The following morning, long before Stella or her aunt rose from their beds, Victoria summoned Dora to help her dress in a plain navy skirt and bodice. With her abundant hair pinned up under a black velvet hat, Victoria whispered her thanks to Dora and donned her long black coat.

'Where are you going so early, miss?' The maid looked worried.

'Just for a walk, Dora. I can't sleep.'

'But it's only just gone six, miss. It'll be chilly out there and with your chest ...'

'My chest is fine. I'm wearing my walking boots, so I might have a steady walk into town.'

'Buy a hot chocolate if you venture that far, miss.' Dora nodded wisely like an old woman. 'Me mam always says a hot chocolate in the morning gave you energy for the whole day.'

At the door, Victoria paused. 'If anyone asks, just tell them I'm gone for a walk into town and may even visit the library.' That would buy her more time.

Rushing, Victoria left the house and walked swiftly down Blossom Street. Across the road, a coal cart stood, the horse snorted in the cool morning air. The coal man and his young helper heaved sacks of coal over their shoulders and took them into the cellar of the Goodwins' house.

She hoped none of the families she knew glanced out of their windows and spotted her. A milk cart passed, the driver waving good morning to her.

She walked under the great medieval Micklegate Bar, and then she was inside the castle's outer walls. She picked up her pace, breathing in relief when a hansom cab came up the rise. She put out her hand to stop it.

'Going into town, miss?' the driver tilted his hat back and squinted down at her.

'Yes, Fossgate. Can you take me?'

'Fossgate?' He scratched his chin. 'Well, you see, I'm booked for a six-thirty pick up.'

'Please, I'll pay you extra.'

'Go on, then. Buttons, here, is fresh so he can get a move on, if you don't mind?'

'Faster the better. I need to go to Wilson's Hospital. Thank you.' She climbed in and held on tight as the cabbie turned Buttons around and spurred him into a trot.

Victoria's heart thumped faster as the hansom crossed Ouse Bridge and carried along Ousegate. In the clear morning air, the horse's hoofs sounded loud on the cobbles.

The city streets were wakening to a new day. Between the buildings, she glimpsed the twin towers of the Minster dominating the skyline. As the sun broke over the rooftops, the stall holders were busily setting up the market. The noise of people and traffic grew louder as they came closer to Fossgate.

This area of town was new to Victoria. There had never been any reason for her to venture into the poorer areas of the city, plus her aunt forbade it. Along Fossgate, they passed several public houses, the smell of stale beer strong in the morning air. The narrow street seemed swarming with people even at this early hour, then she realised they'd be going to their various places of work. Men and boys in working clothes were no doubt heading for the Union Gas Works, which she'd heard mention by her uncle before. Also, she knew the railway workshops and warehouses employed thousands of men.

The driver slowed the horse once they'd crossed Foss Bridge. 'Is here all right, miss?' he called to her. 'This is Wilson's.'

'Yes, thank you.' Victoria paid him and then hid her reticule in her skirt's deep pocket. She'd take no chances on getting it stolen.

Standing on the street, her ears rang with the sound of pigs squealing. Either a market or slaughter house was nearby. Looking up at the red brick house, she gathered her courage and knocked on the door.

It took several minutes for someone to open it and Victoria stood back in surprise when an old woman peered at her.

'Yes?'

For a moment Victoria couldn't speak. 'I've come to help,' she exclaimed.

'Help?'

'Yes. Is there someone I need to talk to about this?'

'The warden.' The old woman, all dressed in dark grey, opened the door wider so Victoria could enter.

Inside, she followed the woman down a short hallway and further into the back of the building.

Coming out of a room on the left, another woman stopped in surprise. 'May I be of assistance?'

'This lady here wants to help,' the old woman said and left them.

Nervous, Victoria forced a smile. 'May I introduce myself? I'm Miss Victoria Carlton, niece of Harold Dobson, banker.'

'I have heard of Mr Dobson and his wife.' The other woman spoke with a strong Scottish accent. 'I'm Mrs Agnes Stewart. How do you do.'

'I apologise for my early call, but Doctor Ashton said he was coming here today and I wish to be of use in some way. However, I wouldn't want to intrude...'

Mrs Stewart indicated for Victoria to enter the room she had been leaving. 'Oh yes, the new doctor. He called briefly last week. Doctor Ashton is a good man, but forgive me, I don't see how you can be of use, Miss Carlton, unless it is monetary. We run a very small establishment here.'

There was a sudden eruption of children's voices running past the door. Victoria looked over her shoulder in surprise as the clatter of boys flowed by. 'Children are here, too?'

'There is a boys' school in a building out the back. It's limited in number and the boys always come in and say good morning to the women when they arrive.' Mrs Stewart glanced at the silver watch on a chain at her waist. 'It's nearly time for morning prayers, would you care to join us?'

Victoria followed Mrs Stewart into an annexed part of the building and was introduced to Mr Smith, a small man with glasses who was the boys' instructor. A moment later, six elderly women entered the room and Mr Smith led them in prayer.

Afterwards, Mrs Stewart escorted Victoria into the women's rooms just as Doctor Ashton arrived.

'Miss Carlton! I did not expect to see you. I am surprised, but happily so.' He gave her a cheeky grin, then sobered. 'What will your cousin and aunt say?'

'They cannot say anything if they don't know.' She smiled back at him, so glad he'd arrived.

'Ah, I see. I am a keeper of secrets then?'

'Would that be too troublesome?'

He laughed. 'Not at all. However, in return I will demand your aid in my endeavours.'

'And you shall have it.' She couldn't wipe the smile off her face.

While the women ate their breakfast of porridge, and Victoria sipped a cup of tea, Mrs Stewart and Doctor Ashton studied ledgers of previous health checks. Victoria felt a little out of place, she had nothing to offer really. Perhaps it had been a mistake to come? How could she help in a well-organised place such as this?

'Miss Carlton?' Doctor Ashton stood next to her.

'Yes?'

'The women here have no medical issues for me to attend to today, which is indeed good news, and a rarity.'

'That is good news.'

'Would you care to come with me?' He led her into one of the communal rooms.

Victoria glanced about, noticing the low fire burning in the grate and the tidiness of the room. Chairs were placed closer to the window for extra light and baskets of sewing sat beside them. 'It is not what I expected, but then I didn't know what to imagine as I've never been in such a place before.'

'This establishment has been running smoothly for some time. Mrs Stewart is a very good warden. It's a small establishment, only ever six women.'

'A small concern then.' She nodded, interested.

'Yes. The donations and stipends it receives gives the women a good life. They have plenty to eat and are occupied with sewing and knitting. Outside there is a kitchen garden where they can grow vegetables and they have their own water pump.'

'Are all the almshouses so well run?'

He shook his head. 'No, not at all, but they do try. However, sometimes the wardens in charge aren't the right people to oversee operations and care only for their own advancement.'

'Shame they all aren't like Mrs Stewart.'

'Indeed. Mrs Stewart has done excellent work here. The women are happy and content. They have their own pew in the church across the road.' He walked her into the hallway. 'This is one of the almshouses which can set an example to others. It reassures me to find places such as these. Believe me, not all of them are so adequately maintained.'

'I feel as though I am not of any use here. I believe Mrs Stewart is not in need of having me follow her about the place,' She told him, smiling at one of the women who entered the room. 'I can give money, but I have no skills which would benefit these women. What can I do here?'

He was silent for a moment and then collected his medical bag. 'Come with me. If you have time?'

She hesitated for only a second. 'Of course.'

They said their goodbyes and left the building. They walked down Fossgate and continued on to Walmgate. The doctor stopped at a small shop that sold bread and other groceries. He bought a loaf of bread and a bag of apples before continuing down the street. They hadn't gone far when Ashton turned left into a narrow dank alley.

'If at any time you feel uncomfortable, you say so instantly,' Ashton said, as the alley opened into a filthy courtyard.

The wooden buildings surrounding the yard looked ancient and dilapidated. Some leaned against each other and she was sure if one beam was taken away the whole lot would crumble into a heap. A cat jumped up on the broken fence, eyeing them with disdain. A mangy dog peed up the side of a water barrel, which collected rainwater dripping from a cracked pipe.

She followed the doctor through another alley at the far side of the yard, holding her breath as rank smells she couldn't identify assailed her nose. The alley widened to about six feet across and timber houses boarded each side. Children ran playing, barefoot and hardly clothed. They all stopped to stare as she passed.

Cries of babies and raised voices filled the air and Ashton stepped up the pace. At the end of the alley, he turned again and went up an outside staircase at the end of a long red bricked building. At the top he knocked on the door. It was opened by a small child.

'Jane, is your Mama about?' Ashton asked, producing a sweet from his coat pocket. The child snatched it and disappeared into the darkness of the room.

Ashton opened the door wider to let in light. 'Mrs Felling?' He entered the room. 'It's Doctor Ashton.'

Victoria stepped into the room, squashing the urge to hold her nose for the smell was disgusting. After a moment, her eyes adjusted to the dimness and she stared in horror.

Several children huddled together on a filthy straw mattress on the floor in one corner. No fire heated the room. In another corner, a pot, full to the brim of urine, was placed next to a broken crate of rotten vegetables oozing mildew. At the back of the room on a pile of torn stained blankets lay a woman, or at least Victoria thought it was a woman, it was hard to tell with the person being so skeletal.

'Where's Polly?' Ashton asked the children as he handed Jane the paper bag of apples and the bread.

The children ignored him and dived into the apples and ripped the bread apart like savages.

Ashton bent to the woman, opening his medical bag at the same time. 'Mrs Felling. It's Doctor Ashton. Do you remember me from last week when I helped deliver your baby?'

The woman on the blankets remained silent, her eyes glazed. In her arms was a tiny baby, the smallest Victoria had ever seen.

Ashton turned to Victoria. 'Can you take the baby?'

She jumped as though he'd asked her to swim in the River Ouse. 'Me?'

'I need to examine her.' He gently lifted the baby from the woman's arms, then paused.

Frowning, he laid it back down again. Hurriedly, he stripped the loose coverings from its tiny body and put a stethoscope to the baby's tiny chest.

Stepping closer, alarmed but absurdly fascinated too, Victoria leaned closer. 'Doctor Ashton?'

'The baby is dead.' He knelt back on his heels. 'Possibly only a few hours ago for he is not discolouring yet.' He covered the baby up again and put him to one side.

Shocked, Victoria turned away, blinking rapidly. Her focus centred on the other children. Four little people, all younger than six she thought, stared at her with large eyes in sunken dirty faces as they chomped on the food. They wore rags, owned no shoes. Her heart broke at the pathetic sight of them.

Suddenly an older girl rushed in.

Doctor Ashton turned to her. 'Polly, isn't it?'

'Yes, sir. Will you make Ma better? She's not moved since havin' the baby.' She eyed the remnants of the bread and apples. 'You'd better have saved some for me!' she screeched, lunging for the one apple that remained and hitting the biggest of the children. 'Greedy pigs!'

Ashton ignored her and continued examining Mrs Felling. 'Your mother is ill. The baby has died.'

'He has? I thought he might. He wasn't feeding.' Polly went straight to the little bundle and scooped him up. 'I'll give him to Mrs Flannery.' She was gone from the room in an instant.

Ashton sighed and continued examining Mrs Felling.

Victoria, light-headed from shallow breathing through her mouth, stepped outside for some air.

In the alley below, women stood in doorways smoking clay pipes, as one they all turned to stare up at her. She looked away, embarrassed. An old man sat on a crate, rubbing the toes of one foot, his boot on the crate next to him. Children ran about, yelling. Two boys began fighting, rolling in the muck, doing their best to beat the other. A man walked into the yard, carrying a basket of sticks, he gave her a glance then went inside one of the hovels.

'Do you feel all right?' Ashton came out to stand beside her.

She nodded, not trusting herself to speak. This was an alien world.

He headed down the stairs. 'Come, I'll guide you back to the street. Go home. Bathe. Eat something.'

'Shouldn't Mrs Felling be in a hospital?' She slipped a little on the slimy stairs.

'Yes.' He huffed, a frustrated look in his eyes. 'However, if I removed her, the children would end up in the workhouse and separated for it would take her many months to be well again. In that time who knows where the children would end up.'

'In the workhouse they would have shelter and decent food!' She hurried to keep up with him.

'And never be a family again.'

'She can die if she's left in that disgusting hovel!'

His jaw tightened. 'I aim to prevent that.'

'Where is their father?'

'Living with a woman in Hungate I'm told,' he said, winding through the alleys.

She followed him dutifully, blocking out the sights and sounds which reeled her senses. Her boots were covered in inches of sludge and it coated the hem of her skirt. She shuddered to think of what it was, or how she would explain the state of them to Dora.

50

On Walmgate, the doctor scanned the road for a hansom cab. 'I apologise, Miss Carlton. I shouldn't have brought you here. You were not ready.'

His words entered her brain, dispelling the shock. 'No. No, Doctor Ashton, I am very glad you did.'

He took his hat off and ran his fingers through his hair. 'It was too much for your first time. I should have left you at Wilson's. You didn't need to see this today.'

'But I wanted to.'

'And what good has it done you? You are stunned by what you've witnessed. You have been protected all your life. It was naive of me to think you could handle such a scene.'

'But witness it I have!' Emotion blocked her throat.

'Yes, I am shocked, appalled. Yet, I cannot ignore it. I cannot pretend this doesn't exist.'

He hailed a passing hansom. 'Again, I am very sorry.'

'Blossom Street, please,' she called up to the driver before turning back to the doctor. 'Where did Polly take the baby?'

'To Mrs Flannery.'

'Why?'

Ashton bowed his head. 'It is known that some people sell bodies to the hospital for research. I believe Mrs Flannery is such a person, not that I have seen her.'

Victoria felt her jaw drop in surprise. 'Sell bodies?' she whispered.

'Polly would have got money from her, not a lot, but enough to buy food for her brothers and sisters. It'll keep them going a while longer.'

She stared at him. 'But the baby needs to be buried. You are a doctor. Surely you would report this?'

'I should, yes. Yet, to do so, would be taking food out of the mouths of those other children. I am unable to do that. The baby is dead. Gone. Just one in among thousands of the slum dead. If a few pennies keep those other children alive then...'

'It is wrong, so very wrong.' How was she going to return home and behave normally? She couldn't ignore what she'd seen. She felt sick. She'd witnessed things her family wouldn't believe even if she told them.

The cabbie's horse snorted and stamped on the cobbles breaking the moment between them.

Victoria opened the hansom's door and climbed in. As the cab pulled away, she thought she heard the doctor call her name.

She didn't look back.

Chapter Four

Music swelled in the grand assembly rooms. Women wearing all the colours of the rainbow paraded the large ornate room, chatting and laughing while the men talked and drank and tried to escape dancing another dance.

Victoria nodded and smiled to those she knew as she made her way through the crowd. Aunt Esther and Uncle Harold had already been drawn away by friends, leaving her and Stella to foray into the mass.

Behind her, Stella called out to people she knew, before grabbing Victoria's arm and halting her. 'We've been here less than two minutes and my dress has already been trodden on!' She whipped the bustle train around her, holding the fabric by the loop at the end and brought it closer into her body.

'You know it always happens.' Victoria smiled at a woman who was someone's wife, but she couldn't recall who it was. 'Let's find the refreshments.'

Stella paused. 'I wonder if Doctor Ashton has arrived. He promised me a dance.'

Victoria stiffened. Her mind and heart was in tor-
ment concerning the doctor. He seemed a good and
decent man, but to allow a child to sell a baby? It defied all her logic.

'Oh, there is Lucy Sykes. I need to speak to her
about her garden party next month.' Stella left Victoria and disappeared into the crowd.

She sighed, knowing this happened at every function but still it annoyed her that Stella would abandon
her and she'd not see her again until they left for
home.

'Miss Carlton.' John Fielding appeared by her side
and bowed to her with a smile.

'How nice to see you, Mr Fielding.'

'Care to dance?'

She returned his smile, liking the man whom she'd
known for years. He was one of her uncle's friends
and a shareholder in his bank. 'I was just about to find
some refreshments.'

'Shall I accompany you?'

She nodded and together they left the main room
and found the refreshment tables in a small adjoining
room. Several of the tables in the middle were taken.
People could talk easier here, away from the music
and dancers.

Mr Fielding handed her a small glass of elderberry
cordial and as she thanked him, her gaze met that of
Doctor Ashton's. He stood with a group of women by
the door. He bowed his head in her direction and she
replied the same.

Two weeks had passed since the day she went to the
slums with him and not a day of it had gone by where
she didn't think of him and what she'd seen.

Of course, she had no one to talk to about it for her uncle and aunt would be horrified and upset that she had put herself in such a dangerous situation. Stella wouldn't understand in the slightest and be appalled she'd even taken part in the adventure. So, the secret weighed heavily on her, and quite possibly gained more of her attention and thoughts than it warranted.

'You seem far away tonight, Miss Carlton.' Fielding raised an eyebrow. 'Does my company bore you intolerably?'

Snapped out of her thoughts, Victoria smiled brightly at him. 'Heavens, no, not at all. In fact, shall we have that dance?'

Not waiting for his reply, she placed her glass on the table and headed for the ballroom, making sure she went through another doorway far from the doctor. She had successfully avoided him the day the family went to Scarborough. She'd pleaded a headache and stayed at home. Stella had worn her new dress and looked spectacular and Victoria hadn't want to try and compete with her for Doctor Ashton's attention. It irritated her that she'd been a coward and not gone to the seaside town. But she had also been concerned the doctor might have mentioned the day in the slum and then she'd have to explain herself to her family.

She needn't have worried, for on arriving home at the end of the day, Stella had praised the doctor solidly for an hour. In her cousin's eyes he was the best of men, so courteous and considerate, taking care of her every need.

If Victoria had lied about the headache at the beginning of the day she certainly wasn't by the end of it after listening to Stella.

Jealousy had ripped through her when Stella announced that Doctor Ashton was escorting her to the theatre the following night – an occasion Ashton had cried off at the last minute due to duties at the hospital. Victoria had hid a secret grin at that.

Shaking her head, Victoria dismissed Stella and Ashton from her mind, determined to enjoy the night.

For the next three hours, she danced and ate and drank and danced some more. She did her best to not stand still long enough to talk to anyone for any length of time. Out the corner of her eye, she kept watch on where the doctor was at all times, noticing every dance partner he had and felt ridiculously bothered if he danced with any woman more than once, especially Stella.

'There you are.' Stella came to stand beside her, hot and flushed. 'We are going home. Papa has an early start for London tomorrow.'

'I'll get our capes.' Victoria left Stella to say their farewells and made for the cloak room near the front of the building.

'Miss Carlton.' Doctor Ashton stepped in front of her.

'Good evening, Doctor.' Her heart thudded in her chest.

'I was disappointed you didn't go to Scarborough. I'd have liked to discuss different topics with you on the train journey. I hope the headache didn't debilitate you too much?'

'I am quite recovered, thank you.' She felt herself blush at the lie she'd told everyone. 'Excuse me. We are about to depart.'

'Please,' he murmured, his hand holding her arm to stop her from walking away. 'I've wanted to talk to you all night. I've not even managed to dance with you.'

'Doctor Ashton—'

He leaned closer and she could smell the slight aroma of a citrus cologne on him. 'Miss Carlton, the incident in Walmgate...'

'Please, let us not speak of it.'

'I know you must have been shocked, but I beg you not to let that one episode cloud your judgement of me or the work that I do.'

She swallowed, unable to break eye contact with him. 'You let a young girl sell her dead baby brother,' she hissed through clenched teeth. 'How can I not judge you on such a thing?'

'It was to save the others.'

'A few pennies? Really, will it save them?' she snapped. 'They should be in a workhouse!'

'Not all poor people can live in a workhouse, Miss Carlton, for overcrowding is already at a premium.' Anger narrowed his blue eyes as he stared at her. 'Don't make conclusions on something you know very little about.'

'I may not have much knowledge of the poor now, but I assure you that I will educate myself on the situation as much as I can.'

'How? By attending a few ladies' meetings about fundraising for an almshouse?' he mocked.

'Don't you dare patronise me!' Her harsh whisper caught in her throat. She was mortified that he'd made her so angry.

'I'm sorry.' He ran a hand through his black hair.
'All I do is apologise to you.' He looked around the
crowd, but no one was paying them any attention. 'If
you truly want to help, then you need to know exactly
what it is that you are dealing with.'

'I *will* visit the workhouses,' she told him, head
held high defiantly.

'Visit? Simply visit a workhouse?' His eyebrows
rose mockingly.

'No, I mean, I'll help and I'll give where I can.'

'That is not enough. The aid is needed *before* these
people are forced to give up everything and enter the
workhouse. If we can help them stay in their own
homes, find work, take care of their families, that is
what has to be achieved.'

His passion for the subject moved her. Compassion
replaced her anger. 'How? How do we try to deal
with a problem on such an enormous scope?'

He shrugged. 'One family at a time, I suppose.'

'Speaking of families, is Mrs Felling...'

'Still alive. I—'

'Victoria!' Stella called from near the front doors.
'Where are our capes?'

Blushing, Victoria ducked her head. She'd forgotten
all about the capes. 'I must go. Good night.'

~ ~ ~ ~

Joseph watched her leave the room and sighed
deeply. He'd been all kinds of fool in regards to Miss
Carlton. He'd been too eager and determined to show
her things she was not ready to take in.

She'd been raised as a sheltered daughter of an influential family. Why had he thought that taking her into the slums would have been a good thing to do? He was used to seeing such deprived conditions, she was not. He'd done more harm than good that day and now she thought him despicable, which was upsetting.

Her attentiveness to the poor was commendable and he felt it could be developed even more.

He'd seen her compassion and believed she could handle more in-depth situations. But he could have managed the Felling situation better.

He should have taken her to other less shocking places.

What a fool he'd been.

All he'd done was drive her friendship away before he'd had chance to prove himself. He wondered if she'd forgive him. He had to show her that his methods were not as depraved as she thought.

He took a glass of champagne from a passing waiter's tray and drank it in one go. Victoria Carlton was getting under his skin and he wasn't sure how to cope it.

~ ~ ~ ~

The following afternoon, Victoria stood on Walmgate staring at the alley she'd gone down with the doctor.

She'd told those at home that she was on an errand to take books back to the library. She lied, a habit she was forming.

In her basket weren't books but as much food as she could squirrel away without being noticed.

She'd dressed in an old dark grey skirt and bodice, which Stella once scathingly said she wasn't to be seen wearing outside of the house. Donning old boots and a long black coat, she'd taken extra money from the drawer in her bedroom as well.

The day was dull and overcast with a chilly breeze. It was a day to stay inside, not be out making her way down a grimy alley as rain clouds threatened.

She kept walking, hoping she was going the right way as the alley twisted and turned. When the first courtyard opened out before her, she congratulated herself on finding it.

A scream pierced the air from behind one of the doors, making her jump. Frightened, she hurried her pace, going through the opposite alley and nearly bumping into a man coming the other way.

'Hey up, missus!' he muttered, barrelling past her, reeking of stale body sweat and ale.

She held her basket tighter and hurried on, grateful to come out at the end. Ahead was the staircase. Two women stood around chatting, smoking clay pipes. One woman sported a black eye and had a baby on her hip while other children ran about playing.

Victoria stopped in her tracks. To get to the staircase she'd have to pass by them and she wasn't sure if she could do it.

These women intimidated her. They might not look like they have a penny between them, but they had an old world knowledge that clearly surpassed her education at Miss Henderson's School for Girls. She might be able to speak limited French and know the kings and queens of England, but these women knew how to survive when everything was against them.

'Can we 'elp you, miss?' the woman without the baby asked.

'Er…um…' Victoria glanced at the staircase and pointed.

'You want to see the Fellings?'

She nodded.

'Aye, go on up.' The woman crossed her arms over her chest. 'She's very popular is Mrs Felling, ain't she, Betsy?'

The other woman called Betsy nodded. 'Aye, the doc is never away from the doorstep. How sick is she anyway? We don't have doctors calling day and night, do we. Rosie?'

Rosie hoisted the baby higher on her hip. 'I think I might get sick if it means that good-looking doctor is touching me!' They both roared with laughter.

Victoria gave them a quivering smile and stepped past them. She felt their eyes burn into her as she ascended the staircase. She knocked on the door and it sounded overly loud.

A tiny face peeped out before opening the door wider and letting her in.

An eye-watering stench filled Victoria's nose of stale bodies and an overflowing chamber pot. Once her eyes adjusted to the dimness of the room, she noticed the children huddled in the same dirty corner. Wide stares in dirty faces. Mrs Felling lay asleep on the floor where Victoria had last seen her.

'Mrs Felling?' For a moment, she was worried the woman had died until a skeletal hand twitched.

'She's sleeping,' a little voice said from the corner.

'Where's your sister?' Victoria stared around the hovel, not knowing what to do.

'Out.'

She nodded. From the corner of her eye, she spied a rat darting out from behind the crate of rotten fruit and stifled a small scream.

Her skin tingled. She looked at the children and they stared dolefully back at her.

What was she doing here? How could she help this family? She was out of her depth.

Realising she still clung to her basket, she stepped to the rickety wooden table placed next to the small and only window. Cobwebs and a film of dust covered the window creating a grey light in the room.

She opened the basket and turned to the children. 'Would you like something to eat?'

In an instant she was surrounded by four little bodies. Ignoring their filthy hands, she passed around the remnants of the breakfast and lunch she'd managed to hide from her family and Mr Hubbard, who had the sharpest eyes in the house.

Breaking up the bread rolls, she gave them out, followed by a few slices of bacon and two boiled eggs, cold now as breakfast had been hours ago. From lunch she'd hid in a napkin, slices of ham, cheese and whole pickled onions. Amazingly enough, she'd been able to hide four scones and two treacle tartlets.

'Don't eat it so fast!' she reprimanded as one of the little boys stuffed so much into his mouth, he nearly choked.

She took some cheese over to Mrs Felling and nudged her awake.

'What?' the sleepy voice was barely a whisper.

'Mrs Felling, you must eat something. Here's some cheese.'

Obediently, the woman opened her mouth, and like a baby, allowed Victoria to place the cheese inside it.

A mixture of emotions swamped Victoria. Compassion, certainly, helplessness, too, but surprisingly a growing amount of anger that this woman had no one to look after her and her children.

'Can you sit up and have some more food?' she coaxed her and was pleased when Mrs Felling raised her head.

'Food?' the woman croaked.

'Yes.' She hurried back to the basket and the children scattered. All the food was gone. She glared at them, dismayed. Yet when the eldest little boy smiled back at her, she instantly forgave them all. How could she deny starving children?

'Mrs Felling, I'm sorry the children ate it all.'

'Tea?'

'Tea?' Victoria glanced around the room. A stone bottle stood on a wooden shelf by the door. She took it down and pulled out the cork. Liquid was inside, not much though and it didn't smell unpleasant no matter what it was.

'Ma's tea.' The oldest girl in the group nodded and Victoria remembered Doctor Ashton calling her Jane.

Taking the girl's word for it, Victoria knelt beside the sick woman and helped her to drink.

Mrs Felling's eyes met Victoria's. 'Thank you.'

The sick woman smelt. Her thin dress was nearly see-through and what skin was exposed was ingrained with grime.

Everything and everyone in the room was dirty. Victoria couldn't stand it, it made her skin crawl and itch. Anger built in her chest again. How could people be allowed to live like this? It wasn't acceptable.

Unsure what to do, but knowing instinctively that something had to be done, Victoria rose to her feet and replaced the bottle back in the shelf. The children watched her and she realised they hadn't had anything to drink. She quickly passed them the bottle.

'No. Ma's tea,' Jane said, pushing her siblings back behind her. 'Polly'll hit us.'

'I'm going to buy more,' Victoria said impulsively. An idea came to her and grew. She smiled at the children, but they huddled back, eyes wide in their pinched faces.

Determined, and not sure where to start, Victoria strode purposely to the crates in the corner and moved them. The rat shot along the wall and disappeared out the door. She shuddered and continued on.

From behind the crates, she uncovered a small stand-alone iron stove, but it had no chimney flue which proved it worthless for the smoke would fill the room as soon as a fire was lit.

Going to the door, she stood at the top of the steps. The women had gone, but the old man she'd seen on her previous visit was down near the alley entrance.

'Excuse me,' she called out to him.

After a moment's hesitation, he plodded to the bottom of the steps. 'Aye, miss?'

'I need a chimney of some kind. The stove in here has no chimney pipe. Do you know someone who could acquire one for me and fit it?'

A slow smile spread across the old man's face. He scratched his long grey whiskers. 'Aye, 'appen I could 'elp yer.'

'You could?'

'It'll cost, mind.'

'I have money...' She paused, wondering if she should say such a thing out loud in this area, but then how would she get him to do this errand for her. 'I'll pay you once you've finished the job.'

'Let me 'ave a look at it then.' He traipsed up the stairs and into the room.

Using the width of his hands, he measured the size of the chimney pipe.

'It's blocked up there.' He pointed to the ceiling where someone had nailed a piece of wood over the hole where the pipe should poke through.

'I see, yes.' Victoria frowned in thought. 'Can you fix this or not?'

The old man scratched his whiskers some more. 'Aye, it'll cost, mind.'

Watching him, Victoria saw the glint in his eye. She might be naive in many things, but she wasn't stupid.

She'd seen Mrs Norman deal with tradespeople for years. 'Very well, but I don't have a lot of money with me. The job has to be done to my satisfaction or you'll not be paid at all.'

He coughed. 'I'm not a young man to be tramping about up on the roof. If I can't fix it from in here, I aint' doing it and I'll *not* do it for nowt.'

She clenched her teeth. 'I can easily find someone else to do it and pay them, if you'd prefer?' She might never have done anything like this before in her life, but she wasn't going to let him get the better of her. He wasn't going to rob her blind.

'Nay, I never said that.' He scratched his chin and she wondered if he had fleas.

'Well?'

'You'll need coal, too,' he muttered, opening the stove and staring into it.

'Do a good job and get this working by tonight and you'll be rewarded accordingly.' She hoped she had enough money in her reticule.

'I'll start tomorrow.'

'No!' Her bark made the children crowd into the shadows even more. 'I mean, I need you to do it now, today. These children need a fire.'

'They need more than a fire, miss.'

'I know and I'm going to rectify that.' How she didn't know, but she had to try.

'I'll go get a pipe then.' He held out his hand for money. 'No one will let me buy on tick, miss.'

'On tick?'

'To pay later. Everyone knows I'm not in work.'

'Oh, I see.' From her reticule, she placed two shillings in his hand, not knowing how much he'd need.

'Any old pipe will do as long as it fits the stove.'

'Aye.' He trudged out and she followed him, standing on top of the stairs.

'Where can I get water from?' she asked his retreating back.

'There's a pump in the next alley. It's turned off until six o'clock.' He looked up at her. 'I'll get yer some, but it'll cost yer.'

She nodded and re-entered the room. So much needed to be done. She'd never cleaned a hovel before. She'd barely cleaned anything at all, except her own body.

Unbuttoning her sleeves, she rolled them up. Tentatively, she began carrying the crates into the middle of the room. Some were empty and other were full of rubbish bits and pieces that she couldn't make sense out of. Dust floated into the air making her cough.

The children laughed at her coughing and she grinned the best she could back at them. 'Will you not help me?'

Their laughter stopped instantly and they huddled back into the corner.

'Hmm, I thought not.' Victoria wanted to wash everything, but without huge amounts of water and soap she was restricted.

Mrs Felling raised her head. 'What…are…you…'

'I'm cleaning your home, Mrs Felling.' She told her and kept on sorting.

In one crate she found an old pot, dinted and missing a handle but usable. She also found a chipped plate and a cracked cup.

Suddenly, Victoria longed for a cup of tea. Guilt quickly clamped down on that desire for she was surrounded by people who'd not had a decent meal for goodness knows how long, never mind a cup of tea.

Holding her breath, she picked up the chamber pot and carefully carried it outside and threw its contents over the edge of the stairs to join the rest of the muck and grime below.

How long would the old man be? Would he even come back? She desperately needed the water to clean. How shocking it was to not have water whenever people needed it. Before today she'd never really known of the frustration of not instantly having to hand whatever she wanted. How did people do it, day after day?

A loud knock sounded on the door and a young woman stood there. 'Sorry for disturbin' yer.'

'Please, come in.' Victoria gave her best welcoming smile. 'I'm Victoria Carlton and you are?'

'Annie Weaver, miss.' She bobbed a small curtsey. 'I live just along the way.' She pointed behind her. 'I usually call in an' make sure Mercy is still alive. The doctor comes in the mornin' an' I pop over in the afternoon. Pays me to come, he does. A few pennies comes in handy.' Annie pushed up a loose strand of hair under the colourful scarf wrapped around her head. 'She's nice enough is Mercy, I don't mind lookin' in.'

'That's good of you.' She frowned in confusion.
She was happy that Doctor Ashton kept such a close
eye on his patient, but to have to pay someone just to
check on Mrs Felling seemed wrong.

Why didn't the neighbours help each other in times
of need? Why was everything about money?

Annie leaned against the door. 'Are yer a friend of
the doctor?'

'An acquaintance.' To say friend felt false.

'I'll head off then, since yer here.'

'Wait! Um ... er ... I need some water, to clean ...'
Time was getting on and she believed she'd never see
the old man and her money again.

'Clean? You?' Annie's eyes widened in surprise.

'I don't see anyone else willing to do it, do you?'

'We all have our own homes to keep tidy.' Annie
became defensive, crossing her arms across her chest.

'I understand, but this woman is very ill. She has
nothing!'

Annie scoffed. 'Do yer think we live in mansions?'

'No, of course I don't ...' Flustered, Victoria wrung
her hands. 'It's simply that ...'

Noise at the door made her turn.

The old man entered carrying a long pipe and a
bucket of water, which he set by the door. 'Here, yer
are then.'

'It'll fit?' Victoria asked. The pipe looked old and
was bent and rusted in places.

'Oh, aye.'

'Where did you get it from, Jimmy?' Annie laughed
at the old man. 'Will some poor sod get home tonight
an' find they don't have a stovepipe?'

Jimmy shrugged and scratched his whiskers. 'Best
get on with it.'

He set to work, making so much noise and dust that Victoria placed a holey rag over Mrs Felling's head. The children refused to move off their bed of filth though and she left them there.

Annie stayed by the door. 'She was lovely, you know, once.'

Victoria turned from pouring water into the dented pot. 'Who?'

'Mercy.' Annie nodded to the sick woman. 'When she first came here, she only had two little ones, and was pregnant with another, but she still stood tall an' smiled at every one. She 'ad good quality clothes. The little ones were smartly dressed with chubby cheeks. Her man, he was a right one for talking. Could charm the birds from the trees, so he could.'

'What happened?' Victoria dunked a rag into the water and started scrubbing the window.

'He lost his job. Took to drink.' Annie pushed her hands into the deep pockets of her apron and watched Victoria work. 'These kids don't need a clean window. They need food an' so does she.'

Feeling foolish, Victoria's hand slowed. 'Yes, I am aware of that, but they can't live in such filth.'

'A fire will help for a bit, but they'll run out of coal. There's no money to buy more. There's no money for anything.' Annie sighed. 'Mercy doesn't want to get better. What does she have to live for?'

Victoria stared at her. 'Her children!'

'Children she can't take care of.' Annie walked down the stairs without saying goodbye.

Jimmy continued to bang, standing on the rickety crates piled three high to reach the ceiling. He made so much mess. Soot from the pipe showered the floorboards like black rain.

Victoria felt tears of frustration prick behind her eyes. It was all too hard.

'It ain't perfect, miss, but it'll work.' Jimmy stood back to admire his handiwork.

To Victoria it looked ready to topple over any minute. 'It's safe?'

'Aye. Safe as you'll get with what you've got.'

'Can we make a fire and test it?' she asked. Outside the grey clouds that had threatened all day suddenly opened up and a huge downpour started.

Jimmy opened the door of the iron stove and prodded about inside its belly.

'Here, I brought you this.' Annie had returned and in her out-thrust hands was a large bundle of newspapers and a jug. 'There's water in the jug. For the children to drink, not to clean with.'

Victoria took the things from her. 'Thank you, Annie.'

Annie turned on her heel and went back downstairs in the rain.

'Are you thirsty?' she asked the children, pouring the water into the only cup in the room.

In turn, each child drank a full cup of water, the youngest, a boy no more than two years old she thought, spilt water down his chin leaving dirty streak marks.

Jimmy screwed up the newspaper and broke up the crates to build a fire. He was unsuccessful in the first attempt but, before long, a cheery blaze was burning.

Victoria smiled at the children as they stared at it. The firelight reflected on their faces, showing in stark contrast the grimy skin on each child.

The fire would need to be kept going night and day to keep this place warm, an impossible task.

Gazing at the filth around her, she felt so tired, so overwhelmed. She wasn't responsible for these children, yet how could she forget about them now?

'I'll stay until young Polly gets back, miss.' Jimmy sat on the floor in front of the fire, breaking up the last of the crates.

'Where does she go?'

'Stealing, foraging, anything to bring back a bit of food for her mam an' the young 'uns.' Jimmy poked the fire with a broken bit of wood. 'She's wild that one, but loyal as a dog when it comes to her family.'

Victoria thought of the girl taking her dead baby brother's body away and shuddered. None of this was right.

Thunder rolled overhead. Dark clouds turned day into night as heavy rain fell.

'I need to go home, Jimmy.' Victoria donned her coat and picked up her basket. She couldn't risk being stuck here for hours as night fell if the weather didn't let up. She'd have to chance getting wet and finding a cab to take her home. 'I'll be back tomorrow.'

'Aye, miss.'

She smiled at the children. 'I'll bring more food tomorrow.'

Blank stares met her. The smallest boy was curled up fast asleep on the soiled mattress.

Pity filled Victoria as she walked out into the rain. The courtyard and alleys were deserted, the rain driving everyone indoors. She hurried along, conscious that she'd been gone from home for hours. She hoped she could lie convincingly enough to detract further questions.

On Walmgate she held up her hand at a passing hansom to stop it.

Sitting back against the leather seat, she sighed and closed her eyes.

The events of the day whirled in her mind. She promised she'd return tomorrow. She just didn't know how she was going to do it without drawing attention to herself at home.

Chapter Five

Victoria hurried downstairs, pinning her black velvet hat on as she went.

'Where are you going?' Stella asked, coming out of the drawing room.

'Oh...I'm walking into town.' She looked away.

'Again?' Stella tutted.

'You know how much I enjoy walking.'

'Well, you cannot go now. Mrs Popplewaite and Cynthia will be here at any moment.'

'They will?' Victoria's heart sunk.

'It's Friday, you know how they call every Friday morning.' Stella frowned. 'Why do you need to go into town again?'

'Just to do some shopping and...er...' Lies rolled off her tongue.

'You were gone all afternoon yesterday. You promised to come with me on the calls, remember? I do *not* want to visit Mrs Downing on my own again. She can't hear a word I say, and I spend twenty minutes shouting.'

Victoria unpinned her hat and put it on the hall table, just as the front door knocker sounded. 'I'll visit Mrs Downing after I've been shopping,' she told Stella as they entered the drawing room to join Aunt Esther while Mr Hubbard answered the door.

After greeting Mrs Popplewaite and her daughter Cynthia, Victoria busied herself pouring out the cups of tea from the tray Jennie brought in.

Her gaze strayed to the carriage clock above the mantelpiece. It was gone eleven. She should be in Walmgate by now.

If she had a choice, she'd have gone straight after breakfast, but Aunt Esther and Stella lingered after eating to talk about the invitations coming in for the summer, the dinner party tomorrow night, and the poetry recital they were attending this evening. Now she had the Popplewaites to sit through when all she wanted was to rush off to check on the Felling family. She'd worried about them all night. Had the chimney stayed up? Did rain come through the hole Jimmy had made for the chimney? Was Mrs Felling still alive?

'Victoria!' Stella nudged her, an eyebrow lifted haughtily. 'Cynthia asked you a question and we are all very interested to hear your answer.'

'Please forgive me, Cynthia, what was your question?' She placed the teapot back on the tray.

'I was simply remarking that I saw you yesterday in Walmgate. My driver took that way coming back from Selby. I wondered what you were doing there in the pouring rain.' Cynthia smiled, but it didn't reach her eyes, which stared coldly at her. 'I cannot think why anyone of our society would be in such a place.'

Shocked, Victoria tried to think of something quick to say. 'I...you saw me?'

'In Walmgate, exiting an alley.'

Stella waved her hand dismissively. 'I think you were mistaken, Cynthia. Victoria has no need to venture to that part of town by herself.'

'I'm sure it was you.' Cynthia waited for Victoria to confess.

She forced a smile. 'I was in the library yesterday afternoon and nowhere near Walmgate. It must have been someone else.' She couldn't believe how easy it was to lie to Cynthia's face. 'Would you care for some lemon cake?'

For twenty-five long minutes, she sat listening to Mrs Popplewaite telling Aunt Esther all about her nephew who was about to marry an American from New York. By the time they left, Victoria knew more than she ever wanted to about this American woman. Cynthia had given her odd looks the whole time and Victoria knew she'd not believed the lie.

'Mrs Popplewaite talks for far too long than is polite,' Stella announced as soon as the door closed behind them. 'Not once did she let us speak for longer than a minute. I'll not be in next Friday, Mama, when they call again.'

Aunt Esther raised her eyebrows at her. 'You might not want to be here on Friday, daughter, but you'll be returning their call on Tuesday.'

Before Stella could protest more callers arrived and another hour was taken up with visitors and then lunch. Victoria felt she'd never get away.

Finishing their meal, Aunt Esther rose and headed for the door. 'I must be going. I need to visit Holmes House and speak with the committee.'

'May I come with you, Aunt?' Victoria asked, also standing.

She'd missed the opportunity to go to Walmgate but perhaps a visit to one of Aunt's charities would help her see the process of how money or aid was given to the deserving.

Aunt Esther hesitated in the doorway. 'My dear, no, I'm sorry. You cannot enter Holmes House.'

'I can help.' She was eager to see what was being achieved so she could talk to Doctor Ashton with more knowledge.

'I'm sure you can, dearest, and at another place you'd be most welcomed.'

'But—'

'However, Holmes House isn't appropriate for you to visit. You may encounter some of the…residents, and that would be unseemly.' Aunt Esther left the room to prevent further discussion.

'Why would you ask to go there? You know it's not allowed.' Stella flicked through a magazine. 'How could you want to be amongst fallen women, I don't understand.'

'No, *you* wouldn't.' Victoria had no patience with Stella's forthright manner of choosing who deserved money or not.

'It is the one charity I refuse to be associated with. Those women are a disgrace. I wish Mama would stop going there.'

Victoria ignored her and hurried after her aunt, finding her in the hall. Mr Hubbard was assisting her in putting her coat on.

'Aunt, can I share the carriage with you then? I'll visit a few of the shops.' She lied again, for she had no intention of shopping, but instead would go to Walmgate after all, despite it being late in the day.

Stella came into the hall. 'We can all go together.'

'Only if you're ready right now, Stella. I'm not waiting,' Aunt Esther said, pulling on her gloves.

Inwardly, Victoria groaned. She didn't want Stella coming with her and preventing her from checking in on the Felling family. She dithered for a moment, trying to work out a plan.

'Actually, girls, you would help me enormously if you go and visit my mother. You know how lonely she gets when she's been kept at home with her poor legs. You can let me out at Holmes House and take the carriage.'

'Oh yes, let us go to Mimi's house instead.' Stella quickly donned the coat that Mr Hubbard held out for her.

Victoria loved Mimi. Like the rest of the family, Mimi, Esther's mother, had welcomed Victoria all those years ago and treated her as a granddaughter the same as she did with Stella. Mimi was in her eighties but still sharp as a tack, and refused to be called 'grandmother' preferring to be known just as Mimi. Usually, Victoria was keen to visit the delightful old woman, but today she was desperate to see how the Felling family fared.

Once in the carriage, Stella held the conversation all the way into the city centre. At the beginning of Church Street, they stopped to let Aunt Esther out before carrying on again.

Fiddling with one of the buttons on her long blue coat, Victoria tried to think of a way to get to Walmgate.

'So, are you going to explain the lie you told to Cynthia and everyone?' Stella suddenly asked.

'Lie?'

Stella glared at her. 'Don't play dumb with me. I know you far too well, better than anyone in fact, and I know when you're lying for your cheeks go red and you don't make eye contact with anyone for a long time.'

Caught out, she didn't know what to say. Her mind froze.

'And don't try to lie your way out of this either! I can see your cheeks going red already!' Stella leaned in close. 'What have you been doing? I insist on knowing! Have you been meeting some gentleman?'

'No!' Victoria gasped. 'How could you even think that of me?'

'It happens. Why do you think Flora Osmond married that gentleman from Harrogate so suddenly last month? Gossip is that she was in the family way when walking down the aisle.'

'Really?' Victoria's eyes widened. Stella always knew the current gossip, whereas Victoria usually had her nose stuck in a book instead.

'So? Tell me everything.' Stella demanded.

'You wouldn't understand.'

'That's twice you've said that to me today.' Stella huffed. 'What wouldn't I *understand*?'

'I want to help the poor of the city.'

Stella rolled her eyes. 'Yes, I know all that. It's all very commendable.'

'It's what I've been doing.'

'You *were* in Walmgate then!' Stella glared at her. 'You did lie!'

'Yes. I was visiting a family who are in desperate circumstances.' The relief of confessing was immense.

'Why have you not mentioned it to us?'

'Because Aunt and Uncle wouldn't want me to go there on my own, and those people need my help.'

Stella shook her head. 'No, those people need *anyone's* help, not just yours alone.'

'While that is true, I can also be of value. I believe I am serving where it is needed most.'

'Serving where?' Stella's eyes narrowed. '*Who* needs your help?'

'A family called Felling. A poor ill woman and her small children.' Victoria gripped Stella's hand, desperate for her to comprehend and believe in the same things as she did just this once. 'You should see how they live! They have nothing. Not a bed, or decent clothes, no food or even water.'

'Good Lord!'

'The woman, Mrs Felling, has been left her destitute by her husband. The children are starving. I have to help them.'

'There are charities we can inform, who will help them. Mama will know what is best to do about them.'

'No, they'll take the children away and put them in one of the workhouses. They'll be split up. I can keep them together. I should be there now, taking them some food and blankets. I want to buy them clothes and a bed to get them off the floor. They need chairs and—'

'Victoria, stop!' Stella demanded, waving her hand. 'You cannot save every family you see who are struggling. There are too many of them. York is full of the destitute classes.'

'I know I can't save every family, but I can do my best to save the Fellings. I intend to.'

Victoria gazed at her cousin with a sudden will of steel running through her. 'I won't be dissuaded. Will you tell Uncle and Aunt about this?'

Stella tilted her head and studied Victoria for a long moment. 'No, I won't tell, as I do like keeping secrets. I have a head full of them. However, I insist on coming with you.'

'Come with me?' Victoria's shoulders slumped. 'I don't think you should. You will not like it.'

'No, I do not think I will. Still, it has to be done and, if I am going to be a part of this secret, I need to know exactly what it is you are doing.'

Ten minutes later, the carriage slowed outside of Mimi's cottage on Monkgate. The housekeeper Mrs Flowers welcomed them in and took their coats.

'Why girls, I wasn't expecting you, only Esther.' Mimi hugged them both from her chair by the fire.

'Mama sends her apologies but she's dreadfully busy today.' Stella sat next to Victoria on the sofa near the window.

'Are you going to the recital this evening?' Mimi asked. 'I was going to attend...' Her voice faded away.

'Do you not feel well enough? Are your legs paining you again?' Victoria asked, concerned. Mimi appeared no different to the last time she saw her a few weeks ago, and she chastised herself for not visiting more.

'My legs are punishing me for a lifetime of dancing with handsome young men.' Mimi grinned. 'And I'm old and creaky, my dear. My head wants to do the things my body refuses to consider. Growing old is a travesty, girls, let me tell you!' She laughed. 'Now tell me all your news and what are Laurence and Todd up to. I never receive letters from them!'

Stella happily filled her grandmother in on family news while Mrs Flowers brought in a tea tray laden with delicious treats.

Victoria glanced at Stella as her cousin piled food on her plate and all she could think of was that the Felling children would enjoy these cakes and sandwiches so much more. Here, they were eating and drinking for the third time today and she fully expected that the Felling children hadn't eaten since she gave them that small amount of food yesterday.

When Stella excused herself from the room, Mimi leaned forward to Victoria. 'What is wrong, my dear? I can see in your eyes that something is troubling you.'

'Oh, no, I'm fine, Mimi.' She played with her napkin.

Mimi leaned back in her chair. 'Don't try to fool an old woman. I see everything.'

'Truly, there is nothing wrong.'

'Victoria, your eyes are too expressive. They speak volumes when your mouth doesn't utter a word.'

She smiled nervously, feeling a little warm. The small room was like an oven with a fire roaring.

Mimi banged her hand on the chair arm. 'I insist on knowing!'

'Well…'

'Ah! So, there is something. I knew it. All the details, now if you please.'

Knowing she had to reveal everything to the old woman made her feel sick to the stomach. She'd gone from no one knowing her secret to two people knowing in less than an hour.

Mimi bent forward, concern in her eyes. 'Are you in trouble, dearest?'

'No! Not at all.' Heavens why did people think she was easily led into mischief?

'It happens, my dear, trust me.'

'The truth is…there is a family, the Fellings, who are poor and in need of aid. I have been visiting them, and I was hoping to go again today, but it's getting late and I don't think I'll be able to go.'

'Your good nature does you credit, my dear.' Mimi sat back and pulled the rug straighter about her knees. 'No one knows of these visits, I take it?'

'Only Stella. I just told her in the carriage.'

'Esther and Harold won't like you doing this on your own. Harold will be appalled. You are too much like your mother and he worshipped the ground she walked on. He'll not want to take any risks in losing you.'

'I can't turn my back on them, Mimi.' She was resolute in that.

Mimi folded her hands in her lap. 'How did you meet this family?'

'Through Doctor Ashton.' She blushed, though it was all very innocent. 'He invited me to visit Wilson's Home for old women, and then afterwards we went to Walmgate. Mrs Felling is his patient.'

'This Doctor Ashton is the same one Esther found a house for, yes?'

'That's correct.'

'He seems to be very agreeable and trustworthy. Esther praised him to me for a good five minutes.'

'He is passionate in his ambitions about helping the poor.'

'Passionate men are too few in the world, in my opinion. There is nothing wrong with a bit of passion, my dear.' Mimi's lips twitched with devilment. 'Stella will not be as committed as you in this endeavour, you know that, don't you?'

'Yes, I do. She doesn't need to be involved, but she has promised to keep my secret...' Victoria looked hopefully at Mimi.

The old woman chuckled. 'Never fear, my girl, your secret is also safe with me. But do keep me updated. I do like a bit of intrigue.'

'Thank you.' Relief flooded her.

Mimi gave her a concerned stare. 'Promise me you'll keep yourself safe.'

'I will.'

'And don't expect Stella to be of any use to you. She'll grow bored within ten minutes if she isn't the centre of attention.'

'I know.' That worried Victoria more than anything.

Stella breezed into the room and declared that she'd torn a hole in her stocking. 'Mimi, I went through your chest of drawers with your maid's help and replaced them. You don't mind, do you?'

Victoria looked at Mimi who winked at her. They both knew that Stella would never devote herself to anything but Stella Dobson.

~ ~ ~ ~

The following morning, Victoria gave in and took Stella with her as she headed for Walmgate.

Yesterday, after leaving Mimi's house a thick fog had descended and whitened the city.

Stella begged her not to go to the slum areas in such foul weather and she had acquiesced, though it had pained her conscience to do so. She'd slept badly because of it.

Now, as they took a hansom cab, Stella chatted about the upcoming Lord Mayor's Ball at Mansion House next month and the dress she was to wear which the seamstresses at Miss Thatcher's Salon were currently creating. 'I do think the deep rose colour of the silk will suit me very well, do you not agree?'

'Yes, I'm sure it will.'

'I saw your dress on my last visit and the emerald is perfect for you.' Stella peeked out of the window. 'Your dress colour is a suitable contrast to mine. Though mine has more lace.'

Victoria tuned out as Stella extolled the virtues of Irish lace compared to Italian as the hansom cab travelled along High Ousegate.

'I want to stop and buy a few things for the Fellings,' Victoria said suddenly.

'What?' Stella blinked, not following her.

Victoria knocked for the cabbie to slow the horse. 'I need to stop and buy some things.'

'Such as what?'

At the end of Parliament Street, the hansom stopped and Victoria climbed down. 'Stay here, I won't be long.'

'Victoria!'

Ignoring her cousin, she hurried through the market stalls. Her first purchase was a large basket. In this she placed a blanket she impulsively bought, not of great quality, but one that was better than the children had now.

Next, she bought some matches, candles, cups and plates from another stall, and from the next stall she bought jars of jam, pickled onions, boiled eggs and a wedge of cheese.

Heading back to the hansom, she paused and bought two loaves of bread and a decent knife from a man who was selling bits and pieces out of an old suitcase.

With the basket bulging and heavy, she managed to buy a bottle of ginger ale and juggling it all she finally returned to Stella.

'Good heavens, why didn't you let me come with you?' Stella admonished as she climbed into the hansom.

'It was quicker on my own.' Victoria smiled to take any offence out of her words. 'You know what you are like, you'd have wandered off and done shopping of your own.'

'Why have you bought so much? I hope these people will be grateful!' Stella searched through the basket. 'We could have taken this from home, no one would have missed it.'

'I know, but well... I didn't think. And I don't want Mr Hubbard to catch on for he'd mention it to Aunt and then there'd be trouble.'

Stella waved a dismissive hand. 'Mr Hubbard is malleable enough if you know how to handle him.'

Once they were travelling down Fossgate, Victoria's stomach churned. She didn't know what she'd face in the Felling's home and having Stella with her only heightened her anxiety. Her cousin was kind enough to those she thought fit to receive her benevolence, but to have the compassion needed for *such* a family in *such* an area might be asking too much of her and Victoria didn't have the energy to worry about her as well as focus on the Fellings.

At the entrance of the alley, Victoria knocked for the cabbie to stop.

Climbing down, Stella looked around her in barely disguised disgust. 'Victoria, I don't think...'

Having paid the cabbie, Victoria turned on her. 'Listen to me, if you don't want to do this get back in the cab now. I am all right on my own.'

Straightening her shoulders and raising her chin, Stella took a deep breath. 'No. I need to know what you are doing. Besides, it will make me look commendable in Doctor Ashton's eyes.'

'Then follow me.' Victoria ignored the mention of Ashton and led the way through the alleys and courtyards.

The deeper into the slums they walked, the more Stella commented about the filth and degradation. She complained about the muck on her boots, the slime on the hem of her dress. She jumped every time someone yelled, or a baby cried, or a woman emptied a bucket of dirty water onto the ground.

'Victoria, really, this is awfully the most—'

'Don't say it, Stella, I beg you,' she snapped, heaving the heavy basket from one arm to the other.

'But—'

'No! I warned you this morning how bad it is. Please, just be quiet, or go home.' Victoria headed up the staircase and then knocked on the Felling's door. She waited a few moments, but no one answered. She knocked again. Frowning, she turned the handle and opened the door.

Inside, the room was dark. Coughing came from the corner. Filtered light from the window and door showed the children huddled on the bed of rags as usual. The iron stove held no fire, the room cold and dank.

'Victoria…' Stella whispered from the doorway.

'Children, do you remember me from the other day?' Victoria asked the cluster of bodies. When they didn't answer her, she turned to their mother laying on the blankets. 'Mrs Felling. I have called again.'

The sick woman raised her head. 'Tea?'

Victoria hurried to the shelf, but the bottle was gone. 'Has Polly gone to get you some more?'

Receiving no answer, she went to the basket and took out the candles. After lighting them, she placed one on the shelf and one on top of the stove. Opening the little stove door, she found the ashes were cold. It had been a while since the fire had been alight. Nowhere in the room could she find newspaper or wood. Frustrated, she turned to Stella. 'Pour Mrs Felling some ginger ale. It's in the basket.'

'Oh, no, I don't think I can.' Stella hadn't placed a foot inside the room.

'Stella, just do it!' she commanded.

'This is beastly of you to make me actually come inside. We'll catch something unmentionable, I'm certain of it. If I die it will be all your fault!'

Ignoring her, Victoria grabbed the blanket from the basket and gave it to the children. As they snuggled under it wordlessly, she began to slice up the bread and using the same knife spread jam across each portion. The children accepted the bread in awed silence.

'Mrs Felling.' Victoria knelt beside the woman while Stella dithered holding the cup.

'She won't wake up.' Stella shrieked. 'Is she dead? Oh, my word, she's dead, isn't she?'

'No, she isn't and lower your voice!' Victoria lifted the woman's head. 'Help me lift her. She needs to eat.'

'I am not touching her!' Stella thrust the cup at Victoria. 'She'll be full of disease and lice.'

'For heaven's sake!' Victoria wanted to shake her cousin.

The door opened, and Doctor Ashton walked in only to stop short on seeing them. 'Miss Carlton. Miss Dobson.'

'Oh, Doctor Ashton.' Stella looked ready to faint. 'I'm so pleased you are here. You must tell Victoria how dangerous this is. Who knows what disease this woman has?'

'Calm down, Miss Dobson. Mrs Felling is recovering from childbirth. She carries no disease, but is suffering from malnutrition and loss of spirit.' He knelt beside Victoria. 'You brought those things?'

'Yes. Are they suitable?'

'Anything is better than nothing, Miss Carlton. Old Jimmy told me what you had done the other day.'

'I thought...I mean...a fire...'

'Yes.' He smiled kindly and then turned his attention to his patient. After a quick examination, he shuffled closer to lift Mrs Felling up. 'Miss Carlton can you help me prop her up, please?'

Victoria pushed up the filthy blankets Mrs Felling was lying on to use as a prop to keep the woman upright. The foul stench of body odour nearly made her gag, but she fought it.

'Mrs Felling.' Doctor Ashton tapped her cheeks. He took the cup from Stella and held it to the poor woman's cracked pale lips. 'Drink, Mrs Felling.'

Sluggish and barely sensible, the woman sipped, though most of the liquid spilled down her chin.

'That's it, keep drinking,' Ashton encouraged.

'I've brought her eggs, boiled eggs,' Victoria whispered, not wanting the children to hear. 'To give her strength.'

'Excellent.' Doctor Ashton tapped the woman's cheek again. 'Mrs Felling. I want you to eat something now. Understand?'

The woman's sad eyes gazed at him.

Ashton glanced up at Stella. 'Miss Dobson, can you bring the basket to me, please?'

Stella grumbled, but did as she was asked, and then went to stand near the open door, holding a lacy white handkerchief to her nose.

'Look what we have here, Mrs Felling.' Ashton broke up some of the egg in his hand and pushed it into her mouth. 'Isn't that a good surprise?'

Egg dribbled out of her lips.

'Eat it now, Mrs Felling.' Ashton demanded, pushing more into her mouth. 'All of it. You need your strength back. The children need you. Miss Carlton has been most generous in bringing you this food. Eat it for her at least.'

Mrs Felling blinked rapidly, sagging in their arms, but Ashton forced her back up and gave her more to drink.

'All of it, if you please, Mrs Felling,' he coaxed.

After what seemed an eternity, both eggs were down her throat, swallowed down with another cup of ginger ale.

'We need a fire in here,' Victoria said as she and Ashton laid her back down.

'I'll organise it. Old Jimmy should be about soon. I'll instruct him to purchase some coal. It lasts longer than wood.' Ashton gazed at her. 'I'm very impressed by your activities, Miss Carlton.'

89

She blushed, happy that she had pleased him although that wasn't her intention. 'It isn't much.'

'It's more than you realise, and I'm impressed that you have gone to such effort.'

His words delighted Victoria enormously as she cut some more bread and spread jam on each slice. She gave a second slice to each of the children while Ashton examined them. Quietly, the children allowed him to look at their frail little bodies, content to munch on the food.

When he'd finished, he took the bucket by the fire and left the room.

'I want to go home,' Stella hissed from the doorway to Victoria.

'Then go. I'm not stopping you.' Victoria cut up the pickled onions.

'I cannot leave you here.'

'Of course you can.'

'This is too much, Victoria. You cannot do this. Leave it to Doctor Ashton to attend to them, or the charities, or someone other than you. Mama and Papa will be horrified about this.'

'You will not tell them!' Victoria waved the knife at her. 'You *promised* me.'

'That was before! I never imagined it could be as disgusting as this!' Stella sneered at the filth around her. 'I will not stay quiet.'

'I confided in you.'

'Miss Dobson.' Ashton stood behind her in the doorway, a bucket of water in his hand.

Stella jumped aside as though he carried slops. Tears gathered in her eyes. 'Doctor Ashton, I *implore* you to assist me in making my cousin see sense!'

'Sense?'

'You must assert your authority here and demand she removes herself from this place.'

'Why would I do that, Miss Dobson?' He frowned, pouring water into a jug. 'Miss Carlton is extremely useful. I would be the last person to ask her to resign her services.'

'Victoria is putting herself and our family in danger by mixing with these people. Who knows what they carry?'

'They carry poverty, Miss Dobson.' Ashton turned away dismissively.

Stella stamped her foot. 'She is not qualified to be here!'

'The only qualification needed is compassion.' He eyed her up and down, making it clear he thought she had none.

Victoria closed her eyes for Stella's face had grown fierce and she knew Ashton was skating on thin ice. Stella could like and hate within seconds, and once she'd turned on you, it took a great deal to win her back.

Sighing, Victoria bowed her head. She'd have to leave and take Stella home, soothe her ruffled feathers, and beg her to not mention a word to Aunt and Uncle.

She gave Doctor Ashton a fleeting smile. 'I must go.' She didn't look at him as she left the room and taking Stella's arm, escorted her out of the slums.

Chapter Six

Adding a spray of light floral perfume, Victoria stared at her reflection in the mirror. The pale apple green gown she wore suited her. Dora had washed and brushed her hair and pinned it up on the top of her head. Copper tendrils hung down around her ears. She had applied a light powder and a tiny amount of blush to her cheeks. She wanted to look her best tonight for the dinner party because Doctor Ashton was attending. She'd not seen him since she was at Walmgate last week.

For days, Victoria had been kept busy in the house and with calls. She was certain Stella did it on purpose.

Every call, every invitation was eagerly accepted by Stella and she included Victoria in all that she organised.

Stella encouraged Aunt Esther to take them on outings and even managed to coerce Uncle Harold in taking them on a picnic after church on Sunday.

At no time did Victoria feel confident enough to slip away and return to check on Mrs Felling. So, she had smiled and pretended that she didn't want to be anywhere else. Yet the whole time she felt guilty for not going back to Walmgate.

Victoria had been expecting Stella to berate her or not talk to her about Walmgate. However, she definitely hadn't expected her to be over-friendly and act as though nothing had happened.

The consequence was Victoria constantly being on edge, waiting for Stella to mention the Felling's hovel to her parents and what she had been doing there.

This act Stella was playing confused and worried her. She didn't know where she stood.

The clock chimed seven o'clock. Taking a deep breath, she left her bedroom and headed downstairs. Guests were mingling. Aunt Esther drifted from person to person, while Uncle Harold was in deep conversation with a visiting Member of Parliament from London.

After kissing Mimi, Victoria said good evening to old family friends such as the Smiths and the Osborns, but kept on walking, looking for the doctor. She found him by the fireplace talking to the awful Miss Rachel Stephens, the daughter of one of her aunt's friends. Her heart did a little skip as she neared him. When he looked at her, she smiled widely, happy to see him.

'Miss Carlton.' He bowed slightly, his eyes warm.

'Good evening, Doctor Ashton. Good evening, Rachel.' She kept smiling though she didn't like how close Rachel was standing to him. She took a glass of champagne from the tray Jennie circulated.

'Your gown is very pretty, Victoria,' Rachel said, though her cold eyes told a different story as they raked over her. 'Such a basic colour, yet done so effortlessly.'

'Thank you, Rachel.' Victoria could have commented on the other woman's gown, a shimmering soft gold, but refrained for that was what she wanted and Victoria was tired of pandering to people. Besides, she didn't even like the woman. Rachel Stephens made Stella look a child when it came to insults and putting people in their place. For years, Victoria and Stella had done their best to stay away from her at social events.

Rachel took hold of the conversation, telling Ashton about her latest trip abroad to Paris and Rome. After ten solid minutes of her talking, Victoria wanted to throw a glass of champagne over her, anything to shut her up.

She and Doctor Ashton exchanged glances and shared a small smile full of meaning as Rachel continued talking.

From nowhere, Stella appeared in their group, her eyes over bright as she stared at the three of them. 'What are we discussing?'

'We aren't discussing anything,' Victoria told her. 'We were listening to Rachel talk about her latest trip to Paris and Rome.'

'How delightful.' Stella sipped her champagne. 'I do think both of those cities will be on my honeymoon list.'

'You are getting married?' Rachel stared at her in surprise.

'No.' Stella laughed. 'At least not yet. I'm waiting for the doctor to ask me.'

Doctor Ashton choked on his champagne while Victoria blinked rapidly to process her words. What game was her cousin playing?

'I do jest.' Stella laughed again, then gave the doctor a flirtatious smile. 'But should you want to, Doctor Ashton, I will consider it.'

Victoria was relieved when dinner was announced. She hoped to be seated next to Doctor Ashton, but instead, she was placed next to Mr Osborn on one side and Mr Smith on the other.

She noticed Stella firmly place herself between Doctor Ashton and Mr Stephens and wondered why. Surely the doctor was the last person she'd want to sit next to after the day at the Fellings' room.

Extensions had been put into the dining table for the extra guests and unfortunately for Victoria, she was at one end of the table and Stella and the doctor were at the other. She couldn't hear a word being said by them but throughout the first and second courses they talked quietly to each other the whole time. During the third course Stella turned to talk to Mr Stephens but as dessert was brought through, her attention was once more back to the doctor. He attentively listened to her while Victoria seethed with envy.

At the end of the meal, Victoria happily left the table to join the ladies in the drawing room and no sooner had the door shut behind them, she caught Stella's arm and pulled her to one side. 'What were you and Doctor Ashton discussing so intimately all through dinner?'

Stella gave a sly grin. 'A great many things.'

'Stella!' Victoria hissed between her teeth.

'Why are you so interested?'

'You monopolised his attention all through dinner.'

'I was being the perfect hostess to a guest.' Stella's eyes narrowed. 'Why are you so het up about it?'

'Doctor Ashton and I...' she faltered. What did she and Doctor Ashton have? Nothing. Simply a common goal to help others.

'Do you have affection for him?' Stella's voice was a harsh whisper. 'You *do*, don't you?'

'No.'

'Liar! You think you can capture a doctor? With your parents' history?'

'What do you mean my parents' history?' She had no idea what Stella meant by that. Why on earth was she bringing her parents into this?

'It doesn't matter.' Stella tossed her head. 'Why are you so interested in the doctor?'

Victoria thought quickly. 'I-I simply wanted to know what you talked about since your last meeting wasn't pleasant.'

'I apologised for my behaviour the other day.' Stella waved a dismissive hand. 'I told him that it was the shock of seeing such dire circumstances and I wasn't prepared for it. He forgave me, naturally. Do you know he wants to build his very own hospital for women? It's an area he wants to specialise in.'

Jealousy ripped through Victoria. She wanted to be the one he told such things to, not her cousin who didn't care a whit.

Stella patted her curls into place. 'I mentioned that my family would be very generous with donations to fund this endeavour of his when the time came. He was most appreciative. He is such a caring gentleman, full of ideas and...passion.'

'Did he mention me?' she whispered, hating that she asked, but she needed to know if he spoke of her.

'You?' Stella frowned. 'No. Why would we talk about you?'

'Because of my helping Mrs Felling.'

'Dearest, you weren't even thought of. We had far more important things to discuss other than one particular slum family.' Stella smiled sweetly, though falsely, and Victoria knew it.

'Of course.'

'Not everything is about you, you know,' Stella said waspishly. 'And before you get any ideas into your head, remember *Ashton* isn't *yours*. He'll look higher than an orphan living in her uncle's house.' Stella walked away as the coffee trolley was brought in.

Victoria could have laughed if it weren't so tragic.

Nothing was ever about her, nor was anything ever hers. She'd come into this family with nothing. Everything she owned was given to her by her aunt and uncle. She belonged to no one and no one belonged to her. She'd known that for a long time.

An hour later, the men joined them, and Victoria watched as Stella immediately took Doctor Ashton's arm and drew him away from the others. Stella laughed gaily at something he said and he grinned back at her. Victoria caught her aunt's knowing smile at Uncle Harold and his return nod.

The blood ran cold in her veins. They were happy to see Stella and the doctor together. A deep sadness welled in her chest. How silly was she to expect the doctor to seek her out just because she'd helped a poor family? It wasn't enough obviously. She needed to have Stella's beauty and poise. Stella had a confidence men enjoyed, knowing that such a woman could run their household and be the perfect hostess to further their career. None of those qualities did she possess.

Uncle Harold joined Stella and Doctor Ashton and their laughter filled the room.

'What a charming man, Doctor Ashton is,' Mimi said, coming to sit beside her. She fluffed out her burgundy coloured gown and then smoothed its lace ruffles on the bodice. 'You think so, too, don't you, my dear?'

'Yes, Mimi, he is most charming.'

Mimi leaned in close. 'Stop watching him, sweet girl, or the whole room will know your feelings instead of just me.'

Horrified, she spun to stare at her. 'I-I—'

'You watched him and Stella all through dinner. If I had sat closer to you, I would have nudged you under the table. My eyesight isn't as it once was and without my glasses, I can't see my hands in front of my face, but from far away I can see as keenly as a fox. Strange I know.' Mimi patted Victoria's hand. 'Haven't I always said to you that your face is too expressive?'

Victoria nodded, feeling sick inside.

'Learn to school your expressions. Sometimes, you must fool even those you are closest to. Stella saw you looking at them.' Mimi gazed about the room, taking it all in, but her words were for Victoria's ears alone. 'I love my granddaughter very much, but she is not always likable, and you know what I mean by that.' She squeezed her hand, but kept her gaze on the other people in the room. 'Stella can read people. She's good at it, that's how she can always get her way. She's the best I've ever seen at it, actually. Better than me and that's admitting a lot.' Mimi glanced at her. 'She knows *you*. Remember that.'

Mimi moved away and Victoria fell into conversation with Mrs Smith, who had much to say about last Sunday's church sermon. When Victoria finally broke free, Doctor Ashton was saying goodbye to those closest to him. She turned away, disappointed that not once had he tried to seek her out after dinner.

The following morning, Victoria was at the breakfast table early. She ate bacon and kippers with slices of toast and wondered how she could get to Walmgate today without Stella knowing.

Uncle walked in and pulled out his chair. 'Good morning, dear girl.'

'Good morning, Uncle.' She fiddled with the tablecloth and made it straighter. 'Did you sleep well?'

'Very well.' He poured himself a cup of tea while Mr Hubbard brought in fresh scrambled eggs.

Uncle piled a plate with food and sat back at the table. He opened his newspaper, giving Victoria an idea to ask Mr Hubbard for all the old newspapers.

'May I share the carriage with you, Uncle?' she asked.

'Yes, absolutely, though I am leaving very soon.' He read and ate at the same time. 'If Stella is coming, too, you'd better hurry her up.'

'No, I'm going on my own. I want to do some shopping and Stella takes too long everywhere we go.'

'Yes, that is true indeed,' he chuckled, 'which is why I refuse to accompany any woman shopping.'

'I'm ready to go whenever you are.'

'Good. I'll be five minutes. I have a meeting this morning.' He didn't look up as he spoke.

Taking advantage of his interest in the newspaper, Victoria slipped from the dining room and hurried into the hall.

She pinned on her hat and then donned her coat and gloves, before swiftly walking along the corridor and down the backstairs to the kitchen.

'Good morning, miss.' Mrs Norman smiled, kneading bread on the large pine table.

'Good morning, Mrs Norman. I am paying a visit to a family who I recently found out is suffering some financial difficulties. I don't wish to go empty handed…'

'That is sad news indeed, miss, and bless your heart for your charity. Of course, you can't go empty-handed. Flo,' she waved towards the young scullery maid who was peeling a mound of apples, 'stop that for the minute and go fetch the leftover meat and potato pie from the larder, and there's a pot of carrot soup, tie a lid on it.' Mrs Norman looked at Jennie as she came into the kitchen from the back door. 'Ah, Jennie, find Miss Victoria one of our shopping baskets and put the currant loaf in it. I was going to use it today, but I've changed my mind.'

Within five minutes, Victoria held a large basket full of delights, as well as a bundle of newspapers and more candles. It was heavy and she'd have to carry it, but it'd be worth it to see the children's faces.

She asked Mr Hubbard to put the basket in the carriage and joined her uncle as he climbed in.

Uncle Harold frowned at the basket. 'What is that for?'

'I'm visiting a poor family, Uncle. I cannot call with nothing. You don't mind that I take unwanted food from the kitchen, do you?'

'Heavens, no, not at all. It's very good of you to be so considerate.' He patted her hand.

'Visiting those in need is something I am keen to continue to do. I feel it is my duty.'

'Good works is an admirable quality in a lady. Naturally, you would wish to do all you can. You have a kindness in you that does you credit.'

'I have your support, Uncle, to help people less fortunate?'

'Absolutely, just as I fully support your aunt in her generous efforts. If you need my aid, please let me know.'

'Thank you.' She sat back against the leather seat and congratulated herself on letting the secret out. Stella no longer had the surprise to use on her now. True, her uncle didn't know all the details and likely expected her to visit good families in respectable areas of town, who just happened to be struggling at the moment. Good works like Aunt Esther did every day was commendable. However, he'd be dismayed to know that she visited the slums.

Not to raise any suspicions, Victoria left the carriage at the end of Parliament Street, and Uncle Harold went on to his meeting none the wiser of her real direction. The basket was too heavy for her to carry along the streets and she hired a hansom to take her the rest of the way.

The sun shone brightly as she exited the cab at the entrance to the alley. Walmgate was full of active people going about their day. The strong smell of hops cooking came from the brewery, and the carts rolled in and out of the timber yard. A landlord of a public house rolled empty barrels along the path while a postman made his rounds.

She received the odd glance as she entered the alley laden with her goods. The warm day brought out the women and their washing. Clothes and sheets hung between the buildings above Victoria's head. Children ran about, yelling at nothing like children do.

The courtyard seemed full to the brim of people. A man nailing a sole to the bottom of a boot nodded to her as she passed. Several women bent over washing tubs paused in their chore to stare at her. An ancient old man sat in the sunshine on a wooden stool near the entrance to the next alley. Victoria smiled at him and kept going.

A large woman, banging rugs against the fence, stopped to watch Victoria. Many of the residents she hadn't seen before were out in the warm weather.

Feeling as though she was an exhibit at a show, she quickened her steps and reached the staircase, her arms aching from the heavy basket.

The door at the top was open and she peeped in, wondering if Doctor Ashton was inside, but he wasn't and she took a deep breath to steady her rapid heartbeat. She had to put the doctor out of her mind. Stella was intent on claiming him for her own and what Stella wanted Stella always got!

Once her eyes had adjusted to the dimness, she made out the children sitting on the mattress, but to her surprise Mrs Felling was sitting amongst them.

'Mrs Felling!' Joy filled her that the woman was sitting up.

'Miss Carlton, yes?' Mrs Felling asked quietly.

'Yes, I am.' She gratefully placed the basket on the floor near the table, her arms burned with the strain of carrying it.

'Thank you.' Mrs Felling smiled, her face dirty, hair lank and straggly. 'You saved my life.'

'Oh no, not me. That was Doctor Ashton.'

'Doctor Ashton is a fine man, but I've been told you came often and brought food.'

'It was nothing.' Victoria paused in opening the basket. The Felling woman spoke softly and well, not at all like the people in these slum parts of town. Intrigued, she took out the roll of newspapers and placed them near the fire, which again was out.

'I'm also told you tried to tidy the place up and paid old Jimmy to fix the stove.' Mrs Felling held Victoria's gaze. 'Thank you.'

'I did very little.'

'You did a lot. More than anyone else has done for me.' A tear ran down the woman's cheek.

Embarrassed, Victoria sorted through the basket. 'I've brought you some food. Soup and pie. Oh, and some candles and a full box of matches.'

Weakly, Mrs Felling stood, the children helping her up. She took a step towards the table and wobbled so badly, Victoria dashed to her side and kept her upright.

'I don't think you should be out of bed,' Victoria said.

Mrs Felling gave her a slow smile. 'I don't have a bed.'

Seeing the funny side of it, Victoria chuckled and when Mrs Felling snickered, they started to laugh even more. Several moments passed before they could talk.

Wiping her tears away, Mrs Felling sighed. 'Tears of laughter. Who would have thought?'

'Sit down and I'll serve you some soup.' Victoria eased her down on the only crate left in the room. The others having been fed to the stove.

'You're back again then?' Annie Weaver stood in the doorway.

Victoria looked over her shoulder at her. 'Yes, as you can see.'

'I've been keepin' an eye on them.' Annie nodded towards the children.

'For the doctor?' Victoria poured some of the soup into a cup and passed it to Mrs Felling.

'Aye, the doctor asked me to an' as a good neighbour I did it.' Annie took a step closer to the table.

Victoria handed out slices of cold toast and bacon to the four children on the mattress. She refrained from saying any more to Annie for the woman had only looked in on Mrs Felling because Doctor Ashton paid her to. Victoria would have respected her more if she'd done it out of kindness.

'That looks good.' Annie pointed to the basket of food.

'It does, yes.' Victoria, hands on hips, faced her. 'Do you have any food of your own?'

'No, not much. Porridge.' Annie's stomach rumbled. 'The porridge is for me 'usband though.'

Victoria emptied out the basket. 'Do you have plates or bowls?'

Annie frowned. 'Aye.'

'Go get them, and you can have some pie. I didn't think to bring any bowls.'

Annie dashed downstairs before Victoria had finished talking.

Mrs Felling sighed. 'Annie's not a bad person. Her husband beats her and she's lost every baby that's started to grow in her belly.'

Instantly contrite, Victoria wiped a hand across her forehead. She'd never understand this world that existed right next to her own.

'I'm sorry I don't have enough things,' Mrs Felling said. 'Everything has been sold for food since I stopped working.'

'I'll bring you some plates.' She began cutting up the pie as Annie returned carrying four clean plates and two bowls.

'This is all I have,' Annie said, clunking them down on the table, her eyes not leaving the pie.

'Water, do you have any?' Victoria scanned the room and saw the bucket by the stove.

'Aye, but not enough for two families,' Annie muttered defensively.

'I didn't bring anything to drink.' Victoria served portions of pie to the children and Mrs Felling, giving the last piece to Annie.

'I'll make a pot of tea in a minute.' Annie sniffed the pie and gave a large contented sigh.

'We need a fire in here.' Victoria glanced around the bare room. Food wasn't enough, they needed so much more.

'You need more than a fire in here,' Annie scoffed, forking pie into her mouth. 'Cor, this is good, ain't it?'

'The best I've tasted in a very long time,' Mrs Felling agreed.

Victoria smiled, happy to bring such simple pleasure to people, and all she had done was ask Mrs Norman for food. If that was all it took, then she could do so much more.

'What are you lot doing?' Young Polly came marching in and eyed them all suspiciously. She held a dead rabbit by the ears.

Victoria stared at the girl, whose dirty torn dress was too short, displaying most of her thighs. She wore no boots or stockings and her hair hung down in matted lengths. 'You are Polly?'

'Aye.' The girl sauntered nearer to her mother. 'You doin' fine, Ma?'

'Yes, my lovely, I am. Look at what Miss Carlton has brought us?'

Polly peered at the food on the table and the candles in the basket. 'We'll have light tonight then.'

'I can read the newspaper to you all.' Her mother gestured to the roll of newspapers Victoria left by the stove.

Polly raised the rabbit. 'If I can get the fire going, I can cook this.'

'We've no coal left.' The joy left Mrs Felling's face.

Victoria pulled out her small purse from her pocket. 'Here, Polly, go buy some coal.' She gave the girl a few shillings not knowing how much it would cost.

Eyes round as saucers, Polly grabbed the money and the empty bucket and dashed from the room.

'You'd be dead without that girl,' Annie announced, scraping the last crumbs from her plate. 'Or in the workhouse.'

'I know. All of us would be,' Mrs Felling whispered, gazing at her children on the mattress. 'And I don't know which would be the worse result.'

Moved by the haunting words, Victoria tidied up the table. 'You mustn't fear that now. I'll help you.'

'I just need to get my strength back and find work, then we'll be fine.'

A shout came from below.

'Lord, that's me 'usband. What's he doin' home at this time?' Annie snatched her dirty plates back and ran from the room.

'Shouldn't he be at work?' Victoria asked. 'Does he even have work?'

'Yes, he works on the boats that travel from York to Hull,' Mrs Felling replied, slowly eating more of her pie.

'He's unpredictable in his movements and temper.'

'Will Annie be all right?' Victoria asked.

'Let's hope so.'

The two women shared a look which was broken by the children squabbling.

'Would you call me Mercy?' Mrs Felling said to Victoria once the children had quietened down.

'Yes, that would please me, and I am Victoria.' She smiled. 'What are the children's names?'

'Polly is my oldest child, then there is,' Mercy sat straighter and pointed to the eldest of the four sitting on the mattress, 'Jane, then Bobby, then Emily and finally little Seth.'

'Polly should be in school.' Victoria watched the other children, who were becoming sleepy after eating more food today than they'd had in weeks.

'I need her to look after the children. I'll teach her what she needs to know.'

'You can read,' she stated. 'You said you'd read from the newspaper.'

Mercy nodded. 'I was educated. My family are Quakers. My father believed in education for all.'

'Where are your family now?'

'Gone to America.' Mercy scratched her head.

'America? Heavens, that is a distance.'

'They begged me to go, but I thought myself to be in love. I chose to stay and marry the man who confessed to loving me and wanting to look after me for the rest of my life. He lied.'

'I'm so sorry.' She had no idea what it felt like to love a man and lose him, but she felt she soon would. Not that she could compare her situation with Ashton in the same way as Mercy could feel being abandoned by her husband.

Mercy sighed deeply. 'He has gone. Another woman has him now and she is welcome to him. He is of no use to me when I can't trust or rely on him.' Mercy shrugged. 'I have mourned what I've lost. First my family, then him and lastly my baby.'

'Yes, I was here that day, when your baby…died…though you may not remember I was.'

'I don't, please forgive me.' Mercy stared at the floor. 'I'm sure you were helpful.'

'No, I did nothing. It was Doctor Ashton.'

'Now I am better, the kind doctor will stop visiting, which is a shame.'

Victoria's heart fluttered at the mention of him calling here. 'Perhaps that is so, but I will not stop. That is if you wish me to keep visiting you?'

'Oh yes, please. I would like that very much.' Mercy smiled and underneath the dirt and despair, Victoria could see she was a pretty woman.

Victoria picked up the empty basket. 'I should go. If I am gone too long my family will not like it.'

'Thank you for everything.' Mercy stood and held out her hand.

Victoria shook it gently. 'I'll be back soon, hopefully tomorrow, but I'm not sure.'

'I understand. You have a life to live.'

With a final goodbye, she left the room and met Polly on the staircase, hauling up the bucket full of coal. 'Can you manage, Polly?'

'Aye, miss, thank you.'

Victoria walked down to the courtyard and lifted her face to the sun which shone bright and high in the sky. Sheets flapped in the breeze. The courtyard didn't look as intimidating when the sun shone and clean washing hung like banners.

'Miss Carlton!' Doctor Ashton appeared from behind a line of clothes at the entrance to the alley.

She stopped abruptly, hating that her silly heart skipped a beat at his presence. 'Good day, Doctor.' She forced her feet to move.

'I didn't expect to see you here.'

'I will not turn my back on them,' she said it harsher than she meant, but she still hurt after his lack of attention at dinner.

His blue eyes gazed at her, his expression unreadable. 'You are leaving?'

'Yes.'

'Miss Carlton—'

'I must go, Doctor.' She side stepped him and carried on through the alley.

~ ~ ~ ~

Joseph watched her figure retreat down the alley until she was gone from sight. He didn't want to be at odds with her, quite the opposite in fact, but she'd built up a defence against him and he didn't know how to get through to her.

He turned and went up the staircase and into the Fellings' room. Immediately he could see a difference in the squalid hovel. Polly knelt before the stove, getting a fire going, while the other children had food smudged on their faces and for once looked alive, instead of giving him an uninterested stare. The most improved was Mrs Felling.

He smiled at her. 'You look well, Mrs Felling.'

'I'm better, thanks to you and Miss Carlton. She keeps bringing us food and with what Polly finds, we are getting by.'

Joseph glanced at the dead rabbit on the table. 'That needs to be put into a pot quickly before it goes off.'

Mercy nodded. 'I'll do it in a minute.'

Joseph lowered his voice so the children wouldn't hear him. 'Are you certain all is well? Your body is healing from the birth?'

'Yes.' She couldn't meet his eyes. 'I think the dark days are over, Doctor.'

'How so?'

'I suppose it's instinct.' Mrs Felling shrugged. 'Meeting Miss Carlton has been a wondrous thing. She's been sent from God.'

'God?'

'I may not be a practising Quaker, or as devoted as my parents, but I think Miss Carlton was sent here to help us.'

'She is a good person.' Joseph smiled, proud that Miss Carlton had made a difference to one family.

'I will consider myself fortunate to call her a friend, if she allows it.'

'I'm sure she would.'

Mrs Felling gestured towards the children. 'She brings the one thing I truly need…food for my children, but she always talks to me like an equal and not something to be pitied, like a homeless dog.'

'You must eat well, too, you need your strength back. Do not give it all to the children. You cannot look after them if you starve yourself.' Joseph ran a practiced eye over the children, noting their under-nourished bodies.

She nodded and watched Polly blow on the fire which made the flames leap and sway. 'Yes, for I must get back to work as soon as I can.'

He swapped his medical bag over to the other hand and flexed his fingers. 'And perhaps we can get young Polly here into school and learning.'

'Not bloody likely!' Polly jumped up and slammed the stove door shut. 'I'm not going to any school.'

'You'll watch your language, girl and be quiet!' Mrs Felling snapped.

'How can I earn money if I go to school?' the girl argued.

'I'll find work and you'll watch the little ones.' Her mother eyed her sternly.

'I bloody won't!' Polly ran from the room.

'Polly!' Mrs Felling called her back but the child was gone. 'I'm sorry, Doctor.'

'Don't apologise, Mrs Felling.' He made a move for the door. 'I'm happy to see you looking much better.'

'I am.'

'Well, if you feel my services are no longer needed, then I'll be on my way. I'm due at the Union Work-house.' As he went down the stairs, he nodded to the women standing around gossiping.

One of the women laughed at him. 'You were quick today, laddo, getting tired of her now, are you?'

He knew what they meant and shuddered. They had a low opinion of him if they thought he went to Mrs Felling for sexual pleasure. He sighed and continued on through the alley. He knew gentlemen came to these parts to visit the brothels, but he wasn't one of them. He was no saint at university, and enjoyed the nights of drinking and carousing with his friends, and in London he'd kept a mistress for a few months be-fore she found someone far more entertaining than him. His work always came first, but was it enough? The image of Victoria Carlton swam before his eyes. No, his work didn't fully consume him as it once did.

Chapter Seven

On her birthday, Victoria woke to blue sky and warmth in the air. May brought sunny days giving her the perfect excuse to say she was going for long walks. In reality, she spent most of her days in Walmgate with the Fellings.

She'd asked for no special party for her birthday, for her relationship with Stella had become frosty since the dinner party. Victoria didn't ask what Stella did with her time, though she knew she was involved in Aunt Esther's charity works, and Stella didn't seem concerned about Victoria. However, Doctor Ashton's name was dropped in many conversations around the table and Victoria had a feeling that Stella was going out of her way to be in contact with him.

Aunt Esther was so busy that she barely noticed Victoria's absence from the house. As long as she was there at mealtimes, no one was any wiser where she went. She suspected Stella knew all too well, but for now she was keeping her secret, and Victoria didn't understand why when they were barely speaking to each other.

Going down to breakfast, Victoria expected to see her family waiting for her as was tradition on birthdays. A fuss was always made at breakfast, but today only her Aunt and Uncle sat eating.

'Victoria, dearest. Happy birthday.' Aunt Esther hugged her and Uncle kissed her cheek.

Uncle Harold patted her shoulder after pulling out her chair. 'Twenty-one today. Where have the years gone?' He shook his head. 'After you've eaten, I would like a word with you in my study.'

'We can talk now, Uncle, if you want?'

'Well, if you're sure.' He led the way down the corridor to his study, a dark red wallpapered room that was his domain alone.

He went behind his desk and opened a drawer. From it he passed her a folder document. 'That is your father's will. He left me instructions that you weren't to have it until you turned twenty-one.'

'My father?' The man she barely remembered. 'I never expected a will. I assumed he didn't have much to leave…'

'He didn't, not an estate as such.'

Heart in her throat, Victoria opened it and began to read. She read the two pages twice before staring up at her uncle. 'Am I reading this correctly? I have half a house?'

'Yes, you own half share in a house.' Uncle nodded but his expression wasn't enthusiastic. 'However, it's not a suitable house for you though. It is not what you would want to live in, but we can sell it.'

'I cannot believe it.' And she didn't. Not a word of it. She had a half share in a house. She'd never owned anything before. 'This house, it isn't my former home?' she asked hopefully.

Sighing, Uncle Harold eased his bulk behind the desk and waved to the chair for her to sit also. 'No. That was sold after your mother died. Your father had very little left. I helped him buy this house, but he lived in it only a month before he passed away.'

'You never said a word.' She wanted to be angry with him, but found she was too happy to have this gift to be annoyed with her uncle.

'I didn't mention it because there was no point. You couldn't inherit until you were twenty-one. I didn't want to give you false hope.'

'False hope?'

'Victoria, my dear, this house is not something to be proud of. It was all your father could afford...'

'Afford? We had a lovely house in Escrick.' She remembered the house had a big garden.

Uncle Harold folded his hands over his rotund stomach. 'Your father was deeply in debt when your mother died. If your mother hadn't died when she did, you'd have moved from Escrick and into York, likely into one of my houses.' Uncle fiddled with the edge of a ledger on the desk. 'I bailed your father out of financial situations many times during his marriage to my sister.'

'I never knew.' Her parents had been financial trouble.

'We, your aunt and I, decided you didn't need to know. After all, you were only a child.'

She raised her eyebrows. 'I'd like to know now.'

Uncle shrugged. 'It makes little difference now. It is in the past.'

'But it's a past I am not aware of. *My* family's past.'

Taking a deep breath, Uncle nodded. 'Very well. Your father made mistakes, invested in the wrong schemes. He lost a lot of money over the years. I couldn't see my sister and her family go without. I helped him to help her.'

'That was so good of you.'

'Then when she and your brother died, your father brought you here to me, as another of his ventures had failed and he couldn't look after you. He was lost in every way, mentally, physically and financially. He adored your mother and her death drove him to drinking excessively, then when his latest financial venture failed it broke him.'

Victoria gazed down at the document in her hand. She had no idea about any of this. 'My poor father.'

'He had to sell your home and pay his debts. With my help, he managed to buy a small house here in York.'

'Your help?'

'He didn't have enough money to buy it, so I bought half of it with him, so he'd have somewhere to live.'

'I am so shocked. I wish I had known.' But she had a feeling that Stella had known, hence the barbed words she sometimes uttered about her parentage.

'Your aunt and I wanted to shield you from it. You are innocent to all the problems your father incurred in his life. We didn't want your future to be tarnished...'

'How did he die? I've never been told the full story. I know he is buried in Escrick with Mama and my brother.' She looked at Uncle Harold and noticed he couldn't meet her eyes. 'Uncle Harold?'

'It's your birthday, a celebration, shall we not talk any more of this today?'

115

'I would rather know, if you don't mind? My father has given me this gift, yet I feel so detached from him. I feel as though I never really knew him, and I should know more about him, shouldn't I?'

'My dear...'

'You've spoken of my mother over the years, how much you loved her and how beautiful she was, how well she played the piano and she could sing like a bird. None of those traits I have inherited, so possibly I am more like my father, the man you never speak of.'

'No, you are nothing like him,' Uncle said sternly.

'Please tell me how he died.' He was keeping something from her and she wouldn't rest until she knew what it was.

'Do you really want the details?'

She nodded.

'He took his own life.'

The words entered her brain and filtered down to her heart.

For his large size, Uncle Harold quickly came around the desk to take her hands. 'Victoria, you were too young to know the truth back then. It was hard enough for you to lose your whole family within six months. I couldn't burden you with the truth of it.'

'I understand.' She did understand his reasoning for not telling her when she was twelve, but she should have known before now. It made sense why she always felt as though she was on the edge of this family – a part of it but not a part of it. Her father committed suicide. The scandal had to hushed up. Society couldn't be told else it might damage the family's reputation. 'Who else knows the truth?'

'Not many people. We kept it quiet, within the family, obviously.'

'Stella knows?'

'Only recently. Your aunt told her for she was asking questions about your father. Why I do not understand, she never cared before.'

Not until Doctor Ashton started to call and that's when Stella began to change towards her. Victoria closed her eyes. So much made sense now.

Uncle Harold kissed the top of her head. 'This is not how I wanted this meeting to go. It's your birthday. Let us go back to Esther and—'

'Where is the house located?' she asked suddenly.

'Oh, er, not a good area. As I said, you'll not want to live in it. But I could sell it for you and invest the money, which is far more beneficial.' He smiled affably.

'Perhaps, but first I'd like to see the house.'

'Why? It means nothing to no one. It was a desperate purchase by your father. He'd never want you to stay there.'

'Who has been living in the premises?'

'It's been rented by a variety of people since your father died and I took over the upkeep of it. To be honest I'll be glad to get rid of that house. It's a noose around my neck sometimes. I don't have the time to deal with it, I've other houses in better areas whose returns are much higher.'

'I'd like to go and see the house before it's sold.'

'Victoria, trust me in this, please?' Uncle Harold walked to the door. 'Let us go back to Esther.' He walked out of the room and along the corridor to the dining room.

Victoria had no choice but to follow.

At the dining table, Stella had joined Aunt Esther and was eating her way through a plate of eggs and bacon. She looked up at Victoria. 'Happy birthday.'

117

'Thank you.'

Stella smiled, but there was no warmth in the action. 'Oh Papa, can I share the carriage with you into town please? I simply must go and buy a new hat to wear for afternoon tea with Doctor Ashton.'

'Of course.' Uncle Harold looked troubled as he poured fresh tea into his cup.

Aunt Esther dabbed at her mouth with a napkin. 'Victoria, how do you feel about your inheritance?'

'Oh yes.' Stella turned cat-like eyes to Victoria. 'You must be excited to finally own something of your own now, even if it's only a half share in a hovel.'

Victoria stared at her, hating that they had become estranged. How had it happened so quickly? Stella no longer tried to be civil.

She ignored the way her chest tightened at Stella's mention of meeting Doctor Ashton. 'You knew about the house?'

'Mama just told me.' Stella laughed. 'A run-down house in *Fossgate*. What a gift! So ironic!'

'Fossgate?' Victoria looked at her uncle. 'The house is in Fossgate?'

'Yes, dear. However, we'll sell it and that will be an end to the whole affair.' Uncle gave her a sympathetic smile.

Stella snorted. 'I doubt you'll get a shilling for it.'

'Don't be ridiculous, girl!' Uncle snapped, scowling at her.

'What number is the house?' Victoria gripped her hands together. Fossgate. One of the worst areas of town, close to Walmgate. And very ironic as Stella jested.

~ ~ ~ ~

118

After sharing the carriage with Uncle and Stella, Victoria waited at the bank while a reluctant Uncle Harold found the box which held the deeds to the Fossgate house and the keys. He couldn't deny her wishes to see the house on her birthday.

Stella had gone on her way without a goodbye and Victoria was glad to see the back of her. Her cousin had chatted on the journey into town about her and Aunt's plans for the day which of course included charity work, visiting friends and the much anticipated afternoon tea with Doctor Ashton and some other women who were willing to donate their time and husbands' money to good causes.

Aunt Esther had asked Victoria to join them, but she'd politely refused. As much as she wanted to be a part of her Aunt's endeavours to help the poor, she found those meetings long and tedious and not a lot was achieved. She felt that by actually visiting the poor like the Fellings, and helping them personally, she could accomplish so much more. Not that she mentioned this out loud, for her aunt and uncle would soon stop her trips into the slums. It still astonished her that Stella hadn't told them the truth. Why hadn't she?

Now, walking down Fossgate, she looked at the narrow street with new eyes.

Many public houses lined both sides of the road and small shops with their mullioned windows, sold just about anything a person could want. The road was always busy, although a poor district it was industrious too. Timber and brick yards were found down different alleys, the smell of stale ale came from the brewery.

She passed the entrance of the Merchant's Hall on her left and another public house. Then just twenty-five yards from the Foss Bridge, Victoria found her house on the right. It was red-bricked with one window and a door leading straight off the street.

Taking the door key from her reticule, she glanced around. On the other side of the river stood Wilson's Hospital for women, where she'd gone to visit only weeks ago, and from where she had followed Doctor Ashton to the Fellings' hovel. That day had been the start of her education in how some poor people lived. She looked up at the house, all three stories of it. She'd passed it numerous times on her visits to Walmgate, and all this time it had been hers.

Excited, she turned the key and opened the door. Dampness hit her nose. She stood in the small entrance and closed the door behind her. Uncle had mentioned the last tenants left two days ago. In front of her, a steep narrow staircase led up to the next floor. A corridor went along beside the stairs. She entered the front room, a small square room, its window overlooking the street and a fireplace on the far wall. Bare wooden floorboards and peeling wallpaper completed the room. Walking down the corridor, she noticed another small room, perhaps large enough to hold a small dining table. At the end of the hallway, a step led down to a large kitchen with a range. Behind one door was a shallow larder and next to it another door revealed stairs leading down to a black cellar.

Outside were two small outhouses and a privy, plus a water pump in the middle of the cobbled yard.

She walked to the wooden gate and peeped over it. A dirt path ran behind the house going right down to the river and left up towards the brewery.

Houses hemmed in the path. Everywhere she looked
were houses and outbuildings, ugly, rundown and un-
kempt. Children were playing in one of the yards and
a dog barked continually. Hammering came from another direction and she realised a foundry mustn't be
too far away.

Back inside, she went up the staircase. Two tiny
empty bedrooms opened off the small landing. An
even steeper, narrower staircase went up to the next
floor. Here she found one large room, completely
empty. Dormer windows overlooked the street.

She took another tour of the house, before walking
out and locking the front door. Her mind whirled with
thoughts as she walked over the bridge and along
Walmgate. A bud of an idea was forming, but she
couldn't quite grasp the thought of it just yet.

She turned into the alley and headed for the
Fellings' room.

Screams reached her as she walked into the courtyard. She slowed and peered around. A group of
women stood in the middle of the courtyard, their
children quiet and huddled close. She recognised two
of the woman who'd spoken to her before.

Victoria jumped as another scream pierced the air
followed by a man's yells. Rooted to the spot with
fright, she couldn't go forward and up the stairs to
Mrs Felling or back down the alley.

'Welcome to a little piece of paradise, miss,' said
one of the women.

'Who is screaming and why?' she asked stepping
closer to the woman, remembering her name as Betsy.

'Annie's getting battered by her husband.'

'Annie?' Victoria looked up at the top of the stairs
as Mercy came out, the children clustered around her.
'Shouldn't we do something?' she called up to her.

121

'What can you do?' another woman snorted, folding her arms. 'It's their business.'

'Where does she live?' Victoria asked as something crashed from behind the door to her right. 'In there?' She pointed to the closed door.

Betsy nodded. 'He'll not thank you for interfering!'

'Miss Carlton, I don't think you should go in,' Mercy said, from above.

'I cannot ignore the fact she is getting beaten!' Victoria opened the door without knocking and stepped inside.

The dim room was a mess. The table overturned, a wooden chair broken, cups and plates shattered on the floor. The scream came again from the next room, then all she heard was Annie begging.

Angered, Victoria rushed in and jerked to a halt to see a huge man bending over Annie who lay curled up in a ball on the floor. 'Stop this at once!'

Shocked, the man turned around, one fist raised, the other pulling Annie by the hair. 'Who the 'ell are you?'

'Get away from her now!' White fury at the scene before her made her bold. Next to the bed was a porcelain jug and basin. She picked up the jug and held it high. 'Leave her alone!'

'Or what? Yer'll bash me with that, yer stupid woman?' he mocked, advancing on her, dragging Alice behind him.

'I'll call the police!' Victoria stepped back in fear. The man was like a mountain, his face red with anger, his eyes bloodshot.

He laughed, but let go of Annie's hair. 'I can do what I like with me own wife.'

'You cannot beat her while I'm here to witness it.'

He pulled up his trousers over his round stomach and puffed out his barrel chest. 'Well, madam, yer'll not always be here, will yer! Now get out!' Stumbling drunkenly, he swung a fist at Victoria catching her on the shoulder making her fall against the door.

'Miss, please, just *go*,' Annie whimpered, the cut on her lip bleeding down her chin. One eye was closing rapidly.

'Come with me, Annie.' Victoria held out her hand, the jug still raised. Her shoulder throbbed. She'd never been so frightened in her life, but something made her stand her ground.

'Nay, I'm fine, miss. You go.'

'I'm not leaving without you.'

'For Christ's sake, you bloody women! I need a drink.' Annie's husband pushed past Victoria and stomped out of the room.

Not convinced the threat was over, Victoria waited until they heard the door bang shut before shakily placing the jug back down and rushing to Annie's side. 'Can you stand?'

'Course I can.' Annie smiled then winced as her lip split some more. With Victoria's help, she stood, moaning. 'Aw, me ribs. I can't breathe. Are you hurt bad, miss?'

'No, I'm fine,' she lied. 'I'm calling for the doctor and the police.'

'No!' Annie gripped her hands. 'No police. It'll only make him angrier.'

The bedroom door opened and Victoria spun around ready to defend Annie, but instead Mercy Felling stood there. Her ragged dress hung on her thin frame and her hair a tangled mess about her shoulders.

'Mercy! What are you doing? You're not well enough to be out.' Victoria didn't know who to help first. Mercy looked ready to faint, so pale was she.

'I had to come and see if you needed me.' Mercy held onto the doorframe. 'The whole courtyard could hear him. We thought he'd kill her this time, or you.'

'I'm fine, course I am.' Annie waved away their concerns, despite looking like a loser in a prize fight. 'I've taken worse, now haven't I? At least this time I had no baby inside…' Her voice cracked.

'Come,' Victoria put her good arm around Annie and aided her out of the house. Together with Mercy, the three of them walked past the other women, who muttered and tutted as they hobbled by.

Betsy took a step forward. 'Nay, Annie, he's done a job on yer this time, ain't he?'

Annie shrugged. 'I'll live.'

At the bottom of the staircase, Victoria stopped. 'Mercy, go up and bring the children down.'

'Why?'

'I'm taking you away from here. You, the children and Annie.'

'Away?' Annie's eyes nearly popped from her head.

'I have a house in Fossgate.'

'And we can live there?' Mercy asked in awe.

'Yes. Go and fetch the children and leave everything behind.' She didn't say that whatever was in the room up there was not fit to own anyway, but it was implied.

Mercy needed no second bidding and slowly climbed the stairs calling for the children.

'Not me, miss. I can't leave.' Annie shuffled back. 'I'm a married woman.'

'To a monster who beats you, Annie.'

She shrugged, holding her side. 'He'll leave me alone for a while now. You might be nothing but a slip of thing but you frightened him off. He'll not want the police nosing around.'

'Please, Annie. Come with me. I'll keep you safe,' Victoria begged.

'I can't, miss.' Annie turned and hobbled back to her home as Mercy and the subdued children came down the stairs.

Victoria watched Annie shut the door on them and then turned to Mercy. 'Where's Polly?'

'I don't know. I've not seen her in two days.' Mercy wearily rubbed a hand over her eyes. 'That girl is never here.'

Victoria asked Betsy to tell Polly to go to Fossgate when she got back and if Doctor Ashton called, then to have him check on Annie.

'Why should I do your bidding?' Betsy argued.

'Because, as women, we should all help each other, don't you think?' Victoria snapped.

Chastened, Betsy nodded. 'Aye, right you are then. I'll send the girl along to you.'

'Thank you.' Victoria withdrew a few shillings and handed them to Betsy. 'For your troubles. Perhaps Annie could do with some salve.'

Betsy pocketed the money with a snort. 'Annie needs a bottle of gin, that'll help with the pain better than owt else!' She turned to Mercy. 'Take care of yoursen, lass.'

With a final wave to the gathered women, Victoria led the little party out of the courtyard.

'Annie won't come, will she?' Mercy asked.

'She won't leave him.'

Sighing in sadness at Annie's misplaced loyalty, Victoria took one of the children's dirty hands and led them along the alley towards the street.

'I'll find work, Miss Carlton, to pay for our keep,' Mercy puffed as they slowly walked towards Fossgate.

'Nonsense, Mercy. You can barely stand up, how on earth can you work?'

'I'll get factory work, or take in work I can do at home, like laundry.'

Victoria glanced at her. 'You'll do no such thing, even if you could manage it, which you clearly cannot.'

Pausing in front of a homewares shop, Victoria told them to wait while she went in.

She found the shopkeeper behind the counter and gave him a smile. 'I'm Victoria Carlton, niece to Harold Dobson from Dobson's Bank.'

'Oh aye, miss, how can I help you?'

'Do you have a pen and paper? You'll need to make a list.' She glanced around at the goods for sale. 'Can you deliver today?' She gave him the house number.

'Aye, miss, it's only up the street.'

'Good.' She stepped to a shelf that sold pots and pans. She grabbed three and gave them to the shopkeeper.

'Now, I need six of everything here.' She pointed to another shelf holding plain white porcelain plates, bowls and cups. Further down the shop, she selected three jugs of different sizes, a large earthenware mixing bowl, a wooden tray and a small marble slab. Walking back to the counter she pointed to the selection of wicker baskets on the floor. 'Two of those please. Do you have a meat store, or a cold chest?'

'Yes, miss.' The shopkeeper nodded and wrote quickly on his piece of paper.

'Thank you. Send the bill to my uncle.' She wasn't sure how she was going to explain the purchase to her uncle, but she'd cross that bridge when she came to it. She left the shop and smiled at Mercy. 'How are you feeling?'

'Free. Exhausted, but free. Thank you so much.' Mercy had tears in her eyes. She looked down at her ragged children standing listlessly, glancing around as if they'd never seen energetic and busy people before, and maybe they hadn't in their young lives.

Victoria walked to the next shop, an ironmonger. Inside she felt a little overwhelmed by the array of items on show. A tall thin young man wearing a leather apron came to her rescue and helped her find what she needed. She ordered two buckets, a large kettle, a coal scoop, a fireplace set of tools, three iron framed family beds, a tin bath and a clothes wash tub.

She found that she was actually enjoying this kind of shopping, again something she'd never done before.

'Miss Carlton, you are spending so much money,' Mercy whispered as they continued to walk slowly up the street. Lines of fatigue showed in Mercy's face.

She smiled to reassure her. 'My house is bare, Mercy. All these things are needed. I can't expect you to buy them, can I?'

The children gave a little squeal as a wiry-haired dog bounded up to them and licked Jane's hand.

Mercy struggled to stand as four children grasped her skirt, edging away from the dog. Seth, the youngest, cried in terror.

'They are like ghosts of children, not real children at all.' Victoria bent to pat the dog to show the children he was friendly. 'Look, he is just wanting a pat.'

Mercy hugged the children to her. 'I am to blame. They've hardly been out of that room since we got there. Before, we were always moving, fleeing creditors. Only Polly is strong. Only she could keep us alive.'

'Come along.' Victoria led them over Foss Bridge and to the front door of the house. Polly's long disappearances worried her. Where did the girl go? 'We'll need food.' She gave the key to Mercy. 'Go in and look around. I'll be back shortly.'

Crossing the road, she went into a small haberdashery shop. She could have laughed at the irony of all the times she had passed these shops never expecting in her wildest dreams she'd one day be going inside them and purchasing goods.

'Good day to you, miss.' A small pleasant woman smiled a welcome to Victoria. 'I'm Mrs Drysdale. How can I be of assistance?'

'I'm Victoria Carlton. I have recently come into property across the road and need to furnish it.' She turned and pointed out the large front window. 'That is my house.'

'Yes, I saw you this morning going in there. I wondered what you were doing.'

'A family is moving in today. I need some items, please, Mrs Drysdale.'

'Of course. What would you like?'

'Bedding for three large beds. Towels, curtains, tablecloths… oh, I don't have a table!' Victoria paused in her mental list.

'Gilforth's furniture in Parliament Street, he'll do you a good deal, Miss Carlton.'

'Thank you.' She noticed a rack of clothes hanging at the back of the shop. 'These are children's clothes?'

'They are a mixture. Some women's skirts. Things I've sewed for clients who have not returned to collect.'

'I need clothes for two boys, three girls and their mother, but their sizes escape me.'

'How old are the children?'

Victoria's mind went blank. 'I could not tell you.'

'They are living in the house now? Perhaps I could go across and take measurements.'

'Oh, er, well, no, not yet...' Victoria tried to find diplomacy in her words. 'They need a bath first...and the bath isn't there yet, nor is a fire lit for hot water. I must get coal, you see, oh and soap.' She stopped talking, aware she was rambling. It suddenly became overwhelming to buy everything she needed. She hadn't thought it through. She'd been so eager to save the Fellings from that awful hovel, that she hadn't realised she was taking them into a shell of a house with nothing of comfort in it for them.

'Fitting out a house is a big task, Miss Carlton. You cannot do it all in one day, surely?' Mrs Drysdale smiled kindly. 'I shall go over there in a moment and take some measurements of the children and also the windows. I have the bedding you need.'

'I haven't even bought mattresses.' Her shoulders slumped with the enormity of the mission ahead. 'What good is a bed without a mattress?'

'Go to Gilforth's. He's a good man and will help you.'

She reached out and shook Mrs Drysdale's hand. 'You are very kind.'

Leaving the shop, Victoria hurried to the end of Fossgate and turned left along The Pavement. One of her aunt's friends called out to her, but she simply waved and hurried on. Clouds were covering the blue sky and it looked like rain.

Turning right into Parliament Street, she saw Gilforth's on the left and entered the large shop. An elderly man, bent over a sofa, straightened and smiled at her. 'Good day, miss. Can I be of help?'

Two hours later, Victoria entered the house on Fossgate totally exhausted. Rain lashed down outside and thunder rolled in the distance.

'Oh, Miss Carlton!' Mercy rushed to her as she walked into the front room. 'You are drenched.'

'Just a little, Mercy.' She stared at the roaring fire in the grate and the children huddled around it. 'How did you get coal for the fire?'

'Mrs Drysdale from across the road gave us some. She made it up and got it going for us, then measured the windows for curtains and the children for clothes.'

'And you? You need new clothes too.'

'Yes.' Tears shimmered in Mercy's eyes. 'How will I ever repay you?'

Before Victoria could reply, a knock sounded on the front door. A large cart had stopped in front of the window.

'Delivery!' Victoria answered the door and instructed the two men to take the beds upstairs.

The ironmongers cart had just left when the grocer's wagon arrived and a young boy carried in two crates filled with vegetables and fruit and took them into the kitchen.

Another young boy, wet from riding his bicycle, brought in the parcels of meat Victoria had purchased.

Mercy stood in the entrance, watching the goods being carried in. 'It is all so unbelievable.'

Tired, Victoria wished Gilforth's cart would come soon for she was in sore need of a long sit down. But they still didn't have a sofa, chair or stool to sit on. Looking around the bare front room, she shook her head. 'There's still a great deal left to do.'

'I'm hungry,' Jane cried.

Victoria went into the kitchen and surveyed the few items there. 'Can you cook, Mercy?'

'Not very well. A few basic things.' Mercy leaned against the wall, dark circles bruised under her eyes. She looked incapable of even standing at the moment. 'I've tried to learn since being married, but I couldn't master it. My mother had a cook and so it was a skill I never learned.'

'I have never done it either. Heavens, that is a pickle, isn't it?' Victoria grabbed a bag of apples and passed it to Jane. 'Take it to the others.'

Left alone, Victoria and Mercy unpacked the crate of vegetables onto the larder shelves, though Mercy's energy soon dissipated and she had to rest.

'We need to get that range fire going to cook on.' Victoria glanced at the large black cooker against the wall.

Mercy opened one of the little stove doors. 'We only have a bucket of coal, that Mrs Drysdale left for us.'

'I've been to the coal yard and ordered coal, but they'll not deliver it until the morning.'

The back door suddenly flung open and Polly raced in, looking wet and wild and hunted.

'Polly!' Mercy smiled tiredly. 'You found us.'

'I must hide!' The girl dodged around as though searching for an escape.

'Why?' Victoria frowned.

'They can't find me or I'm dead!'

A shiver of fear ran down Victoria's back. 'Who can't find you?'

'The police!'

Chapter Eight

Victoria woke late the next morning more tired than when she'd gone to bed. Her shoulder pained her but she tried to ignore it best she could. She'd hardly slept a minute during the night, falling asleep as dawn broke. A quiet birthday dinner had greeted her when she returned from the house in Fossgate. The mood had been subdued, for Mimi was ill and couldn't attend. Uncle and Aunt had talked quietly and Stella ignored her completely.

Still concerned with the house on Fossgate, Victoria had hardly eaten as she went over the day's events. After all the deliveries had arrived, she'd made up the beds while Mercy had put potatoes into the coals of the front room's fire since neither of them could use the range even if they had spare coal for it. Gilforth, a decent man, had sent a table and chairs, a dark green horsehair sofa and three good mattresses.

Coming home to the beauty and richness of her uncle's house in Blossom Street clearly showed her the stark difference between the two dwellings. She'd left Mercy and the children with food and fire and beds to sleep in, more than they'd had for years. But it was only the beginning of a long journey to making the house presentable, and then there was the added drama of Polly.

The girl had been accused of pickpocketing and a policeman had chased her through the streets. She'd lost him in the alleys, only to be told that her family had gone to Fossgate.

Running to the house to find her family, she'd literally bumped into the constable as he rounded a corner. She'd run hard along the Foss River, ducking and diving into warehouses until she got to the house.

Dora tapped on the door, breaking into her thoughts, and entered the bedroom. 'Good morning, Miss.' She carried a freshly laundered blue gown and deep cream linen day dress, which she hung in the wardrobe. 'Everyone has left the house already, Miss, so I can bring you up a breakfast tray if you'd prefer?'

'Yes, please, that'll leave Jennie to clear away the breakfast things from the dining room.' Victoria pushed back the bedcovers and sat on the edge of the bed.

'What do you wish to wear today, miss?'

'The navy skirt and the white blouse with the blue fleck pattern.'

'Are you staying home today, miss?' Dora asked, selecting the garments.

'No, I'm visiting the house my father left me in his will.'

'In this, miss?' Shocked, Dora held up the plain skirt.

'The house requires some cleaning and isn't in a fit state for me to wear my best.' She tipped water from the jug into the basin and washed her face.

'Will you want a bath this afternoon, miss, before you attend the Theatre Royal?'

'The theatre?'

'Have you forgotten, Miss?' Dora laughed. 'That's why I've been working on the blue gown, remember? It had a tear in the lace at back.'

'Oh...er, yes.' A night at the theatre was usually one of her favourite evenings, but after hardly any sleep how was she to make it through?

'I need a hansom cab, Dora, and forget about breakfast, I've too much to do.'

Within half an hour, she was riding in a hansom through the city, heading for Fossgate. The Minster and other church bells rang out the tenth hour.

When the hansom stopped outside of her house, she paid the driver and entered the front door. 'Mercy, it's just me.'

She came to an abrupt halt in the front room on seeing Doctor Ashton standing before the fireplace, Mercy crying beside him and the silent children sitting on the sofa in a row. There was no sign of Polly.

'Miss Carlton.' Doctor Ashton bowed stiffly, his blue eyes glacial. 'I see you've been very busy.'

Her heart skipped a beat at seeing him, but his cold indifference made her turn her attention to Mercy. 'What is wrong?'

'Polly has been arrested.' Mercy wiped her eyes, her face pale and blotchy. 'The police came an hour ago.'

Victoria gasped. 'Oh no.'

Doctor Ashton patted Mercy's shoulder. 'I'll go to the gaol now. See what I can find out.'

135

'I'll come with you.' Victoria didn't wait for his response and hurried out.

A hansom cab stood further up the street, outside of the Queen's Head public house, Ashton hailed it and soon they were trundling away towards the prison.

After several moments of silence, Victoria decided she'd speak first. 'How did you know where to find Mrs Felling?

'I happened to see Annie Weaver. She told me. Nothing is kept a secret for long in those parts.'

'How is Annie?' she asked him, trying to steady her racing pulse as they sat opposite each other in the hansom.

'She has bruises, possibly cracked ribs along with her other minor injuries.'

'Poor woman. Her husband is a brute. I wanted to take her to my house as well, but she refused.'

He gave her a level stare. 'It is not for you to decide whether a wife leaves her husband, Miss Carlton.'

She stiffened. Why was he being so severe? 'Do you expect me to leave her there so she can suffer more abuse?'

'It would be a matter for the police, by getting involved all you would do is bring trouble to your own door.'

'But I may have prevented him killing her!'

'And what about you? Annie told me her husband hit you!'

'I'm fine.' She dismissed the memory of that awful man punching her.

'This house of yours…I see the Fellings are happily ensconced, but how long will it last?'

'What do you mean?'

'Mrs Felling hasn't the strength to hold down a job for long. Are you to keep her for the rest of her days, the children too? Are you thinking of turning the house into a place for the desperate?'

She stared at him, confused. The future hadn't been thought about. All she'd wanted was to get them somewhere better to live. His tone made her doubt her actions and that angered her.

'Are you going to try and save every poor family in the slum? Do you have an income that is so great you can put them all in houses?' His blue eyes stared at her.

'You are insulting me, sir.' At that moment she hated him.

He sighed deeply as the hansom rattled down Castlegate and slowed to rumble through the gates of the inner castle wall's. They circled around the high mount upon which stood the imposing Clifford's Tower, before pulling to a stop in front of the large impressive stone building that was the female prison.

Alighting first, Ashton put his hand out to help Victoria down. He hesitated on letting go of her hand. 'Forgive me, please. I speak too bluntly. You have a kindness that is refreshing, but it also makes me worry for you. You went into battle for Annie against a brute of a man. You're lucky he didn't turn on you!'

'I couldn't ignore what was happening.'

'And it does you credit, truly I admire you for it, but Miss Carlton you must not endanger yourself in that way again.'

'I acted on impulse. It wasn't planned.'

'Was it impulse to take the Fellings away too? I couldn't believe you had offered the Felling family a place to live. These people are different from you.'

'Mercy isn't that different. She was brought up in a Quaker's house. She lived a respectable life until she made a bad decision and married the wrong man.'

'But she has lived a life you cannot imagine.'

'Conditions have brought her low, but that doesn't mean she can't ever rise again.'

'Not everyone is like Mrs Felling. The majority of those people are in a desperate state. They will do anything to stay alive. I don't want you getting involved in something that is beyond your understanding. Weaver and his kind wouldn't hesitate to hurt you just as he has hurt Annie. You must have a care.'

'I cannot turn and look the other way. Those people need help and I can give that help.' She liked that he still held her hand, though it was inappropriate and if anyone saw them she'd be the talk of the drawing rooms.

'Not single-handedly.'

'I can try. I've seen my aunt's charities and the little they do on the street. The organisations become bogged down with details and accounts. I would much rather see for myself first-hand the problems and give the aid where I can.'

'You have done that already with the Felling family.'

'And I won't stop there. My uncle will support my activities.'

He gave her a dubious look, then asked the cabbie to wait. They went up the steps and passed the tall columns. Ashton turned right away from the noise of the main cells.

Victoria had never been in a gaol before and shivered at the coldness seeping beneath her coat. 'Do you know where to go?'

'I've been in attendance here once. I was given a tour of the prison, not an enjoyable experience, I can assure you. The conditions here are grim.' He put his hand under her elbow as they walked up the two flights of stairs to the offices on the next floor.

An older man, with long grey whiskers walked towards them, he paused before opening a door. 'You have business here, sir?'

'Yes.' Ashton held out his hand for the other man to shake. 'I am Doctor Joseph Ashton and this is Miss Victoria Carlton. We'd like to speak with someone regarding the arrest of a girl, Polly Felling. She is ten years old. We weren't sure where she would be held.'

'Not here, at least not until she has been sentenced. She'd be at one of the city's holding cells.'

'Holding cells? But she is just a child.' Ashton frowned. 'I presumed she'd be taken here with the other females.'

'Not until she's sentenced. She'll be at a station cell.'

'How do we know which one she is being held at?' Victoria asked, alarmed that a young girl would be placed in a cell with adults.

The man took out his pocket watch and consulted it. 'I really must go.'

'Please!' Victoria pleaded.

He frowned, then sighed. 'Where was she picked up?'

'Picked up?' Victoria looked at Ashton for clarification.

'Arrested.' The older man amended.

'Fossgate,' Ashton supplied.

'She'd likely be at St Andrewsgate then. Good day.' The man gave a departing nod and went into the office and closed the door.

They quickly left the prison and instructed the cabbie to take them to St Andrewsgate police station.

Victoria gazed at the passing buildings, including the milliner she and Stella frequented and wondered what the doctor's thoughts were regarding her cousin. 'Are you going to the Theatre Royal tonight, Doctor Ashton?' It seemed a ridiculous question considering the gravity of Polly's situation.

He nodded. 'Yes, I am making up one of your family's party at the behest of your aunt.'

'I see...' Her family's party?

This news shocked her, but then she was hardly at home these days to find out what the family were organising. Likely, Stella was behind the invitation as well.

The horse slowed and Victoria looked out. This was a day of several firsts for her. She'd never been to a police station before either and imagined her aunt fainting at the thought of her doing so now.

Ashton asked the cabbie to wait again and they went inside.

Instantly they were assaulted by noises and an awful smell. A barrage of abuse came from within another room and an iron door slammed shut. Policemen and accused felons occupied the small room. A woman sat on a stool crying, begging to be allowed to go home to her children - she was ignored.

A man lurched sideways from the young policeman who held him and vomited over the floor. Victoria jumped back and Ashton shielded her behind him.

Victoria felt sick and faint at the same time. She'd been foolish to not have breakfast, but she'd thought she'd share a cup of tea with Mercy as they discussed what else the house lacked.

Never did she expect to be visiting firstly a prison, and secondly a holding cell surrounded by drunken men.

Ashton went to the high wooden counter and spoke to the constable seated there.

'Yes, sir?'

Ashton made the introduction and told him the reason for the visit while the constable twirled a pencil in his fingers.

'I can't let you see her, sir. It's against the rules until she's brought up before the court.'

'And when will that be?'

The constable consulted a ledger before him. 'Two weeks on Friday.'

'Two weeks!' Victoria felt the air leave her lungs. 'No, that can't be. She is but a child.'

'A child who committed a felony.' The constable pushed his glasses further up his long nose.

Angered, she pushed forward. 'My uncle is Harold Dobson of Dobson's Bank. He is also a city alderman. I *insist* you let me see Polly this instant or I will tell him the state of this establishment!'

'Miss, the cells are not fit for you to be down there.'

'Then bring her up to me immediately,' she demanded as one drunk man began singing a rowdy song about putting a woman over his knee.

Ashton touched her arm. 'Miss Carlton, I think you should wait outside.'

'No. I want to see Polly.' She turned back to the constable. 'I am not leaving here until you do. Will you see to it, please?'

'Wait there, miss.' The constable sighed, his expression one of pained tolerance as he went out through a door behind the counter and was gone for a while.

141

When he finally returned, he had Polly by the scruff of her dress collar.

'Polly!' Victoria rushed to her. The girl was filthy, dirtier than she'd ever seen a child to be.

Defiant, Polly stood and stared at her. 'Is me mam alright?'

'Yes. They are staying at my house. I'll take care of them. Don't worry about them. What about you? Are you hurt?'

'No, miss.' Polly looked at the floor and didn't raise her eyes again.

'We'll get you out as soon as we can.' Victoria felt the words were hollow, but she had to say them. She had no power in the courts and she wasn't sure if Uncle Harold did either.

'She's known is this one.' The constable nodded towards Polly. 'She's led my men a merry dance for months. Slippery as an eel.'

'What has she been accused of?' Ashton demanded.

'Pick pocketing. An expensive pocket watch. Not the first time, I'd wager. She's a thief is this one.' The constable rocked on his heels.

'She is a child in reduced circumstances,' Victoria ground out.

'Still a thief. She should be working for an honest wage, not harassing decent people going about their business.'

'Was the watch found on her?' She glanced at Polly, lice roamed over the girl's lank hair.

'No, but the man she stole from said it was her this morning when he came in to identify her.'

'I didn't steal anything!' Polly mumbled, scratching her arm that was full of red blotches.

'I want her released into my care, is that possible?' Victoria asked him.

'No, it isn't possible, miss, I'm sorry.'

Behind them another man was ushered in protesting loudly at his innocence.

The constable grabbed Polly. 'She needs to be down below.'

Ashton stepped forward. 'I want her to have decent food, not the slop that is served here.' He fished in his pocket and took out money which he gave to the constable. 'See that it is done and I'll be back to check.'

The constable slipped the money away quickly. 'Very good, sir. Good day to you both.'

Dismissed and feeling wretched, Victoria thankfully left the building, and once outside, gulped in fresh air. 'I never thought to give him money.'

'That's the way it is, unfortunately.' Ashton sighed.

'Will he do as you asked?'

'We can only hope so. You were wonderful in there, Miss Carlton.' Concern in his voice, Ashton stood close to her, holding her elbow. 'However, let me take you home. This has been too much for you.'

'I'm stronger than I look, Doctor. Besides, I need to go to Fossgate and see Mercy.'

'I can speak with Mrs Felling.'

'No, she is my friend.'

'Your *friend*?'

She looked up at him. 'Yes, she is my friend. The only proper one I have. Does that surprise you?'

'Your cousin surely must be first in your affections, she is—'

'Stella is my cousin. We live in the same house, but are no longer friends.'

'Why?'

'I am not quite sure, Doctor Ashton, but I feel you have something to do with it.'

'Me?' He frowned, surprise showing in his face. 'How so?'

She pulled away from him and climbed into the hansom, she shut the door, shutting *him* out. The cabbie urged the horse on and she rested back against the leather seat. She'd revealed too much. Mimi always said she did that. When would she learn?

Chapter Nine

'Victoria!' Aunt Esther's distressed voice filled the drawing room the following morning.

Shocked to hear it, Victoria paused on the staircase, where she was considering what excuse she could use to escape the house today to go to Fossgate. She'd been late leaving a distraught Mercy, trying to offer her comfort over Polly. Her lateness had displeased everyone who were waiting for her to get ready for the trip to the theatre. Thankfully, Doctor Ashton had sent a note saying he wasn't accompanying them, which both pleased and disappointed her.

Hurrying into the drawing room, Victoria frowned as in front of her stood Aunt Esther, Uncle Harold and Stella. 'What is it, Aunt?'

'Close the door and come and sit down.' Aunt Esther stood rigidly, spots of anger colouring her cheeks. 'You must explain yourself.'

'Dearest girl,' Uncle gave a reassuring smile. 'Reports have come to us of your recent activities and we—'

'Yesterday, you went to St Andrewsgate police station!' Aunt Esther exploded. 'Why?'

Victoria remained in the middle of the room. 'I went there because a young girl needed my help.'

'Who is this girl?' Aunt demanded.

Stella lifted her chin haughtily. 'It will be one of the slum families' children, no doubt. Victoria has become extremely friendly with the poor, one family in particular.'

'I don't understand.' Aunt's eyebrows drew together. 'What could Stella possibly mean by you being friendly with the poor?'

'I have been helping a woman who is—'

'A woman?' Aunt Esther glanced at her husband. 'What woman? Where?'

'In Walmgate, Aunt.' Victoria ignored Stella's sly grin.

'Walmgate? That notorious area?' Aunt gripped Uncle Harold's arm. 'She has been to Walmgate, Harold, *Walmgate!*'

'Aunt, please, if you'd listen to—'

'Listen? What must I listen to? How you are roaming the lanes of a slum area?'

'Aunt, you help the poor all the time!' she defended.

'Yes, through the charities that are set up for that purpose. I don't parade myself in front of the poor wretches in their own environment! There are boundaries, Victoria. I thought you understood that?'

Stella touched her mother's arm lightly. 'Mama, other people we know have seen her coming out of the alleys in Walmgate.

Doctor Ashton told me in confidence that he is mightily worried about Victoria becoming too involved. That she might get hurt. She confronted a man who was *beating* his wife in the slums.'

'Oh, I say!' Uncle Harold rocked back in shock. 'Victoria?'

Aunt Esther looked fit to faint. 'No! That cannot be true? Victoria? Tell me Stella has it wrong. You didn't confront a man who was beating his wife?'

'I did, but—'

'I can hardly believe my ears. This is outrageous.' Aunt placed her hands over her chest. 'A member of my family going about humiliating herself in such a way is intolerable. People must think I cannot run my own household.'

'Aunt, please.' With each passing moment she felt more under fire and sick at heart. The look of astonishment on their faces was hard to accept. 'I'm sorry if my actions have upset you all.'

'You will cease all this activity and will remain in this house. Tell her that is so, Harold.' Aunt Esther glared at her husband as though it was entirely his fault.

'No.' Victoria shook her head.

Stella gasped and Aunt Esther's eyes widened.

'Victoria, dear—'

'I'm sorry, Uncle,' she interrupted him, 'but I will not abandon those who need my help.'

'I beg your pardon!' Aunt Esther's lips thinned. 'You will do as we say, young lady. You will not cavort about the slum district.'

'I do not cavort. I give assistance, if I can.'

'How? A few pennies here and there? That is not helping those people. You are only embarrassing them by displaying your good fortune. It's cruel.'

147

Anger replaced the hurt. Victoria straightened her back. 'How dare you say such a thing, Aunt? How is it cruel to assist those that are in great need? You say it to anyone who will listen how we must all do our duty.'

'Do not disrespect my mother after all she has done for you,' Stella yelled.

'I am not disrespecting, Aunt,' she said through clenched teeth.

Stella laughed mockingly. 'There are limits, rules to how we deal with the underprivileged and you know it. Do you think those people want to see you in your fine dresses, handing out food or money? They don't want to be faced with what they can never have. They don't want you in their homes like a visiting saint!'

Victoria lost her temper. 'You know nothing, Stella, so be quiet!'

'Do not raise your voice in this house,' Aunt demanded, close to tears. 'I do not understand how this is happening in my own household and I knew nothing.'

'It's easy, Mama, her behaviour is to be expected coming from a father such as hers.' Stella sneered, no longer hiding her dislike.

'That is enough!' Uncle Harold bellowed. 'Stella leave the room.'

'Why?' Stella's act of innocence was lost on them all.

'Just go!'

With a huff, Stella paused by Victoria to whisper, 'Ashton will never be yours now.'

With those spiteful words ringing in her ears, Victoria faced her aunt and uncle.

'I apologise if my activities have caused offense and embarrassment to this family. However, I will continue to do whatever I can to aid those who need it most.'

'You certainly will not!' Aunt Esther shook her head. 'Tell her, Harold.'

'My dear girl.' Uncle Harold scratched his whiskers. 'We only want the best for you, and although we applaud your empathy...' He looked lost for words. 'You see, dearest, you are young, and those people could take liberties.'

'I'm not a child, Uncle. I can take care of myself.'

Aunt Esther sat down on the sofa with a deep sigh. 'We are concerned that you did all this without speaking to us, Victoria. I do champion many causes and charities and I'd be only too delighted to take you to every meeting I attend. That is the correct way to do it.'

'But it's not how *I* want to do it, Aunt.'

'You want to be amongst them? There is no need. Good work can be done in other ways.'

'Aunt, please,' Victoria bent in front of her aunt's knees and took her hand. 'I have helped a family, a decent woman and her children. She was a Quaker, well brought up, but made the wrong decisions, and has been cast low.'

'A member of the Rowntree family?'

'No, I think not.'

'Then let the Quakers deal with her.'

'They have turned their backs on her.'

'Then let others help.'

'Like your charities?' Victoria scoffed. 'Your numerous charities didn't even know about her. She nearly died. Where were your charities then?'

'We cannot help everyone, Victoria.'

'No, but I did my bit. I've been there to support her recovery, and to put food in her children's mouths.'

'Well, since you've done all that, now you can cease these visits. She doesn't need you any more and the whole city won't be tattling about your exertions in the slums.'

'I've installed her in the house in Fossgate.'

'You've done what?' Uncle Harold wheezed, red-faced. 'No, Victoria, that house is to be sold.'

She looked up at him. 'I've changed my mind, Uncle. I wish to put it to good use.'

Aunt Esther withdrew her hands from Victoria's and leaned away from her. 'This is too much.'

'Victoria, we need to discuss this.' Uncle sat in the winged back chair near the fireplace. 'Such a decision cannot be considered without knowing all the facts.'

'Uncle, it is half my house, is it not? I am of age. Therefore, I can do with it whatever I want, do you agree?'

'What will people think?' Aunt Esther quickly got to her feet and marched towards the door, where she turned and glared at Victoria. 'No member of my family will house people from the slums! How will we face society? You've taken this too far, Victoria, and I am seriously displeased with you.' She flounced from the room.

Victoria slowly sat on the sofa, exhausted. 'Aunt Esther is a hypocrite.'

'Now, Victoria I won't have you speak of her in that way.'

'But it is true. I also thought her to be a woman of principle and sympathy, but it seems it's only when it suits her. She is a leader in the community and chairs committees, yet it isn't enough. Raising money isn't the only way to help these people.'

Uncle clasped his hands together over his round stomach. 'Your aunt is a lady. She does her best within the limits of what society expects. Ladies aren't meant to be hands on, my dear. You shouldn't expect it from her, and nor should you be so volatile in your exertions. Reputation is everything.'

'Is reputation more important than saving lives?'

'You are being dramatic. Your role isn't to save lives for you are not a doctor.'

'I will continue to do this, Uncle. I cannot give it up.'

'You must, my dear girl. Roaming the alleys of the slum districts will bring you nothing but harm and I promised your parents I would keep you safe. Therefore, I forbid you to continue your endeavours in this manner. Find other, safer and more gentle ways to help those unfortunates.'

She stiffened at his words. 'You cannot forbid me, I'm of age.'

'Victoria, please. Don't be headstrong. You remind me too much of your mother.'

She had no recollection of her mother being headstrong. The few memories she had were of a gentle woman, with soft hands and kind words. 'When was my mother headstrong?'

Uncle snorted. 'When wasn't she? She defied our father and married Carlton, when he was clearly unsuitable.'

'Why? Why was he unsuitable?'

'Because he was a gambler. Your mother was forbidden to marry him, but she eloped and got married. She was gone for months and when they returned she was pregnant with you. She wouldn't give your father up, despite his unstable ways. The man made enemies where ever he went.'

Uncle sighed sadly. 'I do see her in you so very much and it frightens me. I don't want you ending up as she did, ostracised from family and society.'

Silence stretched between them for some moments, each lost in their own thoughts.

Victoria wished she'd been older when her parents died so she could know more about them. All she had were a few childhood memories, but as an adult she'd have known so much more instead of relying on her aunt and uncle to tell her their side of what kind of people they were.

'I will organise the selling of the house first thing in the morning,' Uncle said. 'You'll not have the worry of it any more.'

'No, please. I don't want to sell it.'

'But you must!' He looked flabbergasted. 'Your aunt will not accept you running some sort of alms-house.'

'I insist. Please try to understand that this is what I feel I need to do.' She gripped her hands together, desperate to make him see.

He rubbed his eyes. 'Then if you must, I will be in charge of it. I can assign a manager to oversee it all.'

'I want to do it myself, Uncle. It's important to me.'

'It's impossible!' Uncle banged the table.

She was distraught at making him so distressed. 'But it isn't if you would only try to realise that this makes me happy.'

Stella suddenly appeared in the doorway and snorted in disgust. 'Then you will have to leave this house. Mama is so upset with you, Victoria. I refuse to stand by and watch you embarrass this family with your actions.'

'Stella, this has nothing to do with you,' Uncle Harold muttered.

'I am sorry, Papa, but it has everything to do with me when it upsets Mama.'

'Just return upstairs, I'll be there shortly.'

Stella stamped her foot. 'Do you wish Mama to be humiliated in front of her friends because she,' she pointed at Victoria, 'refuses to behave as a decent member of our society should? Mama is upstairs in such distress that I cannot bear it.'

Uncle pushed himself off the chair and sighed. 'I shall go and see to her.'

Victoria stood also. 'Uncle. I will leave the house tomorrow.'

'No!'

'Yes. It is only right. Aunt Esther has been good to me, as you have, but I will not remain under your roof when I am obviously displeasing everyone.'

Uncle pulled Victoria against his large chest and held her there. 'There will be no hastiness, my dear. I will sort it all out.' He kissed her forehead and left the room.

Victoria, now she had made the decision, felt better. She stared at Stella. Since coming to live here she had put up with her cousin's selfish ways, her demands, her need to come first, her belief that she had to have the best of everything while Victoria should have second best.

'I think you have made the correct decision,' Stella said, sauntering into the room. 'Leaving, I mean.'

Victoria watched her, waiting.

Stella picked up a book left on the small table by the sofa. 'Before you go, you should know that I'm expecting Doctor Ashton to declare his interest in me to Papa any day now.'

153

Her heart pounding, she kept watching her cousin, seeing her for the nasty person she was. Stella had never wanted Ashton until she knew that Victoria admired him. 'Then I wish you every good thing.'

Stella's eyes narrowed. 'You thought he wanted you, didn't you?'

'Not at all.'

'Don't lie to me. I know you too well.' Stella's smug smile stripped her of any beauty. 'You wanted the doctor for yourself since the first moment you saw him. I could see it plainly and I did my best to take every opportunity to turn him against you.'

'Why?'

'Because you cannot marry before me. Because you cannot have the one man in town who is handsome and clever. Because he's too *good* for you'.

'Too good for me?' Victoria frowned. 'How is that so?'

'Without my father, you'd be a nobody, probably in a workhouse yourself. Your parents lived only by my father's goodwill, as *you* have done all these years. How could you possibly believe you deserve someone with breeding and position such as Ashton? Especially now, when you've shown such *passion* for the unfortunates of this city.'

'I admire Doctor Ashton for his work and dedication. That is all.' She hated her and her hurtful words. She'd never forgive Stella for being a spurious friend.

Stella preened. 'I will make him a wonderful wife. He'll be raised as high as possible with our family's support.'

'I think the doctor would believe he is highly positioned already and doesn't need this family's backing.'

'You can always go higher. He could be chief medical officer or serve the royal family. Ambition should never be ignored. And I will help drive him to reach that success. We will be so happy.'

Victoria raised an eyebrow. 'I don't think you even know what happiness is, Stella. I feel sorry for you.'

'*You* feel sorry for *me*?' Stella gaped at her.

'Yes. I see you flitting through life never knowing what it's like to really live.' Smiling a little, Victoria walked out of the room.

The smile froze on her face when a scream rent the air.

Stella joined her in the hallway. 'What was that?'

Another scream came from the rooms above.

'Aunt Esther!' Gathering up her skirts, Victoria dashed upstairs followed by Stella.

She raced into the bedroom belonging to her aunt and uncle and skidded to a stop. Uncle Harold lay on the floor with Aunt kneeling down beside him, begging him to wake up.

'Mama?' Stella cried from the doorway.

'He's dead!' Aunt Esther moaned in despair.

'Are you sure?' Victoria knelt on the other side of her uncle. 'Has he just fainted?'

'He clutched at his arm and then his chest, he dropped...' Aunt Esther wailed.

Hands shaking, Victoria placed her fingers by Uncle Harold's neck trying to feel for a pulse, but she shook so much she couldn't tell if there was one or not.

Mr Hubbard hurried into the room. He bent down next to Victoria and bent his ear to Uncle's chest. 'A mirror.'

Victoria scrambled to her feet and retrieved the hand mirror from her aunt's dressing table and gave it to him.

He held it in front of Uncle's mouth. No breath misted the glass.

Aunt Esther wailed again and Stella pulled her up off the floor and hugged her.

Mr Hubbard stood and dashed for the door. 'I'll go for the doctor myself.'

Standing looking down at her uncle, Victoria knew he was dead. A deep sadness welled in her chest. She retrieved a pillow from the bed and placed it gently under his head, wishing he'd suddenly open his eyes.

'*You* did this!' Stella screamed, pointing a finger at her.

She stared up at her cousin as though she'd lost her mind. 'Me?'

'Yes, you! You caused him to worry over you!' Stella snarled like a dog fighting over a bone. 'All this nonsense about mixing with the lower orders, and that stupid house where you've ensconced the filth from the gutters. It was too much for him. *You* killed him!'

'Stella that is absurd. You're upset.' Victoria trembled. Had she killed him? Worried him to death? Maybe she had? This was her fault.

'Get out!' Stella's shriek echoed about the room. 'Get out and never come back. You are not welcome here.'

Her heart squeezing in her chest, she looked at her aunt. 'Aunt Esther, please, I...' Her words faltered as her aunt stared at her full of hate.

'He was talking of you, trying to convince me to accept your independence...' Aunt Esther gulped. 'He was agitated... *Your* name was the last word he said.' She broke down and cried into Stella's shoulder.

'You will leave this house immediately and never return.' Stella's voice was cold and hard.

Distraught, and with a last look at Uncle Harold dead on the floor, Victoria turned and left the room.

Chapter Ten

Victoria stepped down from her uncle's carriage and stared at the front of her house on Fossgate. It was all she had. She'd never felt more alone in her life.

The door opened and Mercy stood there, terribly thin in her ragged dress, her hair lank and unwashed. 'Are you coming in, Miss Carlton?'

Victoria hesitated, then turned and grabbed her large bag from inside the carriage, while Thornberry, the driver, jumped down to unstrap the trunk from the back. 'Can you take that inside, please?'

'Yes, miss.'

Once inside the house, Victoria felt hot tears well. She glanced about the front room. A small fire burned in the grate and the children sat on the floor. Mercy had used charcoal to write numbers on a piece of board.

'I've been teaching them how to count.' Mercy gestured to the board.

Nodding, Victoria couldn't speak. Emotion clogged her throat. Thornberry dipped his hat at her on the way out and soon her uncle's carriage was trundling up the road, back to the house that had been her home…

'Miss Carlton?'

'Mercy, I…' Tears fell, and she couldn't stop them.

'Come and sit down.' Mercy guided her to the sofa and sent the children out of the room. 'What's happened?'

'My uncle Harold has died, today, just an hour ago.'

'I am so sorry.'

'I am banished from the house.'

'Banished? Why?'

'Because they found out about what I've been doing, helping you, visiting the slum areas.'

'Then you must stop doing it. Go home. Tell them you'll stop.' Mercy paced the floor. 'I can go back to the room…I'll get work…'

She shook her head and wiped the tears away. 'No. No, I cannot go back. Not without my uncle there. My aunt blames me for his death, and so does my cousin. I cannot face them.'

'Perhaps it was the grief which made them act so harshly? I'm sure they'll change their minds once the shock has receded.'

Taking a deep breath, Victoria sighed. 'I don't want to be there. I couldn't live there knowing they secretly blame me.'

'But what is the alternative?'

'I'll live here. It is my house, or half of it is.'

'Here?' Mercy's eyes widened. 'But this is very different to how you are used to living.'

She fished out a handkerchief from her reticule and wiped her eyes. 'I'll have to adjust then, won't I?'

'Oh, miss.' Mercy wrung her hands. 'I'll gather the children and return to our room in Walmgate.'

'It'll be taken by now.'

'I'll find somewhere else if that's the case and you must return home.'

'No, no, Mercy. You are to stay here.'

'It's not right, Miss Carlton. Because of me you have been cast aside, rejected by your family.'

'And do you think I can cast you aside now? No. We will live together. Here.'

Relief made Mercy's shoulders sag. 'Miss Carlton, are you really certain about that?'

'Yes. I couldn't ask you to leave, not after bringing you here in the first place.'

'Thank you, miss. I'll get work, pay my way.'

She stared around at the room, at the peeling wallpaper, the stains on the wooden floorboards, the dirty curtain-less windows. Patches of mould created patterns on the walls and ceiling. Despite the fire, coldness still penetrated the room. The whole house needed work done to it, lots of work, which would cost money. Money she didn't have now her uncle was dead.

Tears burned behind her eyes again. How could she live here? There was no comfort, no joy in this house.

'We all slept together last night for warmth and because the children were scared. The biggest room upstairs has the other bed. I don't need it. I'm happy to sleep in with the children. I actually slept better last night than I had in a very long time. We were warm and comfortable.'

Victoria nodded, not really caring at that moment. 'I'm sure we'll make do.'

'We can use some of the coal to light a fire in your bedroom and get it warm for you.'

'No, I don't need a fire in the bedroom. We need to save the coal for cooking. Did you manage to get the range lit?'

'Yes. Oh, I'd best check it.' Mercy dashed out of the room.

Slowly, feeling depressed in spirits, Victoria followed her into the kitchen at the back of the house.

This was another room which was freezing cold and in a state of shabbiness. The only furniture it held was the wooden table and chairs she'd bought from Gilforth's.

Mercy raked the glowing embers in the range fire and added more coal. 'I can try to cook something.' Her expression was doubtful. 'Are you hungry?'

'No, just some tea would be nice.'

'I can do that.' Mercy busied herself with putting the kettle on the stove top and measured tea leaves into the brown earthenware teapot.

Victoria stared out of the small dirty window overlooking the tiny courtyard. The grey overcast day matched her mood. She shied away from thinking about her uncle, or the future, for both were too sad to contemplate. Her mind was numb, her heart heavy. In one day she had lost everything, her family, her home, Doctor Ashton...

'I think I'll go upstairs and lie down for a bit.' She rose from the chair and walked upstairs, her feet felt laden with every step.

In the largest bedroom, she stared at the bed. Nothing else was in the room, no drawers, wardrobe, basin or jug, no curtains or carpet or pictures on the wall.

Her chest tightened. She stifled a cry and fell onto the bed. Burying her face into the cold pillow, she cried for all she had lost.

When she woke, cold and with a headache, the room was grey with a dim dawn light. Outside it was raining and looking more like winter than spring.

Shivering, she slipped off the bed, her clothes crumpled and her hair hanging loose.

From her trunk, she took out a pale blue shawl and wrapped it around her shoulders.

The house was eerily quiet as she crept downstairs, wincing every time the floorboards creaked.

In the kitchen, the embers in the range winked between piles of thick ash. She raked them with the tongs and added more coal, which made it smoke. Coughing, she looked around for inspiration and saw a pile of broken crate pieces and gathering those, she pushed them into the embers. Shutting the stove door, she hoped for the best.

'Miss?' Mercy stood at the door, dishevelled and pale.

'Lord, Mercy, we need to get you some clothes.' Victoria shook her head at the state of the other woman's ragged, stained dress. She sighed, overwhelmed by the enormity of the situation she was in.

'Mrs Drysdale is finding me a skirt from her old stock.' Mercy came to the range and shook the kettle. It was empty. From the water bucket, she filled the kettle and then put it back on the stove. 'I'll fry some ham.'

Victoria sat at the table. 'Can we spare some water? I need to wash and change.'

Mercy pointed to the bucket. 'Take that. The very best thing about this house is that we have a pump out the back. We will never be short of water. Isn't that wonderful?'

'Wonderful?'

'Yes.' Mercy put a frying pan on the stove and added slices of ham to it from the meat supply Victoria had bought.

'If it makes you happy then I am happy.'

'Where we were living, there was one tap for the whole courtyard and three alleyways. It was only turned on in the morning for a couple of hours. Having water whenever I want it is a luxury I've not had since leaving home.'

Victoria frowned. 'I never even considered not being able to have water.'

Mercy smiled sadly. 'There will be so many changes for you, miss, you'll find it hard to adjust to this kind of life to begin with.'

Victoria's stomach rumbled as the smell of ham wafted about the kitchen. 'Do you ever regret the choices you made. About leaving your family?'

'Now, yes, of course I do. But back then, no. I felt I was doing the right thing. I loved Stephen. I thought him to be decent and kind. And he was, at first.' Mercy shrugged and added fresh tea leaves to the teapot. 'My father was... fanatical about the teachings of his church. I did not agree with him. I was forever in trouble because of it.'

Above their heads they heard the footsteps of the children.

Mercy pushed the ham around the pan. 'When Stephen offered me the chance of another life away from the strictness of my father, I was only too glad to accept. I would be a married woman, elevated from simply being a merchant's daughter in a household ruled by God.'

The door opened and four little faces peeped around it.

Victoria smiled at them. Despite being filthy and thin, they were dear looking children. 'Come in. Your mother is cooking breakfast.'

Shy, they huddled together by the door.

'Come and sit at the table if you want to eat.' Mercy took a loaf of bread and began slicing it up.

'Let me do that.' Victoria was capable of slicing bread and the rest she'd have to learn.

After a humble meal of bread, ham and tea, Victoria went up to her room and washed herself from a bucket.

She changed into clean undergarments and donned a black skirt and bodice. Despite not being at home, she'd still show herself to be in mourning for her uncle. Her hair she pinned up with pale tortoiseshell combs. She felt now she could face the day.

In the kitchen, Mercy sat at the table, washing the plates in a bucket. 'Was your uncle a good man?'

'One of the best. I don't know what I'll do without him. He loved me like a daughter and I'll miss him terribly.'

'That's nice. To have someone who cared for you. I don't even know where my family is. Last I heard they'd sailed to America.' Leaning back in the chair, Mercy wiped her dull hair out of her eyes.

Victoria eyed the tin bath in the corner of the room. 'I think you and the children should bathe today. I have never had lice in my life and I refuse to start now.'

'The younger children have never had a bath before. My husband sold it years ago, along with everything else, to pay his debts.'

'Do you miss him?'

'I miss the old him, the smiling man who said such lovely things to me, and who promised me that we'd have a good life.'

'When did that change?'

'Soon after Polly was born, he lost his job. He changed, become riddled with debts and despair and the old Stephen was replaced by a drunken, evil man I didn't recognise. He left last Christmas when I told him I was having another baby, the one that died. I've not seen him since.'

Victoria stood and put the kettle on the heat. 'Do you think he'll come and find you?'

'No. Why would he? I bring him nothing but misery apparently.' Mercy stacked the plates on the table. 'We need shelves in here.'

Victoria chuckled without humour. 'We need a lot in here!' Then she grew thoughtful. 'Mercy, I will confess this to you now. I don't have a lot of money. With my uncle passing, I will not have my allowance as I once did. Once the money I do have has run out...well...'

Mercy smiled slightly. 'Miss, we'll be fine.'

'I wish I had your confidence.'

'I have been at the lowest I think a person can go. I did not want to live and last month I would happily have died giving birth. Only look at us now! My children have food, a roof over their heads and they are away from that awful room. Once Polly is free, I know things will continue to change for the better. If I believe in nothing else, I believe in that.' She went out the back door to the pump in the courtyard and filled the buckets with water.

Victoria watched her through the window, listening to the children in the front room playing and suddenly she felt better. Nothing would bring her uncle back, but not everything was lost.

Mercy returned to the range, filled the three pans they had with water and put them on the heat.

Puffing at the exertion, she glanced at Victoria. 'I *will* recover my health and get my strength back. I *will* find work. We *will* be fine.'

A terrible thought entered Victoria's head. 'I will have to find work, too.' The realisation of such a prospect rendered her speechless.

'Let me work first, miss. I'll adapt easier than you will.'

'What could I even do, Mercy?'

'Don't worry. We'll find something suiting your station.'

Deflated, she sat on a chair. 'I don't think I have a station in society any more. I'm a nothing. Just… adrift.'

'You're a lady. You'll continue to be one.'

Victoria stared around the dingy kitchen. Ladies didn't live in such places as this. The tears welled again but she fought them.

A knock on the door made her stand and hastily wipe her eyes. 'Who could that be?'

'Maybe Mrs Drysdale?'

'On a Sunday?'

'Shall I answer it?'

Victoria nodded and went into the front room, she quietened the children with a raised a hand, but relaxed when Mrs Drysdale entered carrying a large bag brimming with clothes. 'Mrs Drysdale, it's a pleasure to see you.'

'And you, Miss Carlton.' The other woman placed the bag on the floor.

'What have you got there?'

'I've found some clothes for the children, not much, but I had some old pieces in a trunk in the attic, which I altered last night.'

'That is so very good of you.'

'The main thing I have though are curtains.' She pulled out thick green damask drapes. 'I live above my shop and saw through your windows last night. You don't want people seeing you at home, do you? Did you stay here last night, Miss Carlton?'

'Yes. I will be living here from now on.'

'*Living* here?' Mrs Drysdale's eyebrows rose. 'I see.'

Victoria sensed her surprise. She touched the fabric. 'They are perfect. How much do I owe you?'

'You are in mourning?' The other woman eyed Victoria's black clothes.

'Yes, my uncle died yesterday.' The lump in her throat grew bigger.

'I am sorry to hear it. We'll talk money another day. First, let me get these hung for you. We can't have another night of the whole street being able to see inside your windows. I've brought white lace net curtains too, so during the day people aren't gawping at you as they walk by.'

Mercy gathered the children to her. 'I'll take them into the kitchen and give them a good wash before they put on their new clothes.'

Left alone, Victoria helped Mrs Drysdale to hang the curtains and instantly the room seemed better, cosier.

'You're still short of things in here, aren't you?' Mrs Drysdale said, sorting out the children's clothes.

167

'Yes, a great deal, but I'll have to be careful in how I manage my money now.'

'You have no private income?'

Shocked at how straightforward the woman was, Victoria didn't know how to reply.

'Miss Carlton, I am a little blunt, forgive me, but that is my way. I've been a widow for fifteen years and I have no family. Living on my own all this time means I am lacking in the airs and graces that you would expect.' Mrs Drysdale tweaked the curtains so they hung straight. 'I say what I mean because there is no one I love left to offend.' She smiled a cheeky smile that made Victoria warm to her.

'The answer is no. I do not have a private income.'

'Hmm…this could be interesting then.'

'I have enough to pay you,' Victoria said quickly.

Mrs Drysdale waved her concerns away. 'Sundays aren't the day to talk business.'

She brought out a thinner pair of curtains in dark blue. 'For your bedroom. I'll find some more for the other rooms tomorrow.'

'Thank you, very much, for everything.'

'It'll be nice to have someone decent living in this place for a change.'

'Would you like some tea?'

'That would be lovely. Shall we go into the kitchen and help that poor woman wash those children? She's paper thin and I've never seen children as dirty as them in my life.' Mrs Drysdale gathered up all the children's clothes she'd brought.

Victoria grinned. 'Nor have I.'

In the kitchen, chaos reigned. Mercy, sitting on the floor beside the bath, was as wet as the children. Her bones poked through the wet threadbare material of her dress. She looked exhausted.

Jane sat silently shivering on the floor in front of the range, naked and wet from head to toe.

Bobby stood by the back door, looking ready to make a run for it, while Emily and Seth were in the tin bath splashing and giggling, for once appearing to behave like normal children.

'Oh, Miss Carlton. I'm sorry. I can't get Bobby in the water.'

Mrs Drysdale folded her arms over her ample chest. 'You, young man, get over here and get in that bath.' From the pile of clothes she'd dumped on the table, she held up a pair of grey trousers and a cream coloured shirt. 'Once you're clean look at your new clothes you can wear.'

Bobby's eyes widened. 'For me?'

'Aye, you're the man of the house, aren't you?'

Bobby nodded, quickly stripped off his filthy rags and pushed Emily out of the way to get into the water.

'Come here, pet.' Mrs Drysdale took a towel and started to dry Emily.

'Do we have something for Jane?' Victoria asked, her heart going out to the poor girl shivering.

'Aye, there are a few dresses.'

Victoria searched through the pile and found a blue dress and helped the girl to get dry and put the garment on.

'Once all of you are clean and dressed, I'll bring over my pot of beef stew that I've made for you all.'

'Beef stew?' Mercy looked up, holding a slippery Seth. 'For us?'

'Aye.'

'Thank you, Mrs Drysdale.' Victoria felt close to tears at her generosity. She took a deep breath. She had to pull herself together. Crying wouldn't solve her problems.

Chapter Eleven

A week later, Victoria walked in brilliant sunshine amongst the crowd lining the streets near York Minister. Like a black tide, people in mourning gathered around the Minster to pay their respects and to watch many of the city's important residents slowly making their way inside to find a seat.

Victoria walked down the wide central aisle, in awe of the splendour of the flowers covering every surface.

She gazed up at the vaulted ceiling, finding it hard to believe her dear uncle was being buried today. Sunlight coming in through so many coloured windows brought rainbows to the cavernous Minster, making it look bright and joyful.

If people hadn't been wearing black, it could have been a wedding. Organ music played to those waiting for the hearse to arrive and Victoria kept the black lace veil over her face as she passed family friends.

She didn't want to explain why she wasn't in the family carriage and kept her head down until she reached an empty pew.

Young boys in black gowns occupied the choir stalls, their master quietly giving instructions.

After what seemed an eternity, the Minster filled. Victoria shuffled along the pew as more people came to sit down until no one else could sit in her row.

Finally, the pallbearers carried in Uncle Harold's coffin. Hot tears burned behind her eyes at the sight of it. Her dear uncle, gone forever. The family followed behind it.

Her aunt wore a similar veil to Victoria's but Stella, holding her arm, wore only a short veil, her gaze sharp as she took in the mourners.

Laurence stood on the other side of Aunt Esther and Victoria stared at him. He'd changed since she last saw him; he'd grown fatter living in London and now owned an impressive set of long whiskers. They'd never been close. Laurence was always away at university, then abroad and now London. She looked for Todd but failed to see him and wondered if he'd gone to Italy. Nor could she see Mimi, and this worried her for the old woman had been sick since Victoria's birthday. Behind her family walked Doctor Ashton, he held the arm of an elderly cousin on Aunt Esther's side. Victoria's chest tightened as she gazed at him. He must certainly be in with the family to walk with them into the church.

The organ music changed to accompany the choir as they sang the first hymn beautifully. Victoria stood along with everyone else and sang quietly, conscious that the people next to her were friends of Aunt Esther.

When the Dean started to speak, everyone sat down. Uncle was well respected, and the pews swelled with the rich and powerful of the town and beyond. Tortured with heartache, Victoria tried to listen to his words of comfort, but they did little to put her at ease. She felt alone and unwanted in every way.

'Such a sad day indeed,' the old woman sitting next to her whispered to her friend on the other side. 'Poor Esther, to lose such a decent husband, and he was a good man, was Harold Dobson, I'll not have anyone say anything different. He was a good man who did a lot for this city.'

'Aye, I agree, none better,' her neighbour replied with a serious nod.

'And now Esther is about to lose her dear mother, for I heard just outside that her mother is on her deathbed. It'll be the next funeral we'll attend, just you wait and see.'

Victoria stiffened at the conversation. Was Mimi that ill? She felt the need to hurry from the Minster and go straight to Mimi's house and see for herself.

'And poor Esther's son, the younger one, broken his leg, so he has.'

'Never.'

'I swear. Can't make it to his own father's funeral. Apparently fell down a flight of stairs drunk. Typical, he has no purpose that boy, never has had. He'll fritter his life away in drink and women, you mark my words.'

'Well, he'll never be thought of as responsible, not like the oldest son, will he?' The neighbour nodded in the direction of Laurence. 'He'll take over his father's bank and he's the best one to do it.'

'There's always one rotten apple in the barrel.'

Victoria shuffled on the hard pew. Mimi on her deathbed and Todd had broken his leg. It distressed her that she heard about her own family from strangers. Poor Todd would be devastated not being able to attend the funeral.

The old woman continued, 'And the word is that the niece, Victoria I think her name is, has gone off.'

Victoria barely breathed.

'Gone off? Where?' the other asked.

'Far away obviously, for she's not coming today.'

'How sad.'

'Apparently, she's travelling with some distant relative. From what I hear Esther Dobson was ready to throw her out for wasn't the girl mixing with the dregs of the slums!'

'No!'

'True as I'm sitting here. Apparently, the niece liked to get involved in things that had nowt to do with her. Sticking her nose in where it's not needed.' The woman leaned in closer to her friend. 'Even got involved with a married man and his wife wasn't having any of that. I'm told there was a fight!'

'Poor dear Mrs Dobson, to have such a person in her family! The niece was brought up a lady, too. Mrs Dobson must be beside herself, and after all she's done for that girl, taking her in.'

'It's hardly surprising though, is it? The girl is too like her late mother, she was wild, that one.'

'Families, hey?' the old woman chuckled. 'Whether they've got money or not, there's always drama.'

Victoria sat in stunned silence at the dreadful gossip which no doubt would be echoing around the town. How could she face people if that's what they were saying about her? The music changed, and she forced herself to concentrate on her uncle's coffin.

When the lasts words were spoken, and the final hymn was sung, the congregation filed into the warm sunshine. Birds twittered in the trees around the Minister. Hundreds of people gathered, and the general murmur of voices permeated the air.

Victoria was happy that so many people had come to honour her uncle and that the sun shone for his final day. However, sadness flooded her heart.

Her arm was suddenly grabbed, and she was spun around.

'What are you doing here?' Stella, eyes red from weeping, whispered harshly into her ear. 'How dare you attend this day after what you did!'

Shaken, Victoria wrenched her arm free. 'I came to pay my respects to a man I admired and loved.'

'Did you think your veil would hide you from me?' Stella swiped at the jet brooch Victoria wore. 'I know your clothes and jewellery. You wore this for Grandpapa's funeral two years ago.'

'Go away, Stella. Aunt Esther needs you.'

'Yes, she does. And we don't need *you*, that is for certain,' she hissed like a demented snake. 'Do not come near the house. You aren't welcome. I've told Laurence all about your deplorable behaviour. He agrees with me that you caused our father's death with your antics.'

'That's not fair, Stella.'

'Do you think I care about what is fair? My lovely father is *dead*!'

'Miss Dobson, your mother wants you.' Doctor Ashton called from the edge of another group of people. He looked straight at Victoria with a frown.

Victoria wondered if he knew it was her under the veil.

'I'm coming, Joseph.' Stella smiled sweetly to him. She turned back to Victoria. 'Thankfully no one knows it's you under that veil, but I knew. I would recognise you anywhere in any disguise!' She went to turn away but paused. 'I've told Joseph you have moved away.' Her tight evil smile matched her eyes full of venom. 'Expect to see an engagement notice in the paper before the summer is done. He is mine!'

Victoria stared at her smug face and wondered how she had ever loved this selfish cousin. 'How are Mimi and Todd?'

'They are none of your business any more.' Stella walked away, a black handkerchief held to her nose as though she was crying. Doctor Ashton was by her side instantly.

Distraught, Victoria slipped away from the crowds and headed back to Fossgate.

At the house, she found Mercy asleep on the sofa and the children playing in the bedroom upstairs. She went into the kitchen and checked the fire still glowed enough to put the kettle on to make a cup of tea.

It was over. Her life as she once knew it was gone, finished. She no longer had a family. For a moment she was overwhelmed by wretchedness. Her chest tightened with a deep sadness that she doubted would ever leave her.

She glanced around the ugly kitchen. All she had was a half share in a rundown house.

'Miss Carlton?' Mercy stood in the doorway. 'I didn't hear you come back.'

'I've only just returned. I didn't want to wake you, as you're still recovering your strength.'

'I thought you'd be gone most of the day.' Mercy added fresh tea leaves to the teapot.

'No. I am not welcome there.'

'They said that to you?'

'My cousin, Stella, did, yes.' Victoria moved to the back door and opened it to stare out at the small grimy courtyard.

'But what about your Aunt? She must need you at this dreadful time.'

'Even if she did, Stella would make sure my Aunt soon thought differently. My cousin Laurence will also have been hoodwinked by her lies. They all believe I killed Uncle by my behaviour.'

'You must visit them and tell them your side of it.'

'They are grieving. They will not believe me.' She swallowed back the tears that threatened.

'Miss Carlton, you need—'

'Mercy, please, call me Victoria. We are living together now. We are friends. I think we can drop the formalities.'

'As you wish.' Mercy mashed the tea, sighing deeply. 'I feel responsible. If it wasn't for me, you'd be home with your family.'

'That isn't true. I would have helped another family, no doubt, it just happened to be you that Doctor Ashton took me to that day.'

'Can't Doctor Ashton speak for you?' Mercy passed Victoria a cup of tea.

'No, Stella has managed to get her claws into him as well. He sees me as someone who is interfering. He doesn't agree with me bringing you here. It's not what a lady does.' She shrugged one shoulder, not understanding the man she thought was different to all others. In the end he was just the same as everyone else in their society.

'Well, we'll manage just fine.' Mercy smiled.

Victoria didn't answer. She didn't have Mercy's blind faith. She had household bills to pay for a family to feed. How was she going to do that?

~ ~ ~ ~

The following day, Victoria and Mercy were busy scrubbing the house. Victoria couldn't stand another day of dirty windows and with the sun shining, they'd begun the enormous task of cleaning the house.

She set the children to work, too. Their job was to pull off all the peeling wallpaper in the kitchen. She had thoughts on painting the kitchen but couldn't begin on that in its current state. The walls needed scraping and washing, then she'd buy paint to freshen the room.

Mercy had scrubbed the range, but with her energy waning, Victoria had told her to sit down and try her hand at cooking and so she was making an onion and potato soup.

When the door knocker sounded, Victoria thought it to be Mrs Drysdale, who said she might call with some old sheets.

Wiping her hands on a towel, Victoria opened the front door with a welcoming smile, which froze on her face as she stared at Laurence.

'Good day, Victoria.' He took off his top hat, looking up and down the street as though expecting to be accosted at any moment.

'Laurence. This is a lovely surprise. Please, come in.' Victoria showed him into the front room, conscious of the bareness of the place. 'Would you like some tea? I didn't realise you would know where I was.'

'I've been going through my father's business investments. I saw your father's will and the name on the deed.'

She nodded. 'Would you like to sit down?'

'This isn't a social call.' He stood tall and imposing and completely out of place in the room. His suit and coat were of the highest quality, his grey gloves made of the softest kid and his top hat would cost enough to feed Mercy and the children for a month.

Victoria held her hands together, waiting for him to come to the point of his visit.

Laurence sniffed and she expected he would dearly love to put a handkerchief to his nose. The house smelt of damp, staleness and a lingering aroma of the pig market further along the road.

He coughed discreetly and from his coat pocket pulled out a folded letter, which he passed to her.

'What is this?' She opened the letter but couldn't take in the words.

'I have come to tell you that I am selling this house. That is a letter of my intentions.'

Puzzled, she stared at him. 'Sell this house? You cannot. It is my house.'

'Only half of it.' He couldn't meet her gaze. 'I am selling my half.'

'How is it your half?'

'Everything that was my father's is now mine and, as a courtesy, I am giving you the chance to purchase that half from me.

'Purchase?' She was dumbfounded.

'Yes. Do you wish to do that?'

'How-how much would it be?'

'Three hundred pounds, and that's a bargain.'

'Three hundred pounds!' She blinked at the amount. 'I don't have that much money.' She tried to think how much she did have, maybe a few pounds at most.

'That isn't my problem.' He shrugged, his expression not caring. 'If you don't have that amount I will find someone who does.'

'But you can't!' she cried. 'Laurence, please. I'm your cousin. Uncle Harold wouldn't want this.'

'Who, the man you caused to have a heart seizure?' His look was of utter loathing.

'I didn't.'

'You did! I've been informed of all that has occurred.'

'By Stella, I presume!'

'Yes, by Stella and Mama and others. I know it all and if I needed more evidence of how low you've become, I'm standing in it!' He stared about the room as though any minute he expected to be attacked by a plague of rats or vermin riddled beggars or both.

'Laurence—'

'My father only ever did right by you and your subgrade parents. And what was his reward?' Anger coloured his cheeks and his eyes narrowed to slits. 'All he got from his endeavours was worry and stress! First, over his sister, then her errant husband and now his niece, whom he brought up to be a lady in his own home! You threw it all back in his face by consorting with filth from the gutters. You have humiliated the family and it is not to be forgiven.'

'I never meant any harm.' She wrung her hands.

'Yesterday at the funeral, all we heard were whispers and speculation as to why you weren't there. It was bad enough Todd was sufficiently imprudent to break his leg, the stupid fool, but you! *You* should have been a support to my mother, not a hindrance and a name whispered behind hands.'

'I am sorry I caused such grievance. It was never my intention. I will go visit Aunt and—'

'You most certainly will not!' he barked. 'You will never darken that front door again, do you hear? My mother hasn't stopped crying since that awful day. To see you would only upset her even more if that was possible.'

'I am not to blame, I—'

'You are to *blame* in every way, just as your mother and father were before you. You are no longer a member of the Dobson family. Do not use our name for anything. No bills will be paid that you incur, and since you cannot buy my half of the house, then I will sell it to whomever I see fit.' He stuck his top hat back on his head. 'Good day to you.'

When the door slammed behind him, Victoria's knees went from under her and she groped for the sofa to sit down before she fell down.

Mercy came into the room, her face pale. 'Oh, Miss Carl...Victoria.' She knelt before her and took her hands in hers. 'I'm sorry, but I heard it all. He was shouting so loud.'

Victoria stared at her. 'What are we to do, Mercy? I don't have three hundred pounds.'

180

Chapter Twelve

For three days, Victoria remained in a state of shock and disbelief. She had no idea what to do. Her brain was numb from trying to plan a way to raise the money. She couldn't get a loan for the three hundred pounds, she had no way to repay it. If she sold all of her jewellery and clothes, she'd still not make the amount.

On the third evening after Laurence's visit, a letter came through the last post informing her a buyer had been found and the transaction completed.

'Victoria.' Mercy came into the front room. 'Will you have something to eat?'

'No, thank you.' Victoria had lost her appetite. She'd survived on cups of tea and slices of toast, which considering their predicament, helped to save on food.

'I've put the children to bed. They wanted to say good night to you, but I told them you had a sore head.'

Mercy poked at the fire, which had to be lit even on warm days for the house never seemed to be less than terribly cold.

'I'm sorry, I'll go up and say good night to them.'

'They'll manage without it, don't worry.' Mercy replaced the poker on its stand and sat on the sofa. 'I wish to talk to you about something.'

'Oh?'

'If anything was to happen to me, I'd like to think you'd take care of them for me, would you?'

'What is going to happen to you?' Victoria frowned with worry.

'Nothing if I can help it. Before...well, I was very low, as you witnessed. I didn't want to go on.'

'But you're better now.'

'I am, thanks to you, which has got me thinking that should I ever become sick or meet with an accident then would you take care of the children?'

'Yes, of course.' It was an easy answer to give, for she enjoyed the children's company. They were slowly coming out of their shells. With regular food and a better home, they were starting to talk and play more. They no longer stared at Victoria as though she was an unreal vision. Instead they now asked her the odd question, especially Jane. Whereas Seth, the youngest and just two years old, would clamber up on her lap whenever he got the chance.

'Thank you.' Mercy stood. 'I've got some water heating. I thought you might like a bath?'

Suddenly a bath seemed the best thing in the world. 'I would like that a lot, thank you.'

'Right, I'll go and sort it.'

'And I will go and say goodnight to the children and get my nightgown.'

Within half an hour, Victoria was sitting in the tin bath in the kitchen, soaping up her legs.

Mercy stood at the range, heating more water for she was to have a bath after Victoria. 'I expect Polly will be needing a good wash when she gets home.'

'She'll appear before the judge in the morning. I think you should come with me, or I will stay here and mind the children while you go. She would be so happy to see you, I am sure.'

'No, I couldn't...' Mercy sighed. 'I'm not strong enough to see her in there. It would break my heart to see her so upset.'

Mercy wiped the hair from her eyes. 'But I should go, I'm her mother. But...to see her...there...not being able to help her...'

'It must be terribly difficult for you.' Victoria smiled sadly in sympathy. 'I will go and with luck I will return home with her.'

'Do you think that will happen?'

'If it is a fine, I'll use what money I have left to pay it.' Victoria rose from the water and began drying herself.

'You can't use it all. How will we live?'

'I am hoping the fine isn't large. There is always my jewellery I can sell.' She donned her nightgown and wrapped her shawl about her.

'Oh, Victoria.' Disheartened, Mercy shook her head. 'It is all too much.'

'We cannot leave her there another moment, you know that. The poor girl has suffered enough.'

Suddenly the door opened. Mercy screamed, and Victoria jumped violently. A strange man stood in the kitchen doorway, grinning at them.

'Good evening, ladies.' He bowed and doffed his hat.

183

'Who are you? And how dare you enter our home without permission!' Victoria wrapped the shawl around her tightly, knowing her bare feet were on show.

'Ah, but you see, it is now also my home.' The man sauntered into the kitchen and sat at the table, gazing about. 'I'm Silas Finch, a pleasure to meet you both.'

'*Your* home?' Victoria whispered, a tingle of dread shivering down her spine.

'Fair and square.' He waved a piece of paper in front of her and placed it and the front door key on the table. 'Laurence Dobson and I did a deal and I signed the deeds today.'

'It doesn't give you the right to just walk in here unannounced.'

'It does. Read those papers there. It's all legal.' The man rubbed his nose, eyeing Victoria's legs. 'I think I'm going to enjoy living here.'

'What?' She stared at him in disbelief. 'You cannot live here!'

'It's half of my house, of course I can.' He grinned. 'Make us a cup of tea, lass.' He nodded to Mercy. 'What's your name?'

'Get out.' Anger burned in Victoria's chest. 'How dare you come in here unannounced? That is not the behaviour of a gentleman!'

He shrugged. 'Who said I was a gentleman?'

'Come, Mercy.' Victoria dragged her out of the kitchen. They hurried upstairs to Victoria's bedroom, where she quickly dressed in a shift, petticoat, corset, skirt and blouse.

'What are we to do?' Mercy stood, wringing her hands. 'How are we to live with a complete stranger, and a man at that?'

'I do not intend to.' She pulled on her stockings, tying a ribbon around her thighs to hold them up.

'But what can we do?' Mercy looked back at the door, as though expecting the man to burst through it at any moment.

'I don't know. He has a key and knows Laurence, so it must be true.'

Wrapping a shawl around her shoulders, Victoria looked for her boots, then remembered they were in the kitchen. She selected a pair of house shoes and slipped them on. Fully dressed, she felt a little better. 'Let us go down and talk to him.'

Back in the kitchen, Victoria and Mercy faced the man. 'Will you tell us your plans, sir?'

Finch looked up from his plate of bread and cheese which he'd helped himself to in their absence. 'My plans?' He took a sip of tea. 'My plans are to live here, in my house.'

'But we live here.'

'Then we'll share the house.' He shrugged and continued eating. 'I'm sure we'll get along just fine.' He stared at Victoria. 'Which bedroom is mine?'

'There are only two, which we already occupy,' she snapped.

He laughed and wiped his mouth with the back of his hand. 'Looks like I'm sharing with one of you two then, doesn't it?'

Victoria's stomach churned. 'That is simply not an option.'

He waved a piece of cheese in the air. 'Worth a try though.'

'You are eating our food, sir,' Victoria muttered. 'You'll leave some money on the table to cover the expense.'

He grinned and scratched his chin. 'Feisty piece, aren't you? Oh yes, I'll like living here, I think.' He finished his tea and stood. 'I'm going to sit in the front room before the fire and put my feet up. It's been a long day.'

'No, you won't, unless you're sitting on the floor.' Anger consumed her again. 'You may own half of this house, but you don't own the furniture or food inside it.'

Finch laughed and took a step towards her. 'I'll have whatever I want, miss, and you'll still that tongue in your head if you know what's good for you.'

'Please, what will it take to get you out?'

'Nothing. Like it or not, we are in this house together and you might as well get used to it.' He stomped out of the kitchen and into the front room.

Victoria and Mercy looked at each other. The situation was unbearable.

'I can't stand him!' Mercy whispered, the light gone from her eyes and her face had lost all its colour.

'I don't trust or like him either.' Victoria sighed, her anger leaving and being replaced with such despondency she felt ill. She tried to think and after a moment nodded to herself. 'All I can think of is to go to Mimi's house. Hopefully, she'll see me. If I can talk to her, if she's well enough, then together we might be able to sort out this mess.'

'Do you think she'll see you?'

'I honestly don't know, but it's worth a try.' She glanced at the clock, which showed it was just past eight o'clock. 'I'll go now before it gets any later. You go up and stay in the bedroom with the children.'

They parted at the bottom of the stairs and Victoria left the house and walked up the street.

No hansom cabs were about so she kept walking until she reached the St Crux's Church at the junction with The Pavement.

Near the church, a hansom stood dropping off some passengers and she waved to get the cabbie's attention.

On the ride to Mimi's house, she stared out of the window at the lengthening shadows as night fell. She was afraid of being turned away at the door. Had Stella whispered nasty gossip into Mimi's ears? Was Mimi even aware of what had befallen her? Would she believe the tales being told?

Her stomach was in knots by the time the hansom slowed out the front of Mimi's house. She paid him, conscious of the dwindling amount of money she had. If Mimi saw her, she'd beg to use Mimi's carriage back to Fossgate.

Only one downstairs window shone any light, and she wondered if Mimi had retired for the night. Knocking on the door, she waited some minutes before it was answered by a maid Victoria had never seen before.

'May I help you, miss?' The maid stood holding the door, a small light behind her threw everything into a gloomy dimness.

'I do apologise for the lateness of my call, but I need to see my grandmother...' She was aware that Mimi wasn't really her grandmother, and would the old woman claim that connection any more?

'The mistress?' The maid stared wide-eyed at her.

'Yes. Has she retired for the night?'

'The mistress passed away yesterday morning, miss.' The words were spoken quietly yet they boomed in Victoria's head like someone banging a drum.

She stumbled back from the door, shaking her head. Mimi was gone. Another person she had loved…

She turned and ran up the short drive to the street and kept running.

Much later, listless and despondent, she returned to the house in Fossgate. Silas Finch was snoring on the sofa in the front room. She ignored him and went upstairs.

Mercy sat up and eased away from the sleeping children as soon as she entered the bedroom. 'How did it go?'

'Mimi is dead.' Tears trickled down Victoria's cheeks. 'I didn't even know.'

Mercy climbed off the bed and held her to her thin body. 'I'm so sorry for you, really I am.'

'She was always kind to me, like a true grandmother even though I wasn't blood related to her.' Sniffling away her emotions, Victoria wiped her eyes with the back of her hand. 'It's done. Crying won't help Mimi or myself.' She took a deep shuddering breath. 'We are totally on our own now. There is no one to turn to.' She thought fleetingly of Doctor Ashton but rejected it immediately. He, too, was gone.

~ ~ ~ ~

Joseph raised his hand to knock on the Dobson's door, but Mr Hubbard opened it before he completed the action. 'How do, Hubbard.'

'Good day, sir.' The butler took Joseph's hat.

'Are the family home?' Joseph followed Hubbard into the drawing room.

'No, sir, I apologise. They have gone to the train station to see Mr Laurence on his way back to London.'

'The ladies will be upset at that.' He looked around the room, noticing that etching of Miss Carlton had been removed from the top of the piano. 'Has Miss Carlton returned yet?'

'No, sir. I believe she is to remain away indefinitely. Her room has been packed up.'

Shocked, Joseph frowned. 'Packed up? Why?'

'She isn't coming back, sir. She is travelling with a relative on her father's side, I believe.'

'Yes, I was told that she is travelling... but to be not coming back... That seems so sudden. I thought maybe I saw her at the funeral, but I couldn't be certain. Miss Dobson said she'd not returned for it.'

'No, she wasn't here, sir, which is sad for she loved her uncle very much. I think the mistress would have been happy to see her, but it's difficult to come home when you're travelling, isn't it?'

'Yes, it can be, certainly.' He headed back to the front door and Hubbard gave him his hat. 'So, there is no way to get a letter to Miss Carlton at all?'

'Not that I'm aware of, sir. Miss Stella might know though.'

Joseph nodded his thanks and left the house. Walking down the drive, he couldn't but help think that it was all a bit odd. Why would Miss Carlton go travelling with a distant relative and miss her uncle's funeral? Where had she gone in such a short space of time that she couldn't get back again within a few days? And what about Mercy Felling? Had she simply handed over a house and left them to it? Should he call on Mrs Felling and found out? Would Mrs Felling even know anything? It was all very peculiar, and he felt ridiculously hurt that Miss Carlton hadn't said goodbye to him.

~ ~ ~ ~

The following morning, Victoria, who'd slept in with Mercy and the children, donned her black skirt and bodice and crept downstairs to the front room, but Silas Finch no longer snored on the sofa. She checked the kitchen and courtyard but he wasn't there.

The range fire had died out to ashes, and she quickly put screwed up balls of newspaper and twigs on it to get a fire going for breakfast.

'Where is he?' Mercy whispered from the doorway, holding Seth in her arms.

'No idea. Hopefully, he's seen the error of his ways and left us for good.'

Mercy let out a breath and put the little boy on a chair at the table. 'I'll make some porridge. The other children are getting dressed. I've thought about what you said about seeing Polly—'

A scream rent the air from upstairs.

Victoria and Mercy dashed out of the kitchen and up the staircase only to slam to a halt on seeing Silas Finch standing on the landing stark naked.

He bowed and smiled. 'Good morning to one and all.'

Mercy gathered the children to her and hurried them downstairs.

Victoria averted her eyes from his nakedness and stared at a point on the wall above his shoulder. 'I shall call the police. You are indecent, sir.'

'It's my house and if I want to walk around without a stitch of clothing on, then you can do nothing about it.' He scratched himself and she recoiled.

'Where were you hiding? Is it your wish to scare young children?'

'I wasn't hiding at all. I woke up and came out of the bedroom to find myself a drink.'

'Bedroom?' She frowned in puzzlement.

He pointed to the one behind him, *her* bedroom. 'Lovely comfy bed in there. I had a very good night's sleep.'

'That is my room.'

'We can share it, my girl, just like we share this house.' He winked lavishly. 'That bed is certainly big enough for two!'

She took a step back. 'Mr Finch, would you consider selling your share of the house to me?'

He rubbed his chin. 'Perhaps. Say for…six hundred pounds.'

Shocked, Victoria swayed. 'I do not have that kind of money.'

Finch shrugged and returned to the bedroom and closed the door on her.

Incensed, she rapped her knuckles hard against the door. 'Mr Finch! That is my room!'

After a moment, he opened the door wearing only his undergarments. 'Miss, it is now my room. You can sleep in with the others.'

'This is not acceptable!'

'I do not care.' When he went to close the door again, she put out a hand to stop it.

'Mr Finch, would you consider *buying* my share of the house?'

His eye twitched. 'Buy you out of your share?'

'Yes. Then the house can be solely yours.'

'Very well, I'll give you ten pounds.'

'Ten!' She glared at him, hating him. 'Come now, sir, you know it is worth a great deal more than that. You just asked me for six hundred!'

'Fifteen. That's my final offer.'

'No, you foolish man!' She stomped back downstairs furious. In the kitchen she drank the cup of tea Mercy passed to her. 'He offered me fifteen pounds for my half of the house, or I pay *six hundred* to buy him out.'

Mercy stopped helping Seth to use the spoon for his porridge instead of his fingers and stared at her. 'Fifteen? The rudeness of the man.'

'He had no clothes.' Jane piped up from the end of the table, her eyes wide in her elfin face. 'He scared me.'

'I know, sweetling.' Victoria stroked her head. Her mind whirled with ways to get rid of the man, but nothing was forming as an idea.

'We will all go to the court to see Polly,' Mercy said, wiping food off Emily's chin. 'I won't stay here on my own with him.'

Victoria nibbled on a piece of bread and butter. 'If he gave me a good price, I'd move us away somewhere else.'

'But this is a decent house! We have water and we're close to everything. Mrs Drysdale is just across the road. Why should you have to sell?'

'There are other houses.' Finch fully dressed, came into the room and poured himself a cup of tea. He looked at Victoria. 'I'll give you sixty pounds. I can have the paperwork written up today for you to sign.'

'It's not enough.'

'You'll be able to rent somewhere with that amount of money.' Finch sipped his tea. 'I even have a few properties that you can view in respect of renting, if you wish?'

'One hundred pounds.' Victoria's heart was thumping fast. 'I'll take nothing less.'

'You drive a hard bargain, Miss Carlton.' He smiled. 'Done. I'll go see my solicitor this morning and have him draw up the necessary paperwork. I'll be back this afternoon.' He bowed and left the kitchen.

Not until she heard the front door close did she breathe.

'Do you trust him?'

'I'm not signing anything until the money is in my hands.'

'Then what will we do?'

'After I've been to the courthouse, I'll go look for some suitable lodgings. If Mr Finch owns some houses, we may have to take him up on his offer and rent one.'

'Owning a house to renting one by the stroke of a pen.' Mercy shook her head sadly.

Victoria tried not to think about the turn of events as an hour later, she stood in the courtroom and listened to the first of the cases of the day. She had no idea what time Polly was to be brought up before the judge, so she had to just sit and wait. Thankfully she had convinced Mercy to stay at home with the children, for having four small children sitting in court would not have been ideal.

Near midday, Polly, dirty and terribly thin, was brought up from the cells underground. She was accused of thievery and with no one to defend her she was given a two-month prison sentence as punishment. Polly had scanned the courtroom and found Victoria, she'd simply stared at her and then was taken back down.

Feeling afraid for the poor girl, Victoria wearily made her way out of the building and into the street. She should have sold some jewellery to hire a solicitor for the girl, but with her uncle's death and leaving home to live in Fossgate, Polly had been pushed to the back of her mind and she felt guilty by her lack of consideration.

Walking the streets back towards Fossgate, her mind weighed heavy.

The situation at the house was serious. Should she sell out to Silas Finch? Should she try to talk to her aunt? A flicker of anger at her long dead father flared. If only he hadn't wasted away all his money, he'd been able to buy the house outright and her uncle wouldn't have had to help him. There was no talking to Laurence, he was grieving and blamed her for that grief. It was all such a mess.

Mercy cried when Victoria told her the sentence Polly would serve. 'But she's only a child.'

Victoria poured out two cups of tea. 'She did wrong, Mercy. There's nothing more to say, but when she is let out, we will have to work hard to change her ways. She can't continue breaking the law. She needs schooling and discipline.'

The children came into the kitchen with Seth crying because he'd fallen over and banged his head, while Bobby pushed Emily so he could stand closest to Victoria.

'Don't push your sister. She is smaller than you,' Victoria reprimanded him. 'Say sorry or you'll go hungry today.'

The boy apologised and then smiled beautifully at Victoria.

She turned away from him to hide her grin. He was a scamp that one, but she was finding herself caring a lot for these four children and Bobby was quickly becoming her favourite.

The front door opened and they heard men's voices.

'Sit at the table, all of you.' Victoria hurriedly grabbed the last loaf of bread and cut it into slices. 'Mercy give it to the children before *he* wants it all.'

She scraped the remaining jam from the jar and spread it on each slice of the bread the children had in front of them.

She was just reaching for the cheese when the kitchen door was flung back and Silas Finch walked in followed by four men.

'What is all this?' Victoria stood tall, glaring at Finch.

'My house, my friends.' He looked at the food on the table.

She tensed, ready to fling the cheese over the back fence rather than let him eat it.

Finch turned to his friends. 'Go into the front room and make yourself comfortable. I'll go to the Queen's Heads and buy some bottles of whisky.' He smirked at Victoria. 'We fancy having a party. Care to join us?'

'There are children present.'

'Not my problem.'

'Can you not go elsewhere?'

'I like it here. Besides, you and this one,' he thumbed towards Mercy, 'might like to entertain us. What you say?' He winked at Mercy who clutched Seth to her.

Rage built inside Victoria. 'Absolutely not. How dare you!'

Finch spun on his heel and left the room laughing like a loon.

'Is he our father?' Jane asked in a soft voice.

'No, he is not!' Mercy snapped. 'Eat your bread.' She looked at Victoria, a horrified expression on her face. 'What are we going to do?'

Closing her eyes, Victoria felt the world was crumbling around her. 'I'll have to sell my half of the house to him. We can rent somewhere decent until we work out something else.'

A roar of laughter came from the other room.

Mercy had gone paler than normal. 'I don't feel safe here. If they are going to be drinking all afternoon and evening, by tonight they'll be drunk and will go looking for fun…and us…'

'No, they will not!' Fuelled by rage and injustice, Victoria marched into the front room and faced the men lounging about. 'Mr Finch, may I have a word please?'

'Of course, Miss Carlton.' He followed her into the hall. 'What can I do for you.'

'Have you been to the solicitor?'

'Indeed I have. The papers are ready for your signature.'

'For the agreed price,' she demanded.

'One hundred pounds.' He grinned, knowing he had her in a tight spot.

'That is an indecent offer and you know it. Are you a gentleman or not?'

'I'm not, especially when it comes to business.' He shrugged, pulled out a document and handed it to her. 'Take it or leave it.'

AnneMarie Brear

She read the paper quickly, it was simple enough. She would be signing over her share of the house for one hundred pounds. Instinct made her want to tear it up and throw it in his face but as one of the men in the room laughed, common sense come to the fore. 'Very well.'

Finch rocked back on his heels, not hiding his delight. 'Excellent. And to show you that I am a fair man, I have some rooms you can rent for a good rate. I'll even give you the first week's rent for free. What do you think?'

She nodded with a deep sigh, the anger ebbing away. 'I have very little choice.'

He pulled out a wad of money and placed it in her hands. 'One hundred pounds. Shall we sign now while we have people to witness it?'

Without replying, she followed him into the front room. The men grew silent as from one of their cases they brought out a pen and ink.

In minutes, Victoria had signed away her share of the house.

In the kitchen, she felt numb, the money still in her hands. 'It is done.'

Men's laughter filled the house and she cringed.

'Where will we go?' Mercy murmured.

'Mr Finch has offered a place to rent in St Saviourgate.' She looked down at Bobby who held onto her skirt. 'I'm coming with you, aren't I?'

Her heart melted at his quivering bottom lip as he fought tears. 'Of course, you are. We will all go together. Now, go upstairs with Jane and pack the clothes Mrs Drysdale gave you. I'll be up in a minute.'

Once Jane and Bobby had dashed upstairs, Victoria sprang into action. 'Mercy, we must take everything. I'll go across the road to the pig market and see if I can find someone with a cart to help us. Pack everything quickly.'

'We are going right this minute?'

'Yes.' She paused and looked around the kitchen. 'We don't leave anything behind, not even a spoon.'

Chapter Thirteen

The city's church bells rang twice as Victoria rounded the corner into St Saviourgate. The sun shone from a clear blue sky. Summer always lifted her spirits usually, though not anymore. She had no time for peaceful country walks in the sunshine. Today she had been shopping in the markets buying food. They never seemed to have enough of it.

Since moving to Finch's rented rooms a week ago, she'd done nothing but clean and scrub and wash until her hands bled. They lived in two rooms on the ground floor of a large town house. Once fashionable, the town house would have been someone's grand home, now though, it was walled off into numerous accommodation for the families who could afford the rents. She shared a bedroom with Mercy and the children, and in the other room they cooked, ate and sat together.

'Miss Carlton?'

Victoria turned at her name being called and stopped as Doctor Ashton joined her. 'Doctor Ashton.' She bowed her head slightly.

'It is a pleasant surprise to see you. Indeed, it is most astonishing.' His smile was warm and genuine. 'Stella informed me that you had gone travelling.'

'I'm sure she did,' she said tartly, putting a hand up to her hair which was escaping from her hat. Her black skirt needed washing and her bodice had a stain on it, but she hoped he hadn't noticed.

He frowned, the smile slipping. 'I was told you missed your uncle's funeral because you were in some distant country?'

'How is your work coming along, Doctor?' She changed the subject. She had no wish to indulge in Stella's lies.

'Er...I've been kept extremely busy. I've recently returned from London. I presented a talk at a medical college there.' His blue eyes stared at her.

'Was it well received?' She knew he was puzzled, but she wasn't in the mood to be civil.

'It was.' His gaze softened. 'I never got the chance to say how sorry I was for your uncle's death.'

'Thank you.'

'And your grandmother's too.'

'Mimi wasn't really my grandmother, being Esther's mother, she was no relation to me, but she treated me like a granddaughter and I loved her dearly for it.' The stiffness of her manner dissolved a little on thinking of Mimi.

'Are you back in York for some time?'

She sighed. 'I have never been away. Stella lied to you.'

His eyebrows shot up. 'Lied to me? Why would she do that?'

'Because I am no longer a member of their family.'

'But why? I don't understand. What has happened?'

'They blame me for Uncle Harold's death.' Her voice caught in her throat.

'You?' Ashton jerked. 'He died of a heart seizure.'

'That I caused by mixing with the bottom classes of society. There had been a heated discussion, and everyone was upset. The next moment my uncle was dead.'

Ashton shook his head, amazement written on his features. 'I do not think it would have been down to you. Your uncle probably had a weak heart. Your argument wasn't a direct cause to his death.'

'Are you sure?'

'Harold ate and drank far too much, evidenced by his overweight stature. I warned him previously that he needed to adjust his diet, but he wouldn't listen.'

'They all believe differently, I'm afraid. Stella thinks of me as a murderer.'

'What nonsense. Perhaps her grief has affected her rational thought.'

'I feel Stella wanted me gone, anyway. This was a perfect excuse.'

'I feel saddened by your estrangement from the Dobsons. I am sorry it has come to it. I thought your aunt would have not allowed it to happen.'

Victoria juggled the basket from one arm to the other. 'My aunt thinks more of her charities and what society thinks than she does of me,' Victoria scoffed. 'She could have handled the situation so much better. But she acted as though I was taking in fallen women from the street corners and dining with beggars!'

'I thought better of her.' The disappointment was evident in his tone.

'Doctor Ashton!' A tall gentleman wearing a suit and top hat called from across the other side of the road.

Ashton waved to him, and the gentleman waited for a carriage to pass before crossing the road and joining them.

'My good fellow, so pleased to see you.' He shook Ashton's hand and bowed to Victoria. 'Forgive my intrusion, miss, I simply couldn't let the opportunity to speak to the doctor go by.'

'Then, I'll leave you to it. Good day to you both.' Victoria stepped past Ashton. She sensed he wanted to say more to her, but the gentleman started talking to him and she hurried away.

Her face felt hot as she went over their conversation. She wanted to rant and cry in frustration that her so-called family had turned her out of the house and left her to fend for herself.

There was much she had wanted to say to Doctor Ashton. Yet she had left some unspoken. What good would it have done to have told him the truth about her reduced circumstances? He'd have told Aunt Esther and Stella and she'd be further scorned and ridiculed. She'd wanted him to take her hand and say he'd help her, but that was never going to happen and she had to stop wishing for it.

Climbing the stairs up to the townhouse's front door, she hooked the basket over her arm and went inside. She'd been shopping for the best bargains all morning and her feet were aching. The rooms they rented were on the right and she was pleased they were living at street level and not down in the dank basement, or high up in the attics.

Opening the door, she smiled at Mercy, who sat near the window overlooking the street, with Seth on her knee. The other three children sat on the floor by her feet. Bobby had tears streaking down his face.

'What has happened?' She stared at Mercy as she put the basket of food on the table. A tingle of fear ran down her spine.

'We've been done over,' Mercy murmured.

She frowned, not understanding. 'Done over?'

'Robbed.'

'Robbed?' Again, she didn't understand. The poor weren't robbed. 'What ever do you mean? Who would rob us?'

'Men came. They had knives.'

'I hit one!' Bobby piped up. 'A man knocked me over!'

Like the air had been sucked from her lungs, Victoria fell on to a chair. 'You were in danger...threatened by men with knives?'

Stone-faced, Mercy gazed out of the window. 'They said they'd kill us, or at least hurt us. They knocked Bobby over when he tried to grab one of their legs. He was ever so brave.' She gave the boy a fleeting smile.

Shaken, Victoria glanced around the room. Everything looked the same as when she left. The pot on the stove simmered with a watery stew Mercy had made yesterday. Drying clothes hung from rope above their heads. Then a sickening thought dawned. 'The money!'

'It's gone.' Mercy showed no emotion.

'All of it?' Victoria dashed into the bedroom and lifted up the mattress where she'd stored the money Silas Finch had given her for the house in Fossgate. The metal springs no longer held the black beaded reticule in which she'd hidden the money. Dropping the mattress, she rifled through her trunk searching for her jewellery case. It too was gone.

Slumping onto the bed, she felt sick.

Stunned, unable to think, she sat there for a long time until Bobby came and sat beside her. He slipped his little hand into hers and said nothing.

She wanted to cry and wail and stamp her feet. Yet, she did none of that. Slowly she stood and holding Bobby's hand, she walked back into the other room.

Mercy turned to stare at her. The light had gone from her eyes and she looked like she did back in Walmgate when she didn't want to live.

A knock on the door made them all jump.

Heart in her throat, Victoria picked up the iron poker from the fireplace and then opened the door an inch. 'Who is it?'

'Rent man, miss.'

She blinked in confusion. The rent man? She opened the door wider to reveal a young man wearing a thin brown suit and a bowler hat. He had a satchel slung over his shoulder and he held a notebook and pencil. 'You really are a rent man?'

'Aye, miss, for Mr Finch. He says your first week living here for free has finished. I've come to collect your rent. I'll be calling every Monday from now on.'

'H-how much is it again?' She held onto the door for her legs had gone to jelly. She couldn't remember what she'd agreed with Finch.

'Eight shillings.'

'Eight?' Victoria felt the blood drain from her face. At the time she'd thought it a manageable sum with the sale of her share of the house.

'We don't have it,' Mercy spoke from the window. 'You'll have to come back.'

'Miss, I've many rents to collect today, I can't keep coming back every time someone tells me to.'

Her face pinched and grey, Mercy stared motionlessness at the man. 'I said you will have to come back later.'

Sighing, the man shook his head. 'Right, since this is the first time, I'll give you one hour. When I come again I want the money. Mr Finch is a demanding man and not to be crossed.'

Victoria closed the door on him and leaned her back against it.

'It's started again,' Mercy murmured.

'What has?'

'Everything.' Like a ghost, Mercy drifted over to the fire, picked up one of the baskets and started filling it with clothes she pulled down from the washing line above.

'Mercy, what are you doing?'

'Don't you understand?' Mercy flung plates and cups on top of the clothes. 'We have to go.'

'Go? Go where?'

'Anywhere we don't have to pay eight shillings a week rent.' Mercy passed the children things to hold like pans and the kettle.

'We have nowhere to go.' Frightened, Victoria wanted to shake her. 'Stop, Mercy, please!'

'How much money do you have?' Mercy went into the bedroom and rolled up the blankets into one sheet.

Victoria watched her. 'Not much. I bought a lot at the market.'

'How much do you have?' Mercy dragged Victoria's chest closer to the door.

Opening her purse, Victoria counted the money left from shopping. 'Four shillings and tuppence.'

Mercy swayed and held onto the bed. 'I know where we can get a room for two shillings a week. We need to go before the rent man returns.'

'Perhaps I can go and talk to Silas Finch. He may give us another week rent free.'

'Finch!' Mercy shook her head, fury in her eyes which was worse than the dead like stare. 'Don't you understand? Finch is behind this. He was the only one who knew we had money. Money *he* gave us! Those men didn't go to any of our neighbours, just us!'

The realisation made Victoria shake. She felt a fool. Mercy was clever in the ways that Victoria never would be. Why was everything against them? How much more could they take?

'We haven't a cart,' she said dully.

Mercy laughed a dry mocking cackle. 'Lord above, Victoria, we can't afford a cart now. We walk and we carry!'

In a daze, Victoria packed as much as she could in the trunk, squashing all her beautiful dresses. She dragged it out of the bedroom and into the other room. Mercy put things in towels which she bundled and tied up and placed on the backs of the children, even Seth at two years old was carrying the kettle.

Taking a last look around, Victoria struggled to come to terms with how her life had changed again. They were leaving behind two beds, a table and chairs and the sofa. She glanced at Mercy who was bent over with the weight of the large bundles she carried.

They each took either side of the trunk and somehow managed to get it down the front stairs and onto the street.

A young boy passing stopped and tipped his cap at them. 'Need a hand, missus?'

'Yes, please.' Victoria smiled at him.

'We can't pay you though!' Mercy snapped.

'No pay?' The boy screwed his face. 'Stuff that for a lark then!' He ran off laughing.

'What did you tell him that for, Mercy?'

'Because he'd have been expecting something and when we gave him nothing, he'd have come back in the night and taken what little we have!'

Victoria shuddered. Was there no human decency left?

Puffing and heaving, they walked down the street carrying their loads. Seth cried, not wanting to walk, and scraped the bottom of the kettle on the cobbles, the sound driving them mad before very long.

The sun was warm on their backs, the cobbles hard under their feet.

'Enough.' Victoria panted. 'I can't go another step.'

'We've much further to go.' Mercy remained stooped over. 'Don't stop.'

Victoria held up her hand at a passing cart, the driver pulled his horse to a stop.

'Yes, miss?'

'Would you be so kind as to help us, please?' Victoria asked hopefully.

'Aye, miss, that I can if you aren't going far, as I have to be back at the yard soon.' He jumped down from the cart and picked up the trunk as though it weighed next to nothing. Next, he took the bundles off their backs and placed them up beside the trunk. 'Come on you little 'uns.'

One by one he loaded the children on the cart and then helped Mercy up. 'Now you, miss.'

'Thank you.' Victoria climbed up onto the seat beside him.

'So where are we off to?' the driver said, geeing up the horse.

'Hungate,' Mercy spoke from over his shoulder.

'Hungate?' The driver raised his eyebrows but said no more.

Victoria cringed, knowing that Hungate was one of the worst slum areas. A lot of the Irish railway workers and their families lived there, and the place was notorious for being a den of thieves, drunkenness and prostitutes.

In a short space of time, Mercy told the driver to stop. She climbed down and disappeared down an alley. Seth started crying again and Victoria pulled him onto her lap to soothe him.

'Are you certain this is where you want to be, miss?' the driver asked, his voice full of concern.

'No, it isn't, but we have nowhere left to go.'

'This place isn't for you.' He nodded towards the men leaning against the front of a public house. Ragged-clothed children ran about playing and yelling while women gathered on corners gossiping. 'You'll not last long here, miss.'

She was saved from replying when Mercy came out of the alley. 'I've got us a place.' She lifted the children down from the cart.

With the driver carrying the trunk, and the rest of them carrying everything else, they followed Mercy down the narrow alley between two public houses.

The alley twisted and turned for a while, ending in a squalid courtyard. Mercy turned right and went down an even tighter cut-through running alongside a factory wall.

They passed an open gate to a slaughterhouse and glimpsed the butcher cutting up a pig. Other animal carcasses lay on tables and blood ran freely into the drain running down the alley.

Finally, Mercy stopped at the third door along a row of brick terraced houses in a dead-end alley. A sign nailed to the first terrace proclaimed them to be at Petal Lane. The houses faced a brick wall for half the length of the alley, and the yard of a public house at the other end. Mercy nodded to the driver who placed the trunk on the cobbles.

'Good luck to you.' He tipped his hat and he left them.

Victoria stood holding two large baskets and a sheet bundle slung over her back. Her arms ached, but she hesitated at going inside.

Standing amongst the filth of the lane showed her they were in a place where no person should live, God alone knew what was inside. A pig squealed behind her, making her jump. The animal was large and fat and rooting around in the rubbish that littered the sides of the alley. As if by an invisible force, the six other doors of the terrace opened at the same time and seven women came out to stand on their doorsteps and stare at them.

Mercy ushered the children inside. 'Come, Victoria.'

On the threshold, Victoria paused. The entrance was dark, the smell of damp strong. Ahead was a steep narrow staircase and a group of children sat at the top staring down at them.

'We're in here.' Mercy opened a door on the left. 'It's the last one available in this row.'

Following her into the room, Victoria gagged at the smell. 'What is that smell?'

'It doesn't matter what it is. We have a roof over our heads.' Mercy dumped her bundles on the bed built into the wall. 'And we have a bed.'

Gazing around the room, Victoria couldn't believe what she was standing in. Under the window sat a scratched and stained table with two chairs. And on the other wall was the fireplace. The walls were originally whitewashed, though the paint had yellowed with age and years of smoke from the fire, and mould now created black vein patterns.

'We can't stay here,' Victoria whispered, wanting to scoop the children off the bed they'd clambered onto, for she dreaded to think what they'd catch being in this room.

'We have no choice.' Mercy started to unpack, her movements slow and lethargic. 'This is our life now. You might as well get used to it.'

'I won't.'

'Then go. Go back to your family and beg their forgiveness.' Mercy raked at the pile of dead ashes in the grate. 'The children and me have been in this situation before. At least this time I'm not pregnant and sick. I can cope this time.' Her resigned manner spoke louder than the words she uttered.

'Don't go,' Bobby begged Victoria, running over to grab her hand.

As much as she longed to return to Blossom Street, she knew she couldn't leave Mercy and the children to fend for themselves here. And who was to say that Aunt Esther and Stella would allow her to even enter the house?

Victoria gazed down at Bobby who looked up at her with total trust. 'We'd best make the bed then, hadn't we?'

'Who are you then?' a voice boomed.

They all turned to look at the large woman standing at the door.

Mercy straightened from setting the fire. 'I'm Mercy Felling, this is Victoria Carlton, and these are my children. And you are?'

'Kathleen O'Shea. I live next door with me 'usband Mick an' me two sons, John an' Seamus.' The woman had a strong Irish accent and greying hair that escaped the bun she'd tied it up in. She wore a faded green dress and a large white apron.

'Pleased to meet you.' Victoria smiled.

'No man?' Kathleen looked from Victoria to Mercy and back again.

'No, we don't.'

'My Mick will give you a hand when you need one.'

'Thank you.' Victoria kept smiling not knowing what else to do. She couldn't invite Kathleen in, for she doubted there was room for the big woman to sit anywhere and besides they'd not unpacked any tea things.

'Right, well, I'll see myself off then. I just wanted to show my face and introduce myself so it were.' Kathleen walked back outside and to her own door.

Mercy continued getting the fire going well enough to boil some water and reheat the stew which fortunately had survived the move.

Victoria, hiding her inner feelings of hopelessness and fear of the future, started to make the bed with the help of the children. She ignored the smell of damp and some other stink she couldn't identify that pervaded the room, and she ignored the solitary tear that ran down her cheek.

Chapter Fourteen

Victoria struggled to walk while carrying two buckets full of water, but she was determined not to show it in front of the women who were queueing up for their turn at the water pump.

Kathleen stood at the end of the line, chatting to Eileen O'Meara. 'Morning to you, Victoria. A splendid day, ain't it?'

'It is, Kathleen,' she answered, feeling hot and tired already and it was only midmorning.

The August weather baked the city. There'd been no rain for many weeks and there were rumblings in the alleys that the taps and pumps would soon be only turned on every second day if no rain fell soon.

She didn't know how she'd cope if that happened. Being restricted to water was something she couldn't get used to.

They'd been living in Hungate for months and each day she cleaned the room they lived in as though it was the first day.

Constant scrubbing with carbolic soap had cracked the skin on her hands and some days they would bleed. She'd scrub through the pain, not giving up.

If she'd been told a year ago that her main obsession in life was cleaning a hovel of a room surrounded by the poorest of society, she'd have laughed in amazement. Now she lived the reality.

Every day, without fail, she cleaned the room and everything in it. The children were washed and brushed the moment they entered the room after playing outside.

She broke her back scouring the room's floor and walls. The plaster had come away, exposing brickwork underneath, and she'd sold her last dress and bought lime wash and painted them, much to Mercy's disgust, for she said the money was needed for food and rent and no one cared for whitewashed walls.

However, Victoria cared. Just because she had to live here in a slum alley, it didn't mean she'd had to forget her principles. Hungate was unbearable to her. It made the house in Fossgate look like a mansion and her old home in Blossom Street a palace. The only way she could survive it was by trying to keep to the standards she was brought up with.

She rounded the corner and lumbered into their alley, laughingly called Petal Lane. There were no flowers or petals to be seen in any of the alleys, courtyards and lanes in this area. Any natural beauty of long ago had been replaced by factories, slaughter yards, hundreds of dilapidated dwellings, public houses, breweries and gin houses.

Her arms aching, she gratefully entered the room and deposited the bucket by the fire.

Jane sat on the bed playing with a stick doll Mick O'Shea had made for her. Their neighbours, the O'Shea family, were good people basically, though Kathleen was as nosey as the day was long, but her husband, Mick, loved the children. Often, Victoria found him playing in the alley with them even after working all day in the railway sheds.

'Jane, you should be out in the sunshine, not in here.' Victoria shooed her out the door.

'But the other girls won't play with me.' She remained on the doorstep.

'Then find some different friends.' Victoria had no time for her at the moment, for she needed to cook some sort of meal for them all, and cooking was something she couldn't get to grips with. 'Where is Emily?'

'Playing with Bobby and the other boys.'

'Then go play, too. You should be watching over Emily and Seth. You are the eldest.'

'No, I'm not. Polly is!'

'Polly isn't here!' Victoria closed her mind to Polly. The girl continually found trouble in prison. Her sentence had been extended due to her unruly behaviour. Her last indiscretion was to bite the hand of a prison guard.

'The big boys knock me over.' Jane pouted.

'Then go find me some fuel for the fire. Anything that will burn will do.'

'Do I have to?'

'If you want something to eat tonight, then yes, you do!'

When the little girl had finally gone, a moment of worry bothered Victoria. Bobby had Seth and Emily with him. She hadn't seen them in the alley just now. She wasn't used to being solely responsible for children. However, since Mercy had managed to acquire a few shifts at The Bay Horse public house, she'd soon had to adapt to being alone in the room with the children. But then, she was getting good at adapting.

Who'd have ever thought that she could learn to do basic cooking with a limited amount of food and fuel, or teach herself how to wash clothes in a bucket, or how to make one shilling stretch to do the work of two?

How had she coped from having her own luxurious bedroom to sleeping with five other people on a lumpy mattress? Once she had privacy, now she had none. Before she'd eaten rich fancy delicacies and now she existed on porridge, stale bread and scrag-end pieces of meat floating in a watery stew. The days of buying beautiful clothes had been replaced with darning the same skirts and blouses and hoping they'd last a few more months yet.

There were days when she thought she couldn't go on. When the smoke from the fire filled the room and the children fought and cried for hours, when the unpalatable food was burnt or raw, when the four walls closed in on her and she'd do anything to escape and go somewhere clean and spacious, and where she could forget all she had seen, heard and tasted.

But that wasn't going to happen. To do that she needed money and money was something she no longer had.

She was secretly ashamed of how she had ended up. Petal Lane was her home now. Mercy and the children were her family. All that had gone on before was a distant memory. It hurt to think of the past, of how quickly the Dobsons had washed their hands of her. She had swallowed her pride and sent a letter to her aunt and received no reply. Had could they have so coldly forgotten her?

'Victoria.' Kathleen stood in the doorway.

'Come in, please.'

Kathleen shuffled her bulk into the room with a smile. 'You're not to get rid of your fancy ways, do you hear? It's pleasant to hear your voice an' the nice way you speak.' Kathleen's eyes softened.

'I'll try not to.' Victoria smiled at the other woman, who she knew had a kind heart. For the first few weeks of living in Petal Lane, Victoria hadn't been able to leave the room due to her low spirits. She had pretended that nothing existed on the other side of the door. Mercy and Kathleen had kept her going.

She remembered the first time Kathleen had sat with her while Mercy went looking for work.

'You're like a fish out of water, aren't you?'

Victoria nodded, a lump in her throat.

'How did you get in this muck hole?'

'It's a long story.'

'Sure, an' so it is, aren't they all?' Kathleen smiled, wrapping her hands in her apron. 'You need to keep occupied, lass. The minute you let your mind wander, you're done for. Understand? The rot of this place will grind you down until you're nothin' but a shell of the person you once was.'

'I don't see a way forward. I feel trapped here.'

'Then make the best of it, lass.' Kathleen heaved up her huge breasts with her forearm. 'You've got brains an' can read an' write. Use that.'

'How?'

'Oh, I don't know, that's for you to sort out, so it is.' Kathleen grinned. 'But from the bit I know, what Mercy has told me, you were wanting to help those less fortunate.'

'Yes, that's true.'

'Well look around you, lass. You're in the thick of it now.'

'But I had money back then, money to help buy food.'

Kathleen snorted. 'Money? No one here has money, you get used to that. So use what you do have.'

Confused, Victoria frowned at her. 'Such as what?'

Kathleen tapped her head. 'In here, lass, that's what you use an' you have that for free.'

When Kathleen had gone back to her own home, Victoria sat before the fire deep in thought. What could she do? She'd tried, really she had, but the effort to do anything other than survive exhausted her.

Since then, she and this big loud Irish woman had become friends. 'Want a cup of tea, Kathleen?'

'Aye, an' when have I ever said no, so I have?' Kathleen sat on the stool by the door.

'Is something wrong?' she asked for usually her neighbour didn't stop talking.

'I'm hot an' there's mumblings that some of the men might be put off from the railway.'

Victoria paused from adding water to the kettle. 'Will it affect Mick and your sons?'

'We don't know. I dread to think of my men being out of work.' Kathleen blew out a deep breath and fanned her face with her apron. 'We've been through it before, sure and so we have, but I don't be fancying doing it again.'

'Perhaps it won't come to that.'

Noise from outside made them both go stand at the door. A group of women were arguing with a man in a suit.

Victoria peered around them, wondering if it was the rent man, but he wasn't due for another two days.

Kathleen stood on the doorstep. 'Hettie, what's going on?' she shouted to one of the women.

'He's from the council. They are turning off the water tap. We've only got it for a few hours every second day now.' Hettie fumed.

Another woman spoke from further away. 'They say we've not had enough rain, there's a water shortage.'

A thin little woman, Mrs Flannigan from number eight, broke free of the group. 'They want us all to die of thirst and disease, that's what they want. Kill us all off!'

'Jesus, Mary an' Joseph.' Kathleen crossed herself.

'They can't turn off the taps, can they?' Shocked, Victoria asked Kathleen. 'How will we live without enough water?'

'It's not the first time, lass. Sure, an' it won't be the last.'

The council man tried to make a run for it, but the women, irate and wanting to vent, struck out at him. He stumbled, lost his hat, but managed to run away with a load of abuse following him.

The women, some living in Petal Lane, and others in the adjoining courts, stood together grumbling. Children ran about playing, diverted from their games by the confrontation. One boy had picked up the man's hat and was strutting about with it on his head like a fine dandy.

'This cannot be correct. Perhaps the man made a mistake?' Victoria spoke to no one in particular.

One of the women turned to her. 'The council can do as they like. We don't matter to them.'

Hettie nodded. 'Aye, you can bet none of the toffs in their fine houses have a water shortage!'

Victoria cringed at the mention of what she used to be. However, Hettie was right. She'd never known of a water shortage in her life. It wasn't right. The city couldn't punish those that had less than others.

'We need to speak to someone, make it clear this won't be tolerated.'

Her little speech was met with laughter.

'Oh aye, Queenie, and who is going to listen to the likes of us?' Hettie scoffed.

Victoria took off her apron. 'I know of some people.' She went inside and to her trunk. She shook out one of her last remaining silk black skirts and bodice. Her mourning clothes had been replaced by every day skirts of brown and grey, and her gowns had long been sold for food and rent.

'What are you going to do, lass?' Kathleen stood in the doorway, the women gathered like hens behind her, eager to hear.

'My uncle was an alderman. I will try to speak to his friends.' Victoria changed her clothes quickly. 'Will you watch the children for me until Mercy comes back? She should only be another hour.'

'Aye, lass, of course.'

'Thank you.' Victoria brushed her hair and unable to style it, pushed it up under a black velvet hat, the artificial rose on the side of it was crushed, but she'd ignore that for the moment.

She was cheered as she left the alley. Her determination put purpose in her stride and straightened her back. She had a long walk across town from Hungate, and soon her footsteps slowed as any sudden bursts of energy were soon dissipated. She'd not eaten properly in months for the meals they ate were of small portions and unappetising.

By the time she reached Coney Street, her feet ached in her boots that needed new soles and her enthusiasm had diminished while the hunger pains in her stomach grew.

The sun blazed down on her and wearing black didn't help. Sweat beaded her upper lip.

The Mansion House loomed up before her, and she slipped down the side of it to the large stone building behind.

Several gentlemen and other men of business stood about talking in front of the Guildhall, which sat on the banks of the River Ouse. Seagulls cried over their heads and the smell of the river drifted on the warm breeze.

'Miss Carlton?'

She turned at the sound of her name and smiled at the man walking towards her. David Norbutt was an old family friend and one of her uncle's fellow aldermen. 'Mr Norbutt, I'm so pleased to see you. Has there been a meeting?'

'Oh, nothing that would interest you, my dear. How are you? The whole town believes you to be away. How long have you been back?'

'I never left, Mr Norbutt. My family shunned me because I wanted to help the poor of this city.' She blurted out the truth and didn't know why.

'Dear me, that is a surprise.' His grey eyebrows nearly shot up to his hairline. 'Your aunt is a fine woman. I cannot believe such a thing would occur.'

'Believe me, it is true.'

He shook his head sadly. 'Family break ups are a part of life, unfortunately.'

She didn't want to speak of her so-called family. 'Mr Norbutt, I've come to speak to someone about the water situation in Hungate.'

His eyebrows rose again. 'Hungate? Whatever do you mean, dear girl.'

'A man from the council told us this morning that the water taps and pumps will be turned off every second day for the Hungate area. This is unacceptable to all the people living there. We are restricted as it is!'

'We?'

'Yes, we. I live there now.' She no longer cared that her name would be the talk of drawing rooms now.

'The water restriction will be due to the lack of rain we have had. This summer has been an unusually dry one. I'm sure it's nothing to worry about.'

'Are all the pumps and taps turned off in the city every second day?'

'Well, no, that would not be acceptable.'

'But it's to happen in the poorer districts?'

'The city still needs to function, my dear. Leave it to the men in authority. They will see to it.'

Annoyed by his lack of consideration, her voice became louder. 'Please don't brush me off, Mr Norbutt. I do respect you, as my uncle thought very well of you, but something must be done about the water.'

A small gathering of men discreetly stood about close enough to hear her.

One beady looking chap took a pencil and notebook out of his satchel. 'Miss, I'm Roland Small, a reporter for the *Yorkshire Gazette*. Could I be of assistance?'

Mr Norbutt bristled. 'No, go away, Small. Miss Carlton doesn't need the likes of you getting involved.'

She turned to the reporter. 'Mr Small, I need to raise awareness of the plight of the Hungate area and the lack of water for residents.'

'The slums don't need water for the people don't wash anyway!' a yell from a man several yards away made Victoria's anger boil.

'That is a lie.' Victoria faced the men. 'I live in Hungate. Do I look as though I don't wash?' She secretly hoped he didn't look too close for a quick sponge wash was all she'd had for weeks.

A murmur of voices filled the air.

'People fall on hard times,' she continued. 'Should we be punished because of that? Why should some people of this city have enough of everything, yet others are left with scant offerings? Where is our civic pride in allowing our neighbours to be without the basic elements of living, such as water?'

'Here, here!' Mr Small clapped his hands, then wrote vigorously in his notebook. 'My boss, Mr Foster who owns the *Gazette*, will be highly interested in this, you mark my words.'

Victoria looked at each of the men. 'Can any of you help me?'

Abruptly eyes were downcast, and feet shuffled as no one stepped forward to assist her.

'Are you all willing to stand there and let your fellow citizens suffer?' she demanded.

Mr Norbutt took out a handkerchief and wiped the sweat from his forehead. 'Miss Carlton, if there is no water, then there is nothing anyone can do about it. We cannot make it rain.'

'No, you cannot, nor will you contrive a plan to ease the burdens of the poorest in this city.' She gave them all a scathing glare. 'Go home to your comfortable houses and remember that not everyone in this city has the same luxury!'

She stomped away from them, back up the lane and out into the street. Shoppers jostled around her, eager to be on their way. A carriage went past, the horses' hooves striking the cobbles. Her head swam. She needed to sit down. The York Hotel stood on the corner, but she had no spare money to buy a drink, but perhaps they would offer her a glass of water.

She went inside the hotel, the cool interior a welcome.

The doorman bowed to her, though he frowned and looked her up and down. 'A table, miss, or are you joining someone?'

She looked at the people meandering about, the clean white tablecloths, the shine of glassware, the whisper of conversations. She suddenly felt dirty and out of place.

'Miss?' The doorman gave her an enquiring look.

'I'm sorry...' She turned and walked out, feeling foolish and upset that she no longer belonged to that world of wealth and privilege.

Thirsty and tired, she headed back towards Hungate, not caring when she bumped into people, or stumbled in the gutters. Why had she believed she could make a difference? Who was she anymore to command a gentleman's attention? Why would any of those men do anything for her? She was a nobody.

'Miss Carlton?'

She ignored the person addressing her, for she didn't have the energy to stand and talk.

'Miss Carlton?'

Her arm was taken and she stopped and stared into the blue eyes of Doctor Ashton.

He pulled her into the shade of a shop's awning. 'You don't look well. Please let me escort you home.'

She laughed at that. 'I don't need escorting as though I'm a silly young girl with no brains in my head.'

'I wouldn't think of you as that, more that you look ready to faint. I've been so worried about you. We've not seen you for such a long while.'

'*We*?'

'Your family, society.'

'My family?' She laughed mockingly. 'My family don't care about me. They continue to fool you, Doctor.' Dizzy, she placed her hand against the wall and took a deep breath to clear her head.

'Miss Carlton, please let me take you home.'

'I can manage on my own.' She started to walk away.

'I'll find a hansom cab. Where are you staying?'

She gave him a steady look. 'It would horrify you, if you knew.'

Worry crossed his face. 'I cannot leave you alone in this state. I will come with you.'

'No!' She held up her hand, conscious people walking past were staring at them both. 'Leave me be, Doctor. I don't need you. I only need to find who to speak to about the water.'

'Water?'

'They are turning the taps off.'

'I don't understand.'

Victoria glanced tiredly at his perfect suit and neatly cut hair under his hat, his clean shaven face and the stiff white collar. 'No, you'd never understand. Though you think you do.'

Ashton hailed a hansom to stop and opened the door.

Boldly, he took her in his arms and lifted her up onto the seat. 'If you won't tell me where you live then you'll come home with me until I feel confident that you're not going to faint.'

Chapter Fifteen

Joseph held her in one arm, while he fumbled for house keys in his pocket.

'I am quite well, Doctor.'

'Let me be the judge of that.' Finally, he unlocked the door and led her inside. 'My housekeeper isn't in today, but I know how to make a cup of tea and a sandwich.' Her stomach rumbled as he spoke and Joseph pretended he didn't hear it.

Instead of placing her in a chair in the front room, he guided her down the short hallway to the kitchen, which was a much cheerier open room. His housekeeper had placed flowers in several vases around the kitchen and on the sideboard a resting loaf of bread smelled delicious.

'Sit at the table and I'll make some tea.' He eased her down as though she was as fragile as crystal. It alarmed him how thin she was.

Her clothes were shabby and musty, as though they were stored somewhere damp. Was she living by the river now?

He'd done nothing but worry about her since she disappeared. He poured her a glass of water.

'Thank you.' She sat stiffly at the table, her gaze taking in the contents of the room as she drank.

He quickly added wood to the range and placed the kettle on top. From the larder he took out a marble slab which held cheese and ham. The loaf of bread joined it on the table and a pat of butter. As he cut the bread into slices, he watched her out the corner of his eye. She was staring at the food as though she had never seen such a treat before. His concern grew.

'Tell me about this water problem you have,' he encouraged as he scooped tea leaves into the teapot. He needed her to talk. He missed her voice.

'The council are turning off the water taps every second day. It cannot happen. I wish to speak to someone who can change that decision. I went to the Guildhall hoping to see someone who'd listen to me.'

'And no one did?' He wanted to kneel before her and take her in his arms and ease her suffering. His heart felt close to breaking at finally having her in his home. This was where he wanted her to be, not out there where he couldn't find her, or protect her.

'No. Those men didn't care. Only a reporter from the *Gazette* wanted to hear what I had to say.'

'Write letters. Write many letters. You must know countless people of your uncle's acquaintance who are in seats of authority? Write to them.'

'I do know people, yes.' She seemed to brighten a little at the idea. 'But would they listen to me, someone they would shun now if I entered their drawing room?'

He cleared his throat. He'd heard the rumours, the whispers, and he couldn't squash them all as much as he tried. 'Write letters to the newspapers, not just in York but wider afield. Shame the councillors into taking action.' Could she tell that he was struggling to control his emotions?

'That is a wonderful notion, thank you.' She sounded tired.

Smiling, feeling he had actually done something that pleased her, Joseph mashed the tea and added milk to their teacups. He placed the sandwiches on a plate and pushed the plate closer to her.

When she hesitated to pick a sandwich up, he busied himself with tidying away to save her any embarrassment. She ate quickly, hungrily. Joseph watched her quietly. Something was very wrong here. The gentlewoman he'd met only months ago was gone, replaced by someone who looked haunted and desperate. He had to help her.

'Is your home not far away then?' he asked softly, going into the larder.

She looked up at him like a startled rabbit. 'I really should go.'

He held up his hand to stop her rising. 'No one in Walmgate or Fossgate has seen anything of the Fellings, or you. I went to your house in Fossgate and found it to be full of men and women sleeping off a night of wild behaviour, or so Mrs Drysdale told me. She said you all had left in a hurry and she hadn't seen you since. She was worried, as I have been.'

'Poor Mrs Drysdale. I should go visit her. She was very kind to us.'

'Are the Fellings with you? Is Mrs Felling regaining her health? Where have you been living?' He had a head full of questions.

'Mercy is well.' She pushed her empty plate aside. 'Miss Carlton, please tell me where you live. I'd like to call on you.' He was desperate to mean more to her than just a friendly doctor.

'Call on me?' she mocked. 'I am no longer in any decent society to receive callers, Doctor.' She stood. 'Thank you for your hospitality, but I must go.'

His hopes crushed, he reached out a hand to stop her leaving. 'Why will you not tell me what is happening in your life?'

She couldn't meet his eyes. 'Because you will tell Stella, and I could not bear that.'

'I promise you I wouldn't do that. Please, sit down. Let us talk,' he heard the pleading in his voice, not that he cared. He'd beg and plead and walk on hot coals to keep her with him for another moment.

'I cannot. I need to speak to someone about the water.' Colour had returned to her cheeks.

'Nothing you can say to anyone in the council will change their minds today. A decision has been made. The letters being publicly read is the better solution.' He had no idea if that was true.

'I will write letters then.'

'Allow me to walk with you into town, if you feel well enough, or I'll find a hansom to take you home.'

'I'd rather go on my own, thank you.' She took a step away from him.

'Miss Carlton—'

'Doctor Ashton!' She moved towards the door. 'Your kindness is appreciated, but please, leave me in peace.'

'I don't think I can.' He fought the urge to cup her cheek in his hand, to pull her against him and never let her go. 'I admire you greatly, Miss Carlton. I want to help you.'

She shook her head sadly. 'You cannot help me.'

'You underestimate me.' He gave her a small smile. 'I will speak to your family. Your aunt and cousins, who I'm sure, would want to know how you fare.'

'Do *not* mention my name to them. They have made their point about how they feel about me quite clear.'

'Then tell me what I can do.'

'Speak on my behalf to everyone you see, the aldermen, the mayor, anyone. You mix with those I no longer do. I do not have access into the homes of influential men. But you do. Please, Doctor Ashton, be the voice for the poor.'

Her simple yet ardent request nearly brought him undone. 'I already am, you know that. I do as much as I can. At every hospital I visit I make notes on how to improve the situation. I attend town meetings and speak about my findings, but I am one man, Miss Carlton. It takes more than just me.'

She lowered her eyes and sighed.

His heart constricted at the forlorn sight. 'What can I do to help *you*, no one else, just you.'

'There is nothing.' She raised her chin and looked him in the eyes. 'Thank you. Goodbye, Doctor.'

When she had left, he squashed the urge to follow her. If she saw him, any trust she felt towards him would vanish.

He packed away the rest of the food, his mind whirling with what he'd just learned. Although she hadn't told him much, he was trained to observe.

Her clothes and her hair were clearly not as tidy as he expected to see from her. She was painfully thin, and ate as though food wasn't something she had regularly, or of a plentiful amount. She mentioned the shortage of water.

Turning off taps and pumps happened frequently in the poorer areas. She'd somehow lost possession of her house and left in a hurry, something Mrs Drysdale had been anxious about. Without her uncle's support, she'd be struggling financially, she'd have no money or support...

Miss Carlton was living in the slums!

Joseph grabbed his hat and keys and left the house. York was littered with slums and poor districts. He'd search each and every one until he found her.

~ ~ ~ ~

Victoria walked down Fossgate. She should have gone back to Petal Lane after leaving the doctor's house but she couldn't face the probing stares and questions that she had no answers to. The neighbours had sent her off with a cheer, and she'd felt certain she'd make a difference. She had failed.

Pausing before Mrs Drysdale's shop, she stared across the road at the house she'd owned for such a short time. Looking at it now, she nearly laughed. After Blossom Street she'd been ashamed of that house, but compared to Petal Lane it was paradise.

The shop door opened and two women exited. One held the door for her and Victoria nodded her thanks.

Inside, she spotted Mrs Drysdale rolling up a bolt of white linen, while chatting to another woman.

Victoria strolled the shelves, delighting in the sight of rolls of materials in pretty colours. Tables in the middle of the shop displayed selections of delicate lace collars, handkerchiefs and gloves. She dared not touch any of them, for her own black gloves were worn and the stitching coming undone.

'Miss Carlton.' Mrs Drysdale smiled as she walked to the counter as the other shopper left the shop. 'I am so happy to see you.'

'Forgive me for not coming to see you before now, especially after all the help you gave us. It was extremely rude of me.'

Mrs Drysdale placed her hand on Victoria's arm. 'There is nothing to forgive. But I have been terribly worried.' She glanced out of the shop window. 'And that lot over there, well less said about them, the better.'

'Is it so bad?' She knew that her old house was the subject of that statement.

'Horrendous.' She sighed and put away a case of gloves. 'All night entertaining with loose women and drinking. Anyway, enough of them. They are not important. What about you? Where are you all living now?'

'Petal Lane, Hungate.'

'Hungate?' Mrs Drysdale's eyes widened. 'Oh, Miss Carlton.'

'Yes, it is tragic.'

Mrs Drysdale went to the door and turned the sign around to closed and locked the door. 'Come along out the back. We'll have a cup of tea.'

Victoria followed her gladly. The prospect of another proper cup of tea and not the weak sugarless, milkless tea she now drank with Mercy was a welcome. She'd enjoyed every mouthful of Doctor Ashton's sandwich and wished she'd been able to have more, but it'd have been rude to ask. She felt guilty that Mercy and the children hadn't had any.

In the back room, the ordered neatness of the shop was replaced by chaos. The desk held hundreds of papers in large piles that seemed close to toppling over onto the floor. Not that there would be room for the floor space was covered with bolts of material, cases and boxes.

'Sorry about the mess. I can never get on top of it.' Mrs Drysdale waved towards the clutter.

'One day.' She scooped a pile of newspapers off a wooden chair and invited Victoria to sit.

Mrs Drysdale set about making the tea in a little side alcove that supported a small stove. She handed Victoria a tin of biscuits. 'I made them last night. After the shop has closed I like to keep busy as it can get rather quiet at night on my own.'

'They look delicious. Thank you.'

'Take them home for the little ones. Are they all well?'

Victoria nodded and bit into an oat biscuit sprinkled with sugar. Her mouth watered. 'They are. I think the children cope better than Mercy and I.'

'How is Mrs Felling?'

'She is much better. Nearly back to full health if such a thing is possible considering the little we have to eat. But she has managed to get some work as a barmaid.'

'Good. There are worst things she could be doing.' Mrs Drysdale set out the teacups and saucers. 'Across the road is a haven for prostitutes. I'm sure that Silas Finch has turned your old home into a brothel.'

Victoria shuddered hearing his name. 'We left his rooms without paying the rent.'

Mrs Drysdale laughed. 'Good for you!'

'Finch had said we could live there for a week free of rent, as a goodwill gesture for the low price he got for my share of the house. After that week, just hours before the rent man came, we were robbed of anything valuable, the money Finch gave me for the house, and my jewellery.'

Frowning, Mrs Drysdale poured out the tea. 'You were robbed?'

'Yes. We had nothing. Mercy made us pack everything and flee before the rent man came back.'

'Were other tenants robbed nearby?'

'No. Mercy believes it was Finch who arranged it for only he knew we had that amount of money with us. I was foolish and should have banked the money straight away. To this day I don't understand why I kept it with me.'

'Mercy is probably correct in that it was Finch. He is of a criminal mind. You live and learn, Miss Carlton.'

Victoria spotted a pen and sheets of cream paper. 'Mrs Drysdale—'

'Please, call me Harriet.'

'Thank you, and I am Victoria.' She glanced again at the paper. 'I am not used to begging, and I hate to do so now when you helped us so generously before...'

'What do you need?' Harriet smiled kindly.

'Paper and a pen and envelopes.'

'Of course! I have plenty as you can see.' Harriet gathered together enough for Victoria to write a dozen letters. 'Are you writing to your family?'

'No. I've done that and was ignored. This time I am writing letters about the water shortage in Hungate. Doctor Ashton suggested that I write many letters, and it is a good idea, but I couldn't tell him that I had no money for paper and ink, or envelopes and stamps.'

'No, that would be embarrassing. So, they are turning the pumps off?'

'Yes.'

'It's not the first time, nor will it be the last. As soon as there is a drought the poor suffer.'

'I need to write to the *Gazette* and some of the aldermen my uncle knew.'

'Shall I write a letter of complaint, too?' Harriet sounded determined. 'Surely the more people who voice their objections, the more chance those in authority will listen?'

'That would be so good of you. As a business owner they would take notice of you.' She sipped her tea, enjoying the superb taste.

'Well, we can but try, Victoria. On a night I can write for hours with no one to disturb me.'

'Thank you, Harriet.' The tears welled in her eyes.

The older woman gave her a sad smile. 'You seem done in.'

'I'm fine.'

Harriet raised her eyebrows. 'Truly?'

She shook her head. 'No. It is unbearable, Harriet, all of it. I try so hard to manage each day the best I can but it's all so horrible. I cannot get used to it. I lie in bed at night, squashed in with Mercy and the children and I listen to the sounds of the people all around me. There is so much *noise*.

Drunken men shouting and swearing, women yelling at husbands and children, babies crying. There's banging and crashing, dogs barking, tomcats fighting, the factories, the animals getting slaughtered ... At times I think I shall go mad.'

Harriet refilled her teacup. 'I think you should be proud of yourself, Victoria. You've never known such a way of living and you've been thrust into the centre of it. It's only natural that you feel this way.'

She wanted to cry, something she hadn't done in months, but crying wouldn't help her.

Someone knocked on the shop door.

Harriet sighed and craned her neck to look to the front of the door. 'Can't they read the sign? Oh, it's Mrs Gardener. I'd best let her in, she'll want her order.' She left to go and see to her customer.

Victoria put the lid back on the tin after she'd eaten her third biscuit. She'd eaten better today than she had in months. She tasted again the ham and cheese sandwich, Ashton had made for her. The creaminess of the cheese and the slight salty tang of the ham. It had been heaven, just like these biscuits.

She allowed herself a moment to think of the lovely doctor. His blue eyes had smiled at her, his hands gentle as he held her. He genuinely seemed to care. Then, she thought of Stella and her aunt and Laurence. The doctor was still in their society. Would he tell them he'd seen her? Tell them about the state he found her in? They'd be horrified. No doubt Stella would have some cutting remark about how Victoria deserved to end up this way and that she was simply like her no good father before her. Was she? Was she bound to be forever tainted with making decisions that changed her life, and not for the better?

Chapter Sixteen

Victoria opened her eyes and jumped in alarm at the shadowy figure standing beside the bed. She rubbed the sleep from her eyes and focused, breathing a sigh of relief when she recognised Polly.

'I found you,' the girl said.

'You scared me!' Victoria whispered harshly. She slipped out of bed, letting the others sleep. 'We didn't know you had been released.' She wrapped her shawl around her shoulders.

'It's taken me days to find you.' Polly hadn't moved but watched Victoria with a steel-like stare.

'We sent a letter to the prison months ago, informing them of this address.' Victoria bent to relight the fire. She'd seriously doubted that letter had reached anyone it needed to. The prison wardens wouldn't care about a scrap of a slum girl like Polly.

'I don't believe you.'

Straightening, she lifted the kettle and shook it to see how much water was in it. 'I am not a liar.' She looked at the girl who had grown in the time she'd been away. Her long straggly hair had been cut to her shoulders and the grey dress she wore ended mid-calf and was relatively clean. For once the child looked half decent, and strangely much older. 'Where have you been staying?'

'About.' Polly stared at her sleeping mother and siblings. 'They're alright?'

'They are. Your mother is working as a barmaid and—'

'I know. That's how I found you. I asked around.'

She watched Polly eye the loaf of bread. 'Cut some slices. The others will be awake soon.'

Doing as she was bid, Polly started cutting thin slices. 'I'm not staying here.'

'No? Then where shall you go?' She placed the frying pan on the heat and added dripping fat to the pan. She'd learned how to fry bread from Kathleen.

Polly shrugged her thin shoulders. 'Anywhere but 'ere. London mebbe.'

'It's a long way. You'll need money.' The heat from the fire added to the warmth of the weather despite it being early morning.

'I'll get some.'

'By stealing again? You'll end up straight back in prison, is that what you want? And what about your mother and brothers and sisters?' she whispered, losing patience. The girl needed to settle down and stop being a worry to Mercy.

'They don't need me.'

'I believe they would think differently, especially your mother.' She placed the slices in the hot dripping and the sizzling sound woke Mercy.

'Polly!' She leapt out of bed and hugged her daughter, waking the rest of the children.

The grumblings of the sleepy children were soon quietened as Victoria gave them fried bread.

'You've grown, my girl.' Mercy hugged Polly again and for a moment the child allowed her before she squirmed out of her hold.

Mercy mashed the tea. 'You'll be behaving yourself now. No more dealings with police, that's for sure. I'm working, and you'll go to school. We are a decent family and school will help your future.'

'Ma, I need to lie down.' Polly suddenly announced, making for the bed.

'Aye, pet, you must be tired not having a comfortable place to sleep. Climb in.' Mercy fussed over her, pushing the other children out of the way.

'She looks a bit flushed,' Victoria said, turning the last of the bread in the pan. She felt bad for being short-tempered with the girl.

'A bit of a sleep will do her good.' Mercy brushed the girl's hair from her face. 'Though she is a little hot. It's hardly surprising that she might have a bit of a cold, considering where she's been.'

After breakfast, Mercy went to work, and the sunny day beckoned the children outside to play. Victoria stood on the doorstep, banging the rag rug against the wall to remove the dust from it.

'I'm making another one of those.' Kathleen came outside and gestured towards the rug. 'I've saved up enough rags now I think.'

'Will you show me how to make one too, please?'

'Aye, sure I can. 'Ave yer got some rags?'

She laughed. 'No!'

Kathleen chuckled. 'What am I to do with yer?'

Victoria wiped the sweat from her face. The day was hot with not a breath of air. 'I'll ask Harriet when she next calls by. Harriet is bound to have offcuts of material in her shop.'

'Is that the woman who came back with you last night?' Kathleen brought out a chair and sat against the wall in the shade.

'Yes.' Victoria smiled, nothing got passed Kathleen, even though it was late when Harriet had walked home with her.

'I've not seen her before,'

'She owns a haberdashery store on Fossgate.'

'Aye I've seen it, not been in it though.'

'Harriet Drysdale is a good woman. Together we wrote many letters, and she posted them all.' Victoria still felt the sting of humiliation at realising all the letters they wrote needed to be posted and she didn't have the money for stamps. Harriet, bless her, had done it without fuss.

'Letters! As if they'd do any good? Waste of paper an' ink.' Kathleen fanned her face with her apron.

Leaning against the doorframe, Victoria tried to be positive. 'It's worth the effort. We have to try something. If the letters are published in the newspapers, it might bring our plight to everyone's attention.'

Kathleen scoffed. 'Sure, an' 'aven't I seen it all before, lass. Men in big 'ats come poking about an' muttering things, 'olding handkerchiefs to their noses. Then they walk away an' all goes on as before, so it does.'

'Speaking of holding handkerchiefs to noses, what is that smell? It's worse than normal.' Victoria tried not to take a deep breath. The air truly seemed thick with a disgusting aroma.

'It's the river. When it runs low like it's doing now, the stink gets worse. We need rain to flush the river. All the factories an' slaughterhouses drain into the Foss. In dry weather it's…what's the word?' Kathleen screwed up her face in thought.

'Stagnant?' Victoria supplied.

'Aye, stagnant. Sure an' it's the smell of the very devil 'imself.' Kathleen nodded wisely.

Two young women sauntered past, their giggles loud as a solider hurried by buttoning up his coat.

'Where's 'e come from? They'd best be no knockin' shop in this lane!' Kathleen tutted and glared at the women.

'Knocking shop?'

'Tarts. Sure, an' wouldn't their mammies be ashamed of them earnin' a penny that way, so she would.'

Victoria stared at the prostitutes, the first she'd seen up close. They looked like ordinary women, except for their blouses being undone at the neck, their hair hanging loose and they wore bright rouge on their cheeks. 'I've not seen them before.'

Kathleen's eyebrows rose. 'Those two have come from Walmgate. I heard that the regiment is back at the barracks. The girls will be plying their trade wherever they can, but not in Petal Lane!'

Victoria thought of her house in Fossgate. Best to warn Harriet. If Finch had turned it into a brothel, then Harriet will have soldiers to contend with as well.

Suddenly, Kathleen gave a yell. Victoria jumped and turned to see Mick and his sons walking down the lane.

'They've been let go.' Kathleen crossed herself. 'Why else would they be home in the middle of the day?'

'Ho no, Mammy, don't be getting upset,' Mick O'Shea said reassuringly as he reached his wife. 'We'll be back down at the railway sheds tomorrow. The foreman knows we're good workers and will put a word in for us at another warehouse, so he will.'

'Why 'ave yer been let go today though?'

Mick shrugged his broad shoulders. 'Money's tight the foreman said. The workforce is too large. Sure an' doesn't every man jack go to the railway for work? There's not enough positions.'

Kathleen's sons were small wiry young men, kind and solicitous, both with a shock of red hair like their father.

'We're off away then, Da,' announced the eldest, John.

'Away where?' Kathleen bristled.

'To the pub! We've been paid off, but we'll have jobs in the morning, you see if we don't,' John boasted.

Kathleen leapt to her feet and held her hand out. 'Sure, an' do yer think me a fool, John O'Shea? Give me yer money, I'll not be seeing it pissed up against a wall!'

'Mammy!' John protested and received a slap up the side of his head for his troubles. Seamus quickly handed over his money to his mother while reluctantly John fished in his pockets for coins.

'Now, Mammy.' Mick hugged his huge wife to his side. 'Let the boyos have some fun for one night. We'll have the place to oursens, how about that?'

Kathleen grinned like a young bride. 'Nay, Mick, get away with yourself.' Nevertheless, she returned a few coins to her sons. 'A few pots, that's all, no lasses an' no gambling.'

'Ta, Mammy!' The boys gave her a kiss on each cheek and hurried away.

Victoria smiled at the family scene. The O'Shea family might not have much, but they had a love that was deep and cherished.

'Where's the kiddies?' Mick asked her.

Shrugging, Victoria looked down the lane. 'Off somewhere playing.'

'I'll go find them and take them for a bag of toffee halfpenny bits.' Mick kissed his wife and walked away, whistling.

''Alfpenny bits!' Kathleen mocked. 'Just been laid off an' 'e's buying for the whole lane!'

'He's a good man.' Victoria smiled. 'You wouldn't change him for the world.'

'Sure, so he is. I knew it from the first moment I clapped eyes on 'im.' Kathleen smiled wistfully.

'Miss Carlton?'

Victoria turned at the sound of her name. 'Mr Small.'

The reporter took his hat off and nodded to her and Kathleen. 'Forgive my intrusion.'

'Who's 'e, Victoria?' Kathleen stood close to Victoria as though her protector.

'This is Mr Small, a reporter from the *Yorkshire Gazette*.'

'What you doing 'ere then?' Kathleen scowled at him.

'I received Miss Carlton's letter just before I left the office. It came in the first post. Mr Foster has read his letter, too.'

'Who's Foster?' Kathleen demanded to know, crossing her arms over her ample chest.

'Owner of the *Gazette*.' Victoria placed her hand on Kathleen's arm to calm the woman. 'They might be able to help us. Isn't that so, Mr Small?'

'Indeed, Miss Carlton, we hope to. Mr Foster is keen to meet you and was wondering if you'd be free to come into the office on Monday morning?'

She nodded. 'I would be happy to, thank you.'

'Do you know where the offices are situated?' he asked.

'I do, yes.'

Mr Small gazed around the lane. 'Do you think some of the tenants would answer a few of my questions?'

'If you want to truly help this area, then yes.' Victoria grew stern. 'But we'll not be made fun of, Mr Small. We aren't freaks at the fair. Although it might not be much, these are our homes, our lives.'

'Understood, Miss Carlton.' Small looked around. 'I'll make myself known then.'

Once he'd left to go knock on doors, Victoria went inside with Kathleen following her. 'Shall we have some tea?'

'Lord above, who is that?' Kathleen gasped, staring at the girl in the bed.

'Oh, that's Polly, Mercy's oldest. She has been released from prison and turned up early this morning before dawn.'

'Prison?'

'Stealing.'

Kathleen tutted. 'Why's she's sleeping like the dead in the middle of the day?'

'I don't think she's had a good sleep for some time.'

'Not in prison she wouldn't.' Kathleen snorted in disgust. 'Nasty places, so they are.'

Victoria stepped closer to the child and peered at her. Polly's face was brightly flushed. She'd thrown the blankets off. Victoria put the back of her hand to her forehead and jerked at the heat radiating from the girl's head. 'Kathleen, she's burning up!'

Shuffling her bulk to the bed, Kathleen quickly lifted up the girl's dress to reveal her stomach and chest, which were red and covered in an angry rash. Kathleen crossed herself. 'She's got typhus.'

'Typhus?' Victoria backed away, frightened. 'Are you sure?'

'I've seen it before, too many times.' Kathleen gazed sadly at Polly, her eyes distant. 'The curse of it took my three little girls.'

'Your girls?' She had no idea that Kathleen had more children than just John and Seamus.

'Rosanna, Bernadette an' Aileen,' she whispered their names. 'It's why Mick 'as taken to young Jane an' Emily. 'E never used to want to be near any little girls, it 'urt too much, so it did. Then you lot arrived an' suddenly 'e wants to spend all 'is time with the young 'uns.'

Victoria stared at the girl who tossed and turned on the bed. 'What can we do?'

'Nothing. Let nature take its course.'

'We cannot do *nothing*. We need a doctor.' She instantly thought of Doctor Ashton. 'Polly must go to the hospital.'

'Doctors can't 'elp, I promise you that.'

Kathleen wiped her eyes. 'Cool water to sponge her down when she's hot, an' a roaring fire when she's shivering.' Kathleen peered closer. 'Yer could fry an egg on her face it's that warm. She needs sponging down, so she does.'

Scared, Victoria poured the last of their water from the bucket into a bowl and began sponging the fevered child.

'I'll go to Mercy an' bring 'er 'ome.' Kathleen sighed deeply. 'Poor lass.'

Victoria didn't know if she meant Polly or Mercy.

~ ~ ~ ~

Victoria and Mercy took turns to care for Polly as the hours turned from day into night. Kathleen and Mick took the other children into their rooms where Mick made a fuss of them though Bobby stamped his foot in temper at not being allowed to stay with Victoria.

Polly grew weaker. The thrashing of limbs when the fever burned at its highest soon stopped, and she slipped into an unconscious state.

'I'm going to see Doctor Ashton,' Victoria announced to Mercy as dawn broke the following morning.

Mercy, her eyes haunted, nodded. 'Yes, he will know what to do.'

Within minutes, Victoria was walking through the lanes and courts out of Hungate and towards the centre of the city.

Being Sunday, the streets were eerily quiet. She marvelled at how different the town was without the hum of people and the noise of horse and cart traffic.

The morning was already warm, for the temperature hadn't dropped much overnight. Summer still gripped the land, and the rain still held off. Dust coated people and buildings alike.

Her legs tired before she reached Bootham, but she kept going, her errand too important for her to stop and rest.

For a moment she thought she'd not remember which was his house, but soon recognised it and banged on the door, which echoed through the silent street.

She banged again after a minute, wondering if he slept at the back of the house and would he hear her? Should she throw pebbles up at the window?

As she raised her hand again, the door opened, and Ashton stood in a dark brown dressing gown, his hair messy, rubbing the sleep from his eyes. 'Victoria?'

'You must come quickly.' She ignored the fact he'd used her first name, something he'd never done. 'Polly is very sick.'

'Polly?'

'Yes, she returned from prison yesterday and has been ill ever since. She's had a fever and we've been sponging her down all evening and last night. Kathleen says it's typhus. She can be wrong though, can't she?' She couldn't stop rambling. 'Please will you come?'

'Calm down. Yes, I'll come with you. Let me get dressed. Come inside. Go into the kitchen and pour yourself a drink,' he said as he went upstairs.

She went along the small hallway and into the kitchen, grateful to rest for a moment. A water jug stood on a shelf in the larder and finding a glass she poured a small amount into the glass and drank it.

Her stomach rumbled at the sight of all the food lining the shelves. She itched to take the bread and the jar of jam. It seemed forever since she'd had something sweet to eat.

'Miss Carlton?' In what seemed a very short time, he was back downstairs fully dressed and grabbing his medical bag from the table by the door. 'Let us go.'

They hurried through the streets. Victoria stumbled on the uneven cobbles, exhausted.

Ashton took her elbow and slowed his pace, peering at her. 'Have you been up all night?'

'Yes.'

'What are her symptoms?'

'Fever and a rash to start with then she was very cold during the night and then an hour ago she stopped moving and will not wake up.' She panted, forcing her legs to move. 'It can't be typhus, can it?'

'Quite likely. It's a common thing in prisons.' He frowned. 'Why was she in prison for so long?'

'She kept misbehaving, and they extended her term.'

Ashton tutted. 'Well, at least she's out now.'

Victoria grew nervous as they neared Hungate. Ashton would now know where she lived and the shame of it made her blush with embarrassment. He'd been following her lead, but as she turned into Hungate, he hesitated only for a second.

'I hadn't got this far,' he murmured.

She glanced at him. 'Pardon?'

'Nothing.' He flashed her a smile and walked faster.

She took him down towards the River Foss and turned into the labyrinth of alleys and courts until she reached Petal Lane.

The weight of humiliation bowed her shoulders as she stood back to allow him to walk into the ugly room.

'Thank you for coming, Doctor.' Mercy, looking pale, stood and gave him room to move closer to examine Polly.

For several minutes, Ashton said nothing until finally he'd finished examining the girl and sighed. 'It is typhus.'

Victoria grasped Mercy's hand. 'What can we do, Doctor Ashton?'

'Nothing, I'm afraid.'

'Nothing?' Mercy whispered.

'I'm sorry.' Ashton replaced the tools of his trade back into his bag. 'She's advanced. We need to keep her comfortable, let nature takes its course and hope she wakes.' He stood away from the bed. 'Can I wash my hands?'

'Forgive us, we have no water.' Victoria's cheeks flamed with mortification. 'The tap is turned back on tomorrow morning, but we used what we had to sponge Polly during the night.'

He nodded. 'Where are the other children?'

'Next door with the O'Sheas.' Mercy's eyes widened. 'Will they catch it? Polly was only with them for a short time.'

'It depends, Mrs Felling. I can't give a positive answer either way.' His gaze went from one to the other. 'However, I'm more concerned about you two who care for her.'

Mercy turned to Victoria. 'Then you must go elsewhere. I'm her mother, I'll stay.'

Victoria bristled at being sent away. 'No! We are in this together. I've already been with her all night. There's no point being careful now.'

'I'll organise for her to be taken to hospital.' Ashton wrote in his notebook.

'Hospital?' Mercy sprang forward, startling Ashton. 'No, you're not taking her there. She'll never come out of that place.'

'Mrs Felling, the hospital is the best place for her, so she can receive proper medical attention.'

'I'll take care of her. You say there is nothing to be done so why move her to somewhere to be cared for by strangers.'

'Yes, but—'

'I...we...' she glanced at Victoria 'we are the best people to make her well.'

Ashton's eyes softened. 'Mrs Felling, you are not trained, and in the hospital, she will be closely monitored. Her surroundings will be clean.' He shrugged his shoulders helplessly.

Victoria took Mercy's hand again. 'Mercy, Doctor Ashton is right. Polly needs to be somewhere clean and where she can—'

'No! She's been with strangers for months while in prison and look where that has got her, sick! She needs to be with me.'

'But—'

Mercy's expression became desperate. 'She stays here, and I'll look after her. I am her mother and I've not been the best mother for some time. Now, I can make it up to her.'

'The *best* kind of mother would allow her sick daughter to go to the one place that can help her.' Doctor Ashton's tone became stern.

Mercy shook her head. 'I don't agree.'

Expelling a deep breath, Ashton frowned. 'Very well then, if you are certain she is to remain here, then I'll have to make arrangements.'

'Such as?' Victoria raised her eyebrows, puzzled.

'You need to burn all this bedding and the mattress and scrub this room thoroughly. You'll need a new bed, good nourishing food and plenty of fresh water.'

Victoria swayed, knowing that none of that was possible.

Ashton walked to the door, but paused beside Victoria to whisper, 'Polly is dangerously ill. Her pulse is extremely weak.'

He flicked a glance at Mercy. 'Be prepared for the worst.'

Her heart plummeted.

'I'll be back with those other things I mentioned.'

'You?' Her eyes widened in surprise.

'Well you aren't able to obtain all that she needs, are you?' he said softly with compassion.

'No. Thank you.' She watched him go, knowing he would be true to his word and make it happen for them.

Chapter Seventeen

In a haze of exhaustion, Victoria got to work. She took everything outside, dragging her trunk, which was much lighter now since she'd sold most of her things, anything that wasn't fixed to a wall was moved, while outside, the sun rose and burned fiercely for another day. Mercy tried to help, but Victoria sent her back to the bed to attend to Polly.

Ashton returned a couple of hours later and brought a crate of scrubbing brushes, carbolic soap and rags. With him, a burly man carried pails of water. The man kept disappearing up the lane only to come back with more buckets of water. Another man arrived heaving a new mattress.

Victoria quietly gave one of the buckets to Kathleen to use since she had the children.

'Sure and ain't this heaven sent?' Kathleen said, giving the bucket of water to Mick to take inside their own home. She rolled up her sleeves and started scrubbing the walls.

'Kathleen, I can do it,' Victoria protested. 'You go back to the children.'

'Don't talk soft! I'll not sit on me fat backside while you do this yersen.' Kathleen cleaned more vigorously. 'Fancy sayin' that to me!'

Victoria smiled tiredly at her friend. 'Thank you.'

'Mick's playin' with the kiddies, 'appy as a monkey, so he is.' Kathleen wrung out her cloth. 'We all look after each other in this lane.'

Ashton gathered Polly in his arms and picked her up, while one of the men whipped out the old mattress and blankets and dragged them outside. The other man placed the new mattress on the iron bed frame.

Mercy settled Polly once more, while Victoria continued washing the room. Harriet arrived, hoping to have an hour's chat, but found determined industry instead. She went home to collect new bedding and more rags. Outside the men set fire to the mattress and bedding, which only added more heat to the hot day.

After hours of cleaning and scrubbing every single thing that was inside the room and the room itself, Victoria sent Harriet and Kathleen away to rest, thanking them profusely for their help.

Ashton had paid the men and they too had gone. Victoria joined him outside and together they stood and watched the dwindling blaze.

'Thank you for helping us.' She knew he was a doctor and doctors helped people, but he had gone over and above what a normal doctor would do.

'You are welcome.' He smiled.

They stood in silence for a while before Ashton shuffled his feet. 'I would very much like it if you would marry me, Miss Carlton.' He spoke to the flames.

For a moment she thought she had misheard him until he turned to her and took her callused hand in his own. 'I know this isn't the time or the place to ask such a question, but I couldn't hold it back any longer. Will you please just consider it?'

She nodded, her mind whirling and heart thumping fit to burst.

A cry rent the air.

Ashton bent his head and closed his eyes as Mercy called for him. He squeezed Victoria's hand. They sensed what must have happened.

Victoria pushed Ashton's proposal to the back of her mind as she went inside to comfort Mercy.

Polly was dead. Ashton confirmed it. He left them shortly after to arrange for her body to be taken to the morgue.

Kathleen and Mick kept the children a few hours more, so they didn't witness Polly being collected by the undertaker. With Polly gone, grief and fatigue took over and Mercy cried herself to sleep.

Neighbours, on hearing the news, gathered in the lane as a show of respect. Victoria asked John O'Shea if he'd go tell Harriet the news. He returned with a parcel wrapped in brown paper and string and when Victoria opened it, she found inside two black skirts and bodices for Mercy and herself with a little sympathy note from Harriet. Such kindness, such thoughtfulness touched Victoria deeply. Because of Harriet, they had mourning clothes and would be respectably dressed for the funeral.

Mrs Flannigan gave Victoria a kidney pie she'd just made. 'I know Mercy'll not be in the mood for eating, but perhaps the little ones could do with a bite.'

'Thank you, Mrs Flannigan. That is very kind of you.'

With no nonsense, Hettie attached a black wreath to the outside wall of their room to let people know a death had occurred. 'If I had straw to put down in the lane, I would, lass, but I don't. This here wreath should let others know though, and quieten them down as they pass your room.'

'The wreath is more than enough, Hettie. Thank you.'

It amazed Victoria how her neighbours, who had nothing much themselves, were gifting what they could to ease the suffering of Polly's death.

As night descended Victoria quietly made the room presentable again and then fetched the children and brought them back to the room. She'd given Kathleen more buckets of water to bathe the children in front of their fire.

'Mrs O'Shea says our Polly's gone to heaven?' Jane said, climbing into bed beside her sleeping mother.

'Yes, that's right.' Victoria stroked Seth's head as he sat on her lap. Bobby leaned against her while Emily had stayed with Mick, crying that she didn't want to leave the O'Sheas. It worried Victoria how attached the little girl had become to Mick. He was like a father figure to the children and gave them so much of his attention that Victoria was frightened Emily would never want to live with Mercy again.

She kissed the top of Seth's blond head and popped him into bed. 'Come on, scamp.' She smiled at Bobby and tucked him under the brand new blankets Ashton had bought for them. 'Isn't this nice now? A new bed.'

'You won't go to heaven, will you, Toria?' Bobby's earnest expression tore at her heart.

'No, sweetie, I'll try very hard not to.' She kissed his cheek. 'Go to sleep.'

Sitting before the fire, she watched the children's eyes close. Mercy hadn't moved, but her chest rose and fell and Victoria hoped her dear friend would sleep for hours.

With the room quiet and peaceful, she allowed her mind to drift to Doctor Ashton. Had he *really* proposed to her? Was she *really* the one he wanted? What about Stella?

It was all very confusing, but also tantalising that perhaps, just perhaps she could have Ashton for herself. Surely, he wouldn't have proposed if he was already committed to Stella? Had Stella turned him down? Her tired brain tried to process the many thoughts swirling her mind but she couldn't do it, not now, not tonight. She'd not slept for over twenty-four hours and she was beyond worn-out.

She prodded the coals and stared at the buckets of water still by the door. There were three left out of the dozen the men had carried up the lane. Heating some of the water in a pan, she stripped off her filthy clothes until she was naked. Using the carbolic soap and the warm water, she stood on a bit of rag and using another clean one, washed her body until the water turned murky grey and cold. Feeling better, she donned a nightdress and wrapped a shawl around her shoulders. She'd have liked to wash her hair but that was an effort too far tonight. Tiredness pulled at her bones.

When a tap sounded on the door, she sighed, wishing nothing more than to go to bed. Thinking it was Kathleen or Mick, she rose and answered it.

Ashton stood there, carrying a lantern and a basket. 'I'm sorry to have disturbed you. Well…I'm not really as I wanted to see you. Very much so.'

Surprised to see him, Victoria wrapped the shawl around her tighter and stepped outside, closing the door behind her. 'Is something wrong?'

'No, not at all. I just couldn't go to bed without checking on you all.' He handed over the basket. 'I asked my housekeeper to fill it with food for the children for the morning.'

'That is so thoughtful of you, thank you.' The basket was heavy so she put it down on the doorstep. 'You are most generous, Doctor.'

'I'd do anything for you, Miss Carlton, and that is a fact I can no longer hide nor deny.' The golden light of the lantern threw shadows across his features. His blue eyes looked dark, but were full of emotion. 'Can I not persuade you to move to a hotel. I'll pay for it.'

'Thank you, but no. Mercy wants to stay here.' She placed her hand on his shoulder and reached over to kiss him lightly on the lips, surprising them both.

Ashton put down the lantern and pulled her into his arms. His lips were soft and seeking as his arms tightened around her. 'Victoria...'

For a long moment she gave into the desire that flooded her, the ache and longing. It was glorious to be held, to be kissed by a man who wanted her. Then, when she least expected it Stella came into her head.

She pulled away from him. 'We mustn't.'

'Why?'

'My cousin gave me every reason to believe that you and her were considered to be...that is she hinted, no mentioned, that you and she were..."

'Miss Dobson and I are nothing at all.'

He didn't let her go, instead he smiled. 'If your cousin had…designs on me then they were on her part only. I did not reciprocate at all in such feelings towards her. In fact, I found her rather judgemental and self-centred.'

Her eyes widened. 'Oh, I see.' Happiness swamped her. 'But you paid her so much attention.'

'I was trying to impress your whole family, for your benefit only, of course.'

'It worked, at least my family think very well of you.'

'What do *you* feel?' His eyes never left hers.

'I thought I had no chance at all to earn your affections. Stella made it clear I wasn't good enough for you.'

'Nonsense.' He grinned lovingly. 'You are more than good enough, too good. I'll be the luckiest man alive to have you as a wife.' He frowned. 'You will marry me, won't you?'

'Yes. I will.' A great joy filled her.

He kissed her long and slowly and she savoured every second of it.

He pulled away and smiled. 'I'll call again in the morning. Go and get some rest and tomorrow we'll speak of our future.'

She watched him go, only to startle as Kathleen loomed out of the darkness of her doorway.

'Sure, an' wouldn't yer be simple in the 'ead to let such a fine man slip through your fingers!'

Victoria wanted to be annoyed that such a special moment had been overheard, but there was no point. In the lanes, privacy was unheard of. So she smiled, and despite the dreadfulness of the day, she indulged in a moment of feeling happy and hopeful.

~ ~ ~ ~

'Of course, you should go.'

'It's not appropriate.' Victoria passed Mercy a cup of tea. They'd all slept late. Victoria hadn't felt like cooking and instead gave the children what had been in the basket Ashton had brought the night before. Fresh bread spread with strawberry jam. She'd eaten two slices herself and enjoyed every wonderful sweet mouthful.

'It's important, Victoria.'

'And so are you.' She gave Mercy a stern look. 'I'm not going to see Mr Foster today. I need to be here with you.'

'I'm fine.' Mercy hugged Seth who sat on her knee.

From the basket, Victoria cut a currant cake into slices. Bobby stood by her side watching with interest. She gave him a slice and shooed him out of the door. 'Go find Jane and Emily.'

Mercy gave a slice of cake to Seth. 'You will do more good by seeing Mr Foster than staying here with me. This area needs the support of Mr Foster and his newspaper.'

Victoria wrapped the food up and put it away in the basket. 'I'm not going and that's an end to it. Harriet is coming later, and I'll ask her to send a note on my behalf. I'm sure he'll understand. Besides, there is something important I need to discuss with you.'

The haunted stare returned to Mercy's eyes. 'Polly's funeral, and how are we to pay for it?'

'Yes, there's that, and also something else.' Victoria sipped her tea.

Gratefully, the basket had held a tin of tea leaves. The bottle of milk had been shared between the children, but she didn't mind having black tea as long as it was proper tea leaves, like they were having now, instead of over-stewed days old tea leaves that had been reused repeatedly.

'It's not another problem, is it?' Mercy allowed Seth to climb off her knee and go find the other children who could be heard playing in the lane.

'It's good news.' Victoria smiled softly, hesitant to be too cheerful the day after Polly's death.

'We need good news.'

'Doctor Ashton has asked me to marry him.'

Mercy blinked and stared at her, surprise written all over her face. 'Marry him?'

'Yes.'

'But I thought you said he was your cousin's beau?'

'I thought that was the case. Stella never gives up on something when she wants it.'

'Yes, but Doctor Ashton isn't the kind of man she can walk over. He obviously did not want *her.*'

'No, he doesn't, and never did.' The thought filled Victoria with such happiness she thought she'd burst.

'Oh, Victoria!' Mercy held her close. 'I'm so very happy for you.'

Victoria leaned back. 'The hard times are over now, Mercy.'

'What do you mean?'

Victoria grinned. 'By marrying the doctor, I can save us all from this miserable place.'

'But…he's marrying you, not me or my children.' Mercy sat back down. 'This marriage will save *you.*'

'And as my friend, you and the children will benefit as well.' She couldn't keep the excitement from her voice.

Mercy frowned. 'How can that be? We can't all come with you to your new home with Doctor Ashton. That's not fair on the dear man.'

'Well, it'll have to be for I am not going to leave you in Petal Lane.' She was adamant about that.

'I'll not come, Victoria.' Mercy glanced around the room sadly. 'This is my home. You need to start a new life with Doctor Ashton, just the two of you.'

Annoyed, Victoria paced the small room. 'How can I possibly live in a nice house knowing you are here, amongst all this?'

'You did it before and you will do it again.'

'That was before. Much has happened since then, and I'm not the same person.' She hardly recognised herself as she used to be when living in Blossom Street. That person knew nothing of hardship, of poverty, of survival.

'As long as you come and visit us from time to time, that's all I ask.' Mercy tilted her head thoughtfully. 'How are we to break it to Bobby? He'll refuse to let you go.' She gave a glimmer of a smile.

A knock on the open door revealed Doctor Ashton. Victoria's heart somersaulted at the sight of him.

'Good morning, ladies. Are you well?' He took off his hat and entered the room.

'We are, yes, thank you.' Mercy stood and held out her hand. 'I believe congratulations are in order, Doctor. Victoria has told me about your proposal. It brings me joy at a time when it is sorely needed.'

'Thank you, Mrs Felling.' Ashton, wearing a smart black suit, smiled at Victoria. 'I take it then you've not changed your mind overnight? I was worried you might have.'

'I haven't changed my mind. I would be honoured to marry you.' She felt a flush of heat sear her cheeks, but when he took her work-roughed hands and kissed them both, she melted into a pool of longing for him. 'I was worried *you* might change *your* mind!' She laughed.

'Never!'

Mercy lifted up the teapot. 'Would you like some tea, Doctor, since you did provide it?'

'I would indeed, thank you.' He sat on the stool Kathleen used and from his coat pocket, he brought out a few sheets of paper and passed them to her.

Mercy stared at the papers. 'What is that?'

'Mrs Felling, I've taken the liberty of meeting with the undertaker this morning. I've signed everything that needs to be signed and Polly's funeral can take place.'

'I see.' Mercy passed him the tea.

'Forgive me for taking the initiative, but I've gone ahead and paid for her to be buried at the York Cemetery and for a small service to be conducted at the little chapel there. Is that agreeable to you?' His eyebrows rose in question.

Mercy's eyes widened. 'She'll not be in a pauper's grave?'

'No. She'll be buried properly.' He gave her a sad smile.

Mercy swayed and Victoria quickly put her arm around her. 'Isn't that marvellous, Mercy. Polly will be decently buried.'

Tears rolled down Mercy's cheeks. 'How will I ever repay you, Doctor?'

He shook his head, his eyes full of compassion. 'I don't need repaying.'

'But for you to do this, for me, for my child. It is too much. You are too kind.' Mercy grasped his hands. 'Thank you!'

'I'd like to think I can be more than just medical assistance. You are Victoria's friend, and as such, hopefully mine too.' He looked hopefully between Mercy and Victoria.

'When is the funeral to be?' Victoria asked, loving him more at that moment than ever before.

'Tomorrow.' He sipped his tea.

'So soon?'

'I had to call in some favours.' He took another sip of tea and rose from the stool. 'I must go. I have many places to visit today. I'll hire a carriage for tomorrow and collect you both at two o'clock.'

Still crying, Mercy simply nodded, while Victoria walked him to the door. 'Thank you. There are no words for what you have done.'

He took both her hands. 'You are to be my wife. What makes you happy makes me happy. I'm sorry I cannot come to see you tonight but I'm not certain what time I'll be finished by.'

'I understand.' At that moment she would have forgiven him anything in the world. 'Thank you for everything.' She didn't feel worthy of his devotion and his kindness.

'Until tomorrow.' He kissed her and walked away.

Chapter Eighteen

During the night, thunder grumbled overhead and lightning flashed. The temperature dropped and Victoria fell asleep to the sound of heavy rain falling. Her last thoughts were relief that the drought had broken.

By morning, the dry heat of summer had been washed away in a torrent of rain that overflowed the gutters and found every hole in any roof not patched up correctly. Every household in Hungate collected rain in buckets and pans. The streets, alleyways and lanes were lined with jugs and vessels to catch the runoff water from gutters and drainpipes.

Heavy laden skies of dark grey lowered over the city's rooftops. Rain fell so fast, it reduced visibility. The children played happily inside to begin with, but after a few hours started to squabble and fight. After midday, the rain eased somewhat and Kathleen came to take the children so Mercy and Victoria could get ready.

'Harriet Drysdale is a gift of a woman,' Mercy said, smoothing the black taffeta skirt. 'Because of her, I'm dressed decent for my daughter's funeral.'

Silently Victoria agreed. For her own clothes were too shabby to be worn now after so much cleaning and constant wearing. Harriet's generosity had given them both good quality clothes to wear for some months. She'd not embarrass Ashton today.

Holding an umbrella, Ashton came to escort them back to the main road where he had a carriage waiting to transport them to the cemetery on the outskirts of the city.

The rain fell again as they made their way into the little chapel and heard the short service for Polly. Huddling under umbrellas they watched her coffin be lowered into the ground before Ashton ushered them back to the carriage.

In Petal Lane, the rain thrashed the ground, running in channels down the cobbles. The buckets and pans were soon overflowing, and the noise drowned out conversation unless they raised their voices.

'I don't like leaving you here. Can I pay for you to stay at a hotel?' Ashton asked Victoria as he stood by the door. Worry etched his handsome features.

'No. I cannot leave Mercy, or the children.' She glanced back at the sad little group sitting on the bed, eating the last of the currant cake.

'I'll pay for two rooms then.'

She shook her head. 'Mercy won't go. This is her home. She won't leave it to be reliant on you. I must stay with her. I am sorry.'

'I understand, but I am not happy about it. I don't mind paying for it.'

She kissed him. 'Thank you.'

'We should talk about having the banns read in church on Sunday.' He shrugged on his damp coat. 'I have meetings tomorrow, but I can call in the evening?'

'Yes. That would be lovely.'

'If the weather has improved, perhaps we can go for a walk?'

She nodded. 'I'd like that.'

He kissed her cheek to an audience of little faces watching them.

But the next day brought more rain. As though making up for the dry months of summer, the rain and grey skies seemed never-ending.

As the church bells chimed each hour, the rain continued to fall. Ashton sent an errand boy with a note to Victoria, saying he'd call tomorrow instead when the weather cleared.

Disappointed, she curled up on the bed with the children and told them stories she'd remembered reading as a young girl. The pinging of water dripping through the roof into the buckets situated around the room became intolerable, but there was nothing that could be done about it.

The following day saw no difference in the weather. For half an hour in the morning the rain ceased over York. The residents of Petal Lane came out to gossip and throw away the excess water.

'Who'd have thought last week we'd be doin' this!' Kathleen chuckled as she emptied a pan of water into the flowing drain. 'I've more water than I know what to do with. Every pan an' bucket is full from catchin' drips from the roof. I need the pans to cook in, so I do.'

However, in the distance, black clouds crept towards them.

By midday the rain was pounding the city again.
Mercy went to work, and Victoria envied her the
chance to escape the damp fetid room and the frac-
tious children.

To pass the time, she taught the children how to
write their numbers with bits of charcoal, and then the
letters of the alphabet.

Jane, being the eldest, soon picked it up, but the
others quickly lost interest.

Another sodden errand boy arrived with a similar
note to the day before – Ashton wasn't coming.

She couldn't blame him, after working all day, he'd
not want to sit in a dingy damp room full of com-
plaining children with inadequate seating or refreshments. She'd escape herself if she could.

The evening drew in early, the grey daylight slipping away to be replaced by dark heavy downpours.
Victoria had to find something to feed the children,
but all she had was a few potatoes left. They needed
to go and buy some food tomorrow when Mercy got
her wages.

The rain fell so heavily, that she didn't hear the
door open and glanced with a start when Kathleen
entered the room. She wore a canvas sheet over her
head and shoulders.

'The Foss is fair ragin', so it is. We'll all be needin'
bloody boats if this keeps up!' Kathleen plopped onto
the stool.

'I thought I heard the river last night. Is it very
high?'

'We'll need to keep an eye on it, for sure.' From
under her arm, Kathleen brought out a newspaper
wrapped parcel. 'Careful, it's rice and it's seeping
out.'

'Rice?' Victoria took the parcel. She'd never cooked rice before.

'Aye. Mick an' the boys are gettin' shifts at one of the railway warehouses. When something spills, they clean it up an' also bring what they can home. Today it was rice.'

She fished in her apron pocket and brought out a twist of paper. 'Here's a bit of salt. Boil the rice in the pot with a bit of salt to give it flavour. It'll fill you all up.'

'Thank you. I've got some potatoes, so we'll be full tonight.' Victoria set a pan of water to boil. 'Staying for some tea? I have some left from the basket.'

'Aye, sure an' that'll be grand.' Kathleen smiled at the children. 'If the rains stop tomorrow, in the afternoon Mick'll take these lot out for a bit to give yer some peace. Is yer doctor comin' to pay a call tonight?' Kathleen grinned.

Victoria filled the kettle and put it on the heat next to the pan of water. 'No, he has sent another note. He'll come tomorrow if the weather is better.'

'Are yer going to marry 'im?'

'Yes. I hope so.' She hardly dared to expect it could happen. She thought him lost to her, that he was Stella's. It was taking some effort to truly believe he cared for her.

'There's no hope about it, lass. Get yourself wed an' live the life yer meant to.'

'Mercy won't come with me.' She sighed, confused with a mixture of happiness and worry.

'An' nor should she. She's got regular work an' a roof over her head. Me an' Mick are next door should she need anything, so we are. Yer need to see to yoursen now.'

'I cannot leave her behind.'

269

Kathleen snorted. 'Lass, yer to be married. Besides, yer can still call and see us. We ain't goin' nowhere, are we?'

Yes, I suppose...'

'An' being a doctor's wife, yer'll be able to talk to those that matter about the water situation and all the rest. Yer be taken notice of now. That Mr Foster will be having yer to dinner, so he will.'

'True. I will be able to converse with more people on the subjects that affect the poor areas.' Victoria stared at the boiling water. 'I'm feeling such trepidation at being back in society again and we aren't even married yet.'

Kathleen sniggered. 'I'd like to be a fly on the wall when yer family see yer on the doctor's arm, so I do.'

Pouring the rice into the water, Victoria shied away from thinking about her family's reaction when they heard the news. Stella would ignore her, and she couldn't think what everyone else will say.

~ ~ ~ ~

Wet and hungry, Joseph put his head down against the rain that blew under his umbrella. The street's gutters ran like tiny streams, washing away the rubbish and soaking the feet of the unexpected.

He'd just spent the day at the Union Workhouse assisting the doctor there who was swamped with an outbreak of bronchiolitis and chest problems of the very young and older inmates. Damp weather caused no end of difficulties with the frail. They'd had two deaths that morning and he'd be surprised if there wasn't another half a dozen in the next few days.

He rounded the corner on to Bootham, glad that home wasn't far away.

The bad weather was keeping him from being with Victoria, but he knew there'd be no point in going to Hungate, becoming dreadfully wet on the way, only to sit in that tiny room feeling cold and damp wouldn't be fun. If Mercy was working, then Victoria would have to see to the children and they'd not be able to talk freely. No, it was best to wait until the weather permitted them to go walking alone.

Suddenly he was knocked into by a man exiting a building.

'Oh, I do apologise, sir. I slipped on the step.' The man stepped back, adjusting his hat, his umbrella dripping on Joseph's boots.

'It's quite alright. This weather is treacherous.' Joseph went to move on, but the man forestalled him.

'Aren't you, Doctor Ashton?'

Joseph nodded, trying to place where he'd met the man before. 'I am.'

'Forgive me, I'm Arthur Bartholomew, solicitor. We met at a dinner party around March, I think, and we were introduced by the late Mr Harold Dobson.'

'Ah, yes, now I remember.' They awkwardly shook hands juggling cases and umbrellas.

'I am...er...was Mr Dobson's solicitor.'

'I see, yes.' Joseph hoped the man would hurry up and be on his way, the wind was driving the rain horizontal and he was getting severely wet.

'You wouldn't happen to know the whereabouts of Mr Dobson's niece, Miss Victoria Carlton, would you?'

'Miss Carlton?'

'I'm at my wit's end, and that's the truth.'

'How so?'

'I've searched as much as I can to find her with the scant details the family have given me, but they don't seem to know where she has gone. I'm now reduced to asking anyone who happened to have met her at all.' He shook his head clearly dismayed.

'What would it be about, sir?'

'Why her uncle's will, of course. She has an inheritance sitting there waiting for her to claim. Laurence Dobson promised me he'd track her down, but I've heard nothing.'

'An inheritance you say?' Joseph stared at the solicitor hardly believing his words.

'That is all I can tell you, sir, you understand.'

Joseph smiled. 'I know exactly where Miss Carlton is, Mr Bartholomew.' He looked up at the stone building. 'Is this your office?'

'Indeed, it is, sir.'

'Then I'll bring Miss Carlton to you tomorrow.'

'You will? But I heard she was travelling, away somewhere exotic her cousin, Miss Dobson, told me.'

'I assure you, sir, Miss Carlton is nowhere more exotic than York itself!'

'Nay, that can't be.' Mr Bartholomew looked incredulous.

'Shall we say, two o'clock?' Joseph shook his hand and left the man gaping in the rain. Victoria had an inheritance. She could be free of the clutches of poverty. For a moment, another thought entered his head. Having her own money now, would she want to still marry him?

~ ~ ~ ~

Victoria woke to muted noise. She opened her eyes, confused. Darkness shrouded the room. Mercy and the children still slept. Had she been dreaming? Turning over in the bed, she moved Bobby's hand which had slipped under her shoulder.

The noise came again. What was it? She leaned up on one elbow, squinting in the dark. Out of the window the night was black as coal and rain pitted the glass. Was it a rat? Tomcats fighting? Suddenly shouts became clear, then a woman's cry. The sound of splashing reached her. Puzzled, she sat up properly. The noise was becoming louder, more people's voices could be heard mingling with the rain and splashing. Something was definitely happening outside or in the courtyard at the top of the lane.

A scream made her jump.

Mercy sat up. 'What is going on?' she asked sleepily.

'I don't know,' she whispered, trying not to wake the children, but also wanting to be heard over the rain lashing the window.

Rubbing her eyes into wakefulness, Mercy peered at each of the children. 'They are fine.'

'It's not the children, it's coming from outside.'

'Outside? Who'd be outside in the middle of the night in this weather?'

Victoria peered out of the window. Someone went past holding a lantern high. For a moment the glow of the light lit up the room and Victoria stifled a cry.

'What is it?' Mercy asked as they were plunged into darkness again.

'Water.'

'What?'

Slowly, unable to believe what her eyes just saw for a moment, Victoria reached down beside the bed, but before she'd got to the bottom of the bed frame her hand hit cold water. She jerked back as though burnt.

'Dear God, Mercy!'

'What!'

'We're flooding!'

'What do you mean?' Mercy sat up straighter, disturbing Seth.

The enormity of what was happening overwhelmed Victoria. The room was two feet deep in water. How soon would it reach the top of the bed?

More people ran outside the window.

Victoria knelt up and fumbling in the dark, found the box of matches on the shelf above their heads and struck a match. The little circle of light touched the candle wick and an eerie glow filled the room.

Aghast, she stared at the water shimmering in the candlelight.

'Heaven help us,' Mercy whispered, kneeling up to stare as Victoria did. 'We have to get out. We don't know how far the water will rise. Maybe we can go up to the rooms above. The Rowlings might take us in?'

Victoria shuddered. 'No, I don't like how Phil Rowlings watches me.'

'I know he's a dirty letch, but his wife is nice enough in her quiet way, and they are higher up. The river would never reach the next floor.'

'I'd rather we went to Joseph's house in Bootham.' Victoria's only thought was to go to the man she loved. To impose on their neighbours above didn't seem right, there was no room for those families as it was, never mind taking on another six people.

'Yes, Doctor Ashton will take us in.' Mercy nodded sadly.

'We need to plan before we wake the children.' Victoria grabbed her shawl and wrapped it around her shoulders. Hoisting her nightgown up around her waist, she climbed off the bed.

The cold water reached just below her knees, taking her breath away. 'If this bed wasn't so high, we'd be soaked through by now.' She waded towards the door and retrieved hers and Mercy's coats from where they hung on a nail. 'Wear my coat and put yours around Jane. If you carry Seth, I can carry Emily. Bobby and Jane can hold hands.'

Cries and screams from the lane and courts came louder to them now.

They woke the children, each one not wanting to open their eyes or move from the warmth of the blankets. Victoria picked Emily up and the girl slept against her shoulder. 'Bobby, sweetheart, wake up and put your coat on, darling.'

Mercy hitched up her shift, stepped down off the bed and gasped as the cold water touched her bare legs. She took off the top blanket and wrapped it around Seth who slept on. 'Jane, dearest, wake up and help me.'

'No, Ma, I'm too tired.'

'I know, sweetling, but you must. The river has risen, and water is coming into the room. Be a big girl now and get up and help us.'

Grumbling, Jane climbed out of bed, and when the water reached her thighs she started crying. Bobby joined in too, unable to fathom what was going on. He gripped Victoria's hand, refusing to leave the bed.

'Bobby, I cannot carry you and Emily. You must walk. Hold Jane's hand.' Distracted she noticed another person splash past the window.

'No.' Stubbornly, Bobby refused to move.

'This won't work.' Mercy struggled to get Seth and the blanket fully into her arms and hold onto Jane's hand as well.

'We'll have to do it one at a time.' Victoria carried Emily to the door. 'I'll find one of the women who has made it to high ground and give Emily to her, then I'll come back for Seth.'

'Yes, that's a good plan. I'll stay on the bed with these three. Be quick.' Mercy lit a second candle and placed it on the table, before huddling the children up onto the bed.

Wading through the cold water, Victoria carried Emily on her hip. The little girl was too sleepy to worry about what was happening. Opening the door let in more water. She watched as a small wave raced across the room towards the bed. The water reached the mattress. In the candlelight Mercy stared at her in horror.

Without looking back, Victoria left the room and splashed through the water into the lane. She thought of the O'Sheas. Did they know of the flooding? She banged on their door. No answer. Had they already got out? Rain fell in a light drizzle. No moon lit the night sky. The darkness seemed tangible, enveloping familiar features to make them foreign or invisible. An eerie silence pervaded the area. The screams had died away, the lane was deserted.

Frightened, Victoria trudged through knee deep black water along Petal Lane towards the next court.

Ahead she spotted a lantern, but the person turned into another alley and the glow disappeared. Emily, wrapped in a blanket that dragged in the water, weighed heavy in her arms. She kept going more by feel than sight. She tripped on something and stumbled, her hand banging on the wall to save them both from going down.

At the end of the next alley, people stood on boxes, the water not so high.

An old woman sat on a chair perched on a box and gave orders to anyone who'd listen. 'Where you from, lass?' she asked Victoria.

'Petal Lane.'

'Is it liveable down there?'

'No, unless you're on the higher floors. We are on the ground floor and it's two foot deep.'

'Petal Lane has gone under.' The old women shouted to someone leaning out of the window above her.

'I need help, please. My friend has three children with her. I need to go and get them out.'

The old woman shouted upwards again. 'Dorrie, where's our Ralf?'

The woman pointed beyond the buildings. 'He's gone to The Bay Horse, Mam. They need help with the barrels.'

'Men and their beer!' the old woman muttered.

Victoria shifted Emily to her other arm. 'If someone can watch Emily, I can go back and help the others.'

'The water normally never reaches this far up.' The old woman waved on a young couple who splashed past, then turned back to Victoria.

'Leave her with me. I ain't moving from here.'

'Are you sure?'

'No flood has ever removed me from my home.
She's safe with me. I live up there so even if it did
rise this far, we've got somewhere safe.'

Gratefully, Victoria placed Emily on the old woman's lap. 'Thank you so much, Mrs ...'

'Widow Mac is the name, and you are?'

'Victoria Carlton and thank you again. I'll be back
as quick as I can.'

Returning the same way she'd come, she stumbled
over hidden obstacles. Her feet and legs were so cold,
it made her teeth chatter. Her wet nightgown and
shawl were stuck to her body. Something bumped
into her, a box of some sort and she pushed it away
where it floated up against a factory wall.

A young woman holding a baby waded past her.

'Are you all right?' Victoria asked her, as the rain
began to fall heavily once more. She recognised her
as Nellie from the courtyard near Petal Lane.

'Yes, fine, bloody weather. I'm off to me Mam's,
she lives in Walmgate.'

'Head for Widow Mac, the water isn't so high
there.'

'Aye, thanks. I'll go that way.' Nellie turned the
corner and was gone in the darkness.

In the eerie gloom, she continued on. People were
calling to each other from out the windows of upper
floors, the candlelight spilling out reflected on the ink
black of the water, which gave her some light to
guide her.

In Petal Lane, she felt her way along the houses,
counting the doors.

Darkness seemed to penetrate more deeply here, no
lights helped to direct her. The windows above were
in darkness. Were they sleeping through this disaster?

The water was rising further. It reached to her mid-thigh now, scaring her.

'Mercy!' She called before she'd reached her own door.

'We're here, Victoria!' Mercy's voice was a welcome sound.

Poking her head through the door, she was grateful the candles were still lit. The water had reached the lip of the mattress and Mercy held the children close to her. 'Right, come on.'

'I can't believe this.' Mercy scrambled down from the bed and passed Seth to Victoria. 'Bobby, jump on my back. Jane hold my hand.'

'I can't!' Jane cried, terrified at the black water lapping her island bed.

'Climb on my back then.' Victoria turned so the girl could climb on.

'You can't carry them both.' Mercy fumed as Bobby climbed onto her back, his thin arms tight around her neck. 'Jane, be a good girl now, hop down and hold my hand.'

Juggling Seth into a better position in her arms, Victoria straightened the best she could. 'Hold on, Jane. Quickly now.'

Although the little girl's weight wasn't much, combined with Seth in her arms, Victoria felt as though she was burdened with stones. Bent over, her whole body protested.

'I want to go on Toria's back,' Bobby instantly complained.

'Be quiet, Bobby.' Mercy grabbed a cloth bundle she'd wrapped and left on the bed. 'I packed our food.'

Victoria hitched Jane higher up her back. 'Be careful out there. It's black as pitch and no moon. The rain is heavy too.'

'Where's Emily?'

'With Widow Mac. Do you know her?' Victoria pushed through the water towards the door.

'Yes, I pass her on my way to work. She's always sitting outside on a chair, talking to anyone who walks past.' Mercy stumbled on the doorstep.

'She's still doing that, only she has Emily on her lap.' Outside, she waited for Mercy. 'There is no noise from the O'Sheas. I'm worried.'

'They might have got out early.'

'Without telling us?' She looked at their neighbour's closed door.

'That does seem unlikely of them.' Mercy banged on the door. 'Kathleen, are you in there?'

A tiny sound came from within, but the rain fell so hard Victoria wasn't sure if she'd heard anything or not.

'What was that?' Victoria tried the door handle, the door opened an inch then was stuck. 'Mick! Kathleen!'

Silence.

'Mick and the boys have been working night shifts, maybe they haven't come home yet?' Mercy turned away. 'We've got to get the children out of this rain.'

Reluctantly, Victoria walked away. 'I'll come back and check once you and the children are safe.'

Halfway through the alleys, Mercy took over from carrying Seth to give Victoria a rest. With a child each on their backs, they had no breath for talking.

With one hand reaching out to guide her along the walls, Victoria felt as though her back would break.

She'd lost most of the feeling in her feet. She kept falling over things in the water, items that the flood had shifted and brought along on its snaking journey through the courtyards and lanes.

'Here, lasses. Let me help you.' A man loomed up out of a side alley. He took Jane off her back and put the little girl on his own. Next, he grabbed Seth and held him against his chest.

Relieved of some of the weight, Mercy straightened, holding onto Bobby who clung like a little monkey.

They followed the man until they reached Widow Mac, who now supervised from her chair at the upper floor window. The rain had driven her inside.

Climbing the steep narrow staircase, Victoria pulled up her wet clothes to stop from tripping on the stairs. The room above held a roaring fire and a few people sat about drinking tea, looking forlorn and damp. On a blanket near the fire was Emily, sleeping soundly.

'She's right as rain, that one,' Widow Mac said from her chair.

'Thank you.' Mercy knelt down and Bobby scrambled off her back and stood before the fire, shivering.

'Dorrie, more blankets.' Widow Mac barked the order and a thin woman darted about seeing to everyone and making them as comfortable as she could. Tea was poured, blankets found and more wood stacked onto the fire.

Victoria swapped her wet shawl for a thin grey blanket Dorrie gave her. 'I cannot stay here not knowing what has happened to Kathleen,' she said to Mercy through chattering teeth.

Mercy looked up at her from the floor where she was rubbing warmth back into Jane's arms. 'You can't go back out in that. I'm sure they are fine.'

'I must know if she is safe.'

'I can't hear what you're talking about,' Widow Mac called from the window. 'Speak up.'

'Our neighbours, we don't know if they have got out.' Victoria told her. 'I need to go back and find out.'

'Who are they?'

'The O'Sheas.'

'They didn't go past me. Dorrie, get the lass a lantern.'

'I'll be as quick as I can.' Victoria put on her coat, even though it was wringing wet, thanked Dorrie for the lantern and left the room.

The cold water made her shake even more and it took all of her courage to force her legs to move through the water and back down the dark lanes. More people waded past her, carrying items above their heads and children on their backs.

Pitiful looking dogs found high ground where they could, and miserable cats meowed painfully from fence posts and rooftops.

A dull pewter grey light filtered through the area as dawn edged closer, though they'd see no sun today for although the rain had stopped again, the skies were dull and low.

She made it to the courtyard closest to Petal Lane. It was deserted, the dirty water lapping gently at the walls and invading homes. Two men splashed out of one ground floor boarding house, their arms filled with goods. They stopped and stared at her.

'You didn't see us, missus.' The tallest man sneered.

She shook her head, frightened to say anything which might bring them to violence.

The other man dropped a waistcoat into the water and swore. He left it there and hurried on, splashing past Victoria.

The tall man paused beside her as his friend carried on. 'You're a fine piece, I must say. How about you and me have some fun?'

'No!' She stumbled backwards to get away from him and lost her footing. She went down with a scream which turned into a gargle as water filled her mouth. The lantern went under the water as well, and the light plunged them into darkness. As she came up, coughing, she saw the man splashing his way down the alley.

Shaking from cold and how close she came to harm, she leaned against the wall and spat out the foul taste in her mouth. Her hair dripped into her eyes and disgusted, she angrily pushed it away. How had she come to this? From living a comfortable life on Blossom Road to standing in a thigh deep flood in the middle of the slums. If it wasn't so tragic she'd laugh.

Sighing, she walked on. Her wet coat dragged in the water, slowing her down, and as she reached Petal Lane, she paused for a moment to lean against a wall again to catch her breath. She never realised that walking through water could be so exhausting.

Petal Lane was deserted. Debris from the alleys and the river itself floated and bobbed, objects became clearer as the night receded with the dawn light.

The door to their room yawned open, but Kathleen's door remained shut.

Putting her shoulder to it, she pushed hard. 'Kathleen! Are you in there?'

The door opened a bit wider with each push until finally she was able to slip inside. Water rippled against the furniture. Kathleen and Mick had two rooms. One at the front and one at the back. Victoria stumbled through the front room, banging her already bruised legs on unseen objects below the water. Moving aside the curtain that acted as a door, she entered the back room where the family slept. On the bed lay Kathleen, her eyes open in death.

Rushing through the water, Victoria landed beside her friend and grabbed her hand. 'Kathleen!'

She stared at the big woman's chest, but it didn't rise and fall no matter how hard she willed it to.

'Oh, Kathleen. Why did you have to die? Don't you know how much we all care about you?' Shocked, Victoria sat on the bed and gently closed Kathleen's staring eyes.

Dazed, she looked around the room. Another curtain half screened off the bunk beds that belonged to the O'Shea sons.

The room, if the water was ignored, was tidy and organised, clothes folded or hung neatly. A picture on the wall showed a pleasant countryside scene, which Victoria thought must be of Ireland, and fixed on the other wall was a small wooden cross.

She turned back to gaze at Kathleen. Her chest squeezed with grief, for this woman had been such a good and kind friend, full of useful advice and witty comments, a lending hand and a cherry smile when life seemed determined to make you cry. Mick once said that his wife had a big body to carry around her big heart, and he was right.

Fleetingly, she wondered where the O'Shea men were, did they know about Kathleen? She didn't have the energy to go and find them. Besides, she didn't want to leave her friend alone in a watery room. She'd died alone and that grieved Victoria deeply. The least she could do now was sit beside her until someone came to find them.

Taking a thick blanket from the end of the bed, Victoria pulled her feet up from the water and wrapped the blanket around her. She kept one hand holding Kathleen's and the other hand held the blanket tight about her to try and stop her shivering. She was so cold and tired...

Chapter Nineteen

Joseph left his house as soon as he heard about the flooding from his housekeeper. His mind full of Victoria, he hoped she had not been affected. He hailed the first hansom he saw and paid the cabbie extra to drive fast. The grey skies threatened more rain but as yet it held off.

The devastation of how far the flood surge had flowed from the broken river banks soon became clear. Dirty water marked the white walls of houses and shops, and businessmen shook their heads in despair at the cost of the clean up. People lined the streets, finding advantage points to stare at the spectacle of both the Rivers Ouse and Foss invading the city streets.

At the edge of Hungate, Joseph climbed from the hansom and stood surrounded by displaced people sitting in the streets, wet and dejected.

A man sat in the gutter with a bleeding gash to his forehead. Joseph cleaned the wound and bandaged his head, before moving on to the next person.

A young boy had slipped and fallen, clearly breaking his arm. Joseph spoke to the youth's mother and told them to go to the hospital.

As he moved through the crowd, he asked about Victoria or Mercy, but no one knew them. Worry filled him.

He entered the narrow lanes of the slum where the water hadn't reached. People stood about talking. Children played, babies cried, a dog barked.

He helped an old man who had a cut to his knee by getting him sat down and a bandage applied. A woman had started her labour and he told a panicked husband to get her to the hospital unless she wanted to give birth in the gutter. The husband muttered something about a midwife, and their home being under water.

Joseph looked at the man. 'Your midwife is of no use to you if you don't have a home. Go to the hospital, please.'

He walked away, but soon stopped at the beginning of the flood waters. The devastation of half-submerged houses shocked him. Children threw down rubbish from upper rooms, laughing at the size of each splash, while others had made paper boats and raced them.

Joseph kept walking, finding courtyards and alleys that weren't fully waterlogged, trying to get as close to Petal Lane as he could.

'Doctor Ashton!'

He stopped and looked up. 'Mrs Felling!' He looked at the doorway below the window she leaned out of. 'I'm coming up.'

He took the stairs as fast as he could, dodging the odd person who sat on the treads. Hurrying into the room, he scanned it for Victoria.

'Doctor Ashton.' Mercy, carrying her youngest came up to him. 'I'm so glad you're here.'

'Where is Miss Carlton?'

'I don't know.' Fear clouded her eyes. 'She went back to Petal Lane to try and find out if our neighbours are safe, but that was hours ago and she hasn't returned. I'm so worried.'

Fear ripped through him. 'I'll go find her.'

Returning outside, he raced along, not stopping when he reached the flooded lanes. He went straight into the water-filled alleys and courtyards, wading through the washed-up debris. The cold water shocked him, but he ignored it and kept going. A dead rat floated by and he lifted his medical case high so it didn't become wet. It was enough that his shoes and suit were ruined, he didn't want his medical equipment damaged also.

People called out to him from upper windows, but he hardened his heart to them. If he stopped at every house, he'd never find Victoria. Finally, he turned the corner and waded into Petal Lane. The water was higher here being closer to the river. The brown murky water swirled around him as he stopped at the door leading to Victoria's room. The open door revealed a half-submerged room. There was no sign of her.

Splashing to the next door, he found it open, too, but unlike the Felling's room this one had another room at the back. He pushed his way past floating items and moved the dividing curtain aside.

'Victoria!' Seeing her lying on the bed, he hurried as fast as the water allowed him to move. 'Victoria!' He reached her side and pulled her up. She opened her eyes and blinked.

His heart left his throat so he could breathe again. 'Dear God, you frightened me.'

He crushed her into his arms, worried at how cold and pale she was. 'Are you hurt?'

'Kathleen...' she whispered through blue lips.

He looked at the large woman lying beside her and knew by the colour of her skin the woman had been dead for some time. 'She's gone. We must get you away from here and warmed up.'

'I cannot leave her.' She pushed him away. 'Kathleen needs me.'

'You must. You can do nothing for her now,' he said softly.

'No!' She struggled as he picked her up off the bed. 'I cannot leave her.'

He paused and stared into her eyes. 'I'll send people to come and collect her. You trust me to do that, don't you?'

Her gaze lingered on Kathleen, tears on her lashes. 'Mick, he needs to know.'

'I'll make sure he does. Please, let me help you first. You're freezing and wet.'

She sagged in his arms and he held her closer to his chest. Walking through the water carrying her and his bag was difficult, her dress hung in the water and dragged, making his efforts twice as challenging. Victoria closed her eyes and started shivering, her head lolled against his shoulder and he tightened his grip on her.

'Talk to me. Can you do that? Can you stay awake and tell me what you've been doing?'

She remained silent and heavy in his arms as he trudged back towards the house where Mercy waited. He felt sick at the thought of her being next to a dead woman for hours in the cold, flooded room.

~ ~ ~ ~

Victoria woke, blurry-eyed and fuzzy of mind. She felt hot as though her skin burned. Voices rang in her head, hurting her, too loud, too close. Something cool was placed on her forehead and she liked that. The darkness closed in on her and she welcomed it. When she awoke again, fire raged in her body. She cried out, the agony intense.

Something heavy was pressing on her chest. She couldn't breathe. Her lungs squeezed, not working properly.

She gasped for air. Her eyes wouldn't open, or had they and she was blind? Panicked, she fought to see something, anything. Voices echoed. Darkness filled her brain. She cried out again. Hands touched her, scorching her skin. She'd died and was in hell.

~ ~ ~ ~

Joseph wiped the sweat from Victoria's forehead as she squirmed on the bed. The soft lamp light didn't hide the brutal flush of fever that ravaged her body. Since bringing her back to his house yesterday, Victoria had slipped into an unconscious state as her temperature rose. Both he and Mrs Felling had stayed by her side during the evening and night as Victoria battled a rising fever.

Today, she'd grown worse with every hour. Now, as another night was descending outside, he silently hoped Victoria's fever would break before it killed her.

The victims of the flood had filled the hospitals and spilled into churches and almshouses.

He was sorely needed to help with the hundreds of people who'd been injured fleeing the water, but he couldn't leave Victoria. By having her in his home he could take care of her better than leaving her in a crowded hospital. Mercy and the children had come with him to give the situation respectability, not that he could have left them behind. The whole family had been wet and homeless and frantic over Victoria.

As the little clock on the mantelpiece chimed eight o'clock, he looked at Mercy who sat on a chair on the other side of the bed. She wore an ill-fitting brown dress loaned by his housekeeper Mrs Boden. 'Go and get some rest, Mrs Felling.'

'I'm fine, Doctor.' Her face told another story, however. Her skin was grey, drawn and bruising darkened under her eyes. 'I don't want to leave her.'

'You've not slept in over twenty-four hours, Mrs Felling.'

She sighed. 'I'll have a nap later.'

'I can watch over her. I don't need you falling ill as well. Think of the children.'

'You've had no sleep either, Doctor.' Her eyes looked haunted and reminded him of her daughter Polly when she'd been arrested.

'Mrs Felling, please, go to bed, even if it's only for an hour.'

'Very well.' She rose unsteadily and he rushed around to help her stand.

'Did you eat earlier with the children?'

She shook her head. 'I couldn't. Food gets lodged in my throat… She has to wake up…she is all I have, apart from the children.'

He couldn't chastise her about not eating because he hadn't been able to either. Mrs Boden had been in her element sorting everyone out, feeding up the children and getting them a hot bath ready. Clothes had been stripped off the children and washed. The kitchen resembled a laundry but he didn't care. The only thing he cared about was Victoria's survival.

Joseph escorted Mercy to the other bedroom, where the children slept soundly.

When Esther Dobson had found this house for him, he'd doubted the prudence of having a three-bedroom house just for himself. It seemed a waste of money, but being so busy he'd agreed and taken it. Now the house was full and he rather liked it.

He bid her goodnight and returned to Victoria. He sat in the chair beside the bed and held her hand. She looked so flushed and delicate, belying the strength of will she had. She needed that strength more than ever to beat the infection.

'Victoria, you must wake up.' He stroked her hand. 'We have a wedding to organise. Then there is my family for you to meet. They will come from Lincoln for the wedding. Mother is excited to meet you. I've told her so much about you. She'd be here now, but I forestalled her…' He couldn't say that he didn't know if she was contagious and could spread the disease she fought. His mother would come and help, he knew that without being told, but it was better she stayed away until Victoria was well again.

She flung her hand away from his, thrashing her head on the bed.

He rose and poured fresh water into a large bowl and began to sponge her face and neck.

Heat radiated from her body, the borrowed night-gown slick with sweat. He dribbled water onto her lips, hoping a little would seep into her mouth.

A tap at the door made him turn. Mrs Boden stood in the doorway. He straightened, putting the cloth back into the bowl. 'Yes?'

'I've just come up to say I'll stay the night, sir, in case I'm needed.' She gazed with sadness at Victoria.

'That is most good of you, Mrs Boden.' His housekeeper was a good woman and he thanked the fates the day he hired her.

'How is Miss Carlton doing?'

'Not as good as I'd like.' He sighed. 'The fever still rages. It should have broken by now.'

'Bless her. I'll bring you up a tea tray, sir, and some toast. You need to keep your strength up. I said the same to Mrs Felling.'

When Mrs Boden left, he sat back down and continued sponging Victoria's arms. The back of his neck was tight with strain and he stretched a little. The night would be long.

At some point during the small hours of the night, he must have nodded off, for he woke with a start when Victoria moaned.

He blinked to focus and bent over her to feel her forehead. She still burned and his heart constricted. The fever was taking too long to peak. Her hair was wet with sweat. He sponged her down and then stripped off the top damp bedsheet. Mrs Boden had left clean sheets on the chest of drawers by the door.

As he rolled Victoria onto her side to change the sheet beneath her, her body flopped unresponsively.

He needed to change her nightgown too. The voluminous one she wore was from Mrs Boden, and he doubted his housekeeper had another spare.

'Victoria wake up please,' he pleaded, as he finished changing the sheets.

The clock chimed four times. Another hour and it would be dawn. Tired by his exertions, he sat back on the chair and watched her, waiting for a sign that she was recovering.

When he next woke, birds were chirping outside the window and Mrs Felling sat on the other side of the bed.

He sat up and leaned over Victoria to check her.

'I think she's not as hot as she was, Doctor.' Mercy smiled tentatively, hope in her eyes.

He felt Victoria's forehead. It was still warm but not the fierce heat of before. 'Yes, I think you're right, Mrs Felling.' He used the clinical thermometer to get a better reading but he was certain she looked better than a few hours ago.

'You stayed with her all night. You must be exhausted. I can take over while you rest.'

He shook his head, counting the minutes on his pocket watch to gage the thermometer. 'Thank you, but no, I'm alright. I napped a little. However, I will go and have a wash in a moment.'

'Good. Mrs Boden is cooking breakfast and she says we both must eat or she won't be responsible for her actions.'

He nodded absentmindedly. 'We had better do as she says then.' He waited the full five minutes before removing the thermometer. 'Yes. Victoria's temperature is down.'

'Such good news.' Mercy let out a deep sigh.

'I won't be long.' He paused by the door, watching Mrs Felling leaning over Victoria and tenderly wipe her brow. 'Perhaps you could call me Joseph, since we are both in this together?'

She smiled. 'I'd like that, and I'm Mercy.'

He nodded and left the room to cross the landing to his own bedroom. Mrs Boden had already left a jug of hot water by the wash bowl and a clean towel. Turning his back on his inviting bed, he stripped off his jacket and shirt and began to wash. He wanted to look his best for when Victoria woke up and she *would* wake up.

Chapter Twenty

Joseph sat at the desk in the guest bedroom of his house. He'd just finished writing a letter to his mother. Outside the window, a bird chirped in the tree. It was a glorious September day, full of gentle sunshine and a hint of a breeze. The leaves on the trees were changing colour, but slowly, leisurely, as though not ready to depart from their branches just yet.

He heard the children laughing in the garden and Mercy quieten them down and send them inside. He smiled at their innocent pleas to stay out and play. How different those children were to the ones he first met back in March. Gone were the insipid, listless ghosts hiding in a dark corner. Now they were healthy with rosy cheeks and their voices filled his house.

Glancing towards the bed where Victoria lay, he'd hoped the children's noise might have disturbed her enough for her to open her eyes.

However, she lay still and quiet. It's been five days since he'd rescued her. Victoria had suffered a fever for two days, but when it broke, she'd not woken.

As each day went by he grew more anxious as to the reason why.

A soft knocked preceded Mercy as she entered the room. 'I've brought you some tea, Joseph.'

'Thank you, Mercy.'

She placed the teacup and saucer beside his letter and turned to Victoria. 'Still the same?'

'Yes, no change.' He rose from the hard wooden chair and stood next to the bed.

He felt Victoria's forehead, which was at normal temperature. 'I thought she'd have woken by now. The fever left her three days ago. There should be signs of improvement.'

'You said yourself she was lucky to survive the fever. She was so close to death…perhaps her body just needs to rest now.' Mercy gently took Victoria's hand and stroked it.

'She's wasting away, Mercy.' His voice broke and he hurriedly coughed to cover it up. His heart felt shredded to a pulp by the enormity of nearly losing the one woman he loved more than anyone else.

Mercy sat on the chair by the bed. 'What can we do?'

'I don't know. I've written to my contemporaries to see if they can help me. I've tried everything I know of.' He raked his fingers through his hair, frustrated that he couldn't make Victoria wake up.

'You said yesterday that nature will take over and heal her,' Mercy whispered. 'You promised me she'd be better if she survived the fever, but you can't know that for certain, no one can.'

'I'm a doctor. I should know!'

'Nonsense. You can't know everything. It's not possible.'

Mercy looked up at him. 'I know you have affection for her, as she does for you. Let us hope that is enough to pull her through.' She stood and walked to the door. 'I'd better go and see to the children. Your housekeeper is stuffing them full of cake.'

'Mrs Boden enjoys spoiling them. I think I bored her with my quiet ways.'

'It's no longer quiet here that is for sure.' Mercy smiled. 'My four will keep her very busy.'

She opened the door wider and paused. 'I can never thank you enough for letting us stay here. Petal Lane is free from the flooding, it's all drained away. I will go this afternoon to start the clean up.'

'No, Mercy. I can't let you do that.' He stared down at Victoria. 'I know she would want you to be here, safe. That room in Petal Lane will be full of damp and mould. It's not fit for human habitation. In all consciousness I cannot let you take the children back there.'

'But we are not your responsibility, Joseph. You've done enough. I have to go back to work, and sadly Petal Lane is the only place I can afford to live.'

He glanced at her. 'I will help you find a better home, but until Victoria is well again, I'd be happier if you stayed here with me. Besides, the old gossips would have a fit if you left Victoria without a chaperone while she was under my roof.'

'She should be with her family at Blossom Street.'

'Would Victoria want to be there though?' He'd thought of contacting the Dobsons, but the situation was delicate. They'd made it clear that Victoria wasn't part of their family any more. He suddenly remembered Mr Bartholomew and Victoria's inheritance. The Dobsons had lied to the solicitor about her travelling.

Mercy sighed. 'No, I don't think she would.'

'So, do I let them know?' He folded the letter to his mother and placed it in an envelope.

'Let us wait until she is herself again and then she can make the decision.'

'Before the flood, I met up with the Dobsons' solicitor and he mentioned that Victoria has an inheritance from her Uncle Harold.'

Mercy's eyes widened. 'Good Lord! An inheritance. How wonderful for her.'

'Yes. She will be an independent woman.'

'She'll still want to marry you. I know that for certain.'

'I hope so.' Joseph walked with Mercy downstairs. 'I have a few calls to make, but I won't be long. You'll sit with Victoria?'

'Yes. I take the children in and read to them next to her bed. It might make her open her eyes and Bobby likes being close to her.'

'I'll be as quick as I can. If you need me, I'll be at the Union first, and then at Wilsons.'

'I'll send for you if she wakes up.' Mercy stood at the door. 'You've remembered that tomorrow I attend Kathleen's funeral.'

'Oh yes. A great shame.' He donned his coat and hat and picked up his medical bag. 'Her husband came last night, didn't he? Not that I spoke to him. I saw him from the stairs.'

'Yes, Mick O'Shea. He wanted to check we were safe and well. He is heartbroken.'

'Poor fellow.' Joseph opened the front door, thinking of the big Irishman who'd looked broken when he called briefly the previous night to speak to Mercy and inquire after Victoria.

He seemed a decent enough man and Joseph understood how he felt for if he lost Victoria he'd not know how to cope either.

He walked down Bootham towards the city centre.

He'd scaled back all his activities since rescuing Victoria and asked for forgiveness from the institutes that required his services. Even now he'd rather be beside Victoria than doing his visits, but other people relied on him and he mustn't forget that.

At the end of Bootham he glanced around for a hansom.

'Doctor Ashton?' A man called to him from a carriage, which was slowing down in front of him.

Joseph frowned as Todd Dobson climbed down from the carriage.

Todd bounded forward and shook his hand. 'It's been an age, good fellow. How the devil are you?'

'Well. And you?'

'Fit as a fiddle as you can see.'

'Fully recovered from your broken leg?'

'Completely.' Todd smiled charmingly. 'I've recently come home after travelling to Paris. Stella informs me you've not been to the house in months. She is awfully upset about it. Has the family offended you?'

'I have been terribly busy.'

'Not too busy to dine with good friends though, I imagine? You cannot work the whole day round for that makes a very dull fellow.' Dressed in a black suit of impeccable quality, Todd chuckled at his own words.

'I think I must be very dull indeed.' Joseph inclined his head, ready to walk away.

'Ashton? You don't take offence, surely?' Todd's face fell into seriousness. 'Is everything well?'

Joseph stared at him, seeing his fancy clothes and the carefree spirit of a man who has no concerns or responsibilities in his life.

A man who flits from day to day with nothing more challenging on his mind than to wonder what he was doing for his next instalment of entertainment. 'Do you ever think of your cousin, Miss Carlton?'

'Victoria?' Todd blinked rapidly. 'Oh, er…Mama says she's travelling, and not one letter has she sent me!'

'Pardon?' Surprised, Joseph wanted to hit the man. 'That is the story they are telling *even* you?'

'Story? I don't follow you.'

'They blame Victoria for your father's death,' Joseph spat.

'They do? Why? I know nothing of this. I went to Paris as soon as my leg mended. Mama and Stella, along with Laurence came and saw me on their way to London. They told me Victoria wasn't with them because she had met up with an aunt of her father's who offered her the chance to travel with her.'

'It is a lie.'

'A lie?' Todd screwed up his face in disbelief. 'Why would they lie about such a thing to me?'

'They obviously didn't trust you with the truth.'

'What exactly *is* the truth?' Todd looked around and pointed to a café on the corner of Gillygate. 'Over there, let us talk over refreshments. I am sorely confused.'

'I am due at the Union.'

'Ten minutes, please. I need to know what my family is keeping from me.'

They soon settled at a small table by the window and ordered a pot of tea.

'So, tell me everything.' Todd said, whipping out his napkin. 'I am most concerned something has happened that I've been kept in the dark about.'

'To put it simply, your cousin was helping me, visiting the poor, that kind of thing.'

'Right, I see.'

'Your parents found out and your mother especially didn't like what Victoria was doing. There was an argument and your father died of a heart attack. Your mother and Stella blamed Victoria, and she left the house. They have not seen her since, well, except your brother.'

'Laurence?'

Joseph thanked the waitress as she brought them their tea things. He poured the tea into two cups and then stared at Todd. 'I will tell you everything and then you'll know it all.'

Twenty minutes later, Joseph watched the emotions flit across Todd's face after he had told him all that had happened to Victoria since his father's death.

Todd played with a teaspoon. 'And she's gravely ill, you say.'

'Yes, she caught an infection from the flood. The fever nearly killed her. She's staying in my house so I can tend to her, along with the Felling family.'

'This Mrs Felling has told you all of what occurred with Victoria and my family? She can be trusted to tell you the truth?'

'Yes, of course. Victoria has told me some, but not all. While she's been ill, Mercy has filled me in while we've been sharing a vigil over her and she's told me it all. And now you know the truth.' Joseph finished the last of his tea.

'I cannot believe it of Laurence. To sell his share of the house in Fossgate?'

'It is all true.'

'But he had no reason to do it. He's wealthy beyond his dreams as his inheritance from Papa is vast. Stella and I did exceedingly well, too, but Laurence runs the bank...' Todd looked stricken. 'How could he believe a silly argument would be the cause of Papa's death?'

'A heart attack can happen any time. Although it is true that stressful situations do not help, but to put all the blame on Victoria is unkind and unjust.' Joseph stood, he was very late. 'I must go.'

'May I call on Victoria?'

'Certainly. When she has recovered and is able to receive visitors. I refuse to have her upset.' Joseph fished in his pocket for money. 'I will let you know. Are you staying in York for long?'

'A month or two, depending on how much Mama and Stella wear on me.' Todd slowly got to his feet. 'No, let me get the bill.' He shook Joseph's hand. 'I will get to the bottom of this.'

A waitress brought his hat and coat. 'That is your concern, mine is Victoria. Good day.'

~ ~ ~ ~

Something soft and light tickled her hand. Victoria moved. The tickle came again. Her eyelids felt heavy. It was an enormous effort to open her eyes and leave the peaceful place she'd been. At first, nothing was in focus. Then, little by little shapes turned into furniture and the face peering at her became Bobby.

'You're awake!' He stated and climbed up on the bed beside her.

'Look at this. T'is a feather!' He duly held up a long white feather.

'Yes...'

'It was on the grass. It's mine.' His small fingers ran up and down the feather. 'Jane's not havin' it. I'm hungry. Will you play ball? Seth fell down the stairs, hurt his knee. I didn't push him. Can we go to the river?'

His chatter flowed over Victoria like a wave of childish noise. She had no energy to reply and when he jumped off the bed she closed her eyes again, ready to fall back asleep.

'Toria!' Bobby thrust his small round face an inch from hers. 'Get up!'

Mercy rushed into the room. 'Bobby! Out now. Go and play!' She fell beside the bed, her face beaming and tears shining in her eyes. 'You've woken! Oh dearest.' Mercy cried and kissed Victoria's hand. 'Oh, I can't believe it. Praise God! Joseph will be so pleased when he comes home.'

Joseph.

Victoria smiled inwardly at his name. Joseph who had kissed her. Who had asked her to marry him. Moving only her eyes, she searched the room for him.

'He'll be home soon.' Mercy gripped her hands. 'How do you feel?' She felt Victoria's forehead. 'You're much cooler.' She wiped away her tears and laughed. 'What a wonderful day. I'm so happy. Joseph and I were beside ourselves, praying we wouldn't lose you.'

Like Bobby's, Mercy's words washed over her. She was far too tired to think or understand any of it.

'Are you hungry? You must be, you've not eaten in five days. I'll be back.' Mercy dashed to the door, scooping up Bobby as she went and disappeared calling for someone named Mrs Boden.

As silence settled, Victoria nestled further into the pillow and closed her eyes for welcoming sleep.

When she next woke, two lamps were lit, banishing the darkness. She moved her legs, which felt stiff. She turned her head. Joseph sat on a chair beside the bed, his chin resting on his chest, fast asleep. She watched him for some time, studying the shape of his nose, the curve of his jaw. A desperate need to talk to him filled her.

'Jo…' Her voice came out as a whisper, her throat parched as sand. Licking her lips, she tried again. 'Jos…'

His head snapped up and he was beside her in an instant, the joy shining from his beautiful blue eyes. 'I'm here, dearest. I'm here.' He gripped her hand and kissed it before becoming a doctor and feeling her head and peering at her intently. 'How do you feel? Can you move? Do you know who I am?'

'Drink…' Her throat seemed closed.

'Of course.' He poured water into a glass and then gently held her head up to help her drink.

The water was like nectar from heaven above. She drank until the glass was empty, yet even just that simple action had exhausted her. She stared up at Joseph and received a kiss on her brow. A warm loving feeling filled her, and she smiled. 'Joseph.'

'Yes, my love. I'll not leave you.' He stroked her cheek.

'Good.'

'We will get you well again, my darling. Then we will be wed, and I can take care of you forever.' He cradled her against his chest and she closed her eyes in gratefulness that this wonderful kind man loved her.

Chapter Twenty-One

Victoria sat by the bedroom window and looked on-to the road below. Bootham, like Blossom Street, was a busy thoroughfare, and she enjoyed seeing the carriages and people go by. She didn't feel so shut off from the world when she was sitting at the window. Strong October winds had blown the changing leaves into messy piles in the garden where she watched the children run about and play.

Her recovery was slow, slower than Joseph liked. Some days she could leave the bed and make the short walk to the window, other days she had to sleep all day. Mrs Boden fed her the best of ingredients, yet still she remained reed thin. Like the winter before, she'd developed a chest cold and the dreaded cough had returned, keeping her awake at night. Joseph made her drink foul draughts and eat nourishing food often, but there were days when her appetite failed her completely and she ate because it pleased him and Mercy.

Today, as a weak sun broke through racing grey clouds, Mercy had helped her to dress in a soft lawn gown the colour of pale blue and had wrapped a white cashmere shawl around her shoulders. With a blanket over her knees she sat on a cushion-padded chair waiting for Joseph to return home from one of the hospitals. In three weeks they would be married, and she longed for the security of being his wife and having him as her husband. Once they were wed, no one could take him from her. His love was hers alone, and she basked in it like a cat soaking up the sun.

On the table beside her she picked up a sweet letter written to her by Joseph's mother welcoming her to the family and how pleased they were about the up-coming wedding. She looked forward to meeting Joseph's family, especially since finding out she had an inheritance. Now she could hold her head up high and face the Ashton family with the knowledge that she had money of her own and wasn't a destitute.

As yet she hadn't met with Mr Bartholomew, her uncle's solicitor. Joseph said for her to wait until she was stronger to deal with it, but not knowing was driving her mad. However, what upset her more was the fact that all the time she was living in Petal Lane and suffering the humiliation of being penniless, she had some sort of inheritance which she could have used – money which would have saved them from the flooding, from starving, from Mercy working in a public house at all hours, from living in a disgusting hovel.

'Toria!' Bobby came running into the room and climbed onto her lap. He'd been crying.

'What's wrong, sweetheart?' She stroked his head.

Mercy marched into the room, her face like thunder. 'Robert Felling come here at once!'

Bobby snuggled further into Victoria's arms. 'What has he done?' she asked Mercy.

'He ate all of Mrs Boden's honey cakes, or what was left of them.'

Victoria raised her eyebrows at him. 'Why did you do that?'

'Only four, Toria, only four. Seth had some, and Emmy.' His eyes pleaded with her to take his side.

'Enough!' Mercy snapped. 'Seth is little more than a baby who follows your lead and Emily will do anything you say. You are the big brother! You must show them how to behave.' Mercy pulled him off Victoria's lap. 'For being so greedy you can go without your dinner. Now get to bed!'

He ran crying from the room and Victoria felt sorry for him. 'Don't be too harsh, Mercy, he's only little.'

'He's old enough to know better. Do you think I want to raise a son who steals? Didn't I go through enough with Polly?'

'Polly was keeping you all alive.'

'Exactly, so there was reason behind it, which makes it worse for Bobby as we don't go without anything here. I will not abuse Joseph's generosity. Bobby stole for the sheer pleasure of it.'

Victoria hid a smile, loving how much Mercy thought the world of Joseph. The two people she adored the most were the best of friends and often ganged up on her! It made her so happy. 'He's five years old.'

'Old enough to know better!' Mercy fumed.

They both looked at the doorway as Mrs Boden came into the room. 'Sorry to disturb you both, but there's a gentleman here to see Miss Carlton.'

'A gentleman?' Victoria looked at Mercy. 'Who could it be?'

'Mr Foster from the *Yorkshire Gazette*? You never did get to have a meeting with him.'

'No, I very much doubt it is him. He's probably forgotten all about me.' She felt guilty that she'd never been to see Mr Foster and would make it her business to do so as soon as she was well enough.

'The gentleman said he was your cousin, miss,' Mrs Boden said.

The blood drained from her face. 'Laurence?' She stared at Mercy. 'I don't want to see Laurence. Why would he want to see me? No, I won't see him.'

'I'll go down. He'll not get past me!' Mercy stormed from the room with Mrs Boden hot on her heels.

Victoria waited an anxious few minutes before she heard voices on the staircase. Her heart thumped in her chest. What could Laurence want? She wished Joseph was here. She craned her neck to see who it was and felt a rush of emotion as Todd cautiously stepped into the room. 'Todd!'

'Victoria.' He hurried to her and knelt by her chair. 'Dear sweet Victoria. Are you feeling better?'

'Slowly. Why are you here?' She stared at him. He appeared older, thinner, his hair receding.

'To see you, of course, but also to extend my deepest apologies that you have suffered so much. I didn't know. Not until I saw Doctor Ashton in the street a few weeks back.'

'Joseph mentioned he'd spoken to you. I didn't think you'd come to visit me though.'

'Why would I not come? Joseph only just gave me permission to visit. I've been waiting, but he said you were too ill. I have to travel to London this evening, and I didn't want to leave without talking to you.'

She took his hand. 'I'm so glad you have called. I have missed you.'

'And I you.'

Mrs Boden brought in a tea tray and left them to it.

'Let me.' Todd picked up the teapot and poured the tea, a frown on his face.

'I had no idea about any of what happened until I spoke with Doctor Ashton. I'd been told you were travelling with an aunt. I thought it strange at first, but didn't question it. Why would I think my family were lying to me?'

'Why indeed? It's a good story to spread around, easy for people to believe.' Victoria accepted the cup and saucer. Over the initial surprise of seeing him, she grew nervous of what he had to say. Was he to blame her like the rest of the family? She couldn't take any more condemnation. 'So now you know the truth of what happened. Do you judge me for your father's heart attack?'

'No, not at all. Papa was overweight and worked too hard. Doctor Ashton said it could have occurred at any time.'

'Yet Aunt Esther and Stella refuse to believe a doctor's opinion.' She shrugged, the old hurt rising again. 'I loved Uncle like a father. Never would I want to cause him pain. His death has been difficult for me to accept.'

'It has for us all.'

'Do they know you are here?'

'Yes. I have told them everything Ashton told me, all of what you've endured.'

Once she would have been horrified that they knew how low she had become, but not any longer. She had Joseph's love and admiration. It was all she wanted or needed. 'And their reaction?'

310

'Stunned silence to begin with.' Todd sipped his tea. 'Then Mama became tearful. I think she regrets much of what has happened and how you were treated.'

Victoria hardened her heart. 'They will be mortified to have any family member of theirs living in such reduced circumstances. The shame on the family would be intolerable.'

'Perhaps so…' He couldn't lie to her, she saw through him.

'What is their opinion of Doctor Ashton taking me in?' It gave her ridiculous joy that Stella now knew she had lost Joseph to her. For once, Victoria had beaten her cousin.

'They were very surprised, but acknowledged Ashton is a good and kind man.'

'We are to be married.'

'Really? Congratulations!' Todd leaned over and kissed her cheek. 'I am so happy to hear such wonderful news. It is what you want? I mean, you aren't accepting his offer of marriage because you feel you have nowhere else to go?'

'I don't have anywhere else to go, but that is not the reason. My affection for him is deep and abiding. He is a good man.'

'And he will keep you safe, unlike your family.'

She sipped her tea, not wanting to comment. Her trust in people remained thin on the ground. She could only rely on Mercy and Joseph, two people who last year she did not even know. 'I've been informed that Uncle Harold left me an inheritance. Do you know anything about it?'

'I wasn't at the reading of the will. I was still bedridden but I received a letter from Mr Bartholomew. He mentioned only what I received.'

'So, I am still in the dark.'

'I very much doubt Papa would have seen you go without. He loved you as a daughter.'

'Yes, he did, and I'll always be grateful for that.'

'I leave for London soon. Laurence wants to integrate me into the banking society.'

'Banking? You'll do that?'

He laughed. 'No, it's not for me, and Laurence knows it, too, but he keeps trying. He thinks it'll be the making of me.'

'What will you do instead? Not the navy?'

'No, not the navy.' He smiled. 'That was a silly statement I made when I could think of nothing else.'

'What will you do then?'

'I'm going to start an import and export company in India.'

'India?' He had surprised her, and she started coughing on the intake of breath. She held a handkerchief to her mouth as the coughing continued.

Todd poured her a glass of water, his face full of anxiety. 'Shall I fetch someone?'

She took a steady breath and drank some water. 'I'm fine. It comes and goes.'

'You were the same last winter.' Todd topped up her cup of tea.

'Joseph says my chest is weakened, but I'll be fine. Joseph wants us to honeymoon somewhere warm to aid my recovery.'

'That sounds good advice to me.'

She sipped her tea. 'You were telling me about India.'

He smiled and relaxed against the chair. 'I'm going to move there and start a business. I cannot stay in England with Laurence's constant disapproval, and Mama telling me I should marry this or that heiress.'

He shuddered dramatically. 'No, I need to do something substantial before I think about getting married. I have some contacts and while I'm in London, I'll put my plans into motion.'

'That sounds so interesting and exciting, Todd. I really hope it is a huge success.'

'Thank you. I'll return to York in a few weeks. May I call on you again?'

Her heart softened at the wariness in his eyes. 'Of course. You are my cousin and you've done no wrong to me.'

'I would have come home when Father died if I'd known what happened to you. My leg was in a very bad state and walking was extremely painful. The doctor kept me on laudanum for days, but I would have made the journey somehow. I suppose I should have really, for Father, but Laurence sent a letter saying to stay where I was and heal. I shouldn't have listened to him.'

'Laurence says a lot of things he shouldn't.' She couldn't hide the dislike for her older cousin.

'He does. I'll not forgive Mama or Laurence for ejecting you from the family like that. All I can say is that they were grieving and not thinking straight.'

'That doesn't excuse them in my eyes. What Laurence did by selling the half share of the house on Fossgate to such a man as Silas Finch is beyond forgivable.' The loss of that house still upset her greatly.

'I agree. It is inexcusable.'

'They are no longer my family, but you are and, if you are willing, I'd like you to give me away at my wedding.'

He grinned, showing a trace of the old Todd. 'I would be honoured indeed.'

She relaxed. 'Good. Now tell me about Paris and all that you did there.'

~ ~ ~ ~

Bells rang above their heads as Victoria and Joseph exited the church. The children ran ahead throwing rice and petals over the newlyweds. Seth didn't understand the concept and threw the rice at anyone near as well as stuffed some in his mouth. Jane, wearing a new white dress with a blue sash, pirouetted along the path, excited at how pretty she was. Mercy kept hold of Emily's hand to stop her from following Bobby who was running through the gravestones, glad to be free from the restriction of being quiet during the ceremony.

Victoria paused as so many people congratulated them. Joseph had mentioned the wedding to all the people he'd met at the hospitals, the society he mixed in, old friends from university and many more family and friends. The church had been full. It had overwhelmed her to see that amount of well-wishers.

She smiled at those who came up to them and Joseph shook hands. Although it was the beginning of November, the sun peaked between white clouds. A small breeze lifted the white lace of her veil that flowed down her back.

From the side of the crowd she spotted Mick O'Shea and his two sons. They waved as they walked away and she waved back. Kathleen would have enjoyed today and Victoria missed her.

It still saddened her that she not been present at Kathleen's funeral.

That dear woman had made her life in the slums bearable. She would never forget Kathleen.

Harriet slipped to her side. 'It all went beautifully, Victoria.' She adjusted the fine Irish lace on Victoria's bustle, taking pride in the beautiful lace and silk wedding dress she had made as a gift for Victoria.

'It did, and I only coughed once!' Victoria let out a long breath, thankful at last that Joseph was her husband and her future was secure. The memories of Petal Lane would recede in time.

Mercy came to join them. 'Are you tired, dearest? You look a little pale.'

Harriet peered at Victoria. 'Yes, you do. We should get you home.'

'Joseph!' Mercy called to him for he'd moved away to chat with his older brother. 'We should be getting Victoria home.'

'I'm quite well, Mercy, don't make a fuss.' Though in truth she felt tired and longed for a cup of tea. She'd been awake just after dawn to bathe and then Harriet had arrived to style her hair and make any alterations to the wedding dress.

All concern, Joseph was by her side in an instant, but she raised her hand to stop his forthcoming lecture of taking it easy. 'I am all right. I promise you.'

He tenderly cupped her cheek. 'Let us go home, wife. You need to rest.'

They walked from the small church back up along Bootham to Joseph's house, where they were holding a wedding breakfast for a select group, mostly the Ashton family and a few of Joseph's colleagues.

'Are you happy?' Joseph asked her as they walked, her arm tucked into his.

'Happy than I have ever been,' she said honestly. 'This is the best day of my life.' She was frightened to feel such happiness in case it all disappeared like smoke on a breeze.

'That pleases me.' He smiled and kissed her, much to the cheers of their guests who followed them.

For two hours the house was full of laughter and lightness as everyone mingled and ate Mrs Boden's delightful food. Victoria talked with Joseph's parents and found she liked them very much. His brother made her laugh until she coughed.

Todd came to Victoria and took her hand. 'I must go now, cousin. I'm away to London, then Southampton and on to India.'

'It will be some time before we see each other again.' Tears pricked behind her eyes.

'I will write once I'm settled and tell you everything.' He kissed her cheek. 'Perhaps one day you and Joseph will come visit me?'

'I would like that very much.' She watched him leave and tried not to be sad, but he was the last link to her old life.

Victoria forced a smile as other guests came to say farewell. Before very long the noise had dwindled down to quietness. When the final guests took their leave, Mercy and Mrs Boden began to clear away while the children were sent outside to play in the garden.

She watched her husband as he came back into the room after seeing out his family who were staying in a hotel, but he wasn't alone.

'Mr Bartholomew?' She was surprised to see her uncle's solicitor enter the room.

'Good day to you, Mrs Ashton, and congratulations on your marriage.' The solicitor bowed before her, a leather satchel in his hand. 'Your husband said that I would be welcome to come today and speak to you of your inheritance at last.'

Joseph grinned. 'I thought it would round off a wonderful day, Victoria, and put your mind at rest.'

She smiled at him, excitement rising. 'Yes, it's a perfect idea. Do sit, Mr Bartholomew. Would you like some refreshments?'

'I've only just eaten with my wife, so no, thank you.' He sat on the winged back chair opposite her and pulled a few sheets of paper from the satchel. After placing his gold-rimmed spectacles on, he looked at her. 'I shall read your uncle's will if you're ready?'

She nodded and held Joseph's hand as he sat beside her on the sofa. Listening to the solicitor, she heard Uncle Harold's voice in the words he read. The will was straight forward, everything about the businesses went to Laurence, with provisions for Todd and Stella and Aunt Esther. Next, came the personal items for his wife and children, then finally Mr Bartholomew read out her name. '*To Victoria Sarah Carlton, my niece, the daughter of my late sister and who has been in my care since she was orphaned at twelve years of age. I bequeath to you five acres of land on Haxby Road, details and map are with Mr Bartholomew.*'

Victoria gasped in shock, which made her cough. For a moment she couldn't catch her breath as a coughing fit seized her.

Joseph poured her some water from a jug on the table. 'Here, dearest, try and drink.'

She sipped at the glass but the coughing jarred her whole body and she spilt most of it down her chin. 'Forgive me...' She was embarrassed that the solicitor was witnessing such a scene.

'Deep breaths, darling.' Joseph murmured. 'Nice and slow.'

After a few more minutes, she gained control of herself and wiped the spilt water with a handkerchief. 'I am dreadfully sorry, Mr Bartholomew.'

'There is nothing to apologise for, Mrs Ashton.' He smiled and pushed his glasses further up his nose. 'Shall I continue?'

She nodded and calmed her breathing.

'I also bequeath my niece, Victoria, two thousand pounds to use in her own right and with her own judgement. I hope she is happy in her life and let it be known that I loved her as if she was my own daughter.'

Tears ran down Victoria's face. 'What a dear and generous man he was. I miss him very much.'

Mr Bartholomew replaced the papers in his satchel. 'He was a good man in every sense.' He rose from the chair. 'If you would care to visit my office next week, I can organise the transferral of the money into your account and give you the deeds to the land.'

She and Joseph also stood. Victoria shook his hand. 'Thank you, that would be most agreeable. Say, Wednesday at two o'clock?'

'Wednesday two o'clock. See you then.'

While Joseph saw the man out, Victoria took a deep breath, the familiar tickle in her throat warning her that the frightful cough had not entirely left her.

She couldn't believe what a generous thing Uncle Harold had done.

'Well, my darling wife, you are a woman of means.' Joseph chuckled as he came to her side.

'I cannot tell you how relieved I am.'

He frowned. 'You don't need money now you're married to me. I make a good living for us both and I have shares in my family's company. We won't go without anything, I promise you.'

She kissed him. 'I understand what you're saying but this land and money is a safeguard for me should anything happen to you.'

'I will speak to Mr Bartholomew about my own will. I never want you to worry about being left destitute. I'll not let that happen.'

'It's easier said than done. I've experienced poverty, Joseph, and I never want to go back.' She thought about the land. Should she sell it and invest the money?

'That's a natural fear, of course. However, it won't happen again. Even if something happened to me, you'd be looked after. Besides, my family like you. They'd never see you go without.'

She gave him a thoughtful look. 'And what about Mercy and the children? I'm frightened that if something ever happens to me, then she will be back in the slums and I couldn't bear to think of the children living there again. I will provide for them, but what is mine is yours…and I'd like to know that you think the same as I do about making sure they are provided for.'

He cupped her cheek, love in his eyes. 'I will provide for Mercy and the children.'

'You will?'

'I like her very much. I couldn't see her go without. Does that satisfy you, wife?'

She grinned, loving him so much she thought she would burst from it. 'You satisfy me very well, husband.'

Chapter Twenty-Two

Victoria left the Terry's sweet shop on Coney Street, pleased with her purchases. Emily was turning four tomorrow, and they were holding a small birthday party for her before Victoria and Joseph left for their honeymoon. She'd also bought a box of chocolates for Joseph to eat on the train as she knew her husband had a sweet tooth, despite his denials.

She smiled, pulling her fur-lined coat up around her chin. The dull weather forecasted that winter was very close, and she was glad they were heading south, first to London and then on to France. They were staying for a month in a cottage Joseph's brother had bought on the coast not far from Nantes. Excitement filled her at the thought.

For one whole month she'd have Joseph all to herself. They could eat, drink and relax and simply spend time just the two of them, with no patients for Joseph to worry about, or appointments to keep.

She couldn't wait to explore the French countryside and little towns.

They could lie in bed all day if they wished, or laze around the cottage and enjoy the freedom of doing nothing at all.

Whenever she thought of her husband a warm glow spread throughout her body. Their wedding night had changed her into a woman who now knew the intimacies of a man and the act of love. Joseph had been kind and gentle and so very loving that she'd not wanted him to ever leave the bed, much to his amusement.

She headed along the street, thinking of the purchases she still needed to buy for the honeymoon when she heard her name called. She turned and smiled at Mick O'Shea. 'How lovely to see you, Mick. Are you well?'

'Aye, not too bad.' He smiled, but looked older and sadder. 'I'm glad I've seen you.'

'Oh? Has something happened?'

'That journalist you spoke to, Small.'

'Yes, from the *Gazette*.'

'Sure an' hasn't he been pokin' his nose around again. He's wantin' to do another article in the paper about us lot in the lanes.' Mick scuffed his boot along the cobbles. 'None of us are wordy, not like you. We wondered if you'd speak to Small an' see if someone takes notice this time.'

'I can try.' It concerned her how thin he'd become and his clothes were threadbare.

'You've lived there, you know the crack, so you do.'

'I promise you I will, but we go on our honeymoon tomorrow. It'll have to be when we come back just before Christmas.'

'Thanks, lass.'

'Have you got work?' she asked him.

'Aye, a day here an' there. Truth is I don't have it in me any more. What reason do I have to work hard? The boyos are thinking of goin' to America, but I'm too old to go with them.'

'You'll stay behind on your own?' Pity consumed her. How would he could survive without his wife and sons?

'Sure, an' I'll be fine.'

'Will you not come home with me and have a cup of tea with Mercy and the children?'

He backed away, his eyes became dull as he shook his head. 'No, lass. Seein' them little kiddies makes me heart hurt. I miss them.'

'Then come and see them,' she urged, but he was already walking away.

'Mebbe next time, lass.'

She watched him go, saddened by the stoop of his shoulders. How could she help him, or those in the lanes? She continued on and turned right. Ahead were the offices of the *Gazette*. On impulse she went inside and at the reception asked to see Mr Foster.

The young man behind the counter pointed to the left where two gentlemen stood talking. 'Mr Foster is over there. The one in the brown suit. He's busy right now, but perhaps if you'd like to leave your name and address?'

Victoria stared at Foster. He glanced across at her and stopped talking to the man he was with and walked over to her.

'May I be of some assistance, madam?'

She stuck out her hand for him to shake. 'I'm Mrs Victoria Ashton, formerly Carlton. I sent you a letter some months ago, you may remember?'

'I do remember, Mrs Ashton. Mr Small has kept me informed on what has been happening.'

'I would like to speak to you about the slum situation in Hunsgate and other areas. Something needs to be done to help these people.'

His greying eyebrows rose with interest. 'Then perhaps you'll accompany me upstairs to my office and over a cup of tea we can talk?'

~ ~ ~ ~

Joseph's back ached from bending over throughout the difficult birth. He looked at Annie Weaver's bruised and battered face. She was at peace now. Her husband would hurt her no more. He finished cleaning her up, making her decent. Once she looked respectable, he wrapped the stillborn baby in a blanket and placed it beside her on the bed. She'd died giving birth, but from the battering she'd received at the hands of her husband it was doubtful she or the baby would have survived.

He left the room and went outside into the courtyard to get the smell of blood out of his nose. The staircase on the right went to the room that Mercy and the children once lived in. Now another family lived there and he could hear a child crying from inside it.

A woman carrying a bucket of coal came through from the alley and paused. 'How's Annie, Doctor?'

'Dead. Her baby son, too.'

The woman crossed herself. 'Poor Annie. She was a good 'un. Not like that beast of a man she married.'

'If I get my way, he'll go down for murder.' Joseph wiped the tiredness from his eyes. He'd have to go to the undertakers and the police. The sky was already darkening. November days were short and cold and he was eager to get to France with Victoria. However, first, he'd probably spend the night writing out reports and dealing with this incident.

The woman had knocked on a few doors to spread the news and as the neighbours came out to gossip, he returned inside to gather his things.

He'd just finished packing up his medical bag when a roar filled the air.

Pulling on his coat, he buttoned it up and with a last look at Annie in the candlelight, he left the room.

He'd only taken a step outside the door when he was struck and fell to the ground. With the wind knocked out of him, he laid in the mud confused at what had happened to him.

'What you done to my Annie?' The roar came again.

Joseph was pulled up from the ground only to be hit in the stomach by a fist from a man so large he resembled a mountain. His lungs exploding, he gasped for air. Joseph tried to put up a defence, but the man was like a thrashing machine and didn't stop thumping him. Blows rained down on him. His brain ricocheted inside his skull. His stomach cramped from the hits. When his legs gave out, he crumpled to the muddy ground. He was dimly aware of the screams, the fuzzy noise inside his head and the blood and muck in his mouth. He couldn't breathe. A kick to the ribs made him curl into a ball. Pain racked his body. Another punch to the jaw and then there was nothing.

~ ~ ~ ~

'Where can he be?' Victoria paced the front room, stopping every now and then to peer out of the window to scan the night-darkened street. 'This is getting ridiculous now. It's gone nine o'clock. If he's been delayed, he always sends a note.'

Mercy sat on the sofa, knitting on her knee, her face mirroring Victoria's own concern. 'And you're positive he didn't have a meeting or a dinner to go to?'

'Yes, I'm certain of it. He'd have told me. I've checked his diary, and this evening is free as we are supposed to be packing for tomorrow.'

'Sit down and we'll give it another half an hour, and if he's not home then, I'll go look for him.'

'How can you do that? You've no idea where he could be.' She sat on the chair near the fire. 'He visits several hospitals daily, plus the almshouses, Hungate, Walmgate and so on.'

'I'll try them all if I have to,' Mercy said stubbornly.

'Then I'll have you to worry about, too!' Victoria snapped. She had a feeling that something wasn't right.

'Well, you aren't going out there in the cold, not with your chest.' Mercy put the knitting back into the basket at her feet. 'Tell me about Mr Foster and your meeting with him. I know you were waiting until Joseph got home, but you'll just have to repeat yourself and tell him later.'

'Very well.' Victoria sighed. 'Mr Foster is going to write an article about the situation in Walmgate and Hungate and publish it in his newspaper. After our conversation he was enthusiastic for us to work together to bring the situation to the public. He is planning on a series of lectures and speeches and he wants me and Joseph, you too, if you want, to talk to the audience on what we've experienced.'

'Me as well?' Mercy looked stricken. 'I can't do that!'

Victoria frowned. 'Why ever not? You've lived it. People need to hear the truth, the reasons why such areas need money spent on them to make them liveable for humans and not pigs.'

Mercy shook her head. 'I'll support you in every way but I can't stand up in front of everyone and speak.'

'I understand.'

'They might ask questions about my husband and why did he leave me and his children. No, it's not something I can do, I'm sorry.'

'I understand.' Victoria reached over and squeezed Mercy's hand in comfort. 'Joseph and I will do it.'

'When is it to be?'

'Mr Foster said he'll arrange for me to speak at the assembly the week we return from France, a few days before Christmas. It might make several members of society feel guilty that their Christmases will be full of food and warmth whereas others are suffering.'

Mercy added coal to the fire. 'I hope some good comes from it. Harriet tells me the smell of damp and rot still lingers from the floods. People are living in terrible conditions. Something must be done.'

'Mr Foster wants me to give a speech at the next council meeting in the new year, too. I said I would.'

Knocking on the door sounded loudly, making them both jump.

Victoria jerked to her feet and raced to the front door with Mercy on her heels. She opened the door and stared at the young man on the doorstep. 'Yes?'

'Mrs Ashton?'

'Yes.'

'I'm Fred Olsen, a wardsman at County Hospital. I've been sent to fetch you by Doctor Harris because Doctor Ashton has been brought in to us.'

'Joseph? What has happened?' Victoria's heart somersaulted. She grabbed her coat from the cupboard.

'He's been beaten, Mrs Ashton. I'm sorry.'

'How bad is he hurt?'

'Very bad, I'm afraid. I've a hansom to take you back with me.'

'Thank you.' Victoria turned to Mercy. 'I'll let you know how he is as soon as I can.'

~ ~ ~ ~

The smell of carbolic soap and bleaching agents were sharp in Victoria's nose as she walked the corridors of the hospital following Fred. Her mind whirled with the terrifying possibilities of how serious the injuries were that Joseph had sustained.

When Fred stopped at the end of a bed next to another man, Victoria steeled herself to look upon her husband of only a few weeks. For a crazy moment she thought they'd made a mistake, for the man in the neatly made bed wasn't her Joseph at all. However, stepping closer on wobbly legs, she recognised under the bruising and swelling, the cuts and the dried blood, the man she loved. She slapped a hand over her mouth to stem a moan of despair escaping. Was he dead? He looked dead! How could anyone have survived such a beating?

The man next to Fred stepped closer the bed. 'Mrs Ashton. I'm Doctor Harris, a colleague of your husband and resident doctor at County.' He smiled gently and shook her hand. 'Please, take a seat.'

Dazed, she sat on the wooden chair and stared at Joseph's misshapen face. Both eyes were closed with the swelling. He wore a collection of cuts, two of which were stitched, one above his eye and another on his cheekbone. 'Will he survive?' she whispered.

'Yes. I'm certain he will.'

'Thank God.'

'The swelling will go down in a few days, and he's going to be in a lot of pain. I'm afraid there is bruising around his ribcage, I suspect there will be broken bones, which will restrict his movements and cause him plenty of discomfort.' Doctor Harris's voice was reassuring despite delivering the awful news. 'Once he has woken again, he'll be able to tell us more of where he hurts.'

'He has woken then?'

'Yes. When he we placed him on the bed. Only for a short time. I gave him laudanum for sleep is the best healer for these types of injuries.'

'How did this happen, do we know?' She held Joseph's hand tenderly, not wanting to wake him.

'The men who brought him to us came from Walmgate. They transported him in on a handcart.'

'Walmgate?' She frowned at that. He'd been visiting the slums. He was known there and liked due to his generosity of waiving his fee. Why would someone beat him?

'The police have been notified, Mrs Ashton. As soon as Doctor Ashton is well enough, they'll want to talk to him about what happened.'

'Can I stay with him?'

Doctor Harris smiled, his eyes kind. 'Of course. I'll have a nurse bring you some tea. Stay as long as you like.'

'Thank you.'

Left alone, Victoria pulled the chair closer to the bed and raised Joseph's hand to her cheek. 'We'll have you better before you know it, my love.'

Long into the night she sat by the bed. The quietness was broken only by the soft rattle of the nurse's trolley, the odd moan or cough from a patient.

A small thin nurse with a gentle touch stopped by often to check on Joseph and say a quick word to Victoria.

Sleep claimed her eventually, napping in the chair, one hand clasped over Joseph's. She woke with a start, a sharp pain spiking down her neck from the angle it had rested on her shoulder. She glanced at Joseph as she rubbed her neck and blinked in surprise when he smiled brokenly at her. 'You're awake!' She leaned over and kissed him, making him wince as his lip split again and bled.

Dabbing the blood away, Victoria apologised. 'I will not kiss you again, I promise.'

'That's the worst sentence I've ever heard,' he croaked, and his lip bled some more. He could only see out of one eye which was red around the iris instead of white.

'Doctor Harris said he'll come and see you this morning. Where do you hurt?'

'Everywhere.'

'My poor darling. Doctor Harris says you've broken some ribs.'

'I agree. It's difficult to breathe or move.'

'Can I get you something? Water? Tea?'

'Tea, please.' He shifted in the bed. 'Can you help me sit up?'

Between the two of them, they managed to sit him up against the pillows.

Joseph puffed, pain etching his features, turning his skin grey. 'I'm sorry we'll not be going on our honeymoon tomorrow.'

'As if that's important compared to you being attacked?' she admonished him gently. 'We can go to France next year, after winter. There's no hurry. I'll get you some tea.'

'Victoria.' He grabbed her hand to stop her leaving.

'What is it?' she asked lovingly.

'You remember Annie Weaver?' His voice was low.

'Yes, I remember her. She lived near Mercy in Walmgate.' She smiled, remembering Annie, another character from the slums. She and Mercy should visit her, take her a basket.

'She died yesterday, as did her child. That's where I was when I was attacked. It was her husband who did this to me.'

It took a moment for his words to register in her brain. 'Annie is dead? Weaver did this to you?'

'Weaver had returned to the courtyard just after Annie gave birth. He went mad when he heard about her dying.'

'Weaver is a monster. He once threatened me.' The memory of that confrontation remained vivid in her mind as it had been the first time anyone had spoken to her like that or made physical violence towards her. 'How terribly sad about Annie. Mercy said she'd lost all her babies due to her husband's fists.'

'And his fists killed her this time.'

Victoria gasped. '*He* killed her? I don't understand.'

'The birth killed her, but she was badly beaten and the baby was stillborn. She'd been in labour for a long time before I got there. She had given up and she couldn't push the baby out, she was in too much pain from her injuries.' Joseph sighed. 'It was pitiful to see.'

'He cannot get away with it this time.' Anger and disgust filled her.

'No, he will not. I'll testify and do all in my power to make sure he goes to jail for it.'

She squeezed his hand. 'You must recover first.'

'I'll be fine enough to talk to the police.' His eyes were full of determination.

She nodded, knowing it needed to be done, and nothing would sway him. 'I'll support you in every way. Women like Annie need to be protected from brutal husbands.'

He closed his eyes, clearly exhausted. She let him sleep, but her mind whirled with what he'd told her and all that she'd seen in the slums herself. Women and children suffered cruelly. How could she make a difference?

As dawn broke and outside the window, birds trilled a morning chorus, Victoria knew what she wanted to do, how she could help.

~ ~ ~ ~

The following day, while taking a break from the hospital, Victoria celebrated Emily's birthday with Mercy and the children and Mrs Boden. Once the cake and been eaten, and the presents unwrapped, Mercy sent the children upstairs to play while she and Victoria shared a pot of tea.

'I've decided to use the land Uncle Harold gave me to build a Home for women and children who have been left destitute or need somewhere to go to escape an abusive husband.'

'Like a workhouse?'

'Heavens, no! This will be much better than a workhouse. This will be a *home,* where destitute women and orphans aren't punished for falling on hard times. Why should a woman suffer because her husband has left her and she has no way to earn a living and bring up her children? I will not have that.'

'There has to be some rules, or they'll all run riot.'

'There will be house rules in as much as common decency and respect. But I won't have children breaking rocks, or women threading kemp until their hands bleed. No, they'll learn how to cook and sew and the children will go to school to better themselves.'

'It sounds wonderful. How will you afford to build it?'

'Donations. It's how the others are built and maintained. I have the land already so that's one expense we don't have to worry about and the money Uncle bequeathed me will go some way towards building the Home. Also, I was thinking we could build two cottages on the grounds, one for Joseph and myself and the other for you and the children.'

Mercy gasped. 'A cottage for me?' She shook her head. 'No Victoria, no. I feel bad enough living here without paying for anything. I couldn't have you build me a cottage.'

'Oh, stop it, do.' Victoria poured more tea.

'Do you honestly think I would ever let you be alone and unsupported again?

You are my very dear friend, more like a sister really, and the children are my nieces and nephews. I love you all and would never want you to have to struggle again.'

'We adore you, too, but it's too much, Victoria, too generous.'

Victoria selected another piece of birthday cake. 'I'm not saying you'll not earn it.'

'What do you mean?' Mercy frowned.

'Well, you'll be helping me in the Home. Someone will have to help with the organisation.'

'I think I would enjoy that immensely.' Mercy smiled, relaxing.

'Good.'

'What will Joseph say about this plan? He may not like it, or want you to save your money.'

'I think he'll support me in this. It is something he has talked about doing as well, but he was thinking of a hospital. I'd rather it be a Home rather than a hospital. By building this Home and the two cottages, I'll always have a roof over my head. I'll never have to live as I have done this year. Look how easy it is to be widowed. I cannot rely on Joseph always being there for me. I don't have a family I can fall back on either.'

'True. Being married isn't a guarantee that life will forever be perfect. It all makes sense.'

'And we'll be helping others, like Annie Weaver.' Victoria let out a deep breath. 'I can do this. *We* can do this.'

'I support you and Joseph will, too.' Mercy nodded. 'And with the town's support as well, we can build a Home to improve women and children's lives.'

'Once Joseph is out of hospital, I will make plans to see an architect.' Her head was full of ideas and she couldn't wait to get started.

An hour later, she sat beside Joseph's bed and relayed all that she had discussed with Mercy, as well as the meeting with Mr Foster. When she'd finished, she waited for his response.

'It sounds an ambitious plan, my love.' He was sitting up and although his face was a mess with cuts and bruises, he seemed a little better.

Her enthusiasm sunk. 'You believe it cannot be done, that I am unable to do it?'

'No, not at all. I think you have the courage and the spirit to accomplish anything you set out to do.'

'I would rather it was something we did together.'

He smiled crookedly and took her hand. 'And we will. As long as we have a small hospital on the grounds for me to see patients, then I'll be happy.'

Relief poured out of her and she reached over and kissed him.

'Oww!' he joked, tenderly touching his cut lip.

'Sorry.' She grinned, feeling the happiest she'd done in a long time.

'I'm telling Harris that I'm going home this afternoon.'

'No, Joseph, you need to rest.'

'And I can do that better at home in my own bed with my wife beside me.'

'Are you sure?' She still hadn't become used to being referred to as a wife, yet it delighted her all the same.

'Very sure. Mrs Boden's good food will get me back on my feet in no time.' He sat up straighter. 'Besides, we've plans and ideas to discuss, letters to write and people to see. I can't do that in a hospital bed and I'm bored being in here. I want to be home with you.'

'I'll go home and prepare the house then and come back for you in a few hours. You'll want a bath?'

A wicked glint flashed in his eyes. 'As long as you share it with me.'

'Joseph!' She glanced around hoping no one had heard him, a blush creeping up her neck.

He laughed and then held his ribs in pain.

'Serves you right!' She grinned. With a kiss she said farewell and left the hospital.

Chapter Twenty-Three

The sun was out, though it held no heat. Winter held sway now, each day grew shorter and colder.

Victoria walked Jane and Bobby to the new school they were attending down near Bootham Bar, and after seeing them to the door, she decided to stroll into town and do some Christmas shopping, for the holiday was only a week away.

With Joseph being home recuperating and the plans for the Home increasing on her time, she realised it had been weeks since she had simply walked for the pleasure of it. The exercise would give her time to think and make more plans. She smiled at herself, as if her head needed more ideas to cope with. Sometimes she felt her brain would explode with all she had to think about.

A carriage rolled past, but it stopped further down the street. The door opened, and a lady descended the steps.

Victoria's stomach churned as Stella walked towards her. She'd not seen her since Uncle Harold's funeral.

Stella looked her up and down with a sneer. 'I thought it was you. I wondered when I'd see you now you've risen from the quagmire.'

Smarting at the insult, Victoria lifted her chin defiantly. Stella had no right to stare at her as though she'd just stepped from a midden. She wore an expensive dark green walking skirt and bodice. Her black coat was ankle length and lined with mink and her hat was of the best quality and style.

Since marrying Joseph, she had returned to the elegant clothes she'd worn before.

'What do you want, Stella?'

'Want? From you?' She laughed bitterly. 'Nothing. There is nothing you have that I covet at all.'

'Not even my husband?'

'Ha! Ashton? No. He was never someone I could seriously consider marrying.'

'Oh, really?' she mocked. 'You could have fooled me and others. You did your very best to ensnare Joseph and try to make him your devoted puppy. But he saw through you to the real person beneath and didn't like what he saw.'

Stella's eyes narrowed. 'Do you think you've won? That you are better than me? You are nothing and no one, you never have been. An orphan my father took in because of duty. The man you killed!'

'Stop it, stop saying that. It cannot be proven the argument we had was the reason for the heart attack. Do you ever listen to reason?'

'I don't care what anyone else says. I know you were the reason and I'll never forgive you,' she spat. 'When I heard you were living in the slums, I laughed until I cried. It was all you deserved and more!'

'I don't have to listen to you.' Victoria strode past her.

'You'll not be successful, you understand.'

Despite common sense telling her to keep on walking, Victoria hesitated and turned back to her. 'I beg your pardon?'

'The talk circulating the drawing rooms is that you are making a speech at the Assembly on Friday night.'

'Yes.'

'No one will attend. I have made certain of that.'

The warmth left Victoria's face.

Stella laughed at her reaction. 'No one wants to listen to you blather on about the slums or the poor. Decent society are tired of listening to constant speeches asking us to do more, give more. We do enough.'

'There's always more to do.'

Stella shrugged. 'Perhaps there is, but no one will help *you!* I've dragged your name through the very muck you lived in. I *told* everyone I could about how you lived amongst prostitutes and drunks. I *told* people that you were not to be trusted that Papa had thrown you out of our house because of your devious ways. That it was you who drove him to suffer such an attack that it killed him.'

She felt sick. 'They won't all believe your lies.'

'Maybe not, but a few will, and the ladies of our society will convince their husbands. Mama and the name of Dobson carry more respect in this town than you do. No one wants to donate money to your new building that is going to house prostitutes!'

338

'You're misinformed, the Home I am to build is for abandoned women and children.'

Stella's eyebrow's rose haughtily. 'I'm not misinformed at all. I just choose to alter the truth.'

A deep sadness entered Victoria's heart. 'Why be so hateful? I've never done anything to hurt you.'

'Is that what you think?' Stella's laugh was ugly.

'Then tell me differently because I do not know.'

'You were the first in my father's affections, always. He loved *you* more than he did *me*.' Stella's hands balled into fists, her anger visible.

Victoria sighed, tired of her cousin's antics. 'He did not. He loved us both equally, or possibly you more for you were his daughter. I was only his niece.'

'Then why did he leave *you* acres of land and two thousand pounds and all I received was one thousand and a small unpleasant townhouse in London? Answer me that!'

Stunned by the revelation, Victoria thought quickly. 'Perhaps because he knew Laurence would look after you?'

'I don't need Laurence. I will marry well, you watch me, and my husband will be richer than a mere doctor!'

Victoria bowed her head. 'Then I wish you well, Stella. I hope you find happiness.'

'Don't you ever *pity* me!' Stella stared at her for a long moment then turned for the carriage. 'Give my regards to Joseph. You're welcome to him.'

Long after the carriage had disappeared, Victoria stood on the pavement lost to the world around her.

How had she loved her cousin all these years only to feel nothing for her now? How could it be possible? She looked up at the sky, feeling tired.

No more. No more would she waste time trying to understand Stella or feel guilty that their friendship was shattered. She had a future now with Joseph and plans that would bring her much satisfaction and joy.

~ ~ ~ ~

Nervously, Victoria sat in the carriage on the short journey to the Assembly Rooms. Joseph had hired it because the weather had turned bitter and sleet had begun to fall.

'You'll do wonderfully well, my darling,' Joseph said holding her hand. 'Won't she, Mercy?'

Mercy patted Victoria's knee. 'Of course, you will. This is what you want, to tell everyone about the conditions in the slums, of how it can be beaten if we all work together.'

She nodded, her throat too full of nerves to speak. She'd seen Mr Foster that morning to go through what would be happening tonight, and he was expecting a good turnout. There'd been newspaper articles and posters put up around town broadcasting the event. She hadn't the courage to mention the argument with Stella to Mr Foster and her cousin's predictions that no one would attend.

But she had told Joseph, and he'd been furious when she'd revealed all that Stella had said. He'd wanted to go to Blossom Street and confront her, but Victoria stopped him. What good would it have done but cause more heartache?

After seeing Stella in the street, she'd spent the next few days in a low mood. Once they had been close, or so she thought, but perhaps that had been all smoke and mirrors?

Their friendship had disintegrated swiftly as soon as Joseph had been introduced to them. So maybe Stella had never really loved her like a sister. How could she have to have turned on her so rapidly when Uncle Harold died?

When the carriage halted before the Assembly rooms, Victoria felt queasy.

Joseph looked out of the window at the lamp-lit street. 'There's a good many carriages and people entering the building. You see, there was nothing to worry about. Stella's vileness doesn't hold the influence she thinks it does.'

He opened the door and helped her down the step. The cold air hit her face and she shivered despite the fur coat she wore.

Joseph helped Mercy down and then took both their arms on either side of him. He smiled encouragingly to Victoria. 'You can do this.'

Walking into the foyer, a few gentlemen shook Joseph's hands and spoke to Victoria about how keen they were to hear her speech, which made her even more nervous.

Mercy took their coats and gave them to the attendant.

'Would you like something to drink?' Joseph pointed to the refreshments table she could see in a break between the crowds.

'Yes, please.' She gripped his hand before he left. 'There is quite a number of people here.'

He smiled. 'As if there wouldn't be. Who wouldn't want to come and listen to a lady who once lived on Blossom Street as well as Petal Lane?'

'Victoria!' Harriet was suddenly by her side and they embraced.

'I'm so happy to see you here.'

'Moral support and all that.' Harriet grinned. 'Mercy and I are your very own right-hand women! Isn't that so, Mercy?'

Mercy glanced around the swell of people. 'I'm so pleased I'm not the one talking to all of these people.'

Victoria's stomach knotted. 'You're not helping!' she whispered.

Joseph brought back a tray of drinks which included one for Harriet. 'I feel I should make a toast.'

Victoria nearly choked on her first mouthful. 'No! Let us not tempt fate.'

Joseph's face grew serious as he stared beyond Victoria's shoulder. She turned to see why and faced Aunt Esther.

'Victoria, dear.'

Steeling herself for a verbal attack, Victoria stiffened. 'Aunt.' She looked for Stella.

'I am here alone,' Aunt Esther said, appearing older and smaller wearing all black. Her hair was completely silver now and her figure thinner than it once was. Fine lines liberally furrowed her face.

'Mrs Dobson,' Joseph butted in, 'this is an important occasion for my wife.'

'And I shall not ruin it, Doctor Ashton, I promise you. Instead, I come to beg forgiveness from Victoria.' Tears filled Aunt Esther's eyes. 'I behaved deplorably, Victoria, and I apologise sincerely. I have no excuse to offer but grief, which was likened to some sort of madness to me. But as the months have gone on and I didn't know where you were, or how you were coping, I was filled with guilt. I am not a nasty person.' A tear rolled down her cheek, and she dabbed it away with a black lace-edged handkerchief.

'It is a shame your daughter isn't of the same ilk, Mrs Dobson,' Joseph snapped.

Aunt Esther bowed her head. 'I've put a stop to Stella's hate campaign. I am sorry it happened.'

A bell was rung indicating for people to make their way inside and take their seats.

Victoria had loved her aunt and admired her. She could be forgiven. 'Aunt Esther will you sit with Joseph and my friends, Mercy Felling and Harriet Drysdale?'

'You are Mrs Felling?' Aunt Esther blinked, taking in Mercy's well-cut dress of midnight blue. Mercy appeared as far away as a woman of the slums as any person could be, until you saw the haunted look in her gaze sometimes.

'I am, Mrs Dobson.' Mercy stood straighter, prouder.

'You're a survivor, too then?' Aunt Esther said with respect.

'Yes, just like your niece.' Mercy smiled.

Aunt Esther nodded. 'I am pleased to make your acquaintance.' She turned to Victoria. 'You will do our family proud tonight, Victoria, especially your uncle.'

Victoria swallowed a lump of emotion. 'I hope so.'

'Let us take our seats before they are gone.' Joseph ushered everyone inside the large ornate room.

Victoria left them to take her seat up on the stage next to Mr Foster.

'Ready, Mrs Ashton?' he asked, checking his notes.

'As I'll ever be, Mr Foster.'

'As we discussed this morning, I'll speak first, welcome everyone, introduce the Lord Mayor who will say a few words, and then it'll be your turn.'

She nodded and felt in her pocket for her notes, the crinkle of the paper was a little comforting.

'Don't be frightened. Everyone has come to see you. To hear your story. You are representing all those who live in harsh conditions. You are their voice. Just think of the good you can do.'

She nodded again, the pressure and importance of what she had to do made her want to be sick all over Mr Foster's shiny black shoes.

Throughout Mr Foster and the Mayor's speeches, Victoria grew more anxious. She doubted her every decision that had led to this moment.

When Mr Foster introduced her, there was a thundering applause. She stepped up to the podium. The clapping quietened. Mr Foster had spoken well about the plight of the poor and now it was her turn.

Her heart seemed lodged in her throat as she stared out over the sea of people. The Assembly room was packed with some men standing at the back of the room because of the lack of vacant chairs.

Victoria swallowed, her hands shaking. Her notes made no sense, the words blurred and became unreadable.

She took a deep breath.

She could do this.

With a glance at Joseph and Mercy, both smiling proudly, she began to speak.

'Circumstances led me to be among the poor people of York, and it was there, amongst them that I learned many lessons…'

Acknowledgments

Thank you to the wonderful members of HistFic Critique, my critique group, whose support gets me through each book. Their encouragement keeps me going when sometimes I think I can't write another word and every story is rubbish!

To my editor, Jane Eastgate, thank you for finding my mistakes when I think there are none!

To my talented cover designer, Evelyn Labelle, you always give me what I want, thank you!

Thank you to my family and friends. Your support means the world to me.

Finally, the biggest thank you goes to my readers. Over the years I have received the most wonderful messages from readers who have told me how much they've enjoyed my stories. Each and every message and review encourages me to write the next book. Most authors go through times when they think the story they are writing is no good and I am no exception. The times when we struggle with the plot, when the characters don't behave as we wish them to, when 'normal' life interferes with the writing process and we feel we haven't got enough time in the day to do all we have to do those messages make us smile! A simple message from a stranger saying they loved my story dispels my doubts over my ability to be an author. I can't express enough how much those lovely messages mean to me. So, thank you.

You can find me on social media at the normal places like Facebook and a list of all my books on my website where you can sign up for my newsletter: http://www.annemariebrear.com

The Slum Angel

Printed in Great Britain
by Amazon